PRAISE FOR EVERYBODY'S DAUGHTER:

"The last time I remember talking about a book this much was after I read *The Help*."
– Rainy Day Reviews

"This is a unique blend of Science Fiction and Biblical Historical Romantic Suspense Fiction, so there is bound to be something for just about every book lover's genre!"
– Reviews from the Heart

"I could not lay it down. I loved it!"
– My Favorite Things

"Michael John Sullivan is a truly gifted writer who brings his story and it's characters to life. One minute I was angry and the next minute tears flowed freely down my face."
– Karen's Korner

"Part mystery, part suspense and filled with exciting time travel, this book kept me interested from beginning to end."
– Just One More Paragraph

"What moved me the most about this book is that it is filled with genuine emotion that isn't overwrought and with a view of faith and forgiveness that feels natural and accessible."
– Susan Petrone

AN EXAMINER.COM BEST BOOK OF 2012

EVERYBODY'S
DAUGHTER

EVERYBODY'S DAUGHTER

A NOVEL BY

MICHAEL JOHN SULLIVAN

THE
STORY PLANT

The Story Plant
Studio Digital CT, LLC
PO Box 4331
Stamford, CT 06907

Jacket design by J. Allen Fielder

Print ISBN-13: 978-1-61188-153-0
E-book ISBN-13: 978-1-61188-154-7

Visit our website at www.TheStoryPlant.com

First Fiction Studio printing: May 2012
First Story Plant printing: September 2013

Printed in the United States of America

Also by Michael John Sullivan

Necessary Heartbreak
An Angel Comes Home

For Cat and Jackie,
My two greatest gifts in the world.
Love, Dad.

ACKNOWLEDGEMENTS

While writing *Everybody's Daughter*, I grew to love the story more and more as the plot moved away from its original outline. Thanks to my relationship with editor Selena Robins, I learned the value of tension between all of the characters as we spent much time over the phone, discussing each plot scene and interaction. Her efforts helped me transform this story into an intriguing thriller. She was tough, too. It's an aspect of her personality that I only started to fully appreciate during the last step of my editing process. Ms. Robins suggested I read the story out loud. When I did so with my wife, Debbie, I was able to recognize with clarity the weaknesses of the story.

I thank my wife for helping me through this tedious part of the process. She also had to endure my many changing moods during the past two years in writing this second book of the trilogy. *Necessary Heartbreak* was certainly an easier task, as much of the material was already written two decades ago.

While I didn't utilize an agent for *Everybody's Daughter*, it is with great gratitude I thank Frank Breeden, who spent some valuable time with me explaining parts of the publishing business I didn't understand.

Simon & Schuster VP Anthony Ziccardi, who signed me for *Necessary Heartbreak*, the first book in the trilogy, continues to be available to answer my questions. He has supported me with unwavering confidence throughout my publishing journey.

I'm excited to have *Everybody's Daughter* published by Fiction Studio and deeply honored that Lou Aronica accepted my manuscript. Lou is someone I trust during this ever-changing time in the publishing industry.

I would have never written this story if not for the continued love given to me by my friends, too many to mention. Bookclub members were a source of information and feedback to me during my *Necessary Heartbreak* journey. I've made some lifetime friends while writing this time-travel series.

I look forward to taking one more journey in book three with Michael and Elizabeth Stewart as they discover that the most valuable part of life is to learn to just appreciate it. That's a lesson I'm trying to embrace myself as I write this series.

CHAPTER ONE

Jingling the silver coins between his fingers that he had re-trieved so many centuries ago, Michael Stewart again thought about what he should do with the blood money. He leaned on his broom, transfixed in his holy land memories, only to be startled by an intruder.

"Hey, Judas. Pastor Dennis told me to bring this down here," the young man said, stomping down the stairs. "Where do you want me to put this?"

"In the corner is fine." He pointed to the area and continued sweeping the church's basement floor.

The teenager set down a candle snuffer and tugged on Mi-chael's Boston Red Sox jacket's sleeve. "Don't work too hard, *Judas.*" He ran up the stairs, repeating Judas' name and laughing. The sound broke the majestic quiet of the church.

Michael never took offense when his fellow Yankee fans teased him, accusing him of being a traitor.

If they only realized he knew Judas. Personally.

He relaxed, allowing the slight pain in his forearm to ease, and slipped his hand again inside the pocket of his worn jeans. He never left home without the ancient relics, touching them periodically, forcing himself to believe that the week he and his daughter Elizabeth lived in first-century Jerusalem wasn't a dream.

It was real. It *did* happen.

On days when his financial responsibilities overwhelmed him, as insurmountable bills piled up on a weekly basis, he had been tempted to ask an antique expert about their value.

No. I could never sell them, no matter how much they could be worth. I'll burn in hell.

He realized he would perhaps have to explain how he had come to own these unholy souvenirs some day.

"But who would believe me?" he whispered. "They'll think I'm crazy."

He heard footsteps upstairs. "Well, well, surprise, surprise," called a voice from above. "Look who's down there, *again*."

Michael went to the stairway and glanced up at his daughter. "How did you know I was here?"

"I'm psychic."

Michael smiled. "So what does my future say?"

She laughed. "I saw your car parked in front."

"Wait a minute. Aren't you supposed to be at your self defense class?"

"That was yesterday. I'm almost done with it. I can push around the biggest guys. But now I'm rocking with the history club. They want you to come in and discuss your coins."

"You can't be serious?" He stared at her in disbelief. "Not only will they not believe me, but they'll think my elevator is not going up to the right floor. Did you tell them where they came from?"

She didn't respond.

Michael walked up the stairs into the church, gave his daughter a hug and kissed her forehead. "Did you show them the coins I gave you?"

"You look good today, Dad."

"Uh-huh." *Wonder what she's angling for?*

He sat in the first pew and gazed at the musical equipment behind the podium, gleaming in the late afternoon sunlight. Thoughts of finding another opportunity to travel to the Holy Land occupied his mind as he absorbed the peaceful beauty.

Elizabeth nudged his shoulder, shaking him out of his trance. "I didn't show anybody the coins you gave me. They'll think I'm crazy too."

He slid over to give her room. "So, what do you need from me today?"

"Nothing," she said. "It's so quiet." She looked around. "I haven't been here in a while."

"I've noticed."

"I think one church nut in the family is enough," she said.

He gave her a surprised look. "Excuse me?"

"Just kidding. Why are you spending so much time in all the churches in town? Even a Temple."

He didn't answer right away, needing a few seconds to think. "I truly believe Jesus doesn't care whether I pray in a Catholic or a Protestant church, or even a Temple or the ice cream shop or a toy store or..."

"Okay, okay, I get the picture," she said.

He touched her hand. "I saw God in Leah as much as any person I know. She showed us so much love. Real love." He let out a sigh. "Going back to that time and witnessing what we did, well, it changed my life."

He rubbed his forehead and closed his eyes for a few seconds. "And losing your aunt also changed the way I think."

"Yeah, I know." She nodded slowly. "I miss Aunt Sammie too. It changed the way I look at things."

For several minutes they sat in silence. Michael found the stillness of the church rejuvenating.

His daughter nudged his shoulder again. "So what's bothering you? That whole Jerusalem trip was incredible. But you're still sad." She chewed her bottom lip. "I know the real reason why you're here."

"Oh, you do?"

"Yup. I do indeed," she said with the grin of a typical fourteen-year-old. "I know everything." She injected an air of pompous self-importance in her tone, but couldn't keep a straight face. The giggle that followed told Michael she was having a good time ribbing him.

She fiddled with a strand of neon pink hair, twisting it into a small bow. "I'm glad we get along better since that trip." She put her hand on his arm. "I'm kind of worried about you. You want to talk about it?"

Michael refused to grab the bait she dangled. "I'm waiting for the service to start."

She clicked her tongue. "There's no service today."

"I enjoy being here. Dennis is one of my best friends now. He's different from the others."

"Oh, yeah, he is different."

"What do you mean by that?"

"Well, he's kind of old to look the way he does."

"What's he supposed to look like?"

"Like a pastor." She faced him and touched her ear. "That earring he wears, his long hair, and the loud rock music he plays on his iPod. It's just weird. And the motorcycle."

Michael touched his ear. "I'm thinking about getting one."

"Yuck. You're old too." She crossed her arms. "No way do I want my old man to wear one."

"I'm not old and I'm thinking a gold sparkly one would be nice," he continued, nodding.

"That's not gonna happen." She sighed. "Let's talk about something else, so I can get that gross image of you out of my head. How often do you think about her?"

He twisted nervously, his leg pinned hard against the side of the pew. "Who are you talking about?"

"Leah. Who else?"

He hesitated for a fraction. "I think about her often."

She leaned her head against his shoulder. "I'm sure she's doing okay."

"We didn't see her get away from that Roman soldier." He shifted in his seat to ease his anxiety. "I'm worried that I left her behind to defend herself against that maniac. I should have gone back." He looked upward, avoiding her gaze. "That's why I come here so often."

She pressed her hand around his arm. "Yeah, I get it."

"I should have gone back once I knew you were fine."

Elizabeth's eyes widened and she let out a gasp. "I wouldn't have let you go alone. I love her too."

"I know." He glanced at her sideways and noticed another pink streak near her temple. *Was that there this morning?*

"We also didn't know if that soldier was coming back after us in the tunnel," Elizabeth said.

"I still should have turned around and made sure."

She squeezed his arm tighter. "You're still in love with her, huh?"

He grimaced, uncomfortable with the direction their conversation had taken and remained silent.

"Dad," she said. "Answer me. Are you still in love with her?"

He kept staring straight ahead. "I guess."

"You don't sound sure."

He cleared his throat. "Don't get me wrong. I still miss your mom. I'll always love your mom. I sometimes wonder if I should have let go of her a long time ago." He lowered his voice and changed the direction of the conversation. "I also wonder if we should have waited until Jesus rose from the dead. I think about that a lot. But it would have been a big risk. I certainly wasn't going to put your life in danger any more than I had to."

Elizabeth shrugged her shoulders. "I don't know if there's life after death, or whether someone can really rise from the dead like Lazarus or Jesus. But I do know what I saw. And I'm so happy to be home."

Michael smiled.

"What?" she asked.

His heart swelled with pride. "You said you don't know. But you really do." He ruffled her hair. "By the way, I had to clean up part of your room."

She shot him an angry glare. "What were you doing in my room?"

"You left your lights on. Again. I don't have a money tree in the yard. Our electric bill was obscene last month."

"You didn't have to clean it up though."

"No choice. I had to create a path to get to the lamps." He nudged her. "Just the ones that were still on."

She covered her ears with her hands and said through gritted teeth, "You're going to make me crazy."

"You'll be even more crazy living in a dark house when they cut off our electric bill because I can't afford it."

An elderly man and woman entered the church, tip-toeing up the aisle, putting a temporary halt to their bickering. He whispered, "By the way, who's this Matt fella?"

"Someone I met at school." She shrugged. "How do you know about him?"

"Never mind how I know. Is he a boyfriend?"

"Kinda."

He tilted his head heavenward. "No."

"No what?"

"No. He will not be your boyfriend."

"Why?" Her tone was loud and contemptuous.

He put two fingers against his lips. "Lower your voice." He noticed the old man turning his head, obviously angling for a better position to hear their conversation as the lady gave Michael a disapproving glance.

"I don't care if they hear what we say," she said, raising her voice. "Why can't I see Matt?"

He shushed his daughter again, wagging a finger at her. "I don't like him."

"You've never met him."

"I don't have to."

"Ugh. I like him. He's a great guy."

"You're too young."

"I'm old enough to get married during Jesus' time."

"That was then. Different times, different rules. This is now. My rules."

The elderly man was practically hanging over the pew to catch every word. Michael figured it was probably the most entertainment he had enjoyed in a long time.

"Let's discuss this at home," Michael said, trying to put an end to the conversation.

"I want to date him."

"No."

"Yes."

Michael stood and gave an emphatic response. "Absolutely not."

"Sit down. They're looking at us again."

"I don't care."

"Oh, now you don't care?"

He waved to the elderly couple and sat.

"At least meet Matt," she pleaded.

He looked at her adamant expression and saw how much this meant to her. "Okay," he said, trying not to sound defeated. "I'll meet him."

She smiled. "When?"

"At least give me some time to adjust to the idea."

"How about tomorrow?"

"Too soon," he said. "How old is he?"

"Older than me."

"How much older?"

"He's a junior."

He looked upward, concentrating on the church's beautifully hand-painted ceiling. "Oh, Vicki, look at what your daughter is doing to me." Taking a deep breath, he remembered something he'd been meaning to ask her. "Who gave you the chain with the locket?"

"Where did you find it? Did you go in my drawer?"

"You know I'd never do that. It was on top of your dresser."

She huffed out loud. "A friend gave it to me."

"Friend as in this Matt guy?"

She stared straight ahead, shifting in her seat. "It's not a big deal at all."

He breathed a sigh of relief. "Okay." He winced, afraid to hear the answer to his next question. "Does this Matt guy drive?"

He put his hand under her chin, lifting her head. "Does he?"

"Yes. He drives."

"Do not get into the car with him."

"Yeah, I know."

"I can't lose you. I won't lose you."

"Can you at least meet him?"

"Soon."

"Okay, tomorrow then, right?"

"I'll let you know when I'm ready." He shook a finger at her. "And no dating until I meet him."

"That's not fair," she said, raising her voice again and piercing the sacred silence.

He nodded toward the elderly couple. "Shhh."

"They're old. They can't hear us."

"Have you ever heard of hearing aids?"

She frowned. "We're getting off track. What about Matt?"

"What about him?"

"Ugh. Can I bring him over?"

"Soon."

"You won't meet him. I know you. I know the game you're playing."

"I'll meet him when I want to meet him and not a minute sooner," he said in a stern tone.

"All right. All right. I can wait."

Surprised, Michael made a pretense of checking her forehead for a temperature. "You feeling okay?"

"Very funny." She smiled. "I know you have a lot on your mind, working so hard, trying to pay the bills. You deserve a break." She leaned her head on his shoulder. "How about I cook us a nice dinner tonight?"

He moved away. "You're too obvious."

She backed away and formed an angelic look like she always did when she tried to look innocent. "Obvious? Why, I don't know what you mean, Father."

He shook his head and chuckled. "What do you want now, Elizabeth Ellen Stewart?"

She smiled sweetly. "If it's okay with you, I'd like to go to the concert."

"What concert?"

"The one in New York City."

"Where in New York City?"

"Madison Square Garden."

"Who's performing there?"

"Lady Gaga."

"Lady Gaga? Why would you waste your money on her? Wait until Springsteen tours again."

"I don't think so." She shook her head. "Hasn't he retired? Anyway, I don't want to see an old dude on stage."

"Hey, Bruce is not old."

"Will you let me go to the concert? All my friends are going."

They sat in an uncomfortable silence for several minutes though it seemed like hours. Michael broke the quiet of the now unholy atmosphere. "No."

"What?"

"No concert."

"Why?"

"Two reasons. Number one. You're too young to go into the city with friends. Number two. You're too young."

She rolled her eyes. "What happened to the dad who came back from Jerusalem? That dad was way more easy going."

"I've changed again. I'm a complex person."

"Would you rather have me dating a seventeen-year-old or going to a concert with my girlfriends?"

"Neither. Oh, and he's seventeen? Now the truth comes out."

"Ugh."

"Shh."

"I don't care."

Michael bobbed his head, gesturing to the old man and woman listening. "She wants to go see that Lady Goo Goo person in the city."

The couple half smiled then looked away and whispered to each other as they fiddled with their ear pieces.

Elizabeth took the bait. "Don't you think my dad should let me go? I'm old enough to get married."

"You are not."

"It's in the Bible."

Michael waved to the couple and faced Elizabeth. "Enough. Leave them alone."

"What about the Lady Gaga concert?"

Michael didn't answer. The old man and woman got up, and walked slowly out of the church, taking quick, nervous glances as they went by.

Michael stood. "C'mon. I'll get you an ice cream sundae, whatever toppings you want."

Elizabeth yanked on his jacket, pulling him back down. "I'm not a little kid anymore where you can pacify me with ice cream when we're arguing."

"Chill."

"Stop using that word."

"Chill."

"Stop."

"The offer for ice cream is still on the table. Concert is closed for discussion. End of story."

"I don't want ice cream," she said, folding her arms. "Told you, I'm past that now."

"You're sounding like an ice cream snob now." He jostled her, trying to lighten the mood. "Let's go. I promise it'll be a quick trip."

She looked uncomfortable. "I don't think it's a good idea to go there anymore."

"Why? You always enjoyed going there with me before." He tried to stand up again but Elizabeth pulled him down harder. "Hey, take it easy on the jacket. It's a gift from Susan."

"I saw Linda with a man the other day."

"So?"

"She was holding his hand and they kissed."

Michael was quiet for a moment. "Oh." He stood, banging his knee against the pew. "Ouch," he said, trying to make a joke of it. "Look at that? Hurt twice in less than a minute. I guess I'm striking out in a couple of centuries. At least I'm consistent."

He climbed over Elizabeth, tripping over the kneeler as he reached the aisle and headed toward the basement door.

"Dad, give it up."

Michael stopped. "I need a minute, okay?"

"I know where you're going," she said. "The tunnel's not open."

"I have to finish cleaning the basement."

"There isn't a speck of dust left down there."

He put both hands over his ears, not looking back at her. "You would be surprised how much dirt I find down there."

Michael felt his daughter watching his every move as he veered toward the stairwell. He looked back and saw her shaking her head as she dropped her backpack on the pew and got up to follow him.

He rested his forehead against the door.

She stood beside him. "You're going to go down there and nothing will happen. Just like the other hundred times."

"I have to try one more time. Okay, kiddo?"

"If we had stayed in Jerusalem, we'd never have been safe."

He put his hand on her shoulder and brushed the pink lock of hair from her eyes. For a moment he thought about grabbing a pair of scissors and cutting it off. "I know. But I'd feel responsible if Leah was hurt or had to live a life with that evil Roman. I know we made the right choice to come back. But I wish I'd gone back to be sure about her safety. I'm convinced of that now."

She smiled. "By the way, where is your pastor buddy?"

"He's never here on Friday afternoons. Takes off after lunch. Weird."

Elizabeth laughed. "Probably goes joy riding on his Harley."

"Maybe I'll get one of those hogs."

"Oh please, don't."

"Can you see me zipping along with the wind whipping through my hair? A lady holding onto me riding in the back. Baby, we were born to run…"

She ignored him. "Where does he go?"

"No idea." He shrugged. "He never says and I never ask."

"Huh, you sure you guys are BFFs?" They walked back to the pew and Elizabeth picked up her bag.

He shook his head and turned his back on the basement door. "Come on, I'll drive you home."

"I don't need a ride. I'm going to catch a movie."

"What are you going to do for dinner?"

"Pizza. Going to head over to Gino's. RoRo's working there tonight."

They walked down the front steps to the sidewalk. "I guess you'll need money."

She held out her hand and smiled. "Twenty sounds about right."

Michael took a deep breath, sighed, and pulled a bill from his wallet.

"You could make it easy on yourself and let me have your credit card."

He ignored her. "Be home by nine and keep your cell phone on."

"Relax. It's not like I'm going to get stuck in Jerusalem or anything."

"Very funny. What about your bike?"

"RoRo's dad will give me a ride home. He can fit it in the back of the car."

"Well, call me if you need a ride, okay? And don't get in the car with anyone besides her dad."

She gave a faint smile and Michael watched as she rode away. Once she was out of sight he unlocked the car and got in. The glove compartment door was open again. He saw his cell phone was still inside. He slammed the door three times before the lock finally caught. *Got to get that fixed*, he thought for the hundredth time. But it was never a high priority on his to-do list.

His stomach felt queasy as a sharp pain stabbed his right side. He wondered how he was going to spend his evening. *I've done this routine a few times.*

As he pulled into the driveway, he gazed up at the darkening sky. The stars twinkled more brightly than he had ever remembered. Rolling down his window, he whispered softly over the gentle breeze, "Which star are you under tonight, Leah?"

* * *

After a less than satisfying bowl of Cheerios for dinner, Michael was restless and still hungry. Despite his better judgment, he downed two boiled hot dogs, further agitating his upset stomach. He carried the salty taste in his mouth while walking aimlessly up and down the stairs several times, occasionally clicking on the television to channel surf for a glimpse of hockey and basketball scores. He sat on his chair and perched his laptop on his knees. Just as he started an email, he heard the sound of a car door slamming near his house.

Curious, he got up to see who it was. He opened the blind to the front window. "Great. Here comes hell in heels."

He watched as his sister headed toward his front door. He stared in shock. *What happened to her?* Michael rubbed his eyes in disbelief, squinting to be sure. She carried an extra thirty pounds or so on her once stick-like figure. An oversized man's sweatshirt and loose jeans were clearly an attempt to hide her extra weight. Her blond hair, usually neatly kept, now looked straggly, and the dark roots were visible under the porch light's glare. Age looked like it had not only crept up on Connie but trampled all over her. Her wrinkles had wrinkles, which were usually hidden under a ton of makeup.

His sister had been a thorn in his side since they were kids. She was a control freak in the worst sense, always plotting for ways to hurl verbal shots to get under his skin.

He took his time walking down the stairs. "I need this like I need a hole in the head," he muttered.

Opening the front door, he tried to sound enthusiastic but couldn't control himself. "Ah, the last person I want to see on a Friday night. I'm kind of busy."

She looked at him through the screen door. "Oh, my little brother is doing something on a Friday night? Armageddon must be just around the corner then."

Michael cringed as he held the door for her. He could tell it was going to be a long night. "What do you want?"

She swept past him and into the kitchen. "I need something to drink. I'm thirsty."

He followed behind her and watched as she stared at the dishes piled in the sink and the cluttered countertop. She snickered and his stomach turned. He was acutely aware now of the pot on the stove, with its one remaining hot dog.

She laughed, pointing to the pot. "I see the gourmet cook is hard at work again. Bet you're waiting for the Lifestyles of the Rich and Famous to give you a call for a feature, huh?"

"That show is off the air."

"So, apparently, is your life. How does my niece live in such a pig hole?"

"We like to think of it as a mud hole, and we love it."

"Are you working?"

"Yes."

"Yeah, really? Where?" She reached into a cabinet for a glass and opened the refrigerator. "Oh, dear, Lord. Look at this mess. Old Chinese food, milk that's expired. A cucumber? My poor niece."

He grabbed the milk container away from her. "This is fine." He put it back and closed the door.

She put her hands on her hips, her lips slanted in cockiness. "So where are you working?"

"At the church."

"You? In a church? Hell hath frozen over." She passed him and headed back to the living room. "I heard you talking to someone when I was at the door. Is someone here, or are you talking to yourself these days?" She danced a few odd steps around the room. "Are you finally dating? It's about time. Where is she? Why haven't I met her?" She laughed in the way that always grated on his nerves. "Are you embarrassed? Is she hideous or something? Does she look like one of the Teletubbies?"

I need a drink. "Would you like a glass of wine?"

She sat in his favorite recliner and pushed the footrest up. "Wow, my little brother is asking me if I want to have a drink with him. My goodness, life is certainly getting better for me."

"Do you want a glass or not?" he asked, raising his voice as he headed back into the kitchen.

"I'd better take your offer since it probably won't happen again."

He reached into the refrigerator and pulled out a bottle of white wine. He grabbed a couple of glasses and a corkscrew from the cabinet. He soothed his anxiety with a deep breath before returning to the living room. "Why am I blessed with your visit?"

"Blessed? Since when are you so holy?"

"Why are you here?"

"Do I have to have a reason?"

He plunged the corkscrew in and twisted. "You never stop by."

"You never invite me."

"And you really wonder why I don't?" He pulled the cork out harder than he'd intended. "So, what gives?"

"Maybe I wanted to see how my little brother's doing."

"I'm fine. Nothing for you to worry about."

"I am worried." She crossed her arms over her chest. "When's the last time you were with a woman? Don't tell me you still haven't been with anyone since Vicki?"

He dropped onto the couch, pulled the coffee table closer, and poured them each a glass of wine. "It's none of your business."

She scoffed. "It *is* my business." She gestured toward the wine bottle. "Keep pouring."

He filled the glass nearly to the top and handed it to her. "No, it isn't."

She took a long sip. "Are you going to tell me or not? Or do you spend your nights drinking yourself into oblivion?" She took another sip and placed her feet on the ground as if to make an important point. "Like Dad."

Like Jim? What a sucker punch. "Knock it off."

"Grumpy, just like the old man. And you're living your life in that drunken illusion. How's the writing going? Are you working for the *New York Times* yet? Did you win that Pulitzer?" She slapped her hand to her forehead in mock realization. "Oh, right, right. You're a novelist now. One of those self-published people who can't find a real publisher because your work is *misunderstood*. Shouldn't you be a bestselling novelist by now? Oh, right, I forgot, it takes time," she said, mocking the words he'd said a long time ago. "So, how many copies of the great American novel have you sold? Two? Three?"

Michael hadn't talked much about his book nor had he shared the contents of the story with any member of his family. Apparently, word about the publication of his novel had made its way around his large group of relatives.

"Yup, you're just like Dad." She drained the last bit of her wine.

"You never change, do you?" He shook his head in disgust. "You come to my house, uninvited. And you sit here, drink my wine, and goad me."

"Well, *excuse* me," she said, drawing out the word. "Sorry for caring about you."

"You call this caring?" He waved his finger at her. "I call it hateful."

"Hateful? Oh, please. Come and join me in this great crap hole of life."

She grabbed the bottle and filled her glass half way. They were both silent as he watched her take a long swallow.

"Look," she said, her expression softening. "I really am concerned about you. This is how I show it."

"Worry about yourself. I can handle my own life."

He topped off her glass. *Maybe she'll shut up and snooze if I ply her with more wine. Yeah, a silent Connie.*

She raised her over-plucked eyebrows as he refilled his own glass. "Drinking a lot there?"

"I'm not going anywhere tonight."

"Maybe you should. You can't find a woman while you're sitting in your chair drinking wine on a Friday night."

Can't she stop her needling for five minutes? "Get off it."

"Oh, did I touch a nerve?"

"I had a good woman in Vicki. I had a good woman in Leah . . ."

She slammed the footrest down. "Hold on. Who is Leah?"

He recoiled. He had never told his sister about his trip to Jerusalem, knowing she'd be on the phone to the nut house in a New York minute to turn him in. He struggled to come up with an answer. "She lives far away."

"Far away? Where? California? Europe?" She laughed, sounding like her younger self when she taunted him. "Is Leah your drinking buddy?"

"She's out of my life. Subject closed."

"Yeah, right. Does she even exist? Or is this one of your fantasies?" She shook her head, twisting her mouth in a mean sneer. "Geez. Even Dad doesn't make up this kind of junk."

He held the bottle up. "Why don't you stick this up..." He caught himself and stopped. *She's getting to me again.* Michael stood and walked back into the kitchen.

"Why are you running away?" she called out. "I'm just curious about this Leah woman."

"You'd never understand," he shot back.

"Come back in here. I promise I'll listen. I'll understand. Tell me about Leah."

Michael placed his glass down on the counter. *She's like Lucy to my Charlie Brown, always pulling the football away right before I can kick it.*

He took a long sip of his wine, hoping it would erase the last ten minutes of their conversation and headed back to the living room. He sat and looked into his glass.

Connie threw back more wine as she settled herself comfortably in the recliner, crossing her legs. "C'mon. I promise I won't tease you. Who's Leah?"

Michael hesitated, downed more wine for courage, and chose his words carefully. "You're not going to be a jerk about it?"

"I swear." She put her hand over her heart.

He blew out a loud breath. "Leah is someone I met a few months back. Elizabeth and I took a short trip, we got into some trouble and she helped us out."

"Hold on." Connie leaned forward. "Trouble? Are you broke again?"

"I'm not broke." He scowled. "It had nothing to do with money. She kept us safe."

"Safe from what?" She looked concerned. "And since when did you start traveling?"

Michael sighed. "It's hard to explain. We were in a different town."

"Where? Here on Long Island?"

"Not even close," he replied.

"Were you drinking before I came over? You're not making any sense. I think the wine's making you delusional."

"It has nothing to do with the wine. I'm telling you the truth. We were in a different town and Leah helped us."

"Well, then, where is she?"

"I don't know. I can't get in touch with her even if I wanted to."

He rubbed his forehead. *And I desperately want to know if she's okay.*

"Didn't you get her phone number?" she asked and Michael laughed. "What's so funny?"

He shook his head. "You wouldn't understand."

"Well, where does she live?"

Michael waited for the football to be pulled away. He emptied the remaining wine in his glass. "Jerusalem."

Connie's eyebrows shot up. "Get out of here. When did you find the time and money to fly over there?"

"We didn't fly." He let out a loud sigh.

"You're drunk."

"Maybe I am, but I was there and I know what I saw and who I met." He dug into his pocket and fingered the coins. *Should I?*

She laughed and sipped her wine, choking a few times. Michael stared. Connie continued. "Great fantasy you've got going there. This is better than the movies. So, did you take a boat to Jerusalem or did you drive?"

Okay, this is where I stop. "Actually, we rode our bikes."

"Now you're being a jerk."

"It's called payback."

They sat in silence for a few minutes. After finishing her wine, Connie asked, "Were you serious about this woman?"

"It doesn't matter. She's gone." He leaned back on the couch, rubbing the space between his brows. "I didn't expect you to believe me."

"Then why did you tell me?"

"Probably because I hoped that someday my older sister would be a friend."

"Ouch."

"Now you know how I feel when you're around."

"Then why did you ask me to come in for a drink? Why do you still talk to me if I'm such a pain?"

He opened a drawer in the side table, dusted off an old Bible and waved it at her. "Because I remember a time when we were partners in crime."

Nauseous from drinking too much wine, eating Cheerios, and the hot dogs, he retreated to the bathroom, still clutching the Bible. He splashed cold water on his face, sat at the edge of the tub, smoothed the cover and closed his eyes.

He replayed a memory when he and Connie were kids and with vivid recollection remembered one time when they had each other's back.

The memory was so vibrant, he could still hear his father's deep voice, booming, "Connie. Michael. Get down here now!"

Connie ran from her room to the hallway, almost colliding with Michael. "We're in trouble," she whispered.

He shrugged. She ran down the stairs.

"Hi, Daddy. I'm here," she said, standing at attention.

Michael took his time entering the room. He stood close to his sister and cowered.

Their father reached up and tugged Michael hard on his arm, his face only a few inches away. Jim's eyes were bloodshot and his short sideburns were streaked with gray. The air around him was heavy with the smell of whiskey.

"What was the gospel about today?" Jim demanded.

Michael glanced at Connie.

Her expression mirrored his feelings.

Fear.

His father tightened his grip.

"Ouch." Michael rubbed the sore spot and Jim squeezed harder.

"Go to the basement," Jim yelled. "And don't come back up until you can tell me what you learned in church today."

Jim let go of Michael's arm and he followed his sister down the basement stairs, upset that he'd have to miss the football game on TV.

They headed toward the back room behind the boiler. "What do we do now?" he asked.

Connie fell to her knees, her short black hair bouncing as she peered into the crawl space behind the boiler. "No problem."

"What are you doing?"

"Hold on, give me a sec."

She reached in with her hand. "Got it." She pulled out a small, dusty, pocket handbook.

"What else you got in there?" he asked.

"Nothing."

He shrugged. "Whatever."

Connie hopped up, wiping the dirt from the cover. She flipped through several pages. "Here, look. What's today's date again? Yeah, this is it." Her cheeks were flushed with excitement.

Michael read the page and understood. "Nice."

For the next few minutes, they sat and read the gospel from that Sunday together.

Michael looked at his sister, surprised they'd been communicating without tearing each other apart.

"Are you ready to go upstairs?" she asked, after quizzing him a few times.

He nodded with enthusiasm. "I know it now. It's about Thomas doubting Jesus was alive and he wanted to touch his wounds. It's gross but I guess that's what Dad wants, right?"

"Yeah, right." She dropped her hands down so he could slap a low five. He walloped her hand hard. "Hey, that hurt," she yelled.

Loud, heavy footsteps crossed the floor above their heads. "What's going on down there?" Jim called down.

"Nothing," Connie said. "We're ready to talk to you."

"Then get up here."

They ran up the steps, eager to share their newfound information. Standing before their father, they lifted their heads high with pride as Connie started the story and Michael finished it. They both stood in front of their father, grinning.

Jim stopped rocking back and forth in the recliner, and strained to see, like he did when he was suspicious. "Next week I'll ask you again," he said. "And you better know it the first time. No more trips to the basement." He picked up his paper off the floor and held it front of his face.

"Can we go?" Michael asked with trepidation.

Jim's eyes peeked over the paper. "Go."

As they scurried back up the stairs, Michael leaned over and whispered, "That was a great idea. I really liked teaming up with you."

"Yeah." Connie smiled back. "Me, too."

* * *

"Hey, did you fall in the toilet?" Connie's voice brought Michael back to the present.

He opened his eyes, stood and splashed more cold water on his face, toweled himself off, heaved a deep breath, and returned to the living room.

"What were you doing in there?" she asked. "Did you fall asleep? Did you fall in the toilet?"

"Wasn't sleeping. Just deep in thought."

"I know I don't visit a lot, but I can tell I'm not really welcome here."

"It's because sometimes you can be a pain in the backside," he said. "But I hang on to the good stuff we used to do together."

She put her glass down and wiped the corner of her eyes.

"Oh, no," he said, surprised. "What's wrong? I thought I said something nice."

Tears ran down her face faster than she could dry them. "You don't understand. My life is a mess. I'm lonely and scared." She fumbled with her purse. "I'm sure that makes you happy. Right?"

"Of course it doesn't make me happy. Why would you think that?"

"I'm a loser. My husband left me, I'm eating cupcakes and cookies for breakfast, I don't even feel like putting on makeup anymore and I'm spending Friday night drinking with my little brother."

"Gee, thanks."

"Oh, shut up, you know what I mean."

He burrowed through his pockets and handed her a tissue.

She took it and dabbed her eyes. "Thanks."

They sat in awkward silence until Michael felt she had composed herself. "I'm expecting Elizabeth home soon."

"Oh, great," she said. "I can't let my niece see what a loser I am."

"Stop. You're not a loser. Elizabeth doesn't think that either."

"Why do you say that?"

"You think I don't appreciate the times you helped me with her when she was young? The times you took her to the movies when I had to work. She told me how you spoiled her with candy and popcorn at the movies. She still remembers how you both laughed when you spilled a big bag all over the seat. She'll always have those wonderful memories, and she brags about how fun and cool her Aunt Connie is."

A peaceful understanding of silence fell between them. "Let me call you a cab. You're in no condition to drive and I won't let you anyway. You know how I am about that."

She nodded and her body shook. "I miss Sammie so much."

"I miss her too."

She stood. "Look at me. I'm a mess."

He walked over and hugged her. "I'm not much better."

"Did Dad call?"

"Me?"

"Yes. Did he call you?"

"You've got to be kidding. Why? Is the old man dying?"

"That's not funny."

"Is he dying?"

"Now's not the time to talk about this. I'm sure he'll talk to you soon."

CHAPTER TWO

A glint of light snaked its way through the jagged blinds, striking Michael in the face as he turned over to relieve the throbbing in his head. He slid under another pillow to muffle the sound of the ringing phone on the night stand.

"Who's calling at this forsaken hour?" he groaned. *C'mon, machine, pick up.*

As Michael reached over to check the caller ID, he knocked the receiver from the cradle, sending it crashing to the floor. *Oh great.*

"Hello?" a voice called out from below.

Michael flopped back down onto the bed. "Hold on."

He rubbed his forehead several times with his fingers, and wiped away the grainy residue from his eyes. The pain in his head ricocheted from side to side as he retrieved the phone. "Yeah?"

"Michael?"

"Who's this? Why are you calling so early?"

"It's Dennis. I'm sorry if I woke you. It's half past ten and I thought you'd be up."

"I was getting up anyway."

Michael leaned back on the pillow and closed his eyes.

"I saw you in church yesterday and didn't stop to talk, because I noticed you were spending time with your daughter. Looked like you two were in a deep discussion and I didn't want to interrupt." Michael heard shuffling of paper on the other end of the line. "Is everything okay?"

He sat up, cracking his back against the headboard. "We're fine. Same old stuff. Thanks for asking." He yawned. "I cleaned the basement, too."

"It's the cleanest place in the church," Dennis said with a hearty laugh. "I have a few people coming by to make Thanksgiving baskets for our food drive this morning. If you want to come by later and talk, I'll be free."

"Are we going to talk about the book again? Did you learn anything new about it?"

The old book that Michael found in the basement had been a constant source of conversation and speculation between the two. Over two hundred years old, it contained stories of miraculous events that occurred in the old church. The pastor was protective of the book and had never let Michael read it.

"We should talk later," said Dennis. "I was thinking that perhaps you could share your journey to the past with others."

Michael rubbed his forehead with vigorous strokes. "They'll think I'm nuts."

"You were blessed with the gift of time travel. Think it over and I'll support you if you decide you want to share your story."

Michael didn't respond. They said goodbye and hung up the phone. Stretching his arms out, he yawned again. He hadn't had a solid sleep like that in a long time. He hadn't even heard Elizabeth come home.

Elizabeth? "Oh, the class, shoot." He panicked and staggered down the hallway toward his daughter's room and knocked on her door. "Lizzy? Are you here?"

He burst into her room. "Lord, what a mess." He almost tripped over the assortment of history books and papers scattered all over the floor. Her karate robe hung over the computer. *Yup, this was her private mud hole.* Yet he marveled at the neatly made bed. A small, stuffed Pikachu doll stood guard in the middle, a mainstay from her toddler years.

Those were wonderful days.

He stepped out in the hallway. "Elizabeth? Are you home?" Silence.

He ran down the stairs and into the kitchen. A note was attached to the refrigerator with a calendar magnet.

Dad, gone to class, will be back early afternoon. Auntie C called and said she has to see you when she comes to get her car. You have to be here at 11 to let her in. Have fun. ☺ *Love, Lizzy*

Breathing a sigh of relief, he walked back upstairs into the bathroom and turned on the shower. He wasn't up to shaving, so he skipped it. He let the water slide down his face for a few moments, the warm heat gently massaging his eyes.

My teenager is taking a class and I'm lying in bed all morning. Boy, have things changed.

He stepped out of the shower onto the worn monkey mat, careful not to get the tile wet. *I've got to get rid of this thing.* He considered sneaking it out the door and pitching it into the garbage can when Elizabeth wasn't looking. It was the one childhood decoration she'd insisted on keeping other than her stuffed, spotted purple bear named Lucy and the beloved Pikachu.

Michael looked in the mirror while brushing his teeth and noticed more gray hairs invading his temples. His eyes still felt crusty so he cupped some water from the faucet into his hands and splashed his face. As he dabbed the moisture away, he could feel wrinkles forming at the corners of his eyes. *Man, I look bad.* He wasn't surprised though, since he wasn't used to drinking more than one glass of wine. He got dressed and lumbered down the stairs into the kitchen.

He hoped his sister's hangover was worse than his so she wouldn't show up today.

He surveyed the kitchen. *What a mess.* There were two empty wine bottles on the counter. The odor caused his stomach to lurch. A cereal bowl with hardened Cheerios along with an uneaten hotdog floating in a pot filled with old milk sat in the sink. *Gross. When did I cook that?*

The doorbell rang.

He pivoted around to the front door. He could hear Connie's muffled voice on the other side. "Hey, little brother. Open up."

The night ends and the day begins with Connie. Terrific.

"Hold your horses," Michael said as the bell chimed again.

"Hey, bro," she said, brushing past him and into the living room. She dropped to her knees, moving her hands underneath the recliner. "How's your head feeling? Can't handle your liquor? Boy, were you a mess last night. Where're you going today? Paris? London? I bet the Starship Enterprise will be docking outside any minute."

He plunked down on the sofa, rubbing the back of his neck. "What do you want?"

"I lost my cell phone. Did you see it? Did you call that girl from Jerusalem?" She laughed. "Thought you could pull one over on your big sister, didn't you? So where did you put my cell phone?"

"How in the magical world of Disney would I know?"

She stood, putting her hands on her hips. "Well?"

"Well, what?"

"Aren't you going to help me find it?"

He pulled the pillows off the couch and ran his hands beneath the seat cushions. The sooner he helped her find it, the sooner she would leave.

Sighing, he said, "Nothing over here. You sure you had it last night?"

"Yes, I'm sure. Just keep looking."

As he stood, he let out a load groan.

"Getting old, little brother, aren't you?"

"Not as old as you, *older* sister," he retorted as he took the wine glasses off the coffee table and brought them into the kitchen.

"Very funny. Is it in there?"

He left the glasses by the sink before checking the counter. "Nope." He picked up a cell phone from the counter. "This one's mine." He flipped it open. "Great. Dead."

He went back into the living room and saw all the cushions scattered on the floor. The drawers from his desk were pulled out and she was rummaging through their contents. "What are you doing?" he asked, annoyed.

"Help me."

"It's not in my desk. Listen, I've got to get going. Put the stuff back. Now."

"Sorry I bothered you, little brother."

"Stop calling me little brother," he snapped.

Surprise registered on her face. She slammed the desk drawers shut. "You're more like the old man than you think. So cranky after a night of drinking."

He grabbed his coat from the hall closet. "Close the door on your way out."

"Where are you going?"

"To church."

"Church? But we haven't found my cell phone yet."

He remembered his own cell phone and ran into the kitchen, pulled the charger from the junk drawer and plugged it into the wall. He jotted down a brief note on a sheet of paper and stuck it on the fridge next to Elizabeth's note.

"I'm leaving now," he shouted over his shoulder.

"Wait up."

He blew out a frustrated growl. "What now?"

"My cell phone. I need it," she said, meeting him by the door.

"So call the phone company and get a new one. What's the big deal?"

Her eyes filled with tears.

"It's a stinking cell phone. Look, let me call it. Maybe we'll hear the ring."

"No, it won't work."

"Why?"

"It was dead when I came over last night. I didn't have a chance to recharge it."

"Then why are you getting so upset?"

"I had something important on it."

"What could be so important? You can always get the contact numbers again."

She looked away and wiped her eyes. "I had a text message from Craig on it that I…I saved…and…a photo of us. Our last one. In our favorite restaurant. Can you believe he told me there?"

"Oh."

She twisted her wedding ring. "His text was the last time he wrote 'love you' to me."

He inhaled a deep breath. "I'm sorry. Okay, let's keep looking."

"No." She shook her head and waved her hand. "You have to get going. I don't want to stop you."

He patted her on the back. "We can find it later. Why don't you come with me? The cell phone will eventually turn up and this will get your mind off things for a bit."

"To church?" Her eyes widened. "With you?"

"Yes. Just like old times."

"Old times? More like ancient times. Which church are you going to these days?"

"I'll surprise you. Let's just make sure we lay off the church wine."

Connie actually let out a genuine laugh with no mocking in its tone. A sound he hadn't heard in a long time.

* * *

Backpack in hand, Elizabeth ran outside from her classroom at noon into the crisp, sunny day. She unlocked the chain that secured her red bike against the fence. Zipping up her denim jacket, she tugged down on an old Islanders hockey snow hat and adjusted her earphones. She hit the speed dial to call a friend to find out what time they'd be getting together.

After the phone call, she slipped it into her backpack and hopped on her bike. She pedaled down Larkfield Road, speeding past the candy store. She pushed hard on the brakes and skidded. *I should get Dad his newspapers so it'll give him something to do today. Yep. Keep him busy.*

She raced into the parking lot, flipped a wheelie, catapulted over the curb, and locked the bike against the garbage bin. "Hi, Sam," she called out as she entered the store.

"Well, well, look who it is. My goodness, you've grown so much. I remember when you were just a baby," said the gray-haired man behind the register.

Elizabeth giggled. "You say the same thing every time I come in here. I'm a young woman now."

"A woman? My, you can't be much more than thirteen."

She rolled her eyes. "Fourteen."

Sam laughed. "How can I help you, sweetie?"

"Picking up my dad's newspapers."

"Where's your dad?"

"He was still sleeping when I left the house."

Sam's eyes widened. "Wow, that's a change. So it's your job now to get the papers?"

"Today it is."

He handed her the *Wall Street Journal*, *Investors Business Daily*, the *Northport Observer*, and the *Northport Times*. Elizabeth also picked up two sports magazines. "There," she said. "This should keep him busy this weekend. Right?"

"I guess."

Elizabeth handed him the rest of the pizza money from the previous night. "See ya."

Sam laughed. "See you when you're fifteen."

"I *am* almost fifteen," she said over her shoulder.

She tucked the magazines and newspapers inside her backpack and pedaled her way onto Waterside Avenue, staying in the right-hand bike lane. The riding area was narrow in Northport, keeping her almost pinned against the curb. A loud horn sounded behind her. A few seconds later, it blared again.

"Seriously, how much room am I taking up?" She listened intently to the car gaining on her as she hugged the curb.

The horn sounded a third time.

"Give it a rest, will ya," she yelled as she braked to look behind her.

"Give what a rest?" the driver yelled back as the car pulled up next to her and the passenger window slid down.

She smiled when she saw it was Matt. "Oh, it's you."

"Yeah, it's me."

"I thought you were some jerk trying to run me off the road."

"Wrong on both counts. Right?"

Elizabeth laughed. "Of course."

"You need a ride?"

"I've got my bike."

Matt leaned across the front seat and opened the door. "I know you've got your bike, but I thought you might want to save some energy."

"Now that's 'environmentally-not-so-savvy' of you. Professor Black would be so upset." She smirked at him before noticing another car approaching. He tracked it in his rearview mirror. The woman in the driver's seat scowled as she drove by them.

Elizabeth hesitated. "I don't know, Matt. I think I should just bike it home."

"Why? Come on. Get in. You never let me drive you. What's up with that?"

She shook her head. "Long story. Sad story. A dad story."

Elizabeth saw the dejection in his face. *Oh great. I'll lose a chance to go out with him because my dad is psycho about me getting in a car with any teenager.*

"You haven't had anything to drink, have you?" she asked.

"Like what?"

She felt stupid. "You know. Alcohol."

"What?" Matt looked annoyed. "Do you really think I would drink and drive?"

He started to pull away.

"Stop. Stop, Matt. I just wanted to be sure."

He turned the engine off and clicked his hazards on.

"You know me. I wouldn't drink and drive."

She nodded as Matt opened his door and walked to the back of the car to get her bike. "Ah, I don't know if it's going to fit. Can we take off a wheel or something?"

Elizabeth effortlessly disconnected the brake before removing the front wheel and Matt took the bike frame from her.

As Matt struggled to squeeze the bike frame and front wheel into the trunk, Elizabeth settled into the passenger seat. She pulled her Islander hat off, checking in the side mirror to see if her hair was flat. She buckled her seatbelt and observed the contents of the opened and unused ashtray. *Is that a guitar pick?*

Matt slammed the trunk shut and slid behind the wheel.

"Cool car," she said.

Matt laughed. "You're being nice. It was made before we were born but I guess as long as it gets me around, it'll do."

"Hey, can you teach me how to drive?"

"You're only a freshman."

Elizabeth frowned. "Thanks for reminding me, oh ye great big *high school junior*." She tied her hair back, trying to think of something to say. "How did you like class today?"

"I'm into the whole ancient civilization stuff, so I found it interesting. What got you involved in the subject? Don't you think you're kinda young for a community college class?"

"First, enough about my age. Didn't you ever hear it's just a number?"

He persisted. "How'd you get into the class anyway?"

"A connection through my father." She straightened in her seat. "And, second, I know all about ancient civilizations, more than you think."

"You do?"

"I do."

Matt chuckled. "Sounds like we're getting married."

She nervously pushed the radio station button a few times. "I almost did."

"Get out of here. What are you talking about?"

She pointed to her house up ahead, although Matt knew where she lived. "Over there."

He turned into the driveway and parked the car.

Elizabeth became aware of the short distance between them as she unbuckled her seat belt. "Well," she said awkwardly. "Thanks for the ride."

"Tell me how you know so much, smarty," he said. "I won't even ask you what you meant about the marriage thing."

"Someday I will. But not now."

"When?"

"Not sure." She pushed on the door handle and it flew open, then ricocheted back at her. Desperate to get out of the car, she threw her foot in its path, and tried in earnest not to grimace when she felt the door crunch her foot against the car frame.

"Wait," Matt shouted.

"I got it, never mind." Elizabeth hopped out of the car, landing on her throbbing foot. She limped toward the trunk, hoping that he wouldn't notice her flushed face. She turned to see him looking at her over the roof of his car. "Thanks again."

"Hang on," he said. "I want to ask you something else. How about going to a movie or something?"

She took a few seconds to compose herself. "Sure. I'll let you know. Let me check with my dad and see what's going on today. Can you wait a minute?"

* * *

Outside the church several parishioners milled around the front steps, chatting about what they did the previous night, who they planned on seeing this evening, and their upcoming Thanksgiving plans. Michael was greeted by men shaking his hand and women planting friendly kisses on his cheeks.

Connie gave him an envious stare. "Are you sleeping with that one?" she'd whisper to him after each churchgoer embraced him in a warm hug.

"Would you stop?"

He was an old hand at fending off his sister's sweeping moods and inappropriate quips. But in this case, he actually relished the challenge. He glanced at a woman standing next to Dennis.

Connie perked up, pushing her glasses to the farthest point on her nose. "Who is that?"

The woman wore a figure fitting, attractive, black dress. Italian-made sunglasses shaded her eyes from the bright sun, and her dark curly, brown hair slightly touched her bare shoulders. She spoke in an eloquent, soft voice to Dennis. She didn't look more than thirty-five years old.

"My, oh my," Connie said "Is that the local slut?"

"Watch your mouth. Not that it's any of your business, she's just a friend."

"I don't believe you."

Michael wiggled his eyebrows up and down.

His sister devoured the bait. She smacked him on the shoulder. "No way."

"Keep it down. Only you know about this. The pastor doesn't even know."

She narrowed her eyes in suspicion. "What about Elizabeth?"

"No, not even her."

"You're not lying to me, are you?"

He shrugged. "I'm taking the fifth from here on in."

"Why didn't you tell me? Is she the Leah from Jerusalem? Can I meet her?"

He grabbed her arm in alarm as Connie headed toward the woman. "Her name is Linda. Please don't bother her."

"You're so sensitive. What happened between you two?"

"Nothing I should discuss with you. For once, can you please respect my feelings? Anyway, she's busy with Dennis."

"Dennis?"

"The pastor."

"My, we're on a first name basis with the holy honcho."

His mood switched to one of fake friendliness as he spotted a fellow church-goer. "Hey, Mrs. Fullerton, nice to see you."

"Good morning, Michael," the elderly woman said, pulling his head down to give him a kiss. She gestured to his sister. "Who's your friend?"

"Not a friend. This is only my sister. Connie, meet Mrs. Fullerton."

"Yes, Mrs. Fullerton, I'm *only* his sister," Connie said with a heavy dose of sarcasm.

Michael grabbed his sister, spun her around and gave her a big bear hug. "She's going to help us with the food and clothing drive today."

Connie backed out of his embrace, as if she'd been stung by a disturbed nest of bees. "Oh, please."

Mrs. Fullerton smiled. "You've got such a wonderful brother. See you both inside." She staggered slightly as she turned toward the steps.

Michael reached out to steady Mrs. Fullerton as she clung tightly to the railing with one hand and held a cane with the other. She climbed the stairs slowly, taking measured breaths. "I've got it, Michael, thank you."

Connie gave a low whistle under her breath. "My little brother is quite the Don Juan now, isn't he?"

He flashed a confident smile. "That I am."

"Look, I'm going inside," she said. "It's too cold out here."

It was a brisk November afternoon, with Thanksgiving only a few days away. This used to be Michael's favorite time of the year. The town had an early holiday feeling. His gray sweatshirt felt good in the sharp breeze blowing off the nearby harbor. Michael noticed Linda's cheeks were rosy from the frigid air.

Linda turned and caught him staring at her. She smiled and waved. "Hi, Michael." She walked over and gave him a big hug. He enjoyed it, but pulled away from the embrace.

"Hey, Linda, great to see you again." He flipped his hand toward the church door as he ran up the stairs.

Dennis greeted him at the door with a friendly slap on the back. "Hey, buddy, thank you for coming by to help. I'm glad you're here."

"Happy to help. Where do you want me to start?"

"Since you know the basic layout of this church better than most, I need you to bring some of the old containers and cartons full of clothes down to the basement."

"Sure. Where are they?"

"In my office."

"No problem. I'll get right to it." He hurried to Dennis' office.

Michael retrieved four plastic bins. He could see the clothes were in varying stages, from ratty old robes and cassocks to tattered and beaten sandals. He thought the clothing was similar to what was worn in Jerusalem, conjuring up more memories of his time with Leah.

Lost in thought, he went through the motions of setting the plastic bins down in a corner of the basement.

He opened the top container and touched an old robe lying on top of the heap. He shivered as he bunched the material in his hand. He pushed the robe to the side and grabbed a cassock. Carefully, he pulled it over his head and tightened the belt. *Not bad.* He could walk through a Jerusalem crowd any day and not stand out. The nostalgic thought made him smile.

He returned to the bin and rummaged through it, finding a pair of men's Teva sandals that looked like they were in good shape. Rubbing the straps, the familiarity of the sandals brought back the memory of wearing a similar pair in Jerusalem.

Thoughts of the final seconds of his encounter with the dangerous Roman soldier, coupled with the memory of kissing Leah, paralyzed him for a few minutes. His throat felt dry and his hand shook.

If I could go back I would. But I can't leave Elizabeth. What if I don't get back? I couldn't do that, but I want to.

He let out a breath and inhaled again. Steadying his hands, he leaned down and slipped his feet into the sandals. With slow steps, he walked around the basement, recalling the feel of the rough roads and stones beneath his feet.

"Oh, there you are," Connie said, yanking him out of his reverie as she poked her head through the doorway. "Pastor Dennis told me you were down here." She gave him an incredulous look. "What's with the get-up? Halloween was last month."

Michael ignored her.

"Anyway, I spoke to this Linda woman," she said, sounding triumphant. "Did you know she's over fifty? I bet she's even closer to fifty-five. But she's never been to Jerusalem. And she says you guys have gone out. So what have you got to say now, little brother?"

Michael continued to ignore her.

"Did you hear me?"

"Nope."

"What are you doing?"

"Thinking." Michael continued to rummage through the boxes, not sure what he was searching for. He fingered the coins inside his pocket, jingling them, bringing back more memories of his extraordinary journey.

He knelt down beside the container and removed several items, much of them clothing and old relics, including a wooden cross on a necklace. There was an inscription on the back. *The Lord shall protect his peaceful soldiers.* He slipped it around his neck.

"Isn't this beautiful, Connie?" He struggled to say the words in English but they came out in perfect Aramaic.

"What? What did you say?" Connie asked.

"You don't understand?"

"What?"

"I'm saying your hair looks like a bird's nest on a wet April day."

She scratched her head, looking confused. "I don't understand a word you're saying."

Michael trembled and removed the cross from his neck. "Isn't this beautiful?"

She nodded, still baffled. "Yes it is. But, what were you saying before? What language was that?"

"I was yanking your chain," he said, then ignored her guffaw as a glint of gold caught his eye. He knelt down and looked closer through the bin's clear plastic. At the bottom, he spotted a cross, no more than a foot long and wide.

His heart pounded against his ribs.

He found it.

The steel door to the tunnel lay beneath the box.

All he had to do was open it.

But he didn't.

Still kneeling, he stared at Connie, not saying a word.

"What? What's wrong?" she asked in alarm.

He stood and reached over to the bowl of holy water, sitting on a stanchion by the wall. Michael dipped both hands in it, looked at the water with reverence, and drank some.

His sister let out a loud gasp. "What are you doing?"

"I'm thinking."

"You just drank Holy Water. What could you possibly be thinking about?"

"About this," he said, lifting the box and pointing to the gold cross on the floor.

"So what? It's a cross. We're in a church."

"It's more than that. It could take me back to Jerusalem. It's a chance to see if Leah is safe. A chance to see if Jesus truly rose from the dead."

"Yeah, right." Connie rolled her eyes. "You're talking crazy," she said with a nervous laugh. "I think you're spending *way* too much time in this place and turning into one of those religious freaks." She got up and walked to the door. "I'm going back up-stairs. You're starting to scare me."

"No. Don't leave."

"Let's get out of here and go grab some coffee or something. My head is killing me."

"No, I can't leave."

"Suit yourself, but I'm out of here."

"Connie," he called after her. "Promise me that you'll take care of Elizabeth."

"You should lay off the wine. Your hangover is making you talk nonsense."

"Promise me, Connie."

"Of course, I'll always be there if Elizabeth needs me," she said, trying to placate him.

Michael stood in silence, touching the wooden cross so gently. His mind spun around and he wobbled slightly. He could still see Connie at the doorway and her frightened expression.

The sound of a screaming baby jolted him. His breath lodged in his lungs and he was speechless at the sight before him.

His daughter lay in a hospital incubator, crying. He saw a vision of himself leaning against the window, weeping over Vicki's death that night. He tried to shake himself from the nightmare by reaching for the wall behind him. Elizabeth appeared and wasn't more than five years old, running in the backyard, being chased by Connie. He smiled as his sister picked her up and twirled her in a circular direction like a merry go round.

His head continued to feel like he was in a misty fog. "I do," an older female voice said. He turned to his right and his daughter stood majestically in a beautiful white, long gown. A tall man had his back to him and was holding her hand. The church was filled with well-dressed people, some crying, others smiling. "Do you, Matthew…"

"Where am I?" he asked under his breath.

"Are you all right, Michael?" Connie yelled.

He couldn't answer as he fell to the ground.

She ran over to him. "Are you hurt?"

He stretched his neck and rubbed his eyes. "Just dizzy."

"What happened? I called out to you a few times. Didn't you hear me?"

"I felt light-headed and saw all these images of Elizabeth."

"What kind of images?"

"When she was born, the night Vicki died. When she was older, even when she was getting married."

"Wow. Did you sip the church wine while you were down here?"

"Wasn't the church wine," he said. "My life's with Elizabeth." He gaped at the cross and opened the small door, the stairwell to the tunnel now visible. "But I don't know if I should go down those steps and help a friend. What should I do?"

"You should do nothing. You don't know what's down there."

"I do."

She grabbed his arm and shook him. "Let's go back upstairs. You aren't well. You're scaring the daylights out of me."

He heard a voice from the tunnel.

"Wait." He motioned for her to be quiet.

"For what?"

"I thought I heard someone." He pushed Connie away, putting his ear to the opening of the tunnel. He heard a voice again, what sounded like a plea for help. "Did you hear that?"

"Hear what?"

"A voice in the tunnel." He took a couple of steps down. "Is that you, Leah?"

Connie bent over and listened. "I don't hear anything."

"Leah? Is that you?"

"You're hearing things. It's quiet down there."

Michael came back up. "If I go down there, don't let Elizabeth follow me." He gripped her shoulders. "Look at me. Never let Elizabeth enter this tunnel."

"You're scaring me."

"Make sure Elizabeth's scared. Do not let her go down those steps under any circumstance. Do you understand?"

"All right. All right. I'll keep her away from here."

"Good."

He thought he heard her mumble something about him needing to get a life as she climbed up the stairs. "Have fun down here. You are taking this church thing way too seriously."

Connie's steps grew fainter. His gaze remained transfixed on the tunnel's opening. He took three steps down and lifted the cross to his lips and kissed it.

His knees weakened and he fell, holding onto the top step with his hand. His mind left his body for a few moments. He reached for his cell phone but he couldn't move his arms, forgetting he'd left it at home.

Looking up, he gasped at the reflection he saw in the lone basement window. His eyes shone a bright fluorescent green. Red and orange flames licked his arms. His throat raged with warmth. He heard a voice again. The muffled words were like a summer fly buzzing near his ear.

"Leah, is that you?" He put his ear to the ground. "Elizabeth? My God, you didn't go down there, did you? Talk to me? Who is it?"

"There is no pain here. I miss you," the soft voice fluttered in his head.

"What's happening?" he said. "My legs. I can't feel my legs." But the words weren't audible as he strained to yell. "Something's wrong."

He could feel himself being pulled into the tunnel. He grabbed his chest and gasped for air. "I'm having a stroke. Someone ... help me."

CHAPTER THREE

Elizabeth ignored her throbbing foot and forgot about her bike in Matt's trunk. She headed straight for the front steps to the house. She noticed Connie's car was still in the driveway. *Where's Dad's car?* She examined the living room and hallway and shot her head out the door, smiling one last time at Matt, who was watching from the curb. "Wait one second, okay," she said with a wave.

He nodded.

"Dad? Are you home?" she called out instinctively, waiting for him to respond. There was no answer.

She sprinted up the stairs to the bathroom in search of eyeliner. She found it unopened in the top drawer and hobbled over to the mirror. She pulled her socks off, one of which was bloody and dropped it in a laundry basket.

She washed and bandaged her foot, brushed her hair and straightened her shirt. She didn't want to look like she had tried *too* hard. She admired herself one last time in the mirror.

The eyeliner looks real good.

She ran to her room and determined her father was in it recently. *I wonder what he was looking for now?* She walked further and peered out the window. She was relieved to see Matt still outside, waiting in the car.

She decided to take her glasses off, leaving them on the bookshelf. Then she opened her dresser drawer and rummaged in the back until she found a small box containing a gold locket. She paused a moment and clasped it around her neck, making sure it was clearly visible.

She took a quick look in her father's bedroom before heading down to the kitchen and finding his note on the fridge. "You've got to be kidding me. Church? Again?"

Noticing his cell phone still plugged into the wall, she snatched it up before going outside, locking the front door behind her.

She leaned her head through the passenger side window. "Can you give me a ride to church?"

"Yeah, sure. But what about your bike?"

"I'll get it later. Do you mind?"

"No, no problem."

He waited until she buckled her seat belt before backing out of the driveway. As he put the car in drive, he remained focused on the road.

There was an awkward silence. Elizabeth realized that he might have misinterpreted her request. "Oh, we're not going to a *service* or anything. It's just that my dad left his cell phone on the counter and I should tell him where we're going."

"Your father goes to church on Saturdays?"

"Well, yeah. He goes to church a lot of days."

Matt gave her an odd look as he paused to make the left onto Waterside Avenue. "Really. Is he a religious nut or something?"

She sighed. *Great. Now he thinks my dad is a freak.* "Not at all."

"Then why does he go to church a lot?"

"He does a lot of volunteering. And today he's doing some community service thing." Elizabeth kicked her backpack with her good foot, wondering why she hadn't left it at home.

"So he just likes being there?"

"Forget it. You wouldn't understand."

"Hey," he said with a smile, tapping her gently on the shoulder. "Is that a nice thing to say to someone who's giving you a lift?"

"No, it totally isn't." She giggled. "Sorry about that."

"No harm done."

The curbs on Main Street were lined with cars. Matt looked relieved to see no one was coming up behind him. He parked the car about twenty yards from the main entrance.

"Wait here," Elizabeth said, opening the door and sprinting to the sidewalk.

"Hey, can I meet your dad?"

Elizabeth ran back a few steps toward the car. "Not today. Maybe another time, okay?"

"I guess." He shrugged. "You know, I'd like to meet him someday. Does he even know who I am?"

Elizabeth nodded at him, smiling. She saw her father's Toyota and wondered if she should leave a note. The front passenger side door was unlocked. As she pulled it open, the glove compartment door swung down.

"Geez, he still hasn't fixed this thing," she said in frustration.

She put the cell phone in the compartment and slapped at the door but it fell down again. A few Christmas CDs, a ballpoint pen, and the phone slid to the floor.

Annoyed, she slammed it hard again, pinching her little finger as it shut. "Oh great." She pulled her hand back and some blood hit the floor mat.

She rummaged through the glove compartment for a tissue. She found one and wiped her bloody finger, then tossed it on the floor.

I'll just go give him his phone.

She pocketed the phone and slammed the car door, then raced by a handful of parked cars before crossing the street in front of the church. She noticed Matt had gotten out of his car and was now leaning against the bumper, watching her.

Elizabeth jogged through the front doors of the church, expertly weaving around the people working in the foyer. Some were handing each other boxes and stacking them up against a wall, while others organized cans of food on a table that had several empty Thanksgiving baskets at one end.

Squinting, she scanned the group of people and searched for her dad. *Great.* She couldn't see a thing and fumbled around in her coat pockets before remembering she had left her glasses at home. She could hear him saying, *"I told you to always carry your glasses. Someday you'll need them. What were you trying to do, impress a boy by not wearing them?"*

She walked toward the table with the baskets. "Elizabeth?" a familiar voice called.

Elizabeth looked over her shoulder, surprised to see her aunt. "Aunt Connie? What are you doing here?"

Connie walked into the foyer through the doors leading from the nave of the church. She put down a box filled with cans before hugging Elizabeth. "Stay with me, okay? I'm helping out. Are you looking for your dad?"

"Yeah. Where is he?"

"Downstairs. But he's acting weird."

"Weird? What do you mean?"

"He was talking strange at first. I couldn't understand him. Is he taking a language course?"

"No."

"And then he drank some holy water too. Your dad is spending way too much time in church."

"He drank holy water?"

"Yes."

"Oh, no. Something's happened."

Elizabeth rushed through the doors and into the main church.

"Come back here. Your dad told me to make sure you stay upstairs. Elizabeth, don't you dare go down in that basement."

Elizabeth hurried down the main aisle before cutting through a row of pews to her left. She stopped short in front of the basement door, sighed, then grabbed the handle with both hands, and pulled it open.

"Dad?"

She waited a moment, noticing how he neglected to light the stairway. Even so, the high ground floor window in the basement provided enough sunlight for her to see piles of canned foods stacked neatly on the floor below.

"Dad?" she called out again.

She went down the first few steps, certain that he would be where she always found him, sitting in a corner looking at the floor. But when Elizabeth reached the bottom of the stairs, her eyes widened in surprise.

The tunnel door was open and her father was nowhere to be seen.

Shocked, she ran two steps up the stairs and was met by Connie.

She grabbed Elizabeth's arm. "Come back up here."

"The tunnel's there!"

Connie clutched her arm tighter. "Quiet," she whispered. "Someone will hear you."

"The tunnel is open." Elizabeth squirmed out of her aunt's grasp. "Follow me." She dragged her aunt back toward the hole.

"I can't help but follow you. Stop. Now."

"C'mon, you have to see this."

"I've seen it. Calm down." Connie stopped abruptly. "What is wrong with your dad?"

"Auntie C, that's what I'm talking about. *Look.*"

"I've seen it. He told me to keep you away from it. So let's go upstairs."

"I can't." She tugged on her aunt's arm again, trying to tow her toward the tunnel. "We've got to go after him."

"No. He told me to keep you out of there. So stop. He'll be back soon."

A gust of wind pushed Connie back while the same breeze warmed Elizabeth's body.

"This is incredible," Elizabeth said.

"So what? It's a root cellar. I've seen it. Nana Kehoe used to have one of these in her backyard."

"No, it's *definitely* not that. This leads to Jerusalem."

"Not you too? Is this a joke you and your dad are playing on me?"

"No, this is no joke. He might be in danger."

"Let's go back upstairs. He'll be back soon. I know your dad. He kids with me all the time."

"No, no. I'm telling you, he could be in trouble. I know he told me not to say anything but I think he went back to Jerusalem."

"Enough about Jerusalem. I know all about this nonsense. You're acting like freaks. And I know what he told me. Stay out." Connie's hand caught on Elizabeth's coat pocket. She hauled her a few yards away from the opening as Elizabeth struggled to break free. "No. One weirdo is enough in this family." Her aunt let out an exasperated sigh, turned to the opening in the floor and yelled, "Hey, little brother. Get up here. Now. Your daughter thinks you're in danger. C'mon. Stop jerking me around. The joke's over."

Connie stamped her foot on the top step leading into the tunnel and leaned down. "You hear me, little brother? I'm laughing at you." She let out a raucous laugh. "Very funny. I know you're playing a joke on me."

"Auntie C, it's not a joke. He's been coming down here for the last few months, waiting for the tunnel to open and now it has and…and now…he's…he's gone, I know it." She raised her voice. "He could get hurt. There are dangerous soldiers where he went."

Connie released her grip and waved her hands like an umpire telling a base runner he was safe at home. "I've taken enough of this crap."

"There are soldiers there."

Connie's tone softened. "Oh, Elizabeth. I'm not mad at you. It's just your dad and I like to tease each other. He used to play this trick on me when we were kids when I babysat him. He'd pretend to go somewhere in the house and disappear. Then when I would go looking for him, he'd jump out and scare me out of my wits."

Connie walked back toward the stairway and put her arm around Elizabeth, half hugging and half guiding. "Your dad should be up shortly. Let's go wait for him upstairs."

"No. I can't. I'm going to find him." Elizabeth drew her breath in and out in short spurts. Her palms were sweaty. There was no way she was obeying her aunt. "I really think Dad might be in danger. It wasn't so safe last time we were there. There was this soldier...uh, guy...who wanted to kill him."

"Oh, come on." Connie's eyes shot up toward the ceiling. "Where is this so-called soldier?"

"It's true. The soldier wanted me for his wife and Dad stopped him. I'm not lying. I'm not some small child telling a fairy tale. What did he do besides drink the holy water?"

"Why?" Connie asked.

"It's important. Please tell me."

"He put on one of those cassocks and a cross. He started talking all gibberish, a language I never heard of."

"What kind of language?"

"Wasn't French or Spanish, I know that for sure."

"Oh, wow. He had to be going back."

Connie gently rubbed Elizabeth's shoulder. "You and your dad are playing one big joke on me and I don't appreciate it."

Elizabeth swatted at her aunt's hand.

"Sorry, Aunt C. But my dad could be in trouble."

"No. Stop!"

"Hey, what's going on down there?" yelled the Pastor.

They both looked at each other as if they expected to receive detention. "Nothing, Pastor. Just me and Elizabeth straightening out the boxes."

"Are you sure? Sounded like something's wrong down there."

"Not at all," Connie said. "Just Auntie giving her beautiful niece a hand down here. We'll be right up."

"Okay," the pastor said. "We need some more help with the truck outside. Hurry on up."

"Coming," Connie called up.

She turned toward Elizabeth. "Let's go. Your dad loves playing these idiotic tricks on me. He feels he needs to pay me back after all these years. Big jerk."

Elizabeth nodded. "Let me just clean up the mess here. Okay? The pastor will be upset with us if we leave it like this." She started organizing the opened plastic cartons in a methodical fashion. "Go ahead. I'll be right up."

"Promise?"

"I promise."

"Take this," Elizabeth said, handing her the cell phone. "It's Dad's. He'll be upset if I lost it or dropped it."

"Alright." Connie looked back, took a few steps toward the stairwell, and hesitated.

"Go on ahead, Aunt Connie. I'll be right up."

"You promise, right?"

"Have I ever broken a promise?"

Connie smiled. "No."

Her shoes made a thumping sound on the stairs. Elizabeth listened for a moment. Then she fitted herself with a robe from one of the boxes and slipped on a pair of sandals. She grabbed one of the crosses attached to a chain, placing it around her neck.

Flames flickered, encasing her neck and she staggered backwards.

My throat. My legs.

She fell to the floor, gasping for air, clutching her chest.

"Oh, no. This isn't supposed to be happening." She coughed, feeling a sucking draft pulling her toward the tunnel. "Something's wrong," she said, but she couldn't hear her own voice. "Somebody...anybody...Auntie C...help me."

CHAPTER FOUR

Michael regained his footing and looked up to see the gleaming light slipping through an old metal grate.

How did I get here? I don't remember walking through the tunnel.

He took a few steps back in the direction of Northport.

A gust of moist hot air drove him backwards.

I've got to get back to Long Island.

The voice that drew him toward the tunnel's entrance in the church hadn't belonged to Leah. He was sure of that. Or was he? *I'm so confused. I shouldn't be here. I have to get back to my daughter.*

Again, he moved away from the grate. His legs wobbled and a sharp pain knifed through his side. He fell to his knees. The grate above rattled, first side to side, then up and down, finally bouncing like a hard rubber ball on a concrete street, caroming away.

A hand reached down inside the opening and lifted Michael up. "Who's that?" He dusted himself off and spun his head like a merry go round. There was no one there.

Whose hand was that? Whose voice did I hear?

Michael looked down into the empty opening. He put one foot in but fire filled the entrance. He yanked his foot back and ran to the nearest alleyway. Trembling, he leaned against the wall. *Why can't I go back?*

He tried to compose himself.

Obviously there's a reason why I'm here. I hope I can find Leah and make sure she's okay.

He thought about Elizabeth again. *No. My life is back in Northport.* He jumped down into the tunnel and heard a hissing sound. In the darkness, a cobra slid along the ground, poised to strike. Venom dripped from its mouth.

Hiss. The cobra arched upwards and sprayed, hitting the hem of his garment. He stumbled back out onto the street and grabbed his chest, gasping.

He took a quick glance behind him. The snake was gone. "I'm staying."

Michael retrieved the loose grate and sealed the opening. *I need to make sure I remember which one will get me back. I'm not going to make the same mistake twice.*

He spotted a large rock nearby. *Perfect.* He felt a slight twinge in his back as he leaned down and pushed it over the entrance as a marker. Satisfied, he stood, rubbing his lower back.

Finding Leah and making sure she's fine shouldn't take more than a couple of hours, he convinced himself.

He guessed it was late afternoon in Jerusalem. The sun shone a bright golden hue and its warmth re-energized him. The surroundings were as beautiful now as they appeared the first time he visited. He was confident now, sure of his intention and purpose, and unwilling to settle for anything less than a trip home to Northport with Leah.

I wonder if it's only been a few hours since I left? Everything's the same. The town. The stalls.

The sound of his sandals clapping against the stones on the road added to his anxiety. Not wanting to attract the attention of any nearby soldiers, he tried to tiptoe as much as possible. Heading south, his shadow mimed his every move along the pale yellow walls of the buildings. He noticed the abandoned food market.

Probably closed for the Sabbath. He was surprised they had taken down the archway sign. He shrugged off any concerns as he reveled in his return. His heart bounced around like a marble on a roulette wheel as his emotions danced with joy.

The sun's rays disappeared and the sky turned a dull gray. A loud boom erupted. Michael didn't mind the abrupt change in weather. He was excited to be in Jerusalem again.

This is history I'm living. Maybe I'll have a chance to witness the Resurrection.

"It's so beautiful," he said softly, despite the thunder.

Life is simple here. Dangerous. But Godly simple.

He made several mental notes to himself as he navigated the city streets. His mind operated like a camera, clicking on each of the buildings as he moved toward the area where he knew the aqueduct was located.

He stopped when he approached Pilate's courtyard. Michael remembered the last time he was there, lost in the swarm of people, watching Jesus' trial. But he couldn't see the bloodstained steps.

They must have cleaned them. Or maybe this is four months later like my time back on Long Island.

He sprinted toward the aqueduct. Sweat dripped all the way through his robe. Or was it the light, misty rain descending upon his body? The robe clung to his back as he ran, bounding higher off the dirty stone road with every step. He slowed down as he neared Leah's house, checking the front gate to make sure he had the right place.

The sky continued to paint the ground with moisture as he breathed in the sweet smell of the figs. Brown buds spotted the center tree, glistening like copper as the sun snuck through a fading cloud. He could hear the crackling of the fire. The aroma of lamb stew drew him in.

As he entered the kitchen, Michael heard Leah's light footsteps on the floor above. He sneaked over to the steaming pot, but gasped when he reached for the spoon; it was scalding.

"Who is that?" Leah called out.

He didn't answer. *I want to see the look on her face. I'll surprise her.*

He stepped onto the first rung of the ladder and stopped. *Should I hug her, kiss her, or maybe both?*

Michael touched the top of the ladder with his hand. Leah's back faced him as she arranged the dinner mat on the floor. He could smell her now and placed his hand on her shoulder.

She spun around and knocked several bowls over. One shattered into several pieces.

Backing up, she pushed him away with both hands.

He staggered, nearly falling to the ground. "Leah. Wait. It's me. Michael."

"Get out of here. Get out of my house," she screamed.

"But, Leah. . ."

"I said leave." She picked up a plate from the floor and held it toward him as if she were about to launch it. "I will smash this over your head if you do not leave."

He put his hands up in surrender. "I'm sorry. I didn't mean to scare you."

"I do not want you here. You are not allowed in my house."

"Why, Leah?"

Her face contorted in anger. "How do you know me? Stop using my name."

He shook his head, trying to understand what was happening. "Maybe I look different to you. My hair's longer now." He turned around to show her.

"Leave."

"I don't know what's going on, but can we at least sit down and talk about this?"

"No." She slammed the plate to the floor, shattering it into pieces. "Get. Out."

He backed away toward the ladder, confused and frustrated. "What's wrong?"

He looked at Leah one last time. Her eyes, shaded with rage and frightful determination, glared back. He frowned and climbed down the ladder.

Stunned, he walked aimlessly out into the courtyard. When he looked up, he saw her watching him from the second floor window. "I'm leaving," he said, feeling resentment mingled with disappointment.

He began the long walk back to town.

What's going on here? Why didn't she recognize me?

Michael shook his head several times along the way. The streets were still deserted except for a man leaning against a wall, with his hands pressed to his face.

"Cheer up, buddy," Michael said. "Your day has to be better than mine." He touched the man's shoulder as he walked by.

The man didn't answer.

Michael reached the tunnel's entrance with no problems. He struggled to move the heavy rock marking the grate, leaning his right shoulder into it. When it wouldn't budge, he straightened up for a brief rest, puzzled. Bending down again, he pushed hard with both hands. The rock lay still.

What am I doing? I can't leave until I know she's safe from Marcus. Maybe that's why Leah didn't want me there. Is she trying to protect me? Was she trying to get rid of me so he wouldn't hurt me?

Michael stared at the immovable rock. *Elizabeth. She's already lost a mother.*

Again, he pushed with both hands. He stepped back and kicked on the grate next to it.

"Move on, mister," shouted a soldier several feet away.

Michael panicked and ran into an alleyway.

I can't get back now. That rock won't budge. I'm being kept here for some reason.

The soldier's shouting decided his next move. "Move on or you will die."

With desperate strides, he tore back to Leah's.

I wonder if Marcus hit or touched her. I may be the reason why she's in danger now. I can change this. But I'll need a weapon.

He became enraged with each thought, kicking at a loose rock, watching it roll toward an alleyway. His anger gave him strength as he grabbed it and threw the rock against the wall, splitting it into little pieces. He picked up a few and put them in his pocket.

The sun set amidst the lingering gray clouds. Michael saw lit lamps illuminating the windows as he pushed open the gate. He looked up to the second floor and saw Leah's shadow projected on the ceiling. She looked like she was sitting at the dinner mat.

Was she alone? Was Marcus nearby? What would he do then? How could he defend himself? Surely Marcus wouldn't be without a weapon. *I'll need more than a few rocks.* Michael looked around for a sharp branch from a tree that he could use to defend himself but found nothing.

A soft, low-pitched weeping shook him from his thoughts. He crossed the courtyard, tip-toeing into the house, stopping once more to listen.

Is that Leah crying? I'll hit him if he's up there. If he has his back turned, I'll pound him on the head until he's dead.

With caution, he peered from side to side as he reached the top of the ladder. She sat alone in the corner hunched over, face in her hands.

"Leah, are you okay?" Michael asked as he stumbled slightly onto the second floor.

She lifted her head and gave him a puzzled look. "Why are you back? I told you to leave," she demanded, wiping tears with her dark robe. "What do you want?"

No soldier. It's just her. He saw another dinner mat was laid out. *Who is she expecting?*

"Leave, now."

"Leah, please listen."

"I will not listen to anything you have to say."

"Okay, I'll go, but answer this for me first. Are you in trouble? Did he hurt you?"

"How dare you. No one hurt me. Just go."

"I didn't mean to upset you."

"Then go."

Michael paused. "I hope you're safe."

She didn't answer.

He pressed on. "Let me help."

"You could never help me," she shot back. "No one can."

"I can."

She didn't respond, but he could see her eyes were glued to the other mat.

"Leah, you don't have to do this. I'm here now. I *can* help. We can help each other. You can come with me now and be safe."

"I do not need your help."

He noticed two cups filled with wine. "You don't have to stay here."

She grabbed a cup and hurled it at him.

He ducked as the ceramic figure smashed into the wall, the noise chilling his spine. He backtracked a few steps down the ladder.

She doesn't want me here for some reason. He thought again of the flames in the tunnel, and the cobra. *But I can't get back to Long Island. I feel like I'm supposed to be here.*

He saw her slumped against the wall. He gave up and left the house. Exhausted and overwhelmed, he waited by the aqueduct, and then walked back to the well near Leah's home. It was deserted. Water. He needed water.

Trembling, he splashed water onto his face and sipped. Once composed, he decided again that he wasn't going to sprint out of town and leave her. He recalled the night Leah held him on the rooftop. But why doesn't she recognize me? She was still alone as he gazed up at the second floor. Yet this wasn't the Leah he remembered. She was different – filled with anger and rage.

What happened between the time I was here four months ago and now?

It had to be Marcus.

He returned to her home and climbed the ladder again. She glared and picked up a large cup. Water splashed from it.

"You're coming back with me," Michael said. "We spoke about how much we loved each other. I am sure of this now. I haven't stopped thinking about you. I can take care of you in my home."

Her expression was filled with fear but she quickly replaced it with a stoic stance.

He took a small step toward her. "Do you remember what we said to each other on the roof?"

"I do not know what you are talking about."

"It's that soldier, isn't it? I am not going to stand by and let him hurt you anymore."

"You are scaring me."

"How could you be scared of me? Don't you remember what we meant to each other? What we said?"

She shook her head. Panic flared in her eyes.

"I know you're frightened because of Marcus. But I'm not leaving you here with him any longer."

He took a few more steps toward her.

"Do not come any closer." She held her hand up. "If you do not leave my house, I will do what I need to do to protect myself."

"I don't understand. I'm not here to harm you."

"I only know one thing."

"What's that?" he asked.

"I must protect myself."

She hoisted the cup above her shoulder and hurled it directly at his head.

CHAPTER FIVE

A revolting stench, similar to that of wet animals mixed with rotting meat violated Elizabeth's nose and made her slow her pace. Her stomach lurched and she gagged as the repulsive smell followed her through the tunnel.

The dusty mist that accompanied her on the last trip wasn't present. The air had a cool, crisp feel to it.

"Dad," she called out. "Are you in here?"

She wasn't sure how long the trip was the last time but knew she had some distance to cover. Elizabeth willed herself forward through the darkness, her sandals slapping against the tunnel floor.

It wasn't more than ten minutes when she heard noises in the distance. Unlike the previous journey, these weren't the thundering, sharp sounds of an angered crowd or galloping horses. They sounded like a strong wind, whirling whistles against a window pane on a winter night.

A flash of light glimmered ahead as the tunnel narrowed. When she arrived near the end, it opened to form a small room. Light streamed through a grate.

Cautiously, Elizabeth whispered, "Dad, are you there?"

She peered out through the grate.

I hope you're around here somewhere, Dad. I don't want to be alone in this time period.

She recognized Jerusalem on the other side, bathed in the last light of day. If her father had come this way, he'd head straight to Leah's, she reasoned. She listened for several minutes to determine if it was safe to climb out.

An eerie calm settled in the small room as she waited for the slightest sound. No soldiers were strutting about nor were there any people milling in the streets. It was too quiet. Had she come back to the same place? It certainly looked like the same street she had entered only a few months ago.

She noticed a strand of green string on the floor below her. She picked it up, remembering how her father struggled to free it from the grate the last time they were there. Elizabeth thought it would make her father smile when she brought it to him. *He came back to bring Leah home. I'll find him at her house.*

She tucked the string in her pocket and pushed hard on the grate. *Why isn't this moving?*

Standing on her toes, she used her shoulder to give it a hard shove.

Great. This won't open. She examined the next grate. As she reached up, the grate flew off. An unobstructed light tucked its way through the opening. It looked brighter. As her head poked above the ground, she gasped.

Was that a snake?

Climbing out onto the street, she felt a temperature change as she sprinted into the alleyway for cover. The street was filled with shoppers, bargaining for deals.

Odd. I didn't hear any people before.

She squinted. The pleasant aroma of food reminded her about tasting Leah's cooking again. Now, if only she could remember the way back to Leah's house.

Elizabeth leaned out from the alleyway, trying to pick out some landmarks on the street that she could identify. Everything looked familiar. It seemed oddly safe, like she was taking her evening walk to Crab Meadow Beach. She could blend in with the many crowd clusters too.

Plunging back into the moderate darkness of the alleyway, Elizabeth believed that this must have been where Leah surprised her and Michael as they were trying to get back home the last time. If that was the case, she would only have to follow this path all the way to the end, and then she should be able to see the aqueduct in the distance.

Elizabeth half-skipped, half-jogged past the many shops as the sky softened to an early evening darkness. She hesitated before navigating west into the alley. It only led her again into an unfamiliar area. She thought about asking for help but realized that she didn't even know Leah's last name, or if she even had one. Or what her street number was.

They probably don't even have addresses here.

Elizabeth made a crooked turn down every street, understanding that Jerusalem was surrounded by a wall. Twice she found herself at the wall but there was no exit. The falling darkness made her uneasy and anxious. She squinted to see the low position of the setting sun and recognized the aqueduct to her right.

After following the sloping waterway overhead, she recognized the memorable homestead. Everything around her seemed murky and foreboding. She glanced over her shoulder, making sure she wasn't being followed. Before she could see if anyone was watching her, she sprinted to Leah's home.

She stopped a moment to rest. Then with a burst of renewed energy she sped past the front of the concrete home and through the gate, causing it to slam loudly against the courtyard wall. She didn't stop to re-latch it, dashing straight to the woman in the kitchen.

"I'm back," she yelled, throwing her arms around her.

Leah spun around, eyes and mouth wide open.

"It's me, Elizabeth."

Leah shook her head, her eyes confused.

"Oh," Elizabeth said, pulling out the cross and placing it around her neck. "I've come back. I was so lost. I never thought I would get here. Can you understand me now?" She held on more tightly.

Leah stumbled back, nudging her away so she could look into her eyes. She whispered, "Yes, but what are you doing here?"

"I followed Dad through the tunnel. Isn't he here?"

"Michael?"

"Yes. He came through the tunnel. We were at the church and he went down in the basement and the trapdoor was back."

Elizabeth looked over Leah's shoulder to the ladder leading to the second floor. "Where is he?"

Leah dropped her hands to her side. "He's not here."

"What do you mean? He left before me. He has to be here."

Leah looked confused. "I have not seen him since both of you left. I am glad he is not here. "

Puzzled, Elizabeth asked, "Why would you be glad? I thought you cared about him?"

"I cannot explain it all to you at this moment." Leah paced, rubbing her hands against her robe. "You should not be here either. It is not safe."

"It's never been safe here."

Leah glanced out to the courtyard and toward the gate beyond. In the moonless sky, there were few shadows now, only deep, black darkness. She paused for a moment before grabbing Elizabeth's hand and pulling her to the ladder. "Go upstairs. I have dinner made. I will bring it up to you. Stay away from the window. Please go quickly and do not make any noise."

"What's wrong?" Elizabeth asked, her eyes searching Leah's face for a clue.

"You returning. This is wrong. Do not fear, child. I will get you home soon." She placed her hand firmly on Elizabeth's back. "For now, you must listen to everything I tell you. Now go upstairs and do not make any sounds."

"Why do I have to be so quiet?"

Leah's face flushed, her eyes filled with worry and sadness. "He may see you and that would not be good for you or me."

CHAPTER SIX

The box slipped through Connie's perspiring hands, tumbling and spilling several cans of food across the floor. The crowd hushed and stared.

"What's wrong?" asked Pastor Dennis.

She looked around for Elizabeth, avoiding eye contact with him. "Nothing. Everything's fine. I need to go."

I'll kill her if she lied to me. Bounding down the stairs as quickly as she could in her high heels, she said in a tense, high tone. "Lovely niece, you better be down here."

Her arms flailed side to side as she reached the basement. "I'm gonna kill you, my sweet little niece. You better not have lied to me."

She stood at the lip of the opening and slammed her foot down. "Get up here now."

There was no answer. "Your dad is going to be furious with you." *And me.* "Don't make me come down there and drag your sorry …" She stopped short, realizing she was on sacred ground.

She climbed down a few steps and waved her hands in disgust. *What is that odor? It smells like a dead animal.*

"Elizabeth, are you okay?" She descended two more steps and froze.

What is that sound?

A cold, biting gust of wind shoved her back.

"Elizabeth?"

Hiss.

"What is that?"

She bent over, her face now further inside the stairway that led into the tunnel. "Elizabeth, can you hear me? Do you need help?"

"Stay away!" Connie stumbled back up the stairs on her backside, one shoe falling down into the tunnel.

A cobra's head lurched forward and opened its mouth wide.

"No!" She backtracked all the way to the wall and watched the heinous head creep out. It slithered toward her.

"No. Stop. No."

She grabbed the bucket of holy water and tossed it at the charging snake, soaking it.

The cobra withered and recoiled in pain. Its skin sizzled and charred, then turned to dust.

Connie stared in horror, glued to the wall, her hands stretched out in case the snake somehow managed another attack.

Elizabeth, I hope you're not down there.

CHAPTER SEVEN

Leah was up earlier than usual, washed and dressed, kneeling in the garden, praying. She whispered in soft murmurs, lifting her head skyward, pleading. Having cried herself to sleep, mouth parched, she dragged herself over to the well where the man named Michael lay. His face rested on the spongy ground, muddy from the moist dirt which surrounded the leaking well.

Unsure whether this man was dead or drunk, she approached him with caution, one hand out to protect herself, the other pressing the water jug tightly against her body. She bent over and tilted her head sideways to see if he was breathing.

A rush of pity engulfed her as she noticed a crust of mud above his eyes. "I am sorry for striking you. Are you hurt?"

He didn't answer.

Why is he still here? I wonder if he is lost? Maybe he has nowhere to sleep? But why would he come here? I can understand him but he is not from our town. He looks different from the men in our village. His face. His clothes. His hair. He smells strange, like a woman.

A brief bout of dizziness staggered her. She held her stomach with one hand as a sharp pain punched her side. She leaned over and took a short breath. A sour taste snaked its way up her throat and into her mouth. The jug slipped from her hand and the ceramic vessel clattered against the side of the well.

"Who's that – ?" The man, Michael, awoke, sounding startled.

She hoisted the jug and stumbled away, her steps uneven and choppy. The jug slid from her hands, weighing her down. She managed to steady it.

"Wait," Michael yelled from behind. "Let me help you. The water is heavy. I promise I'll leave once I help you."

She regained her balance and gave a feeble wave. She lifted the jug off the ground with one big burst of energy, swayed sideways a few steps, and collapsed. The side of her face struck the dirt. The jug crashed, splattering the water all over and her world went black.

"Leah," Michael screamed in panic.

He ran to where she lay and rolled her gently onto her back. "Are you okay? Can you hear me? Talk to me." He leaned closer to her chest, placing his head on her side, listening for a heartbeat. She was still breathing and he felt a rush of relief. He touched her cheeks tenderly. "Say something."

Her face was flushed red, reminding him of the times when Elizabeth was a child and her fever would spike. He placed a hand to her forehead. "You're burning up."

He picked her up and carried her past the fig tree and into the house. Near the doorway to her bedroom, he stopped a moment.

Forgive me, Leah, but I have no choice. There's no way I can carry you up another flight. And no, I don't think you're too heavy.

He placed her gingerly onto her bedding. Carefully he draped another two bedrolls across her frame while talking to her. He picked up another jug and hurried to the well and filled it. He'd forgotten how heavy the clay containers were. Awkwardly, he balanced it on his right foot and leg and hobbled back to the bedroom.

He found three cloths in a bowl near the oven and wet them with cool water, placing one beneath her neck and two on her forehead. Michael took her pulse several times and used the back of his hands to gauge Leah's temperature.

Still burning.

He repeated this ritual for the good part of an hour before his legs signaled that he needed to sit. So he did, on a small stool in front of her. He monitored her breathing, allowing his mind to sink in silence. Normally, Michael relished a room filled with peace and quiet. Today, the silence sang a song of sadness. Every so often he stopped to listen to the noises outside as children played and adults scolded them to behave.

If I had only taken some Tylenol with me. Wait. People here have survived without any medical assistance or drugs. Why can't she? Maybe this is the reason why I'm here? Maybe that's why the tunnel opened? I'm supposed to be here. I can't leave until she's better, even if it means I can't take her back.

Confident that he had made the right decision to return, he continued to watch her chest rise and fall in rhythmic fashion. He stretched his neck and stared up at the ceiling and noticed a small crib to the left, empty except for a tiny robe hanging over the side.

She's had such a tough time dealing with her daughter's death. He recalled the day when she'd told him about the tragedy. *I can't imagine losing Elizabeth.* He placed his hands over his eyes and rubbed. "Elizabeth," he said. "I've got to get back."

And I'll take you back with me, Leah.

His heart was overwhelmed with love watching her lay motionless, filled with gratitude that she once provided shelter and food, protecting them against pursuing Roman soldiers. He leaned down, pulled the cloths off, and refreshed them with cooler water.

He carefully laid the damp cloths on her face, tucked the blankets under her neck, and brushed the hair away from her eyes with the back of his hands.

He never left the room except to feed the two lambs who were braying, giving the appreciative animals a healthy amount of feed and a pat on the top of their heads in an everything-will-be-all right gesture.

The day gave up its last light as a sliver of sun glided through the overcast sunset near the aqueduct. Michael filled one more jug of water for the evening as he prepared for a sleepless night. He sat and slanted his body slightly against the wall, facing Leah.

It has to be near two a.m. His body was limp, gradually sliding to one side and then straightening up with a jerk as he slumbered into a shallow sleep. His left hand propped his head up as thoughts about his daughter suppressed any happy dreams.

CHAPTER EIGHT

Angst was on the menu as Elizabeth and Leah prepared their evening meal in silence. Leah stayed near the window, using her eyes like lasers to survey the courtyard. She'd rushed downstairs to fetch an item from the kitchen but hurried back without interruption.

It was a scant and quick meal compared to the ones Elizabeth had enjoyed during her last visit. She couldn't help but noticed that all of Leah's actions showed a sense of urgency.

While peeking out the window between hasty bites, she warned Elizabeth, "If I tell you to go to the roof, do so without any delay."

"I will. But can you tell me why you're so nervous? You're scaring me."

Leah pinned her body against the window to ensure no one could see Elizabeth. "I am in grave danger," she said. "If you stay, you will be in danger as well."

Elizabeth dropped a piece of bread and fingered her cup of water. "What kind of danger?"

Leah lowered her head. "When you and your father left, Marcus started to chase you into that opening. I ran back and pleaded with him to leave you both alone."

"Why didn't you leave him? Run away?"

"I tried one night but another Roman saw me. He reported it to Marcus. And…"

"What?" Elizabeth said. "Tell me everything."

She knelt in front of Elizabeth, holding her two hands firmly. "Marcus. He wanted you. Do you understand? You are young, untouched, and pretty. I told him to take me for now.

And when you came back, he could take you. I did not think you would ever come back."

She laid her head on Elizabeth's hands. "What you did was so brave," Elizabeth said. "I'm so sorry we left without making sure you were safe."

"You would never be safe here. You had to leave. I was happy to help you both go home. Your father helped me too."

"Did you ever think we would forget about you?"

"I do not know. I am only trying to stay away from danger. No one visits me anymore, not with Marcus coming by all the time." She stood and went to the window. "Elizabeth, leave. I love you. I do not want you to get hurt. Marcus is a ruthless man."

Elizabeth shook her head. "My dad is coming for you. He might be lost. Heck, I got lost coming here. And you know how men are about asking for directions."

She looked at Leah for a reaction and got none. "Oh right, maybe men are different here."

Leah was silent.

"I know how much my dad spoke about finding you again, seeing if you were safe. He loves you."

Leah walked back to the dinner mat and wrapped her arms around Elizabeth. "I know he loves me. I love him. I love you. But you must go back."

"My dad came back to take you away from this danger."

"Where would he take me?"

"Home. Where we live."

"Where is home?"

"Far away."

Leah nodded. "It would have to be very far away."

Elizabeth smiled. "It's as far away as one can go. We could have so much fun."

"Fun?"

"Yeah, I could take you to the movies. You could go to the Lady Gaga concert with me and Dad would have no problem.

He won't let me go see her. He's got this hang-up about her. But he's old, you know. Do you like ice cream?"

"I do not know what you talk about."

"Right. But you would love it. We could go to the concert and have a monster-sized sundae."

"I do not understand." Leah retreated back to the window. "Elizabeth, the night is here. Now that it's dark, do you want me to walk you back home? The streets will be empty."

"No. I won't leave until I give my father more time. I need to know he's safe. My aunt told me he went down into the tunnel. Something might have happened. I can't leave yet."

"We do not know whether your father is even in Jerusalem." Leah walked to the end of the floor and retrieved a bedroll. "I think we have done this before," she said with a sorrowful smile. "Promise me if your father is not here by the next sunset, you will go home. Marcus never forgets to come by every couple of sunsets. He spends much time near the place where he first saw you and your father."

"Okay, I promise," Elizabeth said.

Leah spread two bedrolls side by side, laying on the one nearest to the window. "So your father spoke about me a lot?"

Elizabeth smiled without apprehension for the first time since she'd arrived. "Oh yes. All the time." She leaned over and whispered in her ear, "He wants to marry you."

CHAPTER NINE

After he cleansed the cloths in the fresh jug of water, Michael poured himself a cup, relishing the moisture in his mouth. He continued to dote over Leah, still gauging her fever with his hands. *Zithromax. How does anyone survive here without it? Wish I had a couple of pills here now.*

The winds dancing on the roof occasionally disrupted the calm of the evening, creating a hollow yet eerie sound. It conjured up a memory, recalling how he and Elizabeth spent their recent Wednesday nights watching "Ghost Hunters." *This would be a perfect place to do some hunting.*

He strained to listen, jumped up and took a few quick steps to the front door. *What was that sound? Am I hearing things? Was that a wolf? Wait, do they have wolves here? At this time?*

The adrenaline pumped through his body so he meditated, begging his heart to settle down. Several minutes ticked by before he went back to check on Leah. She seemed peaceful as little beads of sweat broke out on the side of her face.

Good. Her fever is breaking. She's getting better.

He placed his hands on her face, wiping away the moisture. Kneeling down beside her, he closed his eyes and kissed her forehead. He struggled to keep his eyes open as he settled into a chair. He folded his arms on the table and put his head down. A feeling of relief washed over him like an ocean wave on a hot August day.

When she's better I'll go home. How do I ask her to join me? I'll also make things better with Elizabeth. Maybe there's a way she can go to that concert. Set some rules up but compromise a little. She needs to have some fun. I do, too. He was at peace.

But what if the person Leah is with now is Marcus? What do I do then? She couldn't possibly be happy with that brute. She'll want to come with me. At least that's what I'm hoping.

Sighing, he shifted in the chair and tried to find a comfortable position as he mulled over his options.

If she decides not to come home with me, then I'll stay and defend her. He noticed her breathing was peaceful, sending a welcome feeling of redemption and easing the guilt he'd felt for so long for leaving her behind. He drifted in and out of sleep, never able to form a complete dream with a satisfying ending, stumbling and falling out of the chair to the floor, too exhausted to get up.

* * *

The smell of porridge and the sound of a crackling fire awakened Michael. As he lifted his head, a soft hand touched the back of his neck, startling him. He shifted, unable to muster enough energy to stand right away.

"I am sorry," Leah said. "Can I help you up?"

"Hey, look at you. You're so much better."

He lifted his head higher, rubbing his neck, aching from the odd angle in which he'd slept. He stood, leaning on the table with one hand.

She gave him a slight bow of her head. "You said your name was Michael?"

"Yes. This you know. Maybe the fever had you confused?"

"Thank you for taking care of me, for keeping me cool with the cloths."

"Just returning the favor. I would have helped you even if you hadn't taken care of me once before," he replied. "Thank you for everything you've done for me."

"I do not know what I have done." She looked at him cautiously and backed away. "Let me prepare you some breakfast."

"That would be great. Do you have the strength?"

She nodded. "You look tired. Go and get some water for your face while I cook the meal."

Handing him a fresh cloth, she stared at him closely.

"Oh, that feels good," he said, letting the coolness refresh his face.

"Sit down." She placed a bowl of porridge and filled a cup with water. "Whatever the reason you decided to help me, I am grateful. But you must go after you eat or the neighbors will be suspicious."

"Suspicious of what?"

"I am a married woman."

Michael's heart sank. He gritted his teeth, folded his toes into the hard floor, and clenched his hands. "You married that soldier?"

"Soldier?" She wore a baffled expression. "I do not understand."

"Marcus. The soldier who was after us."

"I do not know of any Marcus."

"The Roman. The one who chased us. The one that wanted Elizabeth."

"Who is Elizabeth?"

Michael rubbed his chin. "My daughter, of course," he said.

Leah shrugged her shoulders.

He looked around the room. "I guess Marcus is not here?"

She frowned, seeming affronted by his question. "I do not know of this person you speak of. My husband would not approve of you suggesting another man would live here with me."

"Your husband? What is his name?"

"Yochanan."

"What?"

"Yochanan is my husband."

He stood, almost knocking over his dish and cup. "That's not possible." He paced, rubbing his forehead and then it dawned on him. *That's why she didn't recognize me.* He stopped and stared at her. "I came back at the wrong time." He held her shoulders. "I can't believe it. I must have done something wrong."

She pulled away. "It is not proper for you to touch me this way."

"I touched you when I was taking care of you."

"That was a different situation. You had no choice."

He nodded. "How did I end up in the wrong time period?"

"You are not making sense to me." Concern flickered in her stare. "Perhaps you have come down with the sickness as well?"

He shook his head, his voice trembling. "No, I'm feeling fine."

"Then what is wrong?"

"Everything. I have to leave now."

"I would like to offer you breakfast before you are on your way."

"I don't have time. I have to get back home to my daughter."

"Perhaps you can bring your daughter back and join me and my husband for dinner?" she asked. "Yochanan will be back soon and I know he would want to thank you for helping me."

His heart pumped at a fast pace. "Where is your husband?"

"Why?"

"It's important. I need to find him."

"He is probably in the mountains, following some rabbi. He finds much comfort in their words. He is still grieving."

"Grieving over who?"

"Our daughter."

"He needs to get back to you as soon as he can."

She stared at him, alarmed. "Why do you say that? Your words are scaring me."

He didn't want to frighten Leah, but he couldn't tell her the truth – that sometime in the near future her husband would be murdered. "I know everything I'm saying must sound strange. Just trust me without asking many questions as I can't answer them for you right now." He took a deep breath to calm the panic building inside him. "I need to find him and send him home to see you."

"I will come with you."

"No. Stay here in case he comes back. If I don't find him by the next sunset, then look for us. What was he wearing?"

She chewed her bottom lip and closed her eyes, whispering something that sounded like a prayer, but Michael wasn't sure. She opened her eyes and looked at him. She seemed calmer. "He is wearing a light blue robe with a brown belt."

"What color is his hair and what does he look like?"

Leah gave Michael a detailed description. He nodded and tightened the strap on his sandals. "Remember, if I or Yochanan don't make it back by the next sunset find a relative or friend who can help you find him."

On impulse he hugged her. She froze yet didn't pull away this time. He stepped back. "Sorry, didn't mean to. If Yochanan comes home, tell him to carry a weapon. You live in dangerous times."

"We do not believe in killing. We live our life through the Ten Commandments."

"Sometimes you need to defend yourself."

"We will defend ourselves with prayer and love."

"Sometimes you can give someone all the love in the world and it won't be accepted. Please promise me you'll consider it."

She didn't answer.

"I've got to go. You have no idea what you've done for me. I will never forget you."

She gave him a curious look before replying. "Nor will I."

He paused a few seconds and shook her hand. Then he hurried out the front door and through the courtyard. He drank a few cups of water by the well before heading toward Jerusalem.

I can save his life. I have to be smart, careful. I can't come at him with fear or he'll think I'm crazy. Of course I can't tell him I love his wife. I'm not even going to tell him I know her. Now I know why I'm here in this time period.

I'm here to change Leah and Yochanan's life.

CHAPTER TEN

Leah stroked Elizabeth's hair with a wooden brush, smiling uneasily. "When I am done, we should go."

"No," Elizabeth said. "Can we wait until at least tomorrow morn...um, the next sunset? Until my dad comes?"

She stopped grooming her. "It is dark out. We will not go now. You should go at sunrise."

Elizabeth sighed. "I don't know where he could be. I was sure he would have been here by now."

Leah held her shoulders. "We will leave after breakfast." She pulled Elizabeth's hair back. "You said your father wishes to marry me?"

"Yes. I don't think he spent one day without thinking about you. He was always looking to find a way to come back here. He was so upset about leaving you behind."

She rubbed Elizabeth's back. "Are you sure he was coming to my house? This town?"

"I am. The opening was there again. My aunt said she saw him go down the tunnel and was talking about going to Jerusalem."

Leah took a deep breath and sighed. "How long did he leave before you?"

"I don't know. It couldn't have been that long."

Elizabeth turned around and saw Leah slump. "You're worried, aren't you?"

"I love your father."

Elizabeth hugged Leah's arm. "I'm worried too. He's always on time. I'm the one who is always showing up late."

"Maybe he went back?"

"No. He would have come here first before leaving. He wanted to make sure you were safe. It's all he talked about since we got back home."

"Maybe he came when I was not here."

"Were you out of your home for long?"

Leah pondered the question for several moments. "I am not sure."

They sat quietly as she moved her hand from the middle of Elizabeth's forehead to the back of her neck. Finally Leah spoke. "We will get up early and make sure you get home. If your father comes after you are gone, I will tell him you went back."

"Will you go back with him, Leah?"

She winced. "Marcus is a merciless man who comes and goes. He is looking to avenge those who do not obey him."

Elizabeth sat up, distressed. "Then this is no place for you to be. You must come back whether my father arrives or not. Come back with me."

The tension in her voice was clear. Leah wrapped her arms around her. "It would be dangerous for me to go with you or with anyone, even your father."

"Why?"

Leah took an extended breath again. "Marcus will avenge my departure. He will hunt down my brother and his wife and children. He drinks a lot and is violent. He will kill anyone he wishes."

"Does he know where your brother and his family live?"

"Yes."

"Oh, no." Elizabeth rested her head against Leah's shoulder. "Dad was right. He knew you were in trouble." She paused and stood. "We have to do something. Can we go to the authorities?"

"What do you think they will tell a Jewish widow?"

"I don't know. I read up a little about this time and the customs. But there's only so much you can learn from a book."

"I do not understand, Elizabeth."

"Well, we have to think of something," she answered with determination.

Leah shook her head. "Let us speak of other things."

"Sure. It will take our mind off that horrible man."

Leah smiled. "Do you like a man back home?"

"A man? Or a boy?"

Leah looked baffled. "A man."

"Well, he's not quite a man yet, although I guess he is a man for this town," she said, smiling. "Anyway, his name is Matt."

"Matt? That is a strange name for a man."

"His full name is Matthew."

Leah nodded. "Matthew. I like that name. Does your father know about him?"

"Well, sort of. He's heard me talk about him but he doesn't know we've gone out a few times. We're mostly friends right now."

"Friends? How can you be a friend with a man?"

Elizabeth rolled her eyes. "That's something my dad would ask."

Leah continued, "You did not answer my question."

"I'm not sure how to answer it. I do like him enough but I don't know how much he likes me, because he's much older than I am."

"How much older?"

"A couple of years."

"What are years?"

Elizabeth paused for a few seconds. "There are three-hundred and sixty-five sunsets for every year. So he would be over seven hundred sunsets older than me."

"That is not much older. Yochanan was many more sunsets older than me."

"How old are you, Leah?"

She pulled back from Elizabeth. "Are you going to tell your father?"

"No. I promise."

"Many more sunsets than you."

Elizabeth laughed. "You're not going to tell me?"

"No." She smiled. "Around here I am considered old. Will you tell your father about Matthew?"

"I've tried. But he always changes the subject."

Leah nodded. "I know why. He is worried about losing you. It is difficult for any father to see his daughter grow up and find a man. I know it was for my father. Be gentle with him. Men do not like to talk about what is in here." She put her hand over her heart.

"Boy, I could really use you in Northport," Elizabeth said with a wide smile. "It would be easier to explain my boy situation to him. I don't want to hurt his feelings. He makes a face like this." Elizabeth frowned and creased her eyes tightly.

"That looks like someone in pain."

"Nah, it doesn't hurt him. It's his way of showing me he doesn't approve."

"When are you and Matthew getting married?"

"Whoa. Married?" She scrunched up her face. "Not for many more sunsets."

"How many more?"

"Too many to count."

"Your town has many strange customs."

"Yeah, true. But this is one I agree with."

"Will Matthew look for somone else if you do not marry him soon?"

"I doubt it. He's too young to be married."

Leah filled two cups of water and handed one to Elizabeth. "My mouth is getting dry from all this talking."

"I'm sorry."

"Why are you sorry? You do not have to be. I have not spoken to anyone like this since I sat on the roof with your father. It is with much joy we talk."

"You enjoyed talking with my dad?"

"Yes."

"What did you talk about?"

"Life. Our losses. Our loves. Our fears. Our hopes. Our dreams."

Elizabeth went to the window.

"Move away from there," Leah urged, and Elizabeth returned to the mat. "Maybe Matthew could be for you?"

Elizabeth shrugged, not really hearing the question.

Leah encouraged her with a tap on the shoulder. "Talk to your father about Matthew. He is easy to talk to once you find a way inside his heart. It may take a while but it will happen. But marry this Matthew." She placed her hand again over Elizabeth's heart and smiled.

Elizabeth shook herself out of the brief trance. "My dad is *not* going to let me marry Matthew. I'm way too young for that. Hey, I like calling him Matthew instead of Matt. Thanks."

Relief healed Elizabeth's heart as she continued to share her private emotions with Leah. Sure, she had close friends, but talking to Leah gave her a more comforting feeling. Without a mother, a confidant, someone with whom she could share secrets like this, she had always felt profoundly sad. Especially when her father emptied his heart, telling her about the night she was born – the night her mother died.

Perhaps it was her fate to battle life's obstacles with her father at times, and other challenges alone. She wanted a longer conversation with Leah. She felt a bond with this woman, as if they had forged a covenant. Together they drank water in silence, and each sip seemed to solidify their alliance.

Elizabeth felt ready to ask the question that had been bothering her all night. "Has Marcus hurt you?"

Leah put her cup down, avoiding eye contact. "I am fine."

"But that's not what I asked. Did he hurt you?"

Leah stayed quiet.

"Tell me. I'm not a child. I can handle it."

Leah reached over and brushed Elizabeth's bangs away from her eyes. "I know you are not a child."

"Did he hurt you?" she pressed.

"It is none of your concern."

"It is my concern," she said. "I love you."

Leah stood and stared out the window.

Elizabeth joined her, wrapping her in a tight squeeze. Leah quivered.

"How did he hurt you?"

"I do not want to talk about it."

"How bad did he hurt you?"

"After you and your father left and I tried to leave, he was furious. He hit me." Elizabeth hugged her again. Leah pulled back with a cry of pain.

"What's wrong?"

"My back. It is hurting again."

"Let me see."

Leah turned and lifted her robe. An angry red welt streaked across the middle of her back.

Repulsed at the brutality, Elizabeth gasped out loud.

"Is it bad?" Leah asked.

"Yes. Marcus did this to you, didn't he?" Elizabeth felt anger she had never experienced before. "Oh my God, you're bleeding," She retrieved a cloth and noticed more blood on the back of the garment and Leah's legs. "Oh no."

"What is wrong?"

"I think you better stay still." Elizabeth grabbed two more cloths from the dining area and hurried back.

Leah doubled over, holding her stomach.

Horrified at the sight of all the blood spilling onto the floor, Elizabeth tried not to throw up. She swallowed hard and knelt beside Leah, handing her a cloth.

"I will be fine," Leah said. "This has happened before."

It took Elizabeth a moment to fully understand what was happening. "You lost it."

"I know," Leah whispered. "We will need to bury him."

CHAPTER ELEVEN

Vendors hawking their products dictated the street's vibrant pace. Women held small children's hands, promising special treats as husbands haggled for the best price. The barking shouts from the business owners reminded Michael of the times he had attended art auctions with his friend Susan. Clusters of people seemed to move in unison from one storefront to the next as vendors boasted about their special deals.

How am I going to find Yochanan in this mess?

Michael strolled from market to market, dissecting each pile of shoppers while remembering Leah's description and her tale about Yochanan's marriage proposal.

He has a light blue robe, dark brown belt, black hair, brown eyes, and a scar on his right knee. He got the scar the night he proposed to me. He kneeled on the edge of a rock sticking up from the ground as he asked me to marry him. Oh, he was so brave and sweet, his knee was bleeding and he patiently waited for me to answer. But I was too distracted by his wincing and the blood pouring out of his knee. I asked him to let me help. He wouldn't. He stayed down on his knee. I started to cry. I said yes, oh yes, Yochanan. Now get up and let me take care of my future husband.

Michael spotted a large group of men and women, some carrying small children, heading in the direction outside the city and toward the hills in the distance. He could see the stream of people, some with donkeys carrying the elderly, making their way up a long trail leading to a winding dirt road. As he shaded his eyes from the mid-afternoon sun to see if Yochanan was among the group, he caught up to the stragglers. One woman carried a sick girl, her legs badly bruised. An older man limped, guiding himself with a wooden cane but laughing, encouraging the youngsters to keep pace with him.

"Excuse me, sir?" Michael panted.

"Slow down son. Catch your breath. What can I do for you?"

"I'm looking for a man named Yochanan. He's wearing a blue robe, has black hair and a scar on his knee," he said, pointing to his own. "Oh, and a brown belt."

"I am sorry," the old man replied. "I do not know."

"Thank you anyway." He pointed ahead. "Where is everyone going?"

"To see this preacher, Jesus of Nazareth."

"Jesus?"

"Yes."

"He's alive?"

The man laughed. "He better be. Or I have taken a very long walk and got myself an earful from a bunch of young ones too."

Michael realized that if he had traveled back at a time when Yochanan was still alive, this was a different time of Jesus' life too, the period where He preached his important lessons.

This all makes sense now. Leah told me the first time I was here how Yochanan would follow preachers in the mountains. Maybe she was talking about Jesus. She said he was up in the hills looking for answers.

"May I follow you?" Michael asked. "I wouldn't know how to find the preacher."

"Yes. Let us see if you can keep up with me. If you have any trouble climbing these hills, I have a cane." He waved it around and laughed. "Where do you come from? Not from here, I know."

"I am from a place where the water surrounds the land."

The old man touched his hand. "What river do you bathe in?"

Michael smiled. "Not a very big one."

The old man looked mystified.

"My name is Michael and I come from Northport."

"I have never heard of that town. Where is it?"

"Near a very big river. Where are you from?"

"Near Galilee. I am Saul."

"How far is that from Jerusalem?"

"It is close to here."

The crowd grew as Michael and Saul marched up the mountain, taking baby steps, circling a big rock or two obstructing the path, and navigating past a group of tall trees. Although frail from age, Saul possessed a spirited tongue as he told his life story. As he would pause, Michael would ask him questions, further fueling the elderly man's exuberance about living in first-century Galilee.

"You've had an interesting life, Saul. How long have you been following Jesus?"

"I am not sure how much time has gone by. I am thankful I am able to remember where I am going today." He winked. "I do remember the day when our town was filled with many people coming from towns near and far away. They were yelling and screaming in the streets. It was unlike any day I had ever lived.

"There was a big crowd celebrating a young couple's wedding and they ran out of wine. I felt terrible for the man and woman. I saw a woman go up to this preacher, asking him if he could help and wondered how this man was going to help her. He looked like any other guest, except he was with several men, followers or relatives. I do not know. I could tell the woman's request touched his heart. He had a look of concern. I believe he told the woman at first 'it is not my time.'

"But there was something spiritual about him. The hurt on the woman's face moved him. He started telling everyone to fill the jugs with water. When they were full, he told the bride and groom there was more wine. And there was."

Michael stared, mesmerized. "Did you have a chance to drink any?"

Saul nudged Michael with his cane. "Yes. I did not want to be rude."

"What did the wine taste like?"

"Unlike any cup of wine I had. My body felt warm, even hot like the sun was inside me. I felt a little dizzy too."

The old man smiled, his grin revealing a missing tooth. "Maybe I had too much wine? I tell you some believed, some were thinking it was a trick. But I know I was glad to have that cup of wine."

"So it wasn't that miracle that brought you here today?"

"I guess it should. But it did not. I saw the Rabbi talking to a man. He was pleading with him. He told him he had come from another town, not far from Galilee. He was trying to get the Rabbi to come back to his town to help his son who was dying."

"Did the Rabbi go with him?"

"No. The man was so upset. I wanted to go and help him. He was crying, begging the Rabbi for help."

"So he didn't help?"

"He did. He told the man to go back home. His son was alive and not sick anymore."

"So you believed the Rabbi performed a miracle?"

"My son, there is no bigger skeptic than me. I followed the man and took that trip back to Capernaum. I wanted to see this miracle with my own eyes."

"What did you see?"

"The boy was running around, laughing, playing with his friends. The father dropped to his knees, looked at the sky, and praised God. He cried and kissed the ground. When his boy ran into his arms, I started to weep myself. I asked one of the family members what happened. They told me the boy got up out of the bed in the afternoon and started playing." He raised his voice. "A miracle. A miracle."

Michael shook his head in astonishment. "I wish I was there. How did the town react?"

"It was unlike any other day in my long life. Women wept, men shouted with joy. People hugged each other."

A chill ran up Michael's spine. "What did you do?"

"I walked over to the little boy and hugged him. I did the same to the father and his family members. I asked the little boy how he felt. He told me he was sleepy at first, saw this beautiful bright light, and then he woke up and felt fine."

Michael's jaw dropped, unable to muster any audible words as he shook his head in bewilderment. Of course he had read these events in the Bible and had heard them in service, but to actually listen to a firsthand account rendered him speechless.

"I know I have lived longer than most, but my eyes do not deceive me even if my legs fail me at times," Saul said.

"Did the boy's father talk about the Rabbi anymore?"

"Whenever he could. I spent much of the day at this man's house. I had to see if the boy was fine or if he had a temporary recovery. I have seen a few of those in my life. But the boy is truly well."

Saul stopped briefly, catching his breath as they approached one of the steep inclines. "When you live as long as I have, son, you watch people's faces more than you listen to their words. I will never forget the look on that father's face when his son jumped into his arms."

Saul wiped a few tears away with his sleeve. "I always get this way when I think back on that day." He grinned again, his wrinkles stretching from the top of his cheekbones to the side of his chin.

Michael noted he looked more youthful when he smiled. It was reassuring to him, knowing Saul was comfortable in his later years, a subject that dogged him every day as he watched his daughter grow up.

"Did you see the rabbi after that day?" Michael asked.

"I did not. It is why I am here." He stopped and lifted a gray eyebrow at Michael. "Is this not why you are here?"

He helped Saul up the hill, holding his arm, giving him a chance to steady himself on his cane. "I'm also here to help a friend."

"You are a good man, Michael. Not many would travel this far to help a friend."

Saul continued. "You talk strange for someone who is a strong follower of the rabbi. You use words that are familiar but they do not sound right."

"I read a lot."

"You are a wise man. Are you with much gold?"

"No. Not at all."

Saul settled down by an abandoned rock, placing his cane to the side. A tree with several long branches gave the area some shade and soon the group of people he had been walking with joined him. The children were delighted now that the adults had stopped.

"How are you doing, son?"

"I'm achy," Michael admitted.

"Do your legs hurt?"

"Yes."

Saul laughed. "You young ones do not know how lucky you are." He paused. "Is something troubling you?"

"It's important I find Yochanan soon."

"It will be difficult to find him in this crowd. Why do you think he will be here?"

"His wife told me he's been going to the mountains to listen to preachers."

"There are many preachers, Michael." He leaned against his cane, his eyes steadily watching the children. "Come over here, children. Do you want to play a game?"

Smiling boys and girls skipped over to him, yelling, "Grandpa, Grandpa, let me play, let me play."

"Quiet down," he admonished them.

"What game are we going to play?" asked one little girl.

He raised his cane like a parent uses their fingers, placing it across his lips. They fell silent and stood at attention as Saul explained the game. "This is going to be the best game you will ever play." The children squealed. He raised his cane again. "We are going to help my friend Michael here. Say hello to him."

"Hello," they shouted in unison.

Michael waved, uncertain how Saul and the children would be able to help. "He is trying to find a friend. I need you to stand up on the highest rocks you can find, climb the biggest tree and look around."

"What does he look like?" asked the tallest boy.

"I am going to let him tell you about his friend."

Michael smiled. "This is a great idea, Saul." He turned to the group. "Children, he has on a blue robe and a brown belt. He has black hair and brown eyes and he has a scar on his knee."

"What's a scar?" asked the smallest boy.

Michael pointed to his scar above his right eye. "It looks like a mark like this."

The children nodded to each other.

"What happened?" asked a boy with curly brown hair. "Did you fight a Roman? Did you beat him up? Did he hit you?"

"I got this from a hockey puck."

"What is that?" asked a girl, giggling.

"Well, it's this hard black rubber … hmm… it's a long story. It doesn't matter right now. I'll tell you after we find my friend."

The children gave him all their attention. "My friend's name is Yochanan. Call out his name. If you find him, just come back and tell me where he is. Whoever finds him first, I'll give you one of my coins," he said, fingering his stash from the first time he had been to Jerusalem.

The children yelled with joy and Saul shushed them. "Michael, we are happy to help. We do not want any gifts, do we, children?"

"No, Grandpa," several small voices said dejectedly.

"That is correct, my children. Now go off and help my friend."

They scurried in different directions, chanting, "Mr. Yochanan? Mr. Yochanan?"

Michael smiled in amusement.

"Do not stand there," Saul said. "You might walk around to see if you can find your friend too. You have a better chance with more eyes."

"You're so right, Saul."

Michael milled through the crowd, focusing only on the males in the gathering. There were many of varying ages – some alone, several accompanied by their wives and children. The elderly struggled to take their final, energetic steps. Amazed by the size of the faithful, he found himself relishing the atmosphere, feeling the hope in the air, the anticipation and excitement of hearing Jesus speak.

He heard faint cries from the children, saw a few of them standing on their toes on some of the bigger rocks in the area, even admiring the biggest boy's creativity of directing the others from a high tree branch.

I wonder what Jesus will say? Maybe he can help me find Yochanan? I can finally ask him about Vicki, and grandma, and–

"Michael, Michael. Look over there," shouted Saul, who was inching his way toward him.

"Where?"

Saul gestured to the right with his cane. "Up that hill."

A dark haired man in a light blue robe, fitting Leah's description, trudged his way to a steep part of another trail.

"Much gratitude," Michael said as he shook Saul's hand. "Maybe I'll see you again?"

"I hope so, son. If you ever visit Galilee, please come to see me."

"I shall."

He hurried toward the man in the blue robe, pushing his way through the stream of followers.

He looks like Yochanan but I can't see his eyes or the scar on his knee.

Michael stopped, cuffed his hands together near his mouth and yelled, "Yochanan."

The man didn't respond, prompting Michael to shout his name once more.

The man finally stopped and glanced over his shoulder. Before he could turn around to proceed, Michael waved. The man gave him a befuddled look and resumed his trek.

"Wait," Michael ran toward him. "Yochanan. Stop."

The man halted his trip again and took a few steps back to Michael.

"Yochanan?"

The man dipped his head slightly. "Do I know you?"

Now what do I say?

"We have a mutual friend."

"Who is this friend?" Yochanan's stare danced all over him. Michael paused, stalling for an answer. "Does it matter?"

With a look of annoyance, Yochanan spun around and continued walking up the hill.

"Stop," Michael said. "I need to talk to you."

He scurried up the embankment, walking side by side with him. "I need to know where you're going."

"I am going to listen to the preacher talk. Is there anything more you need to know?"

"Where are you going after you hear the preacher speak?"

"I do not know. Wherever my heart tells me to go." Yochanan glared at him with a menacing look. "Why are you interested in where I am going?"

Michael noticed Yochanan's muscular forearms and stepped back. "I'm sorry I've bothered you."

He stayed a few steps behind, cloaked behind a large family, never losing track of the light blue robe. Yochanan settled near a big rock with some shade. Michael remained about thirty feet from him. He watched him drop his head as if deep in thought and caught him twice wiping his eyes with his garment.

He's grieving. Probably over his daughter. This is all making sense now. What do I say? Should I tell him I know Leah? How do I warn him? He'll think I'm crazy telling him what might happen if he isn't careful. I wonder how long it's been since his daughter died?

Watching Yochanan unleashed an avalanche of emotions in Michael. He mulled over what he was going to say, knowing he needed to be sensitive. He laid a hand on Yochanan's shoulder. "I hope you don't mind if I sit with you to listen to the preacher?"

Michael asked. "I'm alone and could use some company. You look like you could use a friend too."

Yochanan's face was smeared from his dirty hands. "Leave me alone."

Michael held out his hand and introduced himself. "Do you want to talk?"

"I do not have much to say."

"You don't need to. I'm here as your friend."

"Why?"

"It's what the rabbi believes. So do I."

"You must be a strong follower."

"Sometimes I am. My faith grows every day. What about you?"

"I have listened to many so-called wise men over the past months but I hear of this rabbi from friends. I am filled with doubt. My heart has been broken."

Michael absorbed the seriousness in Yochanan's voice. He recollected when Leah told him the sad story on the rooftop the last time he visited Jerusalem and how she blamed herself. "What is bothering you?"

Yochanan took a half-hearted breath. "It is my daughter." His body slumped. "One day she was laughing and playing, the next day she was sick. I tried to find someone to help her. I went to many neighbors' houses. I prayed and I prayed. But prayer did not help."

Yochanan lowered his head more. "I did not protect my daughter. I have hurt my wife. I have caused her so much pain."

Michael crouched down to his level. "How, Yochanan? How have you caused her so much pain?"

"I could not help my angel. I have hurt my Leah, my love. I cannot go home," he said, sounding defeated.

The words ripped through Michael's heart. Leah had told him how she'd felt guilty for not reaching Yochanan emotionally. She grieved for years, blaming herself for his terrible fate. And here he was, claiming culpability in his daughter's death.

Yochanan and Leah loved each other so deeply that they were destroying themselves.

"I know having a child leaves us vulnerable in so many ways. The world can be cruel and unfair. But you must not blame yourself."

Yochanan lifted his head. "I could not look into my wife's eyes anymore. I failed her."

"You didn't fail her. She felt terrible about what happened, you –"

Michael stopped himself and backed away.

Yochanan's face reddened. "You know my wife?"

"No, I don't. But I believe she must be feeling terrible and is missing you badly. It sounds like you love each other very much. You must go back and talk to her. Tell her how you feel."

Yochanan nodded. "I will go back tonight. First, I want to hear the rabbi speak."

I knew this was the reason why the tunnel opened again. It's giving me a chance to help Leah and Yochanan.

Michael realized what he had done. His heart absorbed a bittersweet emotion that left him both sad and happy.

It doesn't matter how I feel about Leah. It matters that they have a chance at happiness together again.

The crowd swarmed around Him as He moved up the high hills, the terrain wide, big enough to hold a thousand people. He continued to climb several more feet until He located an elevated area high enough so that the throng could hear His voice clearly. Elderly women, perhaps soon taking their final steps in this world, pushed forward with determination, extending their trembling hands to Jesus.

The apostles acted like security guards, surrounding Jesus as He reached out with visible enthusiasm to touch every loving gesture. A woman nearby with long, straight hair smiled widely, patting the children on their heads, wishing parents strength and happiness.

In awe and unable to move, Michael absorbed the feverish atmosphere.

Yochanan smiled. "There He is, my friend."

Michael didn't answer. He allowed himself to mentally float, soaking up the reactions of the children cheering while the elderly put their hands together, closed their eyes and prayed.

There were skeptics too, displaying expressions of scorn. Jesus worked the crowd like a rock star on stage.

"You do not represent my God," shouted a cynic. "You lead only a group of sheep and not warriors."

Jesus turned and smiled. "There will be many who stand in my shoes and talk for me and shout the same cries. Their gold will glitter and impress you. Beware of those who feel the need to wield their swords in the name of my Father's Kingdom."

Now finished with his climb, He waited a minute longer to give the crowd an opportunity to find a space to sit or stand. Then He addressed His followers, holding His hands up. The final faint cries from the worshippers died down and an absolute hush swept across the small mountain.

Michael and Yochanan half-kneeled and half-sat about a hundred feet away from Jesus. His dark brown, shoulder length hair danced from a sudden gust of wind. His soft brown eyes scanned the masses. He touched his reddish brown beard and held up his hands.

Michael never lost eye contact with Jesus. When his view was blocked, he stood. Yochanan mirrored his every move.

Jesus stared at Michael, taking a few steps forward, His head now above a small group of women huddled near a small tree. "My friends," Jesus said. Then He paused. "Some of you have traveled many steps to join me on our path to salvation."

The crowd stilled. "Many of you are taking your travel slowly as your once strong legs have become weakened from age or sickness. There are those who are without food some days or are without treasures. And there are some here who are children, innocent yet burdened with your plight."

He smiled. "It does not matter. We are here today as one. We are here to join my Father in his Kingdom."

The quiet of the crowd was numbing, more peaceful than Michael ever experienced. Yochanan kept still, eyes closed, whispering soft prayers.

Jesus moved from east to west as hordes of people encircled Him, hoping to touch His hands or robe while the apostles cleared a trail. He stopped in front of two men.

"Why should we follow a man who tells us even the poor and the thieves deserve God's love?" asked one man, his arms folded in defiance.

"My father's Kingdom awaits everyone. Those who have sinned often, those who do not. Ask my Father for forgiveness with your heart."

His feet anchored in the fertile ground, Jesus fixed His gaze on the men. One carried a long, narrow spear. When the man tightened the grip on the weapon, Jesus grasped his arm. Several apostles raced to His aid but Jesus stopped their advance with a wave of His hand. "When the world strikes you with force, seek those who wish to join you in peace. Beware of those who say they believe in my Father's Kingdom but do nothing to find men of peace. Let the swords of hate whither in eternal death as the doves of peace are given a place in my Father's Kingdom."

Jesus released His grip on the man's arm. A dove rose from the spear and floated to the sky. The crowd murmured and rose. Michael's eyes widened as he watched the dove ascend to the heavens.

Jesus strolled several feet higher on the hill. "My children," He said. "Those who believe victory can be won by swords will not find a place by my Father's side." He walked toward Michael and Yochanan. "Seek out those who comfort, those who love, those who provide shelter, those who feed the hungry, and those who clothe the naked."

A man with a scarred face and a mangled leg leaned on his cane and shouted, "You tell me not to use my sword. Look at what the Romans did to me!" His voice shook with anger as his hand fiercely clenched the wooden stick. He tried to limp toward Jesus. "You better tell your Father they should burn in hell for what they did."

Jesus held an intent and sympathetic stare on the man.

"Will I be in heaven for what they did to me?" the angry man continued, ranting. "Will they burn in hell?"

Jesus faced the anguished man and steadied his hand. "My friend," He said, softly. "It is not for us to judge another man's words or actions. When my Father asks us to come before Him, it will be He who makes the final judgment."

The man steadied himself on his cane, his face full of sorrow. He lowered his head and remained quiet.

Jesus flashed a comforting smile and turned away, walking back up the hill. "There is no answer for those who have hurt us," He told the crowd. "The only answer we need is when my Father calls us to his Kingdom. Only He will have the final answer."

His voice became more firm, almost amplified. "Beware of those who judge the weak, the sick, the poor, and the sinners. Beware of those who deceive with false promises in exchange for your treasures." His voice trailed off as He comforted a woman holding a sick little girl. He held the mother's hand, His presence mending the distraught woman's grief. Jesus touched the child's hand for a moment, His face full of empathy. "Woman, do not cry," He said, wiping away the tears under her eyes. "Be strong."

"How can we speak to our Father?" a woman cried out, running a few steps behind Him and kneeling in reverence.

Jesus responded, never losing contact with the mother's hand. "There are many ways," He said. "Comfort your neighbor when she is ill. Feed your brother when he can not work. Clothe your sister when she is cold. Shelter your friends when they have nowhere to go. Love your enemy when he is wounded."

He released His hold on the woman as she screamed in joy. The little girl struggled from her mother's grasp and stood.

Michael's heart raced. "My Lord," he whispered. "My Lord."

"Seek out my Father through prayer," Jesus cried out.

"How?" shouted a man from an area higher up on the hill.

Jesus walked slowly in the direction of Michael and Yochanan.

"Our Father, who art in heaven, hallowed be thy name," His voice boomed. "Thy Kingdom come…"

Michael got to his feet and lowered his head as Jesus stood in front of him.

Yochanan stood too. "I am not sure what to do," he whispered.

"Thy will be done," Michael joined in. "On earth as it is in heaven."

Yochanan's eyes widened. Michael's voice trembled as he said the words along with Jesus. They were the only two speaking. "Give us this day our daily bread, and forgive us our trespasses as we forgive those who trespass against us. And lead us not into temptation."

Michael dropped to his knees as Jesus held onto his arm. "But deliver us from evil."

Jesus paused and signaled the crowd He was done.

"Amen," the crowd yelled in worship.

A woman knelt before Jesus.

Jesus lifted her up with His right hand. "Woman, I see you are troubled today."

"I am, Rabbi."

"Do not be troubled. Pray to my Father, let your heart beat openly for His help, be strong with your faith, disregard the temptations of this world. Go home to your families, cherish these words. Live these words. Beware of the many who speak my words with beauty yet do not live them. Beware of those who attract the masses and ask you for your treasures. Be humble in the face of glory."

Jesus disappeared among the apostles as the crowd began to disperse.

Michael looked at his friend. "Incredible, isn't it?"

"I need to talk to Him, Michael." Yochanan was met by four apostles and a woman with long, brown hair.

"What do you need with the Rabbi?" asked the biggest man.

"He's a follower, Peter," interjected the woman. "Do you want to speak to Him?"

Peter frowned.

"My friend would like to express some thoughts with the Rabbi," said Michael. "He means no harm."

"When the Rabbi is ready, I will ask Him."

Yochanan nodded.

The crowd milled around Him. They could see an old woman with a wooden stick talking to Him while several apostles kept guard like the secret service protecting the President of the United States.

I wonder which one is Thomas? Is that John? He looks the youngest. I know Peter. Where is Judas? I don't see him. I wonder where he is.

Yochanan interrupted Michael's mental guess-the-apostle-game. "My friend, how is it you know what the Rabbi says as He says it?"

Michael hesitated. He looked over at Jesus and shrugged. "I don't. It seemed familiar to me." Yochanan eyed him and Michael admitted, "It was the first time I said it with any feeling in many years."

"Many years?"

"Many sunsets ago."

"So this is a prayer you have heard many sunsets ago?"

"How can I explain? It's something I've heard before but never felt compelled to say from my heart. Until today."

Yochanan gave a confused look. "My friend, each moment the sun moves up or down, as I get to know you, I know less of you."

Michael smiled. "I can see why you say that."

There were only a few more people left chatting with Jesus. "Have you ever spoken to Him?" Michael asked.

Yochanan shook his head.

A few minutes later Peter came over. "My brother, come with me."

"May I come too?" Michael asked.

"The Rabbi requests only this brother."

A hand on Michael's back startled him. "The Rabbi will speak to you as well."

The woman smiled, her long hair falling halfway down her back. Her light blue eyes distinguished her from other women in this time. She spoke with confidence, her body language assertive, unlike the average female in Jerusalem. "What is your name, brother?"

"Michael."

"I am Mary. Some call me Magdalene."

Michael stared at her.

She smiled. "How long have you been following the Rabbi?"

"A long time."

"How did you hear about Him?"

Michael studied her narrow face with its high cheekbones. The wind rustled the bangs over her eyes, and he noticed her lips were small and thin. "My friend told me about the Rabbi teaching in the hills. I wanted to hear Him speak."

She waved her hand around at the crowd. "It was wonderful to see the many children here, listening. He was very pleased today."

"Can you tell me more about Jesus?"

She looked at him with a curious expression. "What do you want to know?"

"Anything, everything. What is it like to watch Him, to listen to His words, see Him among the people?"

"You listened to Him today. He is drawn to the weak, the sick, the oppressed. His message is simple and clear, easy to understand. Love each other, respect each other, help one another. He always warns of those who say they believe but cloud His message with their own desires for power and gold."

"Do you think the Rabbi will let me speak to Him?"

"Michael, you can speak to Him whether you stand with me on this hill or with your family in a far away town. I will see if He is finished talking to your friend."

She walked up the steep incline and disappeared behind a tree. Michael sat beside a rock, the same one used by Jesus as a podium only an hour ago. He leaned against it for support. He pondered Mary's words.

A hand reached down and hoisted him up. Jesus handed Michael a cloth. There were faded spots of red all over it. Michael examined and touched it. It felt soft yet worn as he put it close to his face to breathe in its scent. The feel and smell gave him a warm, sanitizing sense of peace.

"Let this cloth cleanse your soul from the troubles of the past and invigorate your heart," Jesus said. "Why do you burden yourself with so much that you cannot change?"

Michael felt the strength in Jesus' tone. "I don't know."

"I will talk to you the way you can understand. My Father understands our failures. Pray to Him. Be aware of those who stand before you in beautiful and big places and repeat my words with their hands out for gold and silver. They do not represent me. It is not important where you pray to my Father. These are the most important ways you can be with my Father."

Jesus' expression was stern, yet filled with sympathy. "Walk with me, Michael. There is much good happening in this world, even from those who hurt you. You need to open up your heart and find the good around you."

Together they walked side by side up the hill. Jesus led him behind a tree and into a deep cave. Despite being several yards inside the mountain, a light illuminated the massive area.

Michael passed a man who sat on the ground, talking to a few apostles. "I loved picking her up," he said to them. "She had the most wonderful smile. We would take trips to the river. She was a gift…"

His voice faded but Michael recognized it was Yochanan's, his face glowing as he told his story. Jesus led Michael deeper into the cave, passing images of men and women, children chatting and playing. Many lives were being played out before him.

"Michael, let me talk to you man to man. You have spent a good part of your life in worry, fragile from what you believe will happen in the future. You seem to want to live in the days that have passed instead of the one you have now."

Jesus led him into a structure familiar to Michael, one he recalled during his days as a young man in Richmond Hill. Michael leaned against the wall. There in front of him was a scene he had played over in his mind so many times before.

He was mesmerized and stared as he was taken back to his bedroom on the third floor of the house he was raised in. It was there he sought refuge from his father's wrath so many times.

The crammed room was the same as he remembered. A single bed pushed against the wall, a dresser, a record player, one small window, and a tiny black-and-white TV resting on a metal chair, its rabbit ears drooping to the floor.

He was twenty-two and scared, racing up to his room in fear. He slammed his bedroom door shut, preparing for another verbal battering. He spun his favorite record, yet not even the strains of Bruce Springsteen's powerful voice and resounding lyrics from the song *Badlands* could build a wall around him from the mental mauling on this day.

The muffled conversation downstairs between his family and relatives added to his anxiety as the sound of Jim's footsteps stomping up the stairs made his heart palpitate painfully.

Michael lay on his bed motionless – much like his mother had the last two weeks before she wilted away from breast cancer. Unlike his mom, he was able to see and move his arms and legs.

The closer the sound of Jim's thumping footsteps became, the tighter his hands clenched the top of the wooden bed frame, as if he were clinging onto a raft in an ocean storm. Despite the lack of air conditioning and ninety degree heat, he closed the only window in the room and covered himself with three blankets.

Maybe he won't see me. Maybe he'll leave me alone. I hope Aunt Ginny calls him back.

Michael loved his mom's sister, Ginny. She understood him, loved him, and listened to him without judgment. Aunt Ginny gave him his first memorable toy, a Casper the Friendly Ghost doll that talked. It still lay underneath his bed. He reached desperately to touch it. *Yes, Aunt Ginny will talk to him. She'll stop him from coming up the stairs.* Yet the creaks grew louder, tingling his spinal cord and back of his neck.

Slam.

Jim pushed the door open so hard it ricocheted off the wall and back against his shoulder. "What do you think you're doing?"

Michael closed his eyes and held his breath, still clinging to the hope that Jim would leave the room.

Jim grabbed the back of his neck, pulling off the blankets in one motion. "Get up. How dare you come up here and listen to that music. Your mother is dead. Is this how you show your grief?"

"No." Michael trembled, shaking his head. "It's not like that."

Jim stomped over to the record player and turned the music off. "You don't care."

Michael swallowed hard.

Jim yanked on his arm, forcing him to sit up. "How could you relax at a time like this?" He shoved him so hard that Michael fell back on to the bed. "I said get up," he shouted, his face contorted in anger.

"Okay, okay. I'll…come down. I just need a few minutes alone –"

"What is wrong with you? You act like this is just another day. How could you not even be upset over this?" Jim's neck and face turned a deep red. "How? Answer me."

Are you kidding me? How could you even say such a thing? Of course I'm upset. I loved her too. I'm not going to break down in front of you or anybody else in this family just to prove my love for my mother. Michael wanted to say all that out loud but he restrained himself.

Jim let out a furious growl and hovered over him, arms folded, lips stitched together in rage. "You don't want to be part of this family, do you?"

Michael kept staring at the ceiling, mentally willing his father to leave. He knew that it didn't matter what he said. The old man would disagree or ridicule him. Again, he remained quiet.

"I'm not going to waste any more time talking to you," Jim yelled. He stormed out of his room, whacking the door a couple of times with his fists. "He doesn't care or have any respect for what his mother went through, Ginny." The cruelty in Jim's tone slammed into Michael's soul, shattering his spirit. "He doesn't care about anybody but himself."

"Kick him out, Dad," Connie said, walking up the stairs. "He has no heart. He didn't even cry when Mom died."

"He's so cold," Jim said. "He's thoughtless and selfish."

As he'd done many times in the past, Michael put his emotions in lockdown mode, working hard to block out Jim and Connie's continuing conversation. "Kick him to the curb, Dad," she said. "Teach him a lesson."

This time Michael surrendered. *I don't want to live anymore.*

He waited until everyone in the house left. He stood up and made his way downstairs, stopping in the kitchen before heading outside. This was going to be the day.

He headed directly to Forest Park, a nice wooded area filled with brush – a perfect place to die alone.

The sun's rays cast its light onto the quiet of the green grass near a tall oak tree – his final resting place. He pulled out his suicide weapon from his pocket – a knife – the same knife he'd used many times over the years to enjoy grilled steak. It would now be his swan sword.

Two men jogged up the hill and briefly interrupted Michael's plan with their loud chatter. He waited for them to be out of sight, holding his breath in anticipation. He held the knife a few inches away from his heart. "Dear God, please forgive me."

A man on a bike rolled by, startling him again, his boom box blaring the song *Badlands*. Its final verse, a rallying cry to confront the challenges of life, shouted with vigor.

Michael listened to the words and repeated them several times in his head. *For the ones who had a notion, a notion deep inside, that it ain't no sin to be glad you're alive...*

He looked at the steak knife in disgust and threw it to the ground. "No."

I won't let them beat me. Never. I'm not leaving until God tells me it's time to go. And only then will I say goodbye.

Hurtling back to the present in the cave, Michael backed away, embarrassed.

Jesus pushed him back forward. "Michael," He said. "Move on."

"I'm sad that I ever thought to kill myself. If I had done that, Elizabeth would never have been born. I know in my heart that she is destined to do great things."

"Yes, she is. And she will. " Jesus stared at him as if deep in thought before He spoke again. "Life is wonderful. Embrace it."

Michael nodded and followed Jesus through a dark tunnel.

"Sometimes when someone has hurt us," Jesus said, "it is expressed through anger and a need for revenge. This is part of being human and part of having the free will my Father has given to all mankind."

Michael absorbed Jesus' words and wondered what lay ahead for him in this part of the cave.

Jesus pointed. "Look and listen. Most of all see what is before you and hear with both ears." He walked backward and faded into the darkness.

Michael swallowed a lump in his throat as a vision of his mother, Rebecca, appeared on the cave's wall. She wore a plaid dress that had seen better days and a white apron, stained with chocolate. She looked tired and sad. In front of her stood a teenage Connie, her head high in defiance with both hands waving at their mother.

"It's not going to be a long party," Connie said.

"I told you, no." His mom wiped her brow and shook her finger. "No more parties. We can't afford the gifts."

"This isn't like the other parties. This one's important," Connie said, raising her voice. "Cindy's my best friend. She gave me concert tickets to see David Cassidy for my birthday. I have to get her something just as nice."

The dark shadows under his mother's eyes were more pronounced as her face flushed a bright red. "Why can't you understand what this family is going through?" The blue veins popping out of her neck looked like a necklace, choking the life out of her. "We don't have extra money to buy gifts for every stinking birthday party you get invited to. I'm not going to give you hard-earned money to squander away on concert tickets, albums, posters, or whatever you girls waste money on these days."

Connie stomped her foot. "Why can Dad waste money on cigarettes then?"

His mother banged her fist on the table. "Your father deserves to treat himself. He works hard to put a roof over our head and feed this whole family."

"It's not fair." Connie's eyes filled with tears. "Michael gets to go to his ballgames with his friends all the time." She yanked on her pink blouse. "I don't even remember the last time I had a new shirt or pair of jeans and now I can't even go to a party."

His mother poured confectionary sugar into a bowl. "Stop your whining."

Connie wiped her face with the back of her sleeve. "What are you making?"

"A cake for daddy."

"Nice." Connie pursed her lips and rolled her eyes. "So there's money to buy stuff to make a cake for him."

"Connie Kathleen Stewart, that is enough." His mom took out the hand mixer and plugged it in. "If you kids don't behave tonight, you can all stay in your rooms. I will not have your father upset on his birthday."

Connie's lips turned white from puckering them in anger. She fought to hold back more tears, yet they flowed down her cheeks.

As Michael watched the scene on the cave's wall unfold, he realized Connie was probably holding back what they all wanted to say to their mother. Sure, the old man put food on the table; he never let them forget it. Threw it in their face every chance he had. Told them more than once, they should be happy with what they had. Money didn't grow on trees. However, when it came to his cigarettes and liquor, there was plenty of money for him.

"Mom, please." Connie let out a loud sigh. "She's my best friend. She'll be mad at me. Just this one last time. I promise I won't accept any more invitations."

His mom put the bowl aside and wiped her hands on her apron. "You just won't give up. Not only are you not going to the party, you can't go out for the rest of the week. Now go to your room."

"No, no, no." Connie gasped. "The dance is in two days. And Tommy asked me to meet him there. And it won't cost that much. I'll only need a few dollars."

"I told you, we don't have an extra few dollars." His mother leaned against the table and heaved a deep breath. "I don't care about the dance or Tommy or any boy for that matter."

"I'm sorry. I promise I won't bother you anymore. Just let me go to the dance, please? All my friends are meeting at –"

"I don't want to hear it anymore. You're not going anywhere for a week. It's time you helped out more around here anyway." His mother turned her back on her.

Connie ran out, sobbing.

Michael leaned forward to get a better view. *I was about ten or eleven when this happened. It's all coming back to me now.*

He remembered that at the time all he wanted to do was go to the ballgame. He focused on the vision in front of him again.

Connie stormed back into the kitchen. "Mom, there's been something bothering me for a while."

"What now?" his mom said, spinning around quickly.

"Michael broke Daddy's lamp in his office downstairs."

"He what?" His mother threw a dish cloth in the sink. "Michael," she yelled. "Get down here. Now."

As Michael walked past Connie, she snickered. "You're in trouble now." She ran up the stairs, laughing.

"Hey, Mom," he said. "Can we leave for the field soon? It's the biggest game of the year. We have a chance to make the playoffs."

His mother shook her head. "You are not going anywhere until you tell me the truth."

"The truth about what?"

"Did you break Daddy's lamp in the basement?"

He looked down at his feet and stayed silent.

His mother grabbed his chin, hoisting it up. "Look at me. Did you break it?"

"Well, yeah, I did," he said in a whisper.

She smacked the side of his face and nudged him forward. "Go upstairs."

"But the game's in half an hour," he said, rubbing his cheek.

"You're not going to any game." His mom faced him, glaring. "Go to your room and think about what you did. I'll let you know when you can come back down."

Michael stomped out the urge to argue any further. Instead he asked, "Can I at least lick the spoon?"

"No," she yelled and grabbed her head as if it ached. "All of you leave me alone."

He scurried upstairs and stopped at Connie's room. Her door was open. "Why did you tell on me? I can't go to my game and now I'm stuck inside."

"Now you know how I feel." She slammed the door in his face.

"You're a crummy excuse for a sister," he said, banging on her door.

"Yeah, well, you're a crummy ball player," she shouted. "Now go away."

He went to his room and pounded his pillow. Not only was he going to miss his ball game but he wasn't given the opportunity to satisfy his sweet tooth. His mom always let him lick the spoon and bowl. Now she was so mad at everyone that they'd probably not even get a slice of cake.

Michael felt Jesus' presence behind him.

"Connie wasn't mad at me. She was mad at my mother," he said to Jesus.

Michael continued to watch himself as a young boy.

"Hey, Sammie," he said, peering out his bedroom door into the hallway looking for his younger sister. "Are you upstairs?"

"Yeah," she answered. "I'm going to the park with Patty and Karen."

"To the park? Did Mommy say you could go?"

"Yup," she squealed, staring at him with an impish grin. She stuck her tongue out.

"You little brat."

She giggled.

"Um, do you want to play with me instead?" Michael asked. "I'll give you gum."

Gum was to his younger sister like an apple was to Eve.

"Bubble gum?" Her eyes lit up. "What kind?" She headed toward his bedroom.

"Any kind you want. I have a big stash in here." He waved her in. "Come on, I'll show you."

She stepped into his room, her eyes like moon balls, gazing at the big, bright orange bag of treats.

Michael handed her a piece of gum. "If you play a game with me I'll give you more."

Her face shone like a Christmas tree star. "Yay!" she yelled, jumping up and down.

He put his fingers to his lips. "Shhh. We have to play quietly. Now listen to me. We're going to play a secret game. Kinda like Scooby Doo and his friends. We're gonna solve a mystery."

She ripped the gum paper and stuffed the wad of Bazooka into her mouth. "Okay. What do we do?"

"First, go downstairs and find the chocolate cake Mom made today."

"That's easy," she said, smacking her gum loud. "It's on the counter. I saw it."

"See, you're good at this game," he said. "Take a butter knife and just pull some of the icing off. Don't cut the cake or anything. Just slide the knife softly so you stick it with some chocolate and bring it upstairs. But don't let Mom see you. She's in a really bad mood."

Her little forehead frowned, looking confused. "Won't she be mad if I do that?"

"Only if she sees you. That's why I said you have to be real quiet."

"What kind of game is this?"

He rolled his eyes, losing patience. "Mom has to figure out who snuck some of the icing. Then when she can't figure it out, we go and tell her we solved the mystery. We tell her Connie did it. But we both have to keep the truth a secret forever, okay?"

She giggled and Michael gave a sinister laugh, knowing full well Sammie would mess up the cake.

"Okay," she said. "That sounds funny. I'll do it."

Michael turned away from the scene on the cave's wall and looked at Jesus. Sorrow filled his heart. "I miss her so much."

"I know," Jesus said. "Facing your past can be painful. It can also give you a sense of peace and understanding."

The pain of Sammie's death a few months ago hit Michael hard but at the same time watching her as a child brought a smile to his face. How trusting and adorable she was. She would do anything to spend time with him – the same way he used to be with Connie.

Michael forced himself to focus on the wall again. Sammie sprinted down the stairs. She peeked around the corner to the living room. Their mother was nowhere to be seen. She climbed up on a chair, took a butter knife out of the drawer, and slid it across the cake, chopping up part of the top, making a big mess on the counter. She grabbed a piece of paper towel and tried to push the uneven, choppy chunk back and rushed back upstairs.

"Here." She handed the knife to Michael. "Do I get more gum?"

Michael reached into his bag, a treasure trove of sugar and chocolate, and handed her a package of Wrigley's Spearmint gum. Sammie yelped in joy. He stared at the knife, covered in chocolate icing. *Oh, what a glorious sight this is.* His tongue snaked out, caressing it slowly at first, enjoying the initial rush of sweet ecstasy. A chunk fell to his hands. He used his finger to pick it up and twirl it in his mouth, savoring every ounce. "Yum," he said. "Isn't this fun?"

"I guess," she said. "Can I have some?"

"Sure." He gave her the knife. "Be careful."

"I will." She skillfully licked a good portion of the icing, part of it covering her face.

They both laughed as Michael and Sammie battled for some of the icing hanging from the tip of her nose.

"What happened to the cake?" screamed his mother from downstairs.

Michael yanked himself back to the inside of the cave and held his hand up to block out the image on the cave's wall. "We learn through our mistakes," Jesus said. "Keep watching, Michael."

With a slow hesitant movement Michael turned his head toward the cave's wall. Yes, it was a childhood prank but he hurt his sister and now she was dead. He couldn't right this wrong.

"I want to know who ruined your father's cake?" his mother yelled.

Michael was already going to have to face his father's wrath about the lamp. He'd already been punished so he sent Sammie downstairs. She ran into the kitchen with icing still lingering on her nose and smeared on her pink cheeks. She grinned.

"I'm sorry, Mommy," Sammie said. "We were just playing a game. And I can't remember the rules." She smiled and snapped her little fingers. "Oh, yeah, I remember. You have to guess who did it. But I'll help you. Cuz we're playing Scooby Doo." She jumped up and down, happy she remembered the game.

"Connie did it," she recalled, flashing a wider smile with all the innocence and trust a child had in her brother who had roped her into believing it was just a game.

His mother opened a kitchen drawer – the drawer all feared – and took out a black leather belt. "Not only did you ruin the cake." She picked up a paper towel and wiped Sammie's face clean. "You lied to me."

"No, Mommy, it was just a game."

Michael watched the scene on the wall, wincing as he saw his mother flip Sammie over her knee, whacking her little bottom four times.

He took several steps back from the cave's wall as Sammie's wails crushed his heart. "I wanted to get back at Connie," he said to Jesus. "Now Sammie's gone. I should have apologized for that day."

Jesus pointed to the wall. "She knew you were sorry."

Michael stared at the wall. She saw the vision of Sammie running upstairs and into his room rubbing her behind and back. Her tear-stained, red face looked confused. "Mommy said I wasn't supposed to touch the cake. It was for Daddy's birthday tonight. She didn't like this new game."

"I'm so sorry, Sammie," Michael said as his voice started to break. "I really just wanted to get Connie in trouble because she got me in trouble."

Sammie wiped her tears with the sleeve of her sweater and hiccupped. "I don't like this game. Mommy's mad at me."

Michael hugged his little sister. "It's a bad game. We're never gonna play it again. I'm sorry. Does it hurt?"

She nodded. "Yes. But I closed my eyes and thought of something nice, like some day having a Barbie house, and a Barbie car. Just like you taught me to do when we get a whipping. So it wasn't so bad."

Michael smiled. "Tomorrow after chores I'll play with you. Whatever you want to play, even those dumb Barbie dolls. I promise."

She giggled through her glistening tears. "They're not dumb. You'll see it will be fun to dress them up. Can I have another piece of gum? I think it will make my boo boo be better."

Taking out three more pieces of Bazooka, he handed them to her. He swallowed back his guilt. "Here, take the whole bag."

The wall on the cave turned black and as quickly as the scene had appeared, it disappeared.

Michael turned to Jesus. "I forgot that I tried to make it up to her."

"You not only apologized, your actions were loving and she accepted it all," Jesus said. "Sammie never looked back on that day. She moved on and never let it define her future. Now, it is time you do the same."

Michael was silent for a few moments, digesting the scene he had witnessed and Jesus' words. "I never realized that my mom was battling her own anger and disappointments. I guess she took it out on my older sister. Connie took it out on me and I tried to do the same." He shook his head in shame.

"Everyone hurts at one time or another and some use that hurt to hurt others to heal themselves, until a person with courage stops the circle of anger," Jesus said.

"I've done my share," Michael said.

Jesus shook his head. "You have already broken your family's cycle of this behavior, Michael. You've been a supportive, compassionate and loving brother to Sammie, right up until her death. Even though your relationship with Connie is strained, you know in your heart you would always be there to help her if she needed you."

Michael nodded. "But would she?"

"Does it matter?" Jesus continued, "Even with the abuse you endured at the hands of your father, you would help him in his time of need."

Michael looked at Him and didn't waiver. "I'm not so sure about that."

"You are human. It's okay to be unsure of certain things. You will have to work out your relationship with your father your way and in your own time. You are a great father to Elizabeth. You could have laid the same anger given to you on your daughter. You never did. You started a circle of love within your own family."

"Don't give me too much credit. I get annoyed with my daughter at times."

Jesus smiled. "I did not say you were perfect."

Michael grinned, relaxing his shoulders but then his sorrow returned as he thought about his wife. "Why did Vicki have to die so young?"

Jesus guided him to another room. "Michael, everyone is troubled with struggles and hardships. Why must you dwell on those instead of my Father's blessings?"

"I'm a man who falters a lot."

"There are men who represent me who falter many times," Jesus said. "You are human and at times frail, especially when you are without my Father's spirit."

Michael's regret returned. "Why was Vickie taken away from us? She was so young. She never had a chance to hold our daughter."

"You must forgive yourself first before you can forgive others. And when you do, you will discover the answers to your questions."

"I'm the reason why Vicki never got to hold Elizabeth," he whispered. "It's my fault."

Jesus walked ahead and indicated for Michael to follow him. "Why are you unable to live life as my Father intended? Why do you dwell on the past and not let it go?"

"I try, I really do." Michael sighed. "When my salary was cut, I worked two part-time jobs and Vicki worked longer hours. She tended to worry about money more than I did. Can't say I blamed her, we were struggling to pay our mortgage. When we weren't working, we were too exhausted to spend time together. The longer this went on, the longer we retreated into our own little worlds."

"All families have challenges. Why do you think your burdens are more than others?"

Michael shrugged, not sure how to answer. Of course he knew everyone faced heartache and challenges, but when he was knee-deep in his own conflict he would forget about the world around him.

Jesus stopped walking and faced Michael. The intensity in his stare melted him. "We cannot avoid the truth our entire lives. When the sun sets, the truth is still here and will find us. Let my Father's strength open your heart."

Michael's legs weakened. Something in Jesus' tone gave him the courage to say what he'd always wanted to say to someone out loud.

"I never had a chance to ask Vicki for forgiveness," Michael said. "She died before I could apologize to her."

The cave room opened up more as Jesus continued to move forward. Michael could hear voices nearby. He stopped and watched Vicki sitting at a table with Connie. "I don't know what to do," Vicki said. "We don't seem to be happy. We're always fighting."

"Ask him to leave, even if it's for a little while," Connie said. "Teach him a lesson. You're working your butt off and he's out there going to basketball games."

"That's his job. It's what he does."

"Do you call that a job? A real job is working in an office or working on a roof, not sitting in some gym watching teenagers play football."

"Basketball. He watches basketball."

"Whatever," said Connie, rolling her eyes. "You have to go into the city every day while he does this. Shake him up. Maybe he'll get off his lazy butt."

Vicki took a deep breath. "I guess a break would do us both well."

"You're darn right."

Michael pointed at his sister. "Always getting involved with my life. Always."

He turned around and saw Jesus wave to another room. Inside he saw himself alone, drinking, sitting on a metal chair in a small room.

I can't believe Vicki asked me to leave.

He heard the phone ring and watched himself pick it up. "Hello, oh, what do you want now? Do you want me to leave the state?"

"Please, Michael, listen. We can't be mad at each other."

"You kicked me out and now I'm sitting in a small room, eating baloney sandwiches every night. And you say I can't be mad?"

"You need to come home."

"Why? Why do you want me home now?"

"I'm pregnant."

"What?"

"I went to the doctor's today and it was confirmed. We need to be here for each other."

"Are you sure the baby is mine?"

"Michael, stop," said Vicki, raising her voice. "You know me better than that."

He held the phone down at his side for a few seconds. Raising it slowly, he measured his words, filled with anger. "I'm coming home only for the baby, not you, Vicki."

He hung up.

"I was so angry after she asked me to leave," Michael said to Jesus. "We were arguing the day she died, too."

He rubbed his forehead. "If I was in that car, I could have saved her. If only I hadn't argued with her, then she wouldn't have even left the house that day and there would have been no accident. This has been eating me up since the day she died."

Jesus nodded, as if he already knew this.

"Are you able to let her know how sorry I am for that day?" Michael cupped his hands as if in prayer. "I beg you to please deliver my apology to her."

"There is no need for you to beg me," Jesus said. He waved his hand.

A comforting breeze brushed Michael's face as a white vapor swept through the air. He wiped his eyes with the cloth. He thought he heard a female's voice calling his name.

He turned to Jesus. "Is that Vicki?"

Jesus nodded. "Speak to her."

He turned around and looked up but he couldn't see where the voice calling his name was coming from. "I can't see her." Michael wiped the moisture away from his eyes. "Vicki, is that you?"

"Yes," the female voice answered. "It's me."

I can't believe this. My wife is talking to me? He held his breath, hoping the voice would keep talking so he could walk toward her. "Where are you?"

"Look at me, Michael," she called out. It was a voice he'd never forgotten, a voice ingrained in his heart.

"I'm trying to find you," Michael said, his heart in this throat. "But I can't see you. Can you see me?"

"Yes, I can."

The surreal experience made it hard to breathe, but he pushed through the anxiety, embracing the elation at the prospect of seeing her again. "Tell me what to do so I can see you." He knew he was speaking fast and hoped it wasn't incoherent. "I'll do whatever it takes. What is it you want me to do?"

"Close your eyes and say a silent prayer. Do it now for me, please."

"Okay." He inhaled deeply, calming himself. "What do I pray for?"

"Pray for this moment so we can see each other."

Michael took a few more deep breaths as his hands stopped shaking. He closed his eyes and prayed harder than he ever remembered.

The temperature rose and his fingers tingled. He finished the prayer, opened his eyes and gasped in wonder as a vision of Vicki, surrounded by the white vapor, appeared before him.

She looked like a hologram, wearing her favorite faded blue jeans and black shirt. A bright green ribbon held her hair in a long, flowing ponytail. Goosebumps scurried up his spine as a cool mist sprinkled his face.

He felt as if he were in a trance, not believing she was actually in front of him. "Are you in any pain?" he asked.

"No. There is no pain here."

He put his hand out to touch her but his arm wouldn't move. He tried to take a step toward her; his feet were planted to the ground. He bit his lower lip, remembering what Jesus had told him, to be happy with the things he had and not dwell on what he didn't have. Right now, he was given the chance to speak to Vicki. He'd be happy with that for the moment.

She smiled and pushed the hair away from her eyes. "I'm glad you came when I called."

"Called? I don't understand."

"I called upon you through our Father."

"Why now?"

"I still have some remorse I can't remove," she said.

"I don't understand."

"A week before we got married you had gotten your tux and you hadn't said a word about getting shoes. I knew you had a worn pair. I was afraid you'd just wear those shoes with the tux so I said something to your best man."

"To Brian?"

"Yes," she said, lowering her head. "I told him to make sure you get yourself a new pair of shoes that matched your tux."

"Oh yeah, he mentioned something to me," he said, confused. "What does that have to do with us now?"

"You were so angry at me at the time. I thought you would regret marrying me."

"No. I could never regret marrying you. I was angry and embarrassed that you didn't trust me enough to make such a simple decision." He shook his head, smiling through the ache of wanting to hold her. "It's so stupid now that I think about it. It was just a pair of shoes."

"I was a control freak and shoes for our wedding day was serious business." She bent her head to the side, sadness etched in her gaze. "I know that it was my need to control everything, even you and not to fully trust. I know it was a small thing but I've always felt terrible about it."

"It's nothing. Really. I never thought about it much." He let out a short chuckle. "So you called me here to have a discussion about the shoes?"

She paused a moment. "No. There's more." Vicki frowned. "The shoes weren't the only reason I asked our Father to see you." She hesitated for a few more seconds. "I'm sorry for asking you to leave."

Michael's stomach lurched as deep gloom engulfed him. "I'm sorry for what I said."

"What was that?"

"That I was only coming home because of the baby. I wanted to be with you."

"I know."

"I was angry, Vicki. But I'm sad I didn't tell you then that I was saying it out of anger. I was hurt."

"I was hurt too. I was confused. It's why I needed to talk to Sammie so often."

"I thought so." He swallowed back a lump of guilt. "I messed up so much."

"We both did."

He gazed at her, willing his expression to show how contrite he truly was. "I wasn't mature enough to realize that I should have come to you and talk about why we were growing apart."

"We both have regrets, Michael. I neglected our marriage and didn't nurture our relationship." Her eyes held a tinge of sadness. "I was so worried about my pregnancy that I shut you out."

He held his hand up. "You were a wonderful wife. We both lost our focus and let the worries consume us." He took a step toward her. "I don't care about all that. I need you to come back and be with Elizabeth and me. Ask our Father to send you back."

"That's not possible." Vicki smiled. "I'm so proud of Elizabeth. She's beautiful and smart. She's so strong and independent."

Michael trembled. The fear of God gripped him as he formed the words. "She misses you so much. It wasn't fair of God to take you from us."

"God did not take me. An accident did. An accident. It can happen to anybody. Please remember that, no matter what you may find out in the future."

"What do you mean, Vicki?"

She didn't respond.

"It's not fair." He felt a rush of heat travel from his neck to his face. "You never got to hold Elizabeth in your arms. Never got to look in Elizabeth's eyes for the first time. Seeing her first smile, her laughter, the first time she walked. Watching her blow out her birthday candles." He bunched his fists. "Makes me so angry every time I think of how much you've missed."

"Are you angry for me or for you?"

For a moment he was speechless. "For all of us."

She held out her hands, her ring as sparkling as it was on their wedding day. "I miss you both. I'm proud of her. You are a great father."

He stared into her eyes, hoping for a brief touch of her flesh. "I wish I could hold you in my arms."

"Behold," Jesus said, standing behind him. "Love her as my Father had intended. Hold her next to your heart."

Michael's mouth dropped. The mist evaporated and Vicki stood in the flesh before him, wearing the same black and white dress from their first date. Her hair was bouncy, curled at the ends, a little bit of makeup on her cheeks. Her long nails were painted in light green, complimenting her eyes.

"Can I touch her?" He turned to Jesus. "Kiss her?"

Jesus smiled. "It is up to you to make it happen."

"How?" He tried to embrace Vicki but he couldn't. "What do I do?"

"Michael," Vicki said. "If you close your eyes and believe you can touch me, feel me and inhale my scent, then you can."

Michael closed his eyes.

"Touch my hand," she said.

He reached out but felt a cold mist. "I can't feel you."

"Do you remember the day you asked me to marry you?"

"Yes, on the ball field, in the rain." He laughed. "We got so soaked that day."

"It was one of the happiest days of my life," she said. "Take me there again."

"How?"

"Believe you can."

He got down on one knee. "It was the happiest day of my life too."

"Are you asking me to marry you again?"

Michael reached up with one hand. "I am. Touch me, Vicki. Touch my hand. I believe you're real. Marry me again. Love me again. Don't let me go again." He opened his eyes. "I can feel you now, can you feel me?"

She quivered. "Yes."

They embraced.

He buried his head against her neck, breathing deeply to smell her hair. "My goodness, you're cold." He rubbed her back hard, trying to warm her up.

They swayed back and forth as they had on the dance floor at their wedding. She tightened her hug. "This feels wonderful, Michael."

"I can smell your shampoo, oh Lord, I've missed that so much."

Vicki did the same. "Keep rubbing me. It feels so wonderful. I never thought I would get to hold you again."

They rocked back and forth as Michael pressed his cheek against hers. He kept the tempo at a crawl, hoping it would prolong the moment. He leaned back and soaked in her beauty. "I never stopped loving you."

He kissed her. It felt like the first kiss they shared riding up the escalator in Rockefeller Center, the night he truly believed she would be the one he would spend the rest of his life with.

She pulled away.

"What's wrong?"

"I feel sad. I wasn't there to help you raise our daughter."

"Can you see us? Hear us from up here?"

She shook her head. "I don't see you or Elizabeth the way I did when I was in your world," she said. "I can feel your love, your emotions, the love you give to each other is the strongest sensation I have. It strengthens my spirit when you both think of me."

"What kind of sensation is it?"

"The most extraordinary one you'll ever have."

"She's my greatest joy, Vicki. You gave me that. No one else could have ever given me such an incredible gift. I hope you know that."

She nodded and then lowered her head.

"What's wrong?"

"I'm feeling faint. I'm tired." She backed away a few steps. "I need to leave."

"No," he pleaded. "Not again. Please. Stay."

She looked up at Jesus. "Thank you."

Vicki reached up for Michael's hand; a fiery flame massaged his fingers as the mist returned. "Don't waste a moment, sweetheart," she said. "While time is eternal in my world, it's fleeting and fragile in yours."

"How much time do I have with you?"

"None."

"How much time do I have before we are joined together?"

She looked at Jesus. He shook his head. Vicki lowered hers.

"I love you," she said. "Be strong. We all must face tragedy to truly appreciate God's gift of time."

Her image faded.

Michael took a heavy breath. "Did I really see my dead wife?"

"Do you believe you saw her?"

"I don't know what to believe."

"Michael, do not delay any longer. Find your way home," said Jesus, startling him out of his thoughts. "Where there is life, there is death, and when there is death, there is life once more.

Carry my cloth and use it wisely but use it with love, unselfish love. Never use it for personal gain or the hand of Satan will be satisfied."

Michael met Yochanan at the mouth of the cave. Together they watched as Jesus joined the Apostles.

"Let's get you home," Michael said.

"I am glad I met you, my friend." Yochanan's tone held a burst of euphoria. "I hope we can become better friends. Perhaps you can bring your family to my home and we can share the holy days."

Michael grimaced.

"Did I say something wrong? Are you not with a family?"

Michael shook his head. "For many sunsets I felt I didn't have much of a family, but after traveling here, I realized how much I truly have. I wish I could join you. It would be an honor to share the holy days with you. But I live so far away. It would be impossible to keep this friendship."

"I do not understand. You have traveled to my town. Why would you not come back?"

"This is a once-in-a-lifetime trip for me. It's the only way I can explain it."

"This saddens me, Michael. You are a good man, a true friend. I hope you can stay long enough to meet my wife."

I've already met your wife. And I've fallen in love with her.

"Join us for dinner, my friend. My Leah is a wonderful cook. You will feel welcome."

"I'm sure I would. I really do have to get back to my family. I have a long journey ahead. I want to make sure I get home to my daughter."

Yochanan smiled. "How old is your daughter? What is her name?"

"She's going to be fifteen next month. Her name is Elizabeth."

"Fifteen?"

"Oh. Right. She has a few more sunsets than the average child."

"Is she married?"

"No. Not for a while."

He gave Michael a baffled look. "Our customs are certainly different from yours."

"I'll try to visit someday, maybe for the next holy day," Michael said, trying to fend off any more questions. "I promise. The most important thing is that you return home safely to your wife. Yes, your wife, Yochanan." His voice trailed off as the emotional reality chewed away at his heart. There would be no life with Leah. No snow-filled evening walks along Main Street. No sharing meals as a family. No holding hands like teenagers. No kisses under a sparkly tree under a moonlit sky.

The only important thing is making sure Yochanan is home with Leah and returning to Elizabeth. I have to be there for my daughter.

They made their way down the hill and proceeded to the city streets, still bustling with shoppers and vendors being observed by Roman soldiers.

"I will buy some fruit for our meal," Yochanan said. "I owe this to my Leah. We have not shared many dinners lately. She has been so patient and loving with me, allowing me to grieve."

Michael nodded several times as if the movement of his head would accelerate Yochanan's pace. It didn't. Yochanan examined the market place options, picking up some fruit, touching the texture, and placing it back in the basket.

"I test my Leah's patience when we go shopping. She is quick to choose the food while I am slow." He winked and Michael half-smiled.

Maybe this isn't the day. I don't see any danger right now. Leah was never specific about the day and the time. If it isn't, then what do I do? Do I stay? Do I tell him about what I know and how I found out? No, that's crazy. He'll dismiss me as a nut case. He knows about the dangers here. He's a strong guy. And my life is in Northport with my daughter.

Yochanan juggled three watermelons in his hands, feeling the weight of each. He exchanged words with the vendor about the prices and placed them down. Nearby, a scuffle broke out between several men a couple of storefronts away, drawing the attention of two Roman soldiers.

"Yochanan, can we leave? I don't like what's happening over there."

"Do not worry. This happens all the time. Fights happen when people shop." He smiled and slapped him on the shoulder. "Someone must be looking for a bargain."

The noise from the fray grew louder as several men pushed and shoved each other. A Roman soldier wielded his spear at the angry people, trying to disperse the mob.

"Ah, a treat my Leah would love," Yochanan said with joy, ignoring the skirmish. He held up a medium-sized watermelon. "What do you think?"

"Yes, it's good. Can we go? The fight over there is getting worse."

A crowd formed a circle around the Roman soldiers who held their spears at their side. Michael heard the muffled cries of children.

"I wonder what happened?" Yochanan asked.

"I don't know. I don't like this."

"We should see why the children are crying."

Yochanan paid for his watermelon and walked with Michael to the perimeter of the crowd. They peered through several men and women, noticing a few boys and girls weeping, being held by adults.

"Grandpa, you are bleeding," one cried. "Someone help him."

Two men knelt beside the injured man, tending to him. He was mumbling, bleeding from the side of his head.

"Saul? What happened?" asked Michael as he fell to the ground to offer aid.

"Grandpa was hit by that man," yelled a child, the same boy who had tried to help him find Yochanan.

Out of the corner of his eye, Michael saw a tall soldier, now with his spear drawn in combat position. "What's your problem?" he said with some heat. "Why did you have to hit him?"

"He dared to wave his cane at me."

"He's harmless. What kind of a sick man are you picking on someone so old who can barely walk?"

"Move away," shouted a voice as a soldier knifed his way through the crowd on a horse. "Why is this man laying here? Is he drunk? Remove him. Put him in prison."

"What?" said Michael as he stood.

The soldier pointed his spear in a threatening position.

Michael's heart pounded.

It was Marcus.

A soldier grabbed Saul by the legs as the children screamed. "Leave my grandpa alone. He is bleeding. Help him."

Another soldier pulled on Saul's arm and the old man winced.

"Stop," Michael shouted, pushing back at the soldier.

A spear stung him on the side of the head, buckling his knees. Marcus swung again. Yochanan defended the assault with his watermelon as red juice and chunks of fruit splattered in every direction.

Marcus sneered. "I see we have two rebels."

Michael clutched the spear and yanked hard, jerking the soldier off the horse. He fell to the ground, his helmet clanging on the stones.

Three young men picked up Saul and carried him across the street, away from the danger.

The crowd scattered, afraid of retaliation by the Romans.

Marcus was groggy but wasn't injured. He adjusted his helmet. "You will die for interfering with the Roman mission and authority."

Michael didn't have time to rationalize his predicament; he was cornered and acted like a caged animal, swinging the spear wildly to hold off the soldiers.

Yochanan retreated to an alleyway, kicking at the bottom of the wall. He dislodged a piece of concrete and rubbed its edges hard. He took aim and hurled his sharp weapon. The rock struck Marcus, making a loud clanging sound as it ricocheted off the top of his helmet.

Marcus pointed toward Yochanan, who was already several steps down the street, running. "Track him down."

The soldiers charged after him, prompting Michael to follow, still carrying the Roman's spear. Marcus retreated to his horse.

"Come back here, rebel. Drop the spear," he roared.

Yochanan far outpaced the Romans in their heavy armor. He waited several yards away. Michael grew fearful as the heavy footsteps of the horse behind him drew near.

I'm going to have to kill him now. Or he'll kill me.

Michael stopped, spotted Marcus and waited until he could see his eyes. He threw with all his might. "Take that."

The spear sailed over the soldier's head, clattering along a stone road many yards away.

The Roman on the horse backtracked, giving Michael ample time to catch up to the pursuing soldiers chasing Yochanan.

"Run, my friend. Go the other way," Yochanan shouted.

"No. No. I've got to help you."

Michael picked up a rock not far from the well near Leah's house and hurled it at a soldier, connecting with the middle of his back.

"Yochanan," cried a woman from a rooftop. "Yochanan, what is happening?"

Leah?

"Do not stop, my friend," begged Yochanan.

Michael saw Marcus back on his horse, spear in hand. He watched in horror, knowing what would happen next.

The spear struck Yochanan in the leg, staggering him. As he tried to limp away, a large rock smashed into his forehead. Michael raced toward him.

"Yochanan," Leah yelled as another soldier barreled toward him.

"Leah, get help," Michael shouted, fidgeting for his cloth. "I'll help him."

A rock struck Michael's arm. He fell backwards. The cross around his neck dislodged and the cloth flew out of his hand.

Two neighbors dragged Yochanan's body to the well.

"No. Stop," Michael shrieked as he retrieved the cloth and waved it. "Bring him back. I can help him."

The men shouted back in an unfamiliar dialect. They put their hands up to tell him to stay away.

The cross. I've got to get it. He crawled on his knees to pick it up. Leah screamed again. "Yochanan, Yochanan!"

A rock smashed Michael's knee as he put the cross around his neck. "Oh, God."

He picked up the cloth and looked around to find Yochanan.

"Michael," Leah shrieked, "Watch out. The soldiers."

"Get the rebel," Marcus roared. "Take him alive. I want to kill him myself."

Michael ignored the sting in his knee and sprinted for his life back in the direction of the city and tunnel.

This time, he wasn't sure that he was going to get out of this century alive.

CHAPTER TWELVE

Leah stayed on guard all evening, occasionally staring out the window. Relieved when Elizabeth fell into a deep slumber, she eavesdropped on the late-night noises.

I must get Elizabeth back home soon. She must not wait for her father. I will insist she leave. She has no choice.

Then her thoughts drifted to Michael.

What has happened to you? Are you hurt? Are you lost? Did Marcus capture you? No. I must stop thinking this way.

She prayed that Michael wouldn't show up at her house. She knew that if Marcus returned he would kill him.

Leah agonized in silence, not wanting to disturb Elizabeth but also worrying about the danger lurking over her own family. She needed to remain strong so that her brothers and their families could live peacefully. The long, torturous past was only relieved by those few precious moments with Michael and her quiet time in the garden, praying. When Marcus was not around, she drew strength from the Temple, meditating toward the goal of finding salvation and redemption. But the threat of an encounter with the soldier's rage destroyed any long period of joy.

Elizabeth stirred, interrupting her thoughts. "Rest, my daughter," she whispered.

Leah climbed down the ladder holding a blood-stained bedroll. She grabbed an empty jug and carried it into the courtyard.

Before going to the well, she took a small shovel and dug a hole about a foot wide and long. She carefully placed the remains in it, quickly covered the hole with dirt, and said a prayer.

She paused for a moment and listened. The sky was black, the air crisp, and the neighborhood was quiet.

She hoisted the jug and took the final few steps to the well. The creaking of the swinging bucket alarmed her so she only filled it halfway. She cupped her hands and splashed water first on her face and washed the bottom of her garment, trying to dull the red stain.

She retreated a few steps from the well.

A hand clutched her shoulder roughly. "Why are you out here at this time?" Marcus demanded.

Frightened, she backed away. "Oh, it's you. I needed some water."

He slapped her across the face. "Do not lie to me."

She shielded her face from the next blow. "I am not lying." Leah handed him some water and watched Marcus spill most of it on his face and armor.

He glared at her. "Do you have any wine?"

"I am sorry but I do not have any," she lied, knowing wine fed his belligerence.

He whacked her so hard her ears rang from the blow. "Why?" He raised his hand, ready to strike her once more but she managed to stumble away. "Come back here," he yelled, slurring his words.

She stopped, thinking quickly. "Please, Marcus. You have been drinking. Go back to the prison and stay there so the neighbors will not report you."

"Who is going to report me?"

"I do not know. I do not want you to get in trouble."

Marcus let out a sinister laugh. "It is odd that you are suddenly so concerned about me."

He staggered a few steps toward her and fell down. He lay there for several moments before she went over to see if he was hurt. He didn't move.

She left the jug near the well and ran.

"Where are you going?" said Marcus, rising to his knees. "Help me."

Leah grimaced and turned back. She helped him to his feet, hoping he would fall again and hurt himself. But he leaned on her heavily and she had no choice but to half-carry, half-drag him back to the house.

He crashed down on a chair in the kitchen. "Make me something to eat. I am hungry."

With Elizabeth upstairs, Leah was more than happy to keep Marcus occupied downstairs by feeding him. She grabbed several pieces of bread, poured some porridge into a pot, and started the fire. He removed his helmet and his face mashed into the table.

Leah watched him carefully out of the corner of her eye. *I could hit him with something.* But many of the cups and plates were upstairs.

The lamb's occasional braying interrupted Marcus' grunts.

"I am going to kill that animal," he said, then thumped his head down again. "When will you have the food ready?"

"Soon, Marcus. The fire is going."

A short search of her bedroom for a weapon yielded nothing that could deliver a sufficient blow. She heard movement upstairs and ran up the ladder, only her head visible to Elizabeth. "Quiet," she whispered. "Marcus is downstairs. Do not move. I will let you know when it is safe." A hand touched her leg and she jumped. "Oh."

"What are you doing?"

"I am looking for another cup for some water, Marcus. I will be right down. Go back down."

"Hurry."

Elizabeth grabbed a mug and handed it to her. Leah tripped descending the ladder, almost dropping it. "You see, I found one."

He pounded a fist on the table. "Bring me my food. Now."

She returned to the fire where the porridge was almost ready. "I shall be right back. I left the jug outside." She placed her hands on his head, pushing it down on the table. "Rest."

Leah ran outside, picked up the jug and returned inside within minutes.

Marcus sat straight for a second or two and then wobbled.

"Here's a cup of water," she said. "The food is done." She spooned a big portion into a bowl and stayed near the ladder. When she looked up, Elizabeth's worried face stared back. "Go back," she mouthed quietly.

"I want more," Marcus commanded.

Leah obliged. "Are you going back to the prison now?"

"No."

"Are you going to travel and see any friends?" she asked.

"Why are you so interested in what I will be doing?"

"I need to know what I have to pick up at the market tomorrow for dinner."

"We can go to the market together." The ugly twist of his mouth told her he was suspicious. "You are not thinking about leaving?"

"No."

"Good. Because you know what will happen if you do."

"I do."

Marcus finished the last of the porridge and held out his cup for more water.

Leah filled it and the soldier stretched his arms and belched. "I think we will stay together tonight. I need a woman."

Her stomach lurched. She could see Elizabeth's disgusted face at the top of the ladder, peeking down. "Go to the roof," she mouthed.

Marcus spun around. "What did you say?"

"Let us stay down here for the night since you are so tired."

"We always stay down here."

"Oh yes, my mistake."

"You seem more nervous than usual."

"I am. You scared me at the well."

"Come join me when you are done cleaning up."

He retreated to the bedroom and took his armor off and lay on a bedroll.

Leah picked up the cup and bowl and left them on the table. She glanced up at the second floor.

Elizabeth's frightened eyes stayed glued to the kitchen area. "What should I do?" she said in a hushed tone.

Leah motioned to her to retreat and whispered, "Go to the roof."

CHAPTER THIRTEEN

A woman screamed. The thumping sound of a human head hitting the stone ground sent a chaotic chill slithering through Michael's spine as he dashed into an alleyway.

Heart pounding, he managed to mutter a few words. "Now what?"

Sporadic clusters of people ignored the ruckus and continued to mill around at a frantic pace trying to fetch last minute bargains before the vendors closed their shops as if confrontation was part of a normal day. He tried to catch his breath, exhausted and nauseous from the day's tragic events.

This was meant to be. It's time to get home. I can't change time. I need to go home to Elizabeth. Maybe this cloth is needed to save someone else? Or was this cloth for Yochanan?

He watched a Roman beat a man, prompting him to take a few steps closer to the altercation. A weeping woman begged for help. Michael kicked at a loose piece of rock at the base of the wall and dislodged it.

He walked a few steps closer, paused, took aim, and fired.

He ducked back into the alleyway, not sure if his toss made contact with the Roman. After seeing the woman leading the man away, he knew his throw did some damage. He gathered up more courage to view the other side of the street. The soldier who had chased him was now attending to his fallen comrade. Another guard pointed and gestured while questioning a vendor.

They're looking for me. I've got to go. Michael's hurried pace caught the attention of some shoppers. "Over there! There he is," one shouted.

"Capture him," yelled a soldier on horseback.

Michael tore past the last fruit stand on his side of the street and spotted the big rock securing the grate to the tunnel, about a hundred feet away.

Doable. But can I move it?

The soldier on foot aimed his spear and threw.

The sharp weapon skidded on the ground like a small rock skipping on pond water, nipping the back of Michael's leg. He cried out in pain, stumbling several steps before falling.

"I got him," the soldier said in a triumphant howl.

"Good work. I will alert Marcus," said the soldier on horseback before trotting away.

The back of his leg bled. Michael recovered and limped toward the grate now about thirty feet away. The soldier dove at him, securing his arms around his waist, falling on Michael.

"Get off of me," Michael said as he swung his elbows at the soldier's face.

The soldier ducked, avoiding another blow, and hoisted Michael up like a jug. The Roman pulled Michael's arms behind his back like a cop and tightened his hold. "Marcus will reward me for this arrest."

As the soldier jostled him around in the direction of the city's exit, a wooden object crashed into the side of the soldier's face. The soldier let go of Michael and fell to the ground, holding his head, moaning.

Michael scrambled to his feet.

"Go son," a familiar voice urged.

"Saul?"

"Run, my friend."

The old man hobbled away, holding a little boy's hand. "Do what I say, not what I do," he told the youngster.

Michael ran to the tunnel's entrance and pushed the big stone to the side.

With one strong tug, he pulled the grate away. Jumping down into the tunnel, he heard the stern voice of another soldier.

"I command you to stop."

Keeping his hands clamped against the walls, he ignored the pain in his leg, moving forward at a fast pace.

"Stop now," the soldier demanded.

He gained more distance on the soldier, letting the wall work for him to build up speed, only taking short breaths as needed. Within several minutes, Michael's eyes captured a slice of light shining ahead.

The soldier's voice echoed in the cramped darkness. "Rebel, you will not get away. If you do not stop, Marcus will kill you!"

Only a few more yards to go. The light brightening ahead elevated his hope.

"Connie," Michael yelled. "Can you hear me? Connie?"

No answer. Michael was close to the stairway, leading him back up to the church.

What is this? He bent down and picked up a woman's shoe.

"Stop now," the Roman called out. "I will tell Marcus you gave up without a struggle to save your life."

"Drop dead, Roman," Michael said, turning back. "Connie, are you there?" He heard a faint voice respond but the words were unclear. "Throw something down here. Hurry." There was still no response. "Call the cops. Now!"

Michael panted as he took the first steps up. He tripped, resting a moment on the stairs, listening for any movement. He could hear the clanging of the soldier's footsteps nearing. He gathered up his last reserve of energy and rushed the steps two at a time, gaining entrance to the church's basement.

He remembered the metal candle snuffer the young man brought to the church.

Where did he put it?

In a heartbeat, Michael spotted it in the corner, stuck the shoe in his back pocket, picked up the snuffer and faced the tunnel's entrance.

Michael raised his arms in battle position. "You're in my world now, Roman. Let's see how tough you are."

The soldier's footsteps drew closer, then silence.

The crown of the soldier's helmet dazzled in the mid-afternoon daylight, as the sun's light hit it at a sharp angle. The soldier's eyes glowed as he climbed the last rung.

"Come on," Michael said, his adrenalin giving him bravado. "Make my century, Roman."

The soldier lunged forward and trembled. A moment later, his arms and legs stiffened.

Michael stared in astonishment as the soldier's face turned dull white, then yellow, then black.

The Roman's eyes widened in terror as his pupils filled with dark red blood. His bones crackled like firewood and his eyes fell to the floor, rolling toward Michael. He kicked at the eyes in revulsion, propelling them down the stairway.

The soldier's body quivered and disintegrated into dust as his metal armor sizzled on the floor.

Michael continued to clutch the candle snuffer over his head, waiting for the soldier to rise out of the pile of dust. The smell of ashes filled the room and bits of dust fluttered in the air.

The ground shuddered, rattling the containers with the clothes and holy remnants. One of them toppled from the apex of the pile. He lowered his candlestick as the gateway to the tunnel sealed itself shut.

Dennis entered the doorway, holding a carton. "What's going on?" he asked. "Michael, what happened? This place is a mess."

Wiping the sweat from his forehead and gaining control of his breathing, he said, "I went back."

Dennis stood in silence.

"I went back," he shrieked.

"Where?"

"To Jerusalem."

Dennis dropped the box. A can of beans hit the floor and rolled away. "Did you see – ?"

"Yes," Michael said, nodding.

"You saw Christ?"

"Yes!"

"You spoke to him?"

"Yes," Michael said, taking off the robe and removing his sandals. "I can't talk about it now, I have to go."

"Wait." Dennis grabbed Michael's shoulders. "Tell me what He said. Tell me what He said about forgiveness. I want to know everything."

Michael backed away. "It was remarkable. There's so much to tell you." He slipped on his sneakers. "First I need to see my daughter and let her know I saw Leah."

"Leah?"

"Yes, the woman I told you about."

"Where is she?"

"She stayed behind. She had to." He wiped some sweat away from his forehead. "I've got to tell Elizabeth. I have so much to tell her too."

"Your leg," Dennis said. "You're bleeding."

"I'm fine. Where's Connie?" He took the high-heeled shoe out of his back pocket. "This looks like hers. Why would she take it off?"

"No idea." Dennis shrugged. "I haven't seen her in a while. She ran out of here, looking as pale as a ghost, limping. She looked shaken, upset."

"Church always made her nervous." Michael dropped the shoe on the floor, bent down to catch his breath, then straightened. "Anyway, I've got to get going. I have an important message for Elizabeth."

"Really?" Dennis asked. "I am curious. What kind of message?"

"A message from her mom."

"You spoke to your wife?" Dennis' voice sounded unsteady. Michael nodded.

Dennis turned his head away and asked, "What did she say?" His face paled and his bottom lip trembled.

That's odd. He looks like he just saw a ghost.

CHAPTER FOURTEEN

Elizabeth sat motionless, lost in gruesome thoughts for several minutes before pocketing a couple of pins that were used to weave baskets. She clenched one in her hands.

She heard a loud noise, like a person falling on the floor. Worried that it was Leah, she gasped out loud.

"Who is up there?" yelled the soldier.

"Marcus, come here. No one is up there," Leah said. "I need you now."

Elizabeth crawled back to the ladder opening to see Leah luring him into the bedroom by removing some of her clothes.

The soldier edged away several steps from the bottom of the ladder.

"Come and take me," Leah implored softly.

Revolted, Elizabeth took a few steps down the ladder. Broken pieces of pottery were scattered on the floor. She could hear Leah's cries. She tip-toed down and the steps creaked beneath her feet.

She froze.

From the corner of her eye, she saw shadows in the candlelight, like an old movie reel being played on a living room wall. The soldier's silhouette clawed furiously at Leah's clothing, tearing at the top of the garment.

"You are hurting me, Marcus."

"Shut up, woman," he said, accompanied by a low growl.

Elizabeth inched her way through the kitchen.

Marcus pinned his body against Leah and grabbed her breasts, squeezing them hard. "Just like milking a goat." He let out a caustic laugh.

His snarl sounded evil to Elizabeth's ear. She recoiled as the soldier attempted to kiss Leah on the lips.

Leah moved her head sharply, avoiding the torturous touch.

Elizabeth remained rooted in place, her hands covering her mouth, plotting how to hurt him.

Dad, now would be a good time to show up.

Marcus struggled to remove his pants.

Elizabeth picked up a large, jagged piece of broken pottery. Walking on her toes, she stalked the soldier for a few steps and slammed the pottery on the back of his head.

"No, Elizabeth," Leah cried.

Marcus dropped to his knees, holding his head, catching some of the blood in his hands. "It is you!" He turned to Leah. "I knew you were hiding her. This time she will not get away." He struggled to get to his feet.

Elizabeth bashed him in the face with the pottery again and he collapsed.

"Leave, now," Leah screamed.

Elizabeth remained still.

Marcus regained his footing and wobbled toward her.

She swung her right foot with force, whacking him below the belt, sending the soldier wincing to the ground. He doubled over, cringing in pain. Instinctively, she struck again, her foot sending him sprawling backwards.

Leah roared, "What are you doing? You need to go home." When Elizabeth didn't move, Leah dragged her into the kitchen. "We are in terrible trouble. Stay here."

Leah returned to the bedroom. "Marcus, forgive the girl. She is not from this town and does not know our ways. She is just an innocent child."

Elizabeth joined Leah. They watched the Roman crawl on all fours, taking short, quick breaths.

"Try to get up and I'll do it again," Elizabeth warned.

He glared at both of them.

"She didn't mean to hurt you," Leah said.

"Yes, I did."

Leah jerked Elizabeth's shoulders. "Stop." She leaned over him. "She is young, Marcus, and ignorant of our ways." She grabbed Elizabeth's hand and led her back into the kitchen. "You must go. You are in danger now. Run as fast as you can. Go home. Do not come back. Ever."

Elizabeth shook her head. "No. I won't go unless you come with me. You're in danger too. He will hurt you. I'm not leaving you here with this animal."

"If I leave, he will kill my brother, his wife, their children, everybody. Why do you not understand this?"

"Do you want to die too? I can't leave you here with him."

Leah put both hands on Elizabeth's cheeks. "You must go and never come back."

"What about my dad?"

"Your father is not here. He would have been here if he had come. I should have insisted you leave earlier."

Marcus emerged from the bedroom and lunged at them, swatting Leah with his forearm as Elizabeth tried to block him. "Run home," Leah yelled. Marcus smashed her in the head and blocked the opening to the door.

Elizabeth scrambled up the ladder as Marcus halted her ascent, clutching one of her legs. Leah picked up a piece of the shattered bowl and threw it at the soldier, barely scraping the top of his head.

He dragged Elizabeth down two of the rungs.

"Don't touch me, you filthy, ugly beast," she screamed as she felt his body pressed against her. She pulled a weaving needle from her pocket and swung it at him, piercing his cheek.

He roared, sounding like a wounded lion and fell back to the floor, wiping the blood from his face with his hand. Enraged, he hurried back up the ladder.

Elizabeth reached the roof and ran to the far side to determine how high up she was.

Is it safe to jump from here? Dad, I sure do need you right now. I hope you're here soon!

Leah frantically called out. "Leave her alone. Take me. I will stay with you, Marcus. Let me take care of you."

Elizabeth saw the top of Marcus' head easing up above the roof. He surveyed the area for a few moments, making sure the neighborhood was vacant. "Come here, woman. You will be mine. You are fortunate to be with a Roman and not a peasant. You will do as I say. Do not move."

She withdrew to the edge of the roof.

As Marcus finished his climb, Elizabeth sprinted to him and delivered a swift, hard kick to the side of his head.

He let out a small grunt but it didn't disrupt his pursuit.

Frantic, Elizabeth ran to the other side of the roof.

"I will report you," Leah yelled as she appeared at the top of the ladder.

Marcus kicked Leah on the face so hard, she fell and tumbled down the stairs. Elizabeth shrieked out after her. "Leah, are you okay?"

She didn't answer.

Elizabeth looked around, not sure where to go next. *Should I jump? I don't know what's down there. It's so dark out.*

On his hands and knees, Marcus managed to crawl several feet toward Elizabeth. He sat up, rubbing his head. "Where are you?"

Elizabeth charged again, cracking him in the face with her clenched fist, allowing the point from the pin to scuff his cheek. Blood dripped near his right ear.

"Who do you think you are striking a Roman soldier?" he howled.

"Wonder Woman!" She whacked him on the back of his leg as he tried to stand.

He landed on all fours again, wiping away the blood from his face. The sight of it dripping to the concrete roof incensed him. As he stumbled to get up, Elizabeth kicked him in the back.

He grunted in pain. "I will kill you."

"Stop hitting Leah or I'll hurt you more." She kneed him in the face, knocking him flat on his back. "And leave her family alone too."

He lifted his head and then lowered it much like a hyena does before a lion. Elizabeth held the long metal pins in both her hands in a threatening position.

Marcus held out his hands in a gesture of defeat. "No more. You have hurt me." He coughed, spewing some blood. "Look what you have done to me, woman. I cannot move."

Elizabeth wasn't convinced, even as he gagged and spit up more blood. "I just want you to leave Leah and her family alone."

"I will not hurt her. I promise," the soldier said in a solemn tone. "I will leave as soon as I am better." He wheezed and coughed again. "Can you get me a cup of water?"

She hesitated. "Leah, are you okay?"

There was answer.

Marcus wiped more blood away with his arm. "Woman, I am bleeding. It is hard to breathe. If I die, Leah will be hunted down by more Roman soldiers. Do you want that?"

Elizabeth circled him with caution as she approached the ladder. "Don't –"

Marcus swung his leg, knocking her down.

She winced as her head struck the roof. One of the metal pins bounced out of her hands and spun over the edge.

"How dare you strike me," he bellowed.

Marcus jumped on top of Elizabeth, raised her arms over her head, and held them together with one hand. "Let it go." He twisted the last metal pin from her grasp.

Elizabeth moaned.

He leaned over and tossed it a few feet away.

She was still for a moment. Her head pounded and she felt groggy.

Marcus stroked her hair and her cheeks, hissing like a snake ready to devour a mouse. His breath was so foul, she wanted to vomit. She gagged, trying to hold down the day's meal.

"I never wanted Leah," he whispered, his voice full of disgusting menace. "I always wanted you."

Elizabeth trembled. Marcus pressed his body firmly against her.

Her head fuzzy, she mustered up enough strength to jerk Marcus' legs off her and spotted a pin nearby. *I've got to try.*

"Resist me and I will kill you."

Elizabeth jostled him with her knees as Leah reached the roof again. "Get off her," she demanded. Leah swung at him with a plate, cracking it on the back of his neck.

He lost his balance and Elizabeth inched closer to the pin.

Marcus stood and pushed Leah hard to the ground and pressed his boot against her head, stunning her. Leah lay motionless.

He leaned down and swatted Elizabeth in the right cheek with an open hand. "I said stop moving."

"You jerk," she screamed.

Marcus kneeled, clamping his free hand over her mouth. "Quiet, or I will let you watch me kill Leah. Do you want that? Do you?"

She shook her head in fear.

He began to remove his pants as Elizabeth pushed up with her knees again, knocking him over and freeing her hands. With one swift movement she retrieved the pin and stabbed him in the leg. Marcus roared in pain and raged at the blood pouring from his leg. He wiped it away and glared. "I have grown tired of you. You are not worthy to be with a Roman soldier."

Elizabeth scrambled away as he staggered to his feet. Marcus kicked the pin out of her hand, pulled her up like a rag doll, and dragged her to the edge of the roof.

His laughter was filled with scorn. "Enjoy your trip back home."

"Stop, stop," she shouted, clinging to his arm. "I'll do what you want. Just stop."

"My patience is no more. I will keep Leah." He removed her grip from his arm. "You are a problem."

"No."

Marcus held her up by the neck and shook her like a rag doll. Elizabeth's feet bounced up and down.

Her grip on his shoulders loosened, her fingers weakened. She lost her balance and fell. Desperate, she dug her nails into his skin as hard as she could.

He leaned close to her ear. "Your God awaits you."

His swift kicks knocked her hands off his leg as she lay a foot from the edge, breathing hard. He got down on his knees and shoved her, trying to roll her off the roof.

Elizabeth pierced his face again, slicing the skin above his right eye.

Marcus fell on top of her. Together they tumbled closer to the edge.

"Oh God," Elizabeth screamed in horror. "Daddy? Leah? Help me."

"Elizabeth!" Leah crawled several feet and lunged at them. "No. Oh God, no."

CHAPTER FIFTEEN

Michael sped through the streets of Northport, talking to himself about what he had just seen. His emotions zigzagged from gloom of not being able to help Yochanan to euphoria of having spoken to Vicki. He hurried into his house and ran upstairs. "Elizabeth. The tunnel opened. I made it back. I saw your mom. I saw Leah."

He opened her bedroom door. Empty. Inside the bathroom her makeup kit was open on the ledge of the sink. "Lizzy, are you home? I'm back."

He returned to the kitchen and noticed a handwritten note. "Oh no."

Michael dialed his sister's number. She didn't answer. *Great.*

He headed back to the church and arrived as the event was wrapping up. He weaved through a group of teenagers chatting and drinking soda. He checked each group of volunteers, asking if anyone had seen Connie or Dennis. When he couldn't locate either, he rushed to the basement.

The dead soldier's dust was still visible. He knelt and could smell the cooling metal. He poked at it with his index finger. *Still hot.* He slowly moved his hand side-to-side over where the tunnel opening was.

"Michael? What are you doing?"

Startled, he jumped up. "Connie. I'm glad you're here. Where were you?"

"I had to get out of this church."

"Why?"

"This place is spooky. There was this snake."

"What snake?"

"I saw a snake slither out of that stairway. What in the heck is down there?"

"Where did it go?" he asked.

"The snake?"

"Yeah, the snake."

"It just crumbled up and died." She furrowed her brow. "At least I think it died. I don't see it around here because I took off so fast. What is in that holy water? And you drank that stuff. Everyone here is freaking me out."

Michael paused, remembering his confrontation with the snake near the grate. "What type of snake was it?"

"I don't know. A hissing kind."

"What did it look like?"

"It had a huge head and a big mouth."

"You're not hurt?"

"I'm fine but the cops think I'm a kook."

"Cops?"

"I went to the police station and reported it to the cops."

"What did they say?"

"I told you they think I'm a nut job." She looked around the floor. "Ah, there's my shoe." She picked it up and slipped it on. "Oh, by the way, here's your cellphone."

"Where did you get this?"

"Elizabeth gave it to me."

"Where did you see her?"

"Here at the church. Didn't she come back with you?"

He froze. "What do you mean?"

"I told her not to go down there but she was worried about you." She rubbed her forehead. "I think she went after you."

"You think?" he shouted. "Did she go down the stairs or not?"

"She said something about a soldier. I told her not to go because you'd get mad at her."

Michael threw his arms in the air. Exasperated, he yelled, "I told you to keep her out of there."

Connie backed away. "She said you were going to see if some woman was safe. She said she wanted to find you and make sure you were okay."

"No, this can't be happening." Michael collapsed to his knees and clawed at the floor, sweeping away the dust. He dug his nails hard into the ground. "Elizabeth, can you hear me?"

"Maybe –"

"Shut up!" He lay on the floor, his head close to the ground. "Elizabeth, if you can hear me, scratch the ceiling." He listened for a moment. "I don't hear anything."

"What's going on down here?" asked Dennis.

"It's Elizabeth," Connie said, pointing to the ground. "She could be in there."

"Are you sure?"

"I'm not a hundred percent sure." Connie knelt beside Michael. "If she is, it'll open again, right?"

Cold sweat poured down his temples. "I don't know."

He clawed at the ground until a couple of his nails broke out in blood. He stopped, bent his head and wracked his brain for a better solution.

The cloth.

He took the cloth out of his pocket and rubbed the floor in frantic, circular motions. "Work. Work, now!" He shook the cloth out and continued rubbing. "Why couldn't you have kept a better eye on her?"

Connie joined him, pawing at the floor. "It's not my fault. Your daughter's stubborn."

Michael dug harder with his fingernails until one tore off. He pressed his head against the ground. "Elizabeth," he shouted. "I'll get you out. Don't move. Stay there."

"Stop," Connie said through her tears. "We have to get the police to help us."

He took a few more half-hearted digs at the cement before getting to his feet. "Go see if Elizabeth's home. Maybe she returned before I got back." He handed her his keys.

She nodded and ran up the steps.

For a moment Dennis and Michael stared at each other in disbelief.

"Let's go," Dennis said.

"No." He continued digging with his nails as more blood pitched out from underneath his fingertips. "Not now."

"We need to compose ourselves. We need to think and pray."

"Pray?" Michael said in disbelief, shaking his head. "It's time for action, not talk."

"Michael, you need to get hold of yourself and think about this rationally." He held out his hand. "Come to my office before you hurt yourself. Connie will let us know if she finds Elizabeth at home."

Michael tried to catch his breath. Dennis helped him up, guiding him up the stairwell and into his office. He closed the door and locked it. He fell into his seat behind his desk. The old, tattered book that Michael and Elizabeth had found in the basement lay in front of him.

"So what exactly happened?" Dennis asked. "Where did you go?"

Michael paced back and forth. "Jerusalem. But it wasn't the same time. I'm not sure of the exact day or year. But I know I didn't go back after Christ was crucified."

"You saw the Lord, right?"

"I already told you. Yes. I saw him up on a mountain."

"What did he say about forgiveness? Did he say one's actions here can remove one's sins?"

"What?" He wrung his hands frantically. "Look, Dennis, right now I'm worried about my daughter. She could be back there. What should I do?"

"Let's wait and see if she did go back. We need to call her friends and check the places she usually visits. It's easy to lose someone in a crowd like the one we had today." Dennis pointed to a chair but Michael shook his head. "Did Jesus say anything to you about removing one's sins while here?"

What is he talking about? He bit his lip so he didn't utter a strong expletive to let out his frustration. "I don't know. I'm confused right now. I have to talk to Connie again."

Dennis frowned but didn't say anything. "You said you saw your wife. Did she say anything about the accident?"

"What? Um, no. Why? Forget that. I need you to help me figure this out."

Dennis fidgeted with a bookmark inside the black book. "You must think hard about all the people you met, what you saw, what they said to you. There has to be a reason."

There was a knock at the door.

"Yes?" called Dennis.

Michael heard the church secretary's muffled voice behind the door. "There's a police officer waiting to speak to you."

"Tell him I'll be there in a minute."

Michael gritted his teeth. "What do I say to the cops?"

"Nothing. Stay here."

Dennis got up from his seat, unlocked the door, and greeted the cop. "Hello, Officer McDougal. How can I help you?"

"We received a visit from a Connie Donatella. She filed a report about some disturbance in the church's basement."

Dennis smiled but Michael knew it was strained. "It was a misunderstanding. Everything's fine." He attempted to close the door. "Thanks for checking it out."

"Misunderstanding?" The cop blocked the door with his hand and wrote something on his notepad. "Ms. Donatella claimed there was a snake coming out of a hole in the basement."

"A snake? Downstairs?" Dennis looked at Michael. "Your sister must have seen a mouse."

The cop's eyes stared from Dennis to Michael. "Connie Donatella is your sister? Is she here right now?"

Michael shrugged.

"I don't think so," Dennis said. He looked at his notepad. "I've got her contact information." He put his pen in his pocket. "I'm going to take a look in the basement. If she comes back, please send her down to talk to me."

"Sure," Dennis said. He closed the door, leaned his ear against the thick, wooden frame, and locked it again. "Your sister is going to have to talk to the police."

"What can she say?"

"The truth."

"They'll think she's crazy."

Dennis nodded. "That's exactly what we want them to think."

"Why?"

"That way they won't go digging for more information. They'll just put it down to her hysterics. You play along and say she's been under a lot of stress lately and her anxiety tends to make her imagine things. That won't make any news headlines. But if the media gets hold of this story they'll turn this place into a circus. Thousands of people will show up at the church. That's not the best thing for us right now."

"I don't care," Michael said. "I only care about finding my daughter."

"I know. But if she did follow you into the tunnel, you have to find a way back. And you won't be able to do that if this place is crawling with people and cameras."

"Okay." Michael put his hands on his hips and looked upward, blowing out a loud breath, trying to make sense of it all. "Obviously, you believe what I went through down there."

Dennis picked up the old book and waved it at Michael. "I've read about the miracles witnessed by the previous pastors of this church. They're remarkable and amazing accounts."

Michael's heart raced, his body energized with hope that there might be a way back to find Elizabeth if she did follow him. "So there's a chance the tunnel will open again for me?"

"Only God knows." Dennis put the book back on his desk. "I'll keep reading this."

The church phone rang and Dennis answered. "Hello. Yes. Yes. Okay. Thanks." He slowly put the phone down, his expression mournful. "Connie said Elizabeth isn't home."

Michael darted out of the office and back downstairs where he found Officer McDougal rummaging through the containers. He gripped the coins in his pocket along with the wooden cross. "What are you looking for?" he asked the cop.

"Excuse me?" The cop lifted his eyebrows. "I'm investigating a report. What are you looking for?"

Michael grabbed the broom leaning against the wall. "I'm going to finish up cleaning." He noticed the cop staring at the scratches marking the spot where Michael dug. He walked over them and pretended to be concentrating on sweeping.

The cop took a couple of steps back up the stairs. "If you see your sister, let her know we'd like to talk to her again."

Michael nodded. "Will do."

He waited a few minutes to ensure the cop had left and went back to Dennis' office.

"Is he gone?" Dennis asked.

"Yeah, but he'll probably be back."

Dennis shook his head. "We can't let this story get out or this place will be overrun. They'll think we're a bunch of crazy nuts."

Michael glared. "I don't care who finds out about what, or what they think of me. They can call me crazy, call my whole family crazy. I don't care if people want to report this. I just want to find my daughter."

He walked out of the office and to the front of the church, watching the crowd continue to mill along Main Street.

"Hey, Mike, what's going on?"

Oh great, now what do I do? "Hello, Allison. Long time no see."

She stepped away from her friends she'd been chatting with and touched his upper arm.

He backed away as if a wasp stung him.

She frowned. "What's up with that? I'm not going to bite you." She stepped closer to him. "You look terrible. What's wrong?"

He ignored her questions.

"Are you all right? You look like you just saw a ghost."

Allison was the last person he wanted to ask for help, especially if it meant being in a confined space with her. But he was desperate. He chased every face for a sympathetic expression, examining every possible option. He eventually relented.

Allison waved her hand in front of his face. "Hello? Are you there?"

"Can you help me?" he asked.

"You want my help? Depends." She nudged his elbow. "What do you need?"

He tried not to roll his eyes. "A ride home."

"You want to be in the same car with me?"

"Forget it. I'll walk."

"Stop being a baby. Let's go."

They got into her blue Sedan and he leaned over to the far right.

"I'm not going to attack you," she said. "Put your seatbelt on."

He did and pressed his shoulder against the passenger door.

"You know, I could open up the door," she said.

He remained silent, not blinking.

"Truce, okay? What's going on?"

"I don't know where Elizabeth is."

Allison pulled her car over on Ocean Avenue. "What do you mean? What happened to my goddaughter?"

"I don't know. I'm not sure."

"What kind of father are you? Not knowing where your daughter is. Does she have a cell phone?"

He nodded. "I tried calling it a few times but no one answered."

"Keep trying. You know how kids are, sometimes they screen their calls."

"Can I borrow your phone? My phone isn't getting reception. Stupid cheap phone."

She handed him her phone and he punched in Elizabeth's number. The phone rang four times and as Michael was about to hang up, a male voice answered.

"Who is this?" Michael demanded.

"Um, it's Matt."

"Matt, this is Elizabeth's dad. Is she with you?"

"No. Isn't she with you?"

"Would I be calling her if she was with me?" Michael bit down hard on his molars. "Do you know where she is?"

"No, I thought she went home."

"Where are you?" Michael asked.

"At home."

"I need to speak to you right now. Where do you live?"

He gave Michael the information. "Stay there. Don't go anywhere. Don't move." He hung up and gave Allison the address and directions to Matt's house.

She sped through the narrow, hilly streets of the old town. When they arrived, Matt was outside, standing near his car. His trunk was open and Elizabeth's bike leaned against the back bumper.

Michael jumped out before the car rolled to a stop. "Where's my daughter?"

"I don't know. I dropped her off at the church and haven't seen her since."

"Her bike is in your car." He grabbed Matt's shirt, tightening his grip. "Don't lie to me."

"I'm not, Mr. Stewart."

"Michael." Allison clenched his forearm. "Stop. He's just a kid."

He relaxed his grip and backed away a few steps. "How long did you wait for her?"

"About fifteen minutes. I went back inside to look around and couldn't find her. But there were a lot of people in there. I could have missed her. My mom called and needed me to drive her to an appointment. I looked around for a few more minutes and assumed she left with you." Two spots of bright red stained Matt's cheeks. "I know she wanted to talk to you."

"About what?"

Matt looked down at his feet. "She wanted to tell you we were going out to a movie."

Michael scowled. "Stay away from my daughter."

As he started to walk away, he glared at Matt. "Why didn't you answer the phone before?"

"I wasn't sure I should answer it. I was kinda uncomfortable."

"If she calls you, tell her to call home right away."

"Of course." Matt put his hand in his pocket and gave Elizabeth's cell phone to Michael. He retrieved her backpack too and handed it to Allison.

Michael turned to Allison and gave a distraught look. "He doesn't know where she is."

"Well, she has to be somewhere. No one disappears into thin air."

They do if they go into a tunnel back to another century.

CHAPTER SIXTEEN

Allison drove Michael home and he showed her the note Elizabeth had left him. "That's a relief," she said. "This proves she must be around here somewhere."

"No." Michael paced, trying to burn off nervous energy before he exploded. "My daughter's gone."

"Do you think she ran away?"

"Nothing like that." He rubbed his forehead. "It's too complicated to explain right now."

The door opened and Connie rushed inside.

"Where have you been?" he asked.

"I was at the police station," she said, her face flushed. "Is she back?"

"Not yet," he said, feeling the anxiety squeezing his chest. "One of the cops showed up at the church."

"Well, they think I'm crazy." She threw her arms in the air. "They didn't believe me about the snake or the big hole. Or you were going to save that woman." She huffed out loud. "They asked if it was a practical joke we were playing on each other."

Allison looked from Michael to Connie. "What is she talking about?"

Michael gave Connie a sympathetic glance. "My sister's been under a lot of stress lately, her husband –"

"Stop, Michael," Connie said. "What are you saying?" Her voice rose even louder. "You told me about going down to –"

"See," he turned to Allison. "She gets hysterical for no reason lately."

Connie planted her hands on her hips. "I swear if you're pulling a fast one on me –"

A knock on the door interrupted them. Michael opened it and let Officer McDougal inside.

"Yes," Michael said. "Can I help you?"

"Your sister gave us your address," the cop said. "She said you'd want to talk to us about something?"

"She's confused." Michael gave Connie a look that he hoped told her not to say anything. "That mouse she saw in the basement did a number on her nerves."

"Michael," Allison said. "You should tell him that Elizabeth's missing."

"Who's Elizabeth?" the cop asked.

This is going to get even more complicated.

"My daughter." Michael blew out a loud breath. "I've been looking for her. She may be with a friend and forgot to tell me."

"How old is she?"

"She'll be fifteen next month."

"Oh yeah, that's the age when your hair will start turning gray."

"It already is," he said.

"How long has she been missing?" the cop asked.

"A few hours."

He handed Michael a business card. "If she's not home by morning, give me a call. Most times, it's a case of an angry teenager hiding out at a friend's place, but we like to make sure."

"She's a happy kid," Michael said, taking the card. It took all of his strength not to break down, tell him the truth and beg for assistance, even though he knew in his heart they couldn't help him.

"Sure." The cop sounded skeptical. "They're all happy kids when they're your own."

"What do you mean by that?"

The cop didn't answer. Instead, he tipped his cap to Connie and Allison. Michael watched him walk outside. The officer stopped by his car and looked inside the passenger side window.

Michael grabbed his stomach and coughed several times. The sickly feeling churned inside his mouth. He ran to the upstairs bathroom and spit up last night's meal in the sink – a combination of first-century bread and berries.

"Are you all right?" Connie asked, placing her hand on his back. "What the heck did you eat yesterday?"

"Nothing you would find here." He ran cold water, cupped some into his mouth, and spit it all out.

"What was in that hole?" Connie asked.

"Inspiration and beauty at first." His breathing was hard and choppy now and thought if ever he was going to lose his mind it would be today. "Then it turned tragic."

Connie gasped. "Do you think Elizabeth's in danger?"

"I hope to God not." Michael felt his stomach gurgle. He shook his head and with it all the fears inside it. "No. I have to think positive. She's coming back to us."

CHAPTER SEVENTEEN

Elizabeth lay limp on the ground where she fell with Marcus from the roof. Blood seeped from her head and her arms were badly bruised.

Leah raced back and forth to the well, dampening cloths, trying to stop Elizabeth's hemorrhaging. "Speak to me, child," she pleaded. "Say something."

She pulled Elizabeth's head up gently, begging her to wake up.

Elizabeth let out a soft moan. Her arms remained flaccid, her eyes filled with fear as she blinked several times.

Marcus's body partially covered her legs. A gash leaked blood from his forehead, the smell contaminating the air. Leah lifted Elizabeth's head close to her chest and placed two cloths on the ground as a pillow. She knew there wasn't much time before Marcus would regain his senses.

Leah ran to the next cluster of dwellings, stopping at the door of a home not unlike her two-floor stone house. "Samuel," she said in a loud whisper. "Wake up."

A woman wearing a robe and carrying a long candle appeared before her. She shone the light in Leah's face. "My dear, why are you out at this time of the evening?"

"Oh, Maris, something terrible has happened. It is important that I speak to my brother."

"What terrible thing has happened?"

"A friend of mine has been hurt. She fell from the roof. She is only a child and she is bleeding."

Maris put her hand over her mouth. "I will get your brother."

She waved Leah inside the house and told her to wait in the kitchen. A few minutes later, her brother appeared, pushing his brown hair out of his eyes. "My sister, what is the latest tragedy you need to tell me about?"

"Samuel, we are all in trouble."

"Again?"

"My friend is hurt. Marcus is too. They fell off the roof. She is laying by my home, bleeding."

"Where is the soldier?"

"He is laying there too."

"How badly is he hurt?"

"I am not sure. He has not moved."

Samuel put his hands around the back of his head. "This is not good. If he recovers, he will certainly pursue us."

"He is bleeding but the child is much worse. We need to help her."

"Leah, you have always been the one with the biggest heart in our family." He kissed her forehead. "Maris," he called.

His wife came out of the bedroom now with two lit candles. She handed one to Leah.

"Wake the children. Take them to my cousin's house in Galilee."

"Why, Samuel?" she asked. "That is a long trip. Why at this time of the night? Can we wait until the morning when there is light?"

He shook his head. "No. There might not be time. We are all in grave danger. You must leave once the children are ready. Woman, do not question me."

"Why are we in danger, Samuel?"

"The soldier. He has been hurt."

Maris nodded. "I will get the children ready." She climbed upstairs to the second floor. Moments later, Leah heard muffled voices and sounds of movement.

"I will get dressed." Samuel looked at his sister. "Do you need anything?"

"Yes, more cloths. The girl will need them to heal the wound. We do not have much time."

Samuel changed in his bedroom and returned minutes later. He picked up a short spear sitting in the corner of the kitchen and showed it to Leah. "We do not have a choice, my sweet sister. We should have done this a long time ago. We must kill Marcus."

Her heart sank. They were words she thought would never be part of any solution in her life. She was squeamish. "I can not kill. Thou shall not kill. The Ten Commandments. This is part of my faith, my belief. Your belief. Should God not be the only judge?"

"My dear sister, I am a man of faith too. I live my life with the Ten Commandments as my guide. I know all about thou shall not kill. Do you see God here? Marcus must die. Or we will."

"What about my friend?"

He gave a look of despair. "I do not know. Let us see how she is. Were you able to get her inside the house?"

"No."

Maris came down the ladder. "The children are dressing."

"Do not hesitate. Once they are ready, move them quickly to Galilee. Do not tell anyone where you are going."

"I will not, my love."

Maris and Samuel hugged and shared a brief kiss. She stroked the sides of his hair. "When should we expect you?"

"Soon. I will help my sister's friend and I shall join you."

He tightened his grip on the weapon, nodded to a sorrowful Maris and disappeared through the door.

Maris hugged Leah. "I will see you soon too?"

"I hope so," Leah replied wistfully. "If I do not see you again, Maris, take care of my brother. Tell him I love him at every sunset if I cannot anymore."

She met Samuel outside and listened to his plan, gaining confidence and reassurance that he would be able to solve this problem.

In the moonlight she pointed to one body on the ground. "Oh no, Samuel. Marcus must have left."

"He might be in the house."

They crept through the courtyard and into the kitchen. A rustling noise froze them until a woman appeared out of the darkness with a lit candle.

"Are you well?" the woman asked. "I heard screaming and yelling earlier but was too afraid to go out."

Leah breathed a sigh of relief as she recognized her neighbor. "Sarah, I am fine. Did you see where Marcus went? He was in front of the house."

"He was badly hurt but he managed to get up and leave. I ran to the corner of my house to see if you had fallen too."

"Where did he go?"

"I saw him walk toward the city."

"He is too hurt to battle us alone," reasoned Samuel. "But he will get more of them to chase us all down. We do not have much time."

"How can I help?" asked Sarah.

"Get us some more cloths. We need to get Elizabeth inside so we can make her well enough to get her home."

"Where does she live, Leah?" Sarah asked.

"I do not know. I know it is far away."

"This is not good," her neighbor said with a worried expression.

With careful movements, Samuel lifted Elizabeth into his arms and carried her into the bedroom. Leah placed two bedrolls on the floor and he gently laid her down.

Elizabeth moaned.

Leah tried to soothe her. "Do not move, my child."

Samuel knelt beside her and furrowed his brow as he looked at the gash on Elizabeth's head. "She has a terrible wound."

Sarah pulled several pieces of cloth from her pocket. Samuel instructed Sarah to dampen them at the well. He placed his hands on Leah's shoulders. "In life we are all faced with difficult decisions. Your friend cannot be moved because we do not know where to take her. The Romans will surely come back here looking for you and her. You must leave or you will be killed."

Leah stared at the big drops of blood scattered across the stone floor. "I cannot, Samuel. But you must go to Galilee. You have a family, a wife, and children."

She paused a moment, then spoke with strength. "Elizabeth is my daughter, my child too. While she may not have come from my womb, while I may not have known her long, she is a beat in my heart. I cannot bear to leave my heart."

"Is there anything I can say to change your decision?" he asked.

She shook her head. "You must leave, brother. Protect your family."

He swallowed hard several times and stood up. "I will give you my weapon," he said, placing it on top of a table. "Do not hesitate to use it."

Leah didn't answer.

Samuel kissed her forehead twice. "You always had the biggest heart."

"I love you, Samuel."

He headed to the door and faced her. "I love you too, sweet sister."

As he walked out, Sarah passed him with the wet cloths. "Where is he going?"

"He needs to be with his family. And so do you."

"I will help."

"No. You must go home. You must forget what you have seen here. Do not share this with anyone."

"Why?"

"It is not important why. It is important you are safe and your family is safe. Forget what you have seen."

Sarah wrapped her arms around Leah. "I will say a prayer for you in the Temple."

"Say many for me and my daughter."

Leah nursed the back of Elizabeth's head, trying to seal the wound. A mix of blood and water drenched the cloths. She did her best wringing them out at the well, careful not to leave any evidence behind for the Romans. Exhausted, Leah filled a jug and carried it to the bedroom.

She found a clean, dry cloth tucked away in the kitchen. She soaked it and placed it on her forehead. "Talk to me, child." But there was no response.

Leah lay down next to Elizabeth, touching her hair. "You are so brave. I would be proud to call you my daughter. I know if my daughter had lived, she would have grown up like you. Strong, beautiful, and smart."

She kissed her cheek. "I will not leave you. I will fight Marcus if I have to. I will fight the Romans. I will not let them hurt you." Her body shook.

Leah knelt, lifted her head to the ceiling and prayed harder than she'd ever prayed in her life. "She still has many more sunsets to treasure, my God. May she recover with your blessing. She needs to be with her father. I ask you for your mercy."

CHAPTER EIGHTEEN

Michael stood in Elizabeth's bedroom and shut the slightly cracked window. "Tell me where you are, Elizabeth."

"What's going on up here?" asked Connie.

"Are you all right, Mike?" Allison asked, breathing hard from running up the stairs.

"I thought I heard Elizabeth's voice," he said.

"That's your stress talking," said Allison, giving him a stern look.

He stared at both women. "Why are you even here, Allison?"

"I'm worried about my goddaughter."

"There's no story here so why don't you leave."

"Can we hold off with the feuds for now?" Connie asked.

The doorbell rang. "I'll get it," he said in a hopeful tone.

It's got to be Elizabeth. She forgot her key. Let it be my daughter. Please, Lord.

He yanked the door open. "Jim? What the?"

Jim brushed passed him, the smell of whisky on his breath filling the air. "Don't just stand there like a statue. Help me to a chair."

"Why are you here?"

"Can't I stop by and see my granddaughter?"

Michael helped him to the recliner. "She's not here right now."

Jim sat, groaning as Connie and Allison stopped short of joining them in the living room. "Connie? What are you doing here? And who are you?"

"I'm Elizabeth's godmother in case you forgot, Mr. Stewart."

"You are?"

"You don't remember me? Vicki's best friend, Allison."

"Nope. Can't say I do. Where's Elizabeth?"

Michael waved them away. "Can you look upstairs and see if you can find anything with Lady Gaga on it?"

"Seriously?" Allison asked.

"Yeah, I'm serious. It may give us a clue if she's still here."

Connie shrugged and joined Allison who was heading upstairs.

He turned to his father. *Oh, Lord. I don't need this today of all days.*

Michael steadied his voice. "So, you found some time to come and visit us out here in the *boondocks?*"

"I'm a busy man. It's hard to find time to sit in a car on the expressway all day long."

"Right." Michael clenched his jaw. "Too busy to come to one of Elizabeth's birthday parties."

"How is my granddaughter?"

Michael extended his hands in an unconvincing wave. "She doesn't even know you."

Jim rocked back and forth. "Well, it's hard to take care of the house by myself since your mother died. Takes up a lot of my time these days."

"That excuse is getting old. Mom's been dead for twenty-five years."

Jim pushed away a strand of gray hair from his eyes and grinned. He pointed to the paint on the ceiling in the far right corner that was chipping, inflated into a foot wide bubble. Stacks of newspapers rested in no particular order on the coffee table. "You're just like me."

Michael charged him like a soldier claiming a hill. "I'll never be like you." He withdrew, his wall of protection badly needing some bricks. So he headed to the kitchen looking for a corkscrew while his dad whined the battle cry.

"Get me some whiskey while you're in there."

Michael walked back to the room empty-handed and prepared himself for war. "You know, for someone who always told me it was too far to come out here to visit his granddaughter, it's an awfully long trip to make for a glass of whiskey."

Jim stopped rocking and shot back, "What right do you have to talk to me like that? In my day, my dad would wallop me in the face if I spoke like that."

"You've laid your last hand on me. Why are you here?"

Jim took a deep breath. "I'm sick."

"You just asked me for a drink. How sick can you be?"

"Could be serious if I don't get help."

"Then get help."

"That's what I'm doing," he said.

"What do you mean by that?"

"You have to help me."

"I have to?"

The old man nodded. "Yes, you have no choice."

Michael slapped his forehead. "Unbelievable. You can't drive out here to visit with your motherless granddaughter, but you have no problem waltzing into my home and demanding I help you." He grunted in anger. "What a piece of work you are."

Jim stood and walked slowly over to him. "I may need a bone marrow transplant. You might be a match. I need you to come with me and see if you are."

"Is it a life and death situation right now?"

"Not yet."

"Then I'm not going anywhere. I have to find Elizabeth."

"You can look for her after we're done." Jim yanked on his arm. "I'm your father. You're going to do what I say."

"I'm a father too. And I'm doing what a good father does. I'm looking for my daughter. If you want to help, great. If not, go home."

CHAPTER NINETEEN

Leah slipped into a light doze, occasionally waking when Elizabeth flinched or moaned. She lay on top of her pillow and blanket, holding onto her brother's weapon. Her dream took her to a world where Yochanan and Michael courted her, though she could never figure out where she devoted her real love.

They took her on trips to the mountains, finding a soft-sounding stream, a chance to hold each other and talk. Her subconscious visions were in places far away from the city, the shops, and the crowds, a time to enjoy the natural beauty and majestic features of her world.

Leah clung to her subliminal state for as long as possible. She took serene, slow breaths, relishing the man's embrace, his strong arms wrapped around her shoulders, the smell of his two-day old beard, and the touch of his hair. While she couldn't distinguish whether it was Yochanan or Michael, or any other man for that matter, she was blissful to be in this place for just a little while.

"How are you?" a woman asked, disrupting her harmony.

"Oh. It is you, Sarah. I am tired. Why are you here?"

"I am here to see how you and your friend are feeling."

"I am fine. She is not. I do think I did stop the bleeding."

"I think I might be able to help," Sarah said.

"How?"

"I know of a man who might be able to heal your friend. My neighbor Paul travels far and often. He told me about his friend who helps the sick."

Leah stared at Elizabeth. "I do not know how we would get her to travel. How far would we have to go?"

"Not far. He was last seen in Bethany."

"Who is this healer?"

"A preacher, a rabbi. His name is Jesus."

Leah was baffled. "The man who was killed on a cross not too long ago? How can it be this man you speak of?"

"This is what my neighbor told me. He said he has seen this preacher heal many sick children, the old and the lame."

Leah rose and poured water out of the jug, rinsing another piece of cloth. She removed the soiled one that nurtured Elizabeth's head and smiled. "Sarah, look, the bleeding has stopped."

She placed the fresh cloth around the gash and rested her head back on the bedroll. "She is still badly injured. I must get her to Bethany to try and find this preacher. I cannot wait much longer as we are all in danger if Marcus returns."

Sarah nodded. "I remember what you told me. I have not said a word to anyone."

"What about your husband?"

"I have not spoken to him about this."

"You may have to tell him now."

"Why?"

"We need his help to get my friend to Bethany."

"Are you sure you want me to tell Jeremiah?"

She nodded, then leaned down to feel Elizabeth's forehead. "She is still with a fever. This is not good."

Leah filled a cup and lifted Elizabeth's head. She opened her mouth and poured some water, prompting Elizabeth to cough a little. "Can you hear me?"

"Leah?" Elizabeth said in a weak voice.

She patted her cheek gently. "Yes, my child."

"Where am I?"

"You are in my home."

"Where's my dad?"

"I do not know."

She let out a small cough. "I want to go home."

Leah gave her a couple of more sips of water. "We are going to try to get you home. But you must first get stronger. Can you get up to walk?"

Elizabeth closed her eyes.

"Should I get my husband?" asked Sarah.

"Yes. Quickly."

Leah continued to give Elizabeth water when she opened her eyes. Elizabeth swallowed and coughed as she drank. "What happened to me?"

"You fell off the roof. Do you remember how it happened?"

"I remember the soldier. Nothing more."

"You had a terrible fall. You hit your head on the ground. You have a bad wound." She wiped around Elizabeth's mouth where water had spilled. "How do you feel now?"

"Awful. My head is hurting so much."

She groaned as Leah placed her head down. "You must get your rest, Elizabeth. We will have to go on a trip to get you the help you need."

Leah gathered up a few travel items, collecting weaving needles to use as weapons, two of her favorite robes, two bedrolls, some food, and a small blanket that used to lay in the crib. As she finished packing the supplies, she stared out the window at the courtyard and fig tree. She stood silent, misty-eyed at the thought of leaving her adored home, where she had loved and lived for many sunsets.

Sarah and Jeremiah arrived as she came down the ladder.

"I have a strong donkey," he said. "The animal can carry your friend but you must walk beside her. I will walk on the other side. The trip is a short one, not many steps. Once we are there, we must leave. Sarah told me about the injured Roman soldier. They will come back for revenge. We will all be in danger."

Leah agreed and packed up more wet cloths, placing one on Elizabeth's forehead and another on her wound. She tightened it like a bandana.

Elizabeth opened her eyes and attempted to lift herself. "It hurts."

"You must be strong. We must travel now. Marcus could be coming back." Leah put her hand underneath Elizabeth's back. "Try now."

She was able to sit up slightly.

"Jeremiah, can you bring the donkey in here?" Leah asked.

"Sarah," he called out. "Bring the animal in."

"Stay strong, my child," Leah said.

"What about my dad?" Elizabeth's breathing was shallow. "Where is he?"

Leah saw the agony in her face and realized Elizabeth might not want to leave with them. So she did what any mother would do for the sake of her child's health and safety – she lied. "He is at your home waiting for you. We must get you healed so you can be with your father."

"How do you know?"

"A friend told me she saw him go back to the city and leave. He did not know you were here so he left. He is probably most worried about you. Let us help you get better so you can join him at home."

Elizabeth attempted a weak smile. "Okay."

Sarah walked the donkey into the bedroom and Jeremiah used his big forearms to lift Elizabeth up, then placing her on the animal. "Steady, steady," he said, gesturing to Leah to hold her in position.

"That hurts. My leg feels awful. I can't move it."

"My neighbor knows someone who can heal you. We are not far from where he was last seen."

"Is he a doctor?"

"No. A rabbi."

"How is a rabbi going to help me?"

"We have heard stories about him helping the sick and hurt."

Elizabeth winced. "I don't care what he is. If he can help me, let's go."

Leah handed Sarah the basket of items she had collected and gave Samuel's spear to Jeremiah. "We may need this."

He nodded. "Let us move as quickly as we can. There is more light coming."

Leah stayed beside the donkey, keeping her arms around Elizabeth as she wobbled sideways on the animal.

Jeremiah kept his one free arm steadying her other side while looking upward at the threatening clouds. "We may be walking into a storm," he said, pointing to the pitch black sky.

"How are you feeling, my child?" Leah asked.

"I'm woozy. My leg has a bad pain and I still have a whopping headache." She gave Leah a sideways glance. "Why are you smiling?"

"Because you are complaining and using those strange words again. Woozy and whopping." She let out a small laugh. "I now know you must be getting better." Leah held on to the last bit of hope left in her heart.

The bandage around Elizabeth's head loosened from the first leg of the trip, so Leah pulled it off and felt the wound with her hand. Blood stained her fingers. "Sarah, I need another cloth."

Leah wrapped the protective piece tightly around her head. Elizabeth bit her lower lip. "That hurts."

"I am sorry. But I need to do it this way."

"We are not far from Bethany," said Jeremiah.

"Sarah, how will we know where to find the rabbi?" Leah asked.

"I will ask once we get to town. He is said to travel with a group of men and sometimes a woman."

There was a group of homes in the distance, surrounded by small and high hills and mountains outlying the perimeter. Leah absorbed the scenery in front of her and thought briefly how wonderful it would be to live in such a peaceful town.

They stopped at the edge of the neighborhood, resting by a well. Leah and Sarah cupped their hands and drank some water. The smell of porridge wafted through the air and the sound of children and families waking up could be heard.

"I will go and ask about the preacher," said Jeremiah.

He introduced himself to several people, including an elderly man, accompanied by a silver-haired woman. He pointed to the far hills, a good distance from where they were now. Jeremiah made a gesture of gratitude and returned.

"He was last seen up there," he said, pointing to a steep climb as the clouds thickened more near the highest hill.

"How do we know if he is there or not?" Leah asked.

"They do not know for certain. They said that they saw him go up there with a group of men. They saw the men come down before the sun set but the preacher was not with them. So everyone in the town believes he is still up there, perhaps praying."

Elizabeth started to close her eyes.

"Stay awake," Leah implored as she pulled the bandage as tight as she could. "We have to go now."

Sarah cast doubt. "It is a long way up the hill. How do we even know the rabbi is there? How do we even know what my neighbor said was true?"

"You say this now, Sarah?"

"I worry."

"I need to go," said Leah, convinced that her trip was wise. "He may be the only one who can help now." A loud bang erupted from above as a heavy rain flooded the ground. "Go back," she told Jeremiah and Sarah.

"No. We will go too," Sarah responded.

"I'm feeling strange," Elizabeth said.

"How, my daughter?" Leah asked.

"I can't feel my arms and legs. I can't move my fingers."

"We will get you to this preacher."

"Oh God, Leah, I can hear you but can't see you. What's happening?"

"No, my daughter. Stay with me. Do not go." Leah remembered Yochanan's last words, much like Elizabeth had just spoken. Her heart sank.

Elizabeth gasped for a deep breath. "Leah, tell my father I'm sorry. I bought the Lady Gaga ticket. I shouldn't have…I shouldn't have…left on the lights."

Leah rubbed her arms and then her legs. "No. No. You are not leaving me. Yochanan left me. My daughter left me. Michael left me. I am not going to let you leave me. No. No."

"I don't want to leave."

"I will not let you," Leah shouted. "Preacher, where are you? My daughter needs your help."

"Leah, I feel weird. Tell my dad I love him. Tell him." Elizabeth closed her eyes.

"No. Open your eyes. Listen to me."

"Hold me, Leah. Hold me, Mom. I'm scared."

She hugged Elizabeth.

"Don't leave me, Leah."

"I will not," she said. "Do not go. We will find the preacher."

"Tell dad. Tell him. Tell him I …"

Leah pushed Elizabeth's eyes open. "Look at me. Do not leave me."

The wind howled as they reached the top of the terrain, prompting all three of them to shield their faces with their hands against the driving rain. The pace slowed and Elizabeth lost consciousness, the cloths now drenched in fading red moisture. Leah protected Elizabeth's face with her body.

Sheets of rain slapped the trees, bushes and ground, drenching Leah's back. "Wake up. We are here," she repeated over and over. The top of her head was soaked. She let a stream of water run down her nose and onto Elizabeth's face, hoping it would shake her from the slumber.

Sarah and Jeremiah leaned against each other, holding hands. "May God be with her," said Jeremiah.

Leah refused to concede, picking Elizabeth's head up in a merciful plea as the rain dripped from her eyebrows. "Where are you, preacher?" she called out, her voice trembling. "Help my child."

She glanced at her friends hoping they would have an answer. They hung their heads on each question while Sarah meshed her face into Jeremiah's wet garment. "My God, protect Leah's friend," he said. "May you have mercy on us all."

They wrapped their arms around Leah in an effort to pull her away from Elizabeth.

"No. I will wait for the preacher."

"He is not here," said Jeremiah.

She pushed them away.

"Do we know where her family is?" he asked.

"I only know from where she came, a gateway or alleyway somewhere in the city of Jerusalem, near a fruit stand. I do not know how far it would be to travel to her home."

"It would be dangerous for us to go back that way," responded Jeremiah, wiping the moisture away from his eyes.

"Her father must be told what has happened to his daughter," said Leah. "I do not even know if we can find her home."

"Was she of our faith?" asked Sarah.

"She believed in God. But I do know they had other customs."

Jeremiah shook his head. "Oh Leah, I do not know what to say or what to do. But I do know we must not stay here any longer."

"I am not giving up. Help me, Jeremiah." Together they pulled Elizabeth off the donkey and laid her on the ground. Leah staggered a few steps in each direction, then stopped and shouted out for the preacher. The drops doused them harder and she fell to her knees, weeping. Leah lay her head on Elizabeth's chest and gave her a kiss on the cheek.

"You have many more sunsets to see, my child. You never did tell me whether I can meet your Matthew. I hope you let me see him."

She looked skyward, letting the storm butcher her face. "My heart is yours. Oh God, please let my heart beat inside Elizabeth. God, let my soul strengthen her spirit." A laser like light lit the side of Elizabeth's face. When Leah spun around to tell Sarah and Jeremiah, a man with his head covered in a white robe appeared, his garment dry and untouched. Startled, Leah gasped. "Who are you?"

"I am here to take Elizabeth home."

"You know where her town is? Can you find her father?"

"I do."

Leah wiped moisture away from her eyes with her sleeve. "Are you the preacher?"

"I am who you are looking for."

"My friend said you can save her. Can you heal her? She is young. She has much life and love to give."

"I do not need to perform a miracle to convince one of who I am. She has much love to give in my Father's Kingdom."

"Where is this Kingdom you speak about?"

"When my Father calls you, you shall see."

"Get away from her. You cannot help her."

"I can."

"What about her father? He will be broken-hearted. He needs to know."

He placed his hands on Leah's face. "Do not weep, woman, for my Father's Kingdom grants eternal life to all."

Leah gave a puzzled look to the preacher and glanced at Elizabeth's lifeless body. Big puddles formed all around them as the glimmer of white light grew, embracing Elizabeth's face.

"She is dead. You cannot heal her. Sarah's friend was wrong."

"Woman, she is already healed."

The preacher held Elizabeth's hands. "My daughter, your work here is done for now."

CHAPTER TWENTY

Jim left and Michael asked Connie and Allison to scour the kitchen and living room for more notes or clues. Michael returned to Elizabeth's bedroom and tore it apart, rummaging through a pile of papers stacked near her computer.

A few moments later, Allison appeared at the doorway. "Besides Lady Gaga references, anything else in particular you're looking for?"

"I don't know. Maybe I'm missing something. A note from someone that might help me find her. Maybe an email that would tell me who she's been talking to recently. A password to her email account, in case there's something in there that could tell us if she was planning on going anywhere today without telling me."

He pulled out several drawers, the remains fluttering to the floor. He swatted at papers much like an old man shooing away a fly on a humid day, desperate for any sign.

"Was she upset about something?" Allison asked. "Was there another boy she talked about?"

"She only mentioned that Matt kid." He opened books and shook out the pages, hoping something would fall out. "I wonder if she did go to that Lady Gaga concert."

"Lady Gaga? Yeah, she's in the city for her tour. Teenage girls don't confide to their dads about their crushes. Maybe she's talked to one of her girlfriends. Have you talked to any of them?"

He rattled another drawer. "No, I don't think this has anything to do with a boy." He sat on the floor tossing each unimportant item to the far corner of the room. "Wait, this might be it," he said, holding up an email copy of the Lady Gaga concert information. "I bet she decided to go to the city today after I told her she couldn't."

"Why do you say that?"

"This was printed after I told her she couldn't go."

"Well, this reminds me of my younger days," Allison said. "I could tell you some stories of my teenage years."

"You don't have to. Your dad has already filled me in," he said with some edge.

She rolled her eyes. "Don't believe everything you hear."

"Right." He stood and headed to the doorway. "I'm calling the cops."

After speaking to one of the detectives about his theory, he hung up and frowned.

"What did they say?" Allison asked.

"They can't help me. There are thousands of kids at the concert so it'll be difficult to even spot her. They advised me to wait a few hours and see if she calls me."

While waiting, he contacted several of Elizabeth's friends. One parent told him her daughter was supposed to meet Elizabeth at the train station. "I dropped Kacie off but left before the train came. So I don't know. But I can text her to find out," said Mrs. French.

His theory hit one dead end after another. Elizabeth never responded to any of the text messages from the kids meeting her for the concert.

Maybe she was too embarrassed to tell them I said no?

"They thought that she wasn't allowed to go," Mrs. French said in a follow up call. "I don't blame you. I don't like Kacie listening to that kind of music but since there were five of them going together, I gave her permission to go."

Michael sighed in despair. "She bought a ticket but never showed up with the other kids. It doesn't mean she isn't there. Right?"

But he knew the answer.

"Where are you going now?" Allison yelled from behind him.

He yanked the front door open. He ran to the garage, lifted the door, and pushed the lawnmower aside. Kicking at several beach chairs, he cleared a path to the back. "There it is."

He picked the object up and shoved several old bags of clothes aside for good measure.

"What are you looking for?" Allison asked out of breath as she reached the garage.

"This," he said, holding up a shiny, unused ax.

Her eyes widened. "Why do you need that?"

"For the church."

"You're nuts." She pushed her curly, brown hair away from her eyes. "Why do you need that for church?"

Michael flew past her, grabbed his keys and cell phone and hopped into his car.

"Wait, wait for me," yelled Connie, running out the door.

"You're brother's gone crazy. We have to stop him," Allison said.

Michael didn't hear his sister's response as his car screeched, making a sharp u-turn on the narrow street, barreling into a neighbor's mailbox. He made Main Street his personal raceway, arriving at the church in a matter of minutes. Not caring, he snagged a handicapped parking space in front of the church and raced up the steps.

Dennis was at the pulpit, delivering a sermon. "We must forget our disputes, our anger toward each other. This is a time for hope, promise, and love. We are human. We are weak at times. We make mistakes. Forgive yourself. Forgive others."

Michael carried his ax on his left side, trying to hide it from the congregation.

Several in the crowd muttered to each other as the ceiling lights reflected off the pristine weapon.

"…and help your neighbors," Dennis continued, stopping in mid-sentence, as Michael stampeded to the basement stairs.

"Debbie," Dennis whispered, pointing to the podium and moving the microphone closer to her face. "Sing."

"Me?" she said, loud enough for Michael to hear.

"Yes. You. Sing," Dennis repeated. "I have to leave for a few minutes."

"What am I supposed to sing?" she asked.

"You were a DJ at your college radio station. Kumbaya. That's our Stairway to Heaven. Don't stop until I return."

Bam. Bam. Bam.

Michael swung the ax awkwardly against the ground, trying to break up the cement floor.

"Michael," Dennis called out. "What are you doing?"

"Stay out of my way," he said, stopping momentarily to rest his arms. "There's no other choice."

Bam. Bam. Bam.

Dennis held up his hand. "Stop it now!"

Bam. Bam. Bam. Bam.

He pounded the ax against the floor, managing to chop up a few pieces of concrete.

"This isn't the way to get back, Michael."

"I can't wait for your prayers to deliver me the answers I need." He pushed Dennis away, then wound up and swung as hard as he could.

Thump.

The ax vibrated in his hands as it struck the ground, dislodging another small piece. He rested a moment, his arms weary. He rubbed his right shoulder, massaging the pain. Breathing deep, he held the ax to his side. He wiped the sweat from his forehead with the back of his hand. "I know she's alive. I heard her talking to me. She's lost. I know it sounds crazy. But being able to go back to that time is just as crazy." He caught his breath. "You have no idea what it's like to love a daughter and then to think you can't help her when she needs you."

"I do have an idea."

"How?"

"You need to calm down. We must look at this in a rational way or we will never be able to figure out what to do."

"Rational? Is there anything happening to me that is rational?"

"I know this. You need to control yourself."

Michael shook his head.

"I was married and had a daughter many years ago before I found my calling. So yes, I do know what you're talking about."

Skeptical, Michael was unsure how to respond. "What do you mean you were married?"

"I had a family until I ruined it."

"What happened?"

"A long story for another time. Now isn't the time to discuss this."

Michael dropped the ax as Connie and Allison arrived in the basement. They both said something but the only sound he could hear now was the faint muffled voices of Debbie and the congregation, singing Kumbaya.

"I've got to get back upstairs," Dennis said, pointing at Michael. "Stay down here. I'll come back when the service is done and we'll talk. We're going to discuss what happened. I need to find out what Jesus said to you about forgiveness and healing. It's important."

Why is this so important right now? For God's sake, my daughter is missing. He stared at the ax and the fragmented pieces of cement scattered across the floor.

"Thank God," said Connie. "I thought you were going to kill someone."

He leaned against the wall. "I don't have the energy to kill anyone. Go home."

"Michael, call me later," Allison said. "Even if it's late. I can come over if you want. I'll be up and I won't go to sleep until I hear from you. Okay? Text me if you have to. Do you need my number?"

Michael gave her a surprised look. "No. I don't need your number. And there's no story here for you."

He blew out a tired breath.

"What do you want me to do?" Connie asked.

"Go back to my house and wait there in case Elizabeth shows up."

"I don't have my car."

"Take my car," he said, handing her the keys.

Michael kicked at the pieces of cement and swung the ax again.

CHAPTER TWENTY-ONE

"Elizabeth Ellen Stewart, Elizabeth Ellen Stewart." Choruses of voices I don't recognize sing my name.

I feel the wind hoist my feet, the feathery feel sweeping through my arms, my body hovering as I float high.

I drift to the heavens and I see Mommy and Daddy. They look a lot younger, especially Dad. He doesn't have gray hair. They both look beautiful, standing in a packed church. Mommy and Daddy are giving each other shiny and sparkly rings.

Dad, you look handsome in a new suit and Mommy is so pretty in her long, white wedding dress. There you stand, happy, hopeful, and full of dreams. I'm so glad I was part of your dream.

Kiss her, Dad.

Wow, Dad, I've never seen you kiss a woman. I thought it would be gross. But it's a beautiful sight. Can you kiss her again?

I float a bit higher. I can't see them any longer.

Where did my dad go?

Oh, there he is, rocking a baby in his arms. Rocking and singing to the baby. That baby must be me. How lucky I am to be able to see you talking to me when I was so little.

You look sad, Dad. I know in my heart you were happy the day I was born, but it must have been so hard for you to be happy on the day Mom went to heaven. I was a lucky little girl to have you, Daddy, taking good care of me.

I float side to side as I head for the light up ahead, a light that sparkles much like the stars in the night sky. I hug Daddy as I float by. I can see a brilliant star shining, a light blue figure so big yet so far.

I now pass my third grade class. I'm in the school yard, giggling as my best friend sings my favorite song. I'm running around with my friends playing tag. My classmates smile, then fade away and now I see Dad smiling with pride as he watches me graduate middle school.

I see many fruits; big red apples and sunshine yellow pears, apricots and melons, the juices quench my thirst. A lavender smell fortifies me and flowers climb and surround me. Yellow and red roses stroke my face.

My head is free of pain, my legs ready to spring. I'm ready to run a race but don't know where to go. How long is this journey, my Lord? Do I need to run faster?

I soar above heaven's gate; a soft, soothing light pink light shines upon my face. I feel the warmth, unlike any I've ever felt. My skin feels tingly. I absorb the love in my soul. It burns. I need not listen to hear the Lord. His face, calm and assured, points to an angel who will hold me tight as I take a deeper flight. The angel is strong, her hands so firm. She's smiling and singing my favorite songs. My angel gives me a tight hug as we arrive at our final stop. Her face turns Brandeis blue and tangerine. I reach for her and my arms shine like cherries hanging from a branch. A flute hums a familiar tune softly. "How much is that doggy in the window?" she sings. I laugh. Daddy, you sang that to me many times before I fell asleep.

The Angel leads me through this misty fog. Mom is waiting there for me. I see Grandma Rebecca too. She looks peaceful and happy. Their faces glow in light shades of blue. I wave to them and they tell me to sit still.

"Your worries are over, no more tears to cry, no more pain to mend, no more sorrow to console," my Angel proclaims. "Tell your dad you are home."

I'm finally home, Dad. I feel so warm. Mom is right next to me. She tells me she talks to you all the time. She says you need to listen more. She's holding me, Dad. I wish you could hold us now.

I miss you, Dad. Thank you for loving me so much, for always being there. I do wish we could visit our favorite ice cream shop together one more time. I'm sorry I worried you sometimes when I was out so late. I'm sorry I didn't clean my room when you asked. I'm sorry I left the lights on. I'm sorry when I fibbed about where I was going. I always loved you and always will.

I want to cry, Dad, I really do, but where I am right now, there is no sadness, no regrets, no tears, no pain, no sorrow. I still miss you but I know I'll see you again one day.

Please, Dad, try not to miss me or be sad like you were when Mom died, because then I will feel your pain and won't be able to experience this eternal happiness. Remember, you will see us someday.

Some will tell you, Dad, my time was short. It wasn't. I see many young people here. Younger than me. I'm luckier than a lot of people. I had a mother who gave her life for me and you, Dad, who made sacrifices and worked so hard to give me a happy home.

It's time for me to leave, Dad. I'm safe now. I'll see you again. There's more work for you to do. This is what mom just told me. Then we'll hug each other again. I love you, Daddy.

CHAPTER TWENTY-TWO

The strains of music chimed its last cords as Dennis ended the service. Michael stood outside his office and watched as his friend bid the congregation goodbye at the church's front doors. Many in the crowd looked at Dennis with an inquiring expression. Some were blunt enough to ask why Michael came into church with an ax and if it was safe to return.

The latter question surprised Michael. *I haven't been the most social person around but I didn't think these people who know me would think I'd be a danger to them. I don't care if they think I've turned into a lunatic. That's their problem, not mine. I have more important things to worry about.*

Dennis dodged the inquiries with a smile and changed the subject each time Michael's name came up. Michael felt remorseful that Dennis had to keep fielding questions and had to assure his churchgoers that there was no need for them to be alarmed.

I'll have to apologize for putting him in this position.

Dennis opened his office door.

"I'm sorry for hacking at the floor."

"Forget it. There isn't a lot of damage."

"I'm not very good with an ax."

"I'm glad." Dennis walked around his desk and sat. "Do you have a ride home?"

"I'll walk. I'm feeling like a caged lion."

"You need to stay in control." He pulled out a bottle of wine. "Jesus drank wine. So can you."

"Are you going to join me in a glass this time?"

Dennis grimaced. "I prefer water." He avoided Michael's stare and opened the black book. "Besides, one of us has to be stone cold sober in case you decide to lose it again."

Michael dragged his hands down his face. "I'm not sure I can do that."

"You have to." Dennis leaned back in his chair. "People like me are not supposed to show weakness. We're supposed to be strong, like some sort of religious superhero, never doubting when troubles confront us in this world, never losing direction with our faith."

Michael shook his head. "You're stronger than I am. Still don't know how you do it sometimes."

"I remember who is there for me no matter what problem I'm facing. If He isn't, I get on my Harley and take a ride." He smiled, trying to lighten the mood a bit. He uncorked the bottle. The sweet fruit smell of the red wine tingled Michael's senses. "We're human too," he said. "I worry like you. I have sadness like others. I get angry when some dope on the street calls me a child abuser. Do you know how that feels?"

"Who called you that?"

"It doesn't matter who." He poured a few ounces of wine into a glass. "I've spent most of my life trying to bring positive change in this world. I've had many sleepless nights worrying about those who can't clothe and feed themselves, even some right here in our town."

"Why do you continue to do this?"

Dennis handed Michael the glass. "Because I get to meet and help people like you."

"But why me?" Michael asked, taking a sip of wine. "You've been there for me for so long. Even when I ignored you."

Dennis didn't answer.

"I don't deserve it but thank you."

"You do deserve it." Dennis placed his bookmark inside a drawer. "I also hurt and become depressed at times."

"When do you get depressed?"

"When a child runs away from me because his parents told him to stay away from bad people like me."

"When did this happen?"

"Not too long ago. It was at my nephew's birthday party." He opened a bottle of water and took a sip. "I remember being so excited about seeing him. I had just returned from a missionary trip in Kenya. So it had been a while since we've been together. When he saw me arrive, the little guy ran over and jumped into my arms.

"One of his classmates came over and looked at me and said, 'My daddy says you touch children in private places. Why are you touching Danny? My daddy says to stay away from bad people like you.' Well, the boy ran away and my nephew cried. I put him down and walked out."

"I'm sorry."

Dennis crossed his leg and tented his fingers on his lap. "Have you ever looked at me and thought I may be a child molester?"

"I don't think that way."

"Well, you don't because you've gotten to know me. How did you feel about me before that?"

Michael hesitated for a few seconds, weighing his thoughts. "I hadn't gotten to know you as well as I do now."

"You see, we all have preconceived notions of who people are and how they behave."

"I didn't make any assumptions about you in that way."

"But you were suspicious?"

"Yeah, for a split second." Michael shifted in his seat. "Sorry about that."

"Don't be. You're human. I'm human. I've made my share of mistakes." He hung his head for a brief moment. "I felt so sorry for myself after my nephew's birthday that I canceled a prayer meeting." He took a gulp of water. "I sat in my bedroom staring at the walls, angry and bitter. I wanted to quit and even drafted a letter of resignation."

Michael took another sip of wine to wet his parched throat. "Why didn't you quit?"

"Because I remembered the night when I heard God's call. It was shortly after I lost my wife and daughter."

"Lost?"

"Well, my wife left me and took our daughter."

"Why?"

Dennis pointed to the bottle of wine. "I drank too much. Lost my job, ignored my family and hit rock bottom." He took another slow sip of his water. "Then while I was stumbling along one Christmas Eve I heard a choir singing *Silent Night*. I went in and sat in the last pew and listened to the words.

"I saw the happy faces in the church. Many came up to me and said hello. I don't know why I happened to be walking on that street during that time. But there was a reason. Had to be." He lowered his head. "It just had to be that God was asking me into His life despite my weaknesses."

Michael took a few more sips and stopped. "I shouldn't be doing this, too."

"Doing what?"

"Drinking. I'm no different than my father or the creep who killed Vicki."

Dennis' face reddened and he cleared his throat. "It was terrible, I know."

Michael felt the anger that still lingered in his gut, even after all these years, start to surface. "They should have fried the punk for driving drunk and plowing into my wife's car."

Dennis took a deep breath, wiped his forehead and took another sip of water. "Was he drunk? People make mistakes. We need to forgive."

"Well, he wasn't legally drunk. But so what?" Michael raised his voice. "I'm sitting here without my wife and now my daughter is missing. And you're talking to me about forgiving the killer?"

"Killer is a bit extreme."

"What?" Michael slammed the glass on the desk so hard, wine spilled out. "If I had the chance I'd flick the switch myself."

"We're getting off track here."

Michael pushed the glass away. "Don't offer me any more wine."

Dennis corked the bottle and stared at his water.

Michael got up and paced. "I'm not like you. I can't be cool like you. I'm losing my mind. I want to rip that floor up piece by piece. I don't even know why I was there. I know you said there's always a reason when God opens up a path. I can't figure it out."

Dennis pulled out a notebook and pen. "Tell me what happened on the trip. Tell me what Jesus said about forgiveness and redemption. Tell me what your wife said."

"My wife? Why?"

"Just tell me what Jesus said."

Michael rubbed his forehead, tempering his urge to tell Dennis to stop repeating the same question about forgiveness. He knew Dennis was right. Michael had to stay calm. Getting into an argument with his friend wasn't smart. After all, Dennis had the book. Perhaps by talking to him something might click.

As Michael regaled all that he had witnessed, Dennis scribbled his account of the time travel journey. Dennis seemed fascinated by the Sermon on the Mount Jesus delivered and peppered Michael with several questions. By the time he had finished his story, Dennis had filled half of the notebook.

Michael cleared his throat, his voice hoarse from talking. "Do you have any more water in there?" he asked, gesturing to the small fridge.

"Help yourself."

Michael opened the small fridge and took out a bottle of water. After drinking half of it, he continued, "I tried to save Leah's husband but I'm not sure if the cloth I used was given to me to save him. I thought I was back there to change this. But now I'm not sure."

"Let's see the cloth."

Michael showed him.

"This is incredible," Dennis said, seeming to lose his train of thought as he examined it.

"Now what do I do? How do I find Elizabeth?"

Dennis held the cloth close to his nose. "I need to review the book more. Maybe I can find a clue or a special message that can help you get back."

"What if I can't?"

The phone rang and Dennis held up a finger. "Hello. Yes. This is he. Okay. He's here. Why? Sure, I'll tell him." He hung up the phone and rubbed his chin. "Are you sure you didn't see Elizabeth at all today?"

"Yes. Why?"

"That was a Detective Brady from the County Police Department. They've asked for a court order to take your car. They say there's blood in it."

"What?" Michael backed up, knocking over a chair. "Whose blood?"

"He didn't say. Look, I'm not here to judge." Dennis stood. "Are you telling me everything you know?"

"Of course." Michael raked his hand through his hair. "Blood? How?"

"Let me drive you home. The police will be there. Cooperate with them." He put his hand on Michael's back. "I'll be there to support you, no matter what."

"I'll do whatever they want me to do." He concentrated on breathing and not collapsing from fear. "Do they have any proof she might still be here?"

"He didn't say much." Dennis waved him toward the door. "Come on, let's go. The quicker you answer their questions, the quicker you'll get some answers."

The dead end street was illuminated by red and blue flashing lights. Dennis parked the car on the corner and Michael jumped out. His sister met him by the curb.

"Connie, what's going on? What did they say?"

Her hand trembled as she touched his arm. "They said they think there might be blood in the car. I didn't give them the keys."

"Give them to me," Michael said. "I've got nothing to hide."

Connie dug into her pants pocket and handed it to him.

Dennis walked ahead of Michael toward a man wearing a dark suit. "I'm Pastor Dennis of the Lady by the Bay Church."

The man nodded to Michael who stood beside the pastor. "I'm Detective Brady. Is this the person in question?"

"I'm Michael Stewart." He gave the detective the set of keys. "Here, you don't need a court order."

The neighbors milled around, chatting and pointing to his car. A large, wide truck rumbled up the hill, accompanied by a loud siren.

"Let's clear this area," the detective yelled through a bullhorn.

Michael read the lettering on the side of the truck. *Crime Scene Unit.*

"Crime scene?" Michael's voice hitched. "What? Is Elizabeth hurt?" Bursts of bright dots danced before his eyes. "What's going on? My daughter's been a victim in a crime? Has she been found?"

"I'll ask the questions for now." The detective put his bullhorn on the ground and took out a notepad and pen. "What was your daughter wearing this morning before she disappeared?"

Michael heaved a deep breath to calm himself. "I don't know."

The detective stopped writing and arched his eyebrows. "You're telling me you haven't seen her at all today?"

"Yes. No." Michael looked up at the sky. "I mean, she left for a morning class before I got up." He glared at Connie, remembering it was her fault he was hung over. "She left me a note instead of waking me up. So no, I don't know what she wore this morning."

The detective continued writing. "Go inside and get us your daughter's hair brush."

Michael struggled to breathe. "You should be out looking for my daughter, not asking about her hair."

"Have you been drinking?"

"What? No." He rubbed his temple, hoping to clear his thoughts. "I mean, yes a little. I had a glass of wine at church." He stepped closer to the detective. "Give me a breathalyzer if you want. I don't care. I'll do whatever it takes if it'll help you find my daughter."

"Then go in your house and get us her hairbrush," the detective said in a commanding tone. "We'll also need a recent picture of your daughter."

"Can you at least tell me why you need these things?"

The detective looked at him carefully, analyzing Michael's every movement. "We'll need her picture so we can pass it along to the different agencies."

Michael clutched his chest, sure that his heart would crash right through it. "Do you think she's been hurt?"

"We'll know more once we conduct our investigation." For a brief moment, Michael thought he saw sympathy in the detective's eyes. "Things would go a lot faster if you'd get us that hairbrush and picture."

Michael steadied his nerves. "Yes, of course." He raced back inside his house, up the stairs, and into the bathroom. He opened the cabinet door on her side and grabbed two hairbrushes and hurried back.

Panting, he handed the items to the detective. "Here they are."

The detective gave them to a woman, who placed the brushes inside a big plastic bag and labeled it.

Two gloved men opened Michael's car door and scoured through it, taking samples of debris off his dashboard, the seats, and the glove compartment. One of the men handed a crumbled piece of paper to the woman. She deposited it into another plastic bag.

Michael paced, trying to burn off nervous energy. He walked toward his sister. "Did you see any blood when you were in the car? We're the only two who were in it today. I didn't see anything. Did you?"

"There were some dark brown spots on some tissues and on a piece of paper on the floor." Connie shrugged. "It didn't look like blood to me."

"Where on the floor?"

"On the passenger side. I thought it was magic marker so I didn't think anything of it. Your car is such a mess anyway."

"Maybe that's what they're talking about. But I haven't written any notes or remember having any paper on the floor."

Detective Brady walked over to them. "I'd like to take a look inside your house. Do you mind?"

"Come with me," Michael said.

The detective spent over half an hour examining each room on the bottom floor. "Where's her bedroom?"

"This way," Michael said, leading him upstairs.

The detective glanced around the room. "Looks like a hurricane hit this room."

"That's my fault," Michael said, wishing his voice would stop shaking. "I was looking for a clue." The detective stared at him. "Wait for me by your car. I'll be a few minutes."

Michael went outside and watched the crew tediously comb through his car, opening the glove compartment door again, rifling through the many pieces of papers and tissues stuffed inside it. He moved closer. *What are they looking for? When's the last time Elizabeth was in the car? Was it Wednesday when we went to the grocery store?*

Detective Brady returned with a plastic bag filled with some items and went over to Dennis. Michael watched the two speaking but couldn't hear the conversation. Dennis walked away as the detective questioned the woman holding the plastic bags.

The last of the crime unit crew closed his car doors.

"Mr. Stewart," the detective said. "I advise you not to leave Northport. You also need to give us all the phone numbers where you can be reached. And please send me a picture of your daughter."

I'll leave this century if it means saving my daughter, Michael wanted to say, but bit his tongue and nodded.

The detective pulled out his notepad and pen again. "Do you know a Mr. Banks?"

Michael folded his arms over his chest. "No."

The detective started writing. "Mr. Banks claims he witnessed you and your daughter fighting in church." He flipped over a page. "Something about your daughter's boyfriend?"

"I told you, I don't know any Mr. Banks."

"My niece has a boyfriend?" interjected Connie.

"Matt is just a friend," Michael said, losing patience. "And we weren't arguing in church. I have no idea why this man would say something like that."

Connie lifted her brow and remained silent.

Detective Brady rubbed his chin and continued writing. "I need to know whether your daughter was in contact with anyone today?"

"This friend of hers, Matt. He told me they were hanging out together today."

"What's his address and phone number?"

Michael gave him Matt's information and pointed to his car. "What did you find?"

"We're still investigating."

"Did you find blood?"

The detective nodded. "Yes."

"Do you know whose blood it might be?"

Detective Brady regarded him intently. "No. Do you?"

"She wasn't in my car today."

The detective jotted down more notes. "You sound sure about that."

"Because I am."

"Interesting," the detective said, scribbling. "You have no idea what she wore this morning, ate for breakfast, or what time she left for school but you know for a fact she wasn't in your car."

Michael barely hung on to his patience but he chose his words carefully. "Can you tell me where my daughter is based on what you found in the car?"

"Not yet." He looked from Michael to Connie. "Is there something you're forgetting to tell us about today?"

Michael looked away for a moment. "I thought she might have gone to New York City with some friends to see a Lady Gaga concert. I called several of her friends. I did speak to one mother who said her own daughter couldn't reach her. I haven't seen or heard from her all day."

"What about you?" The detective gestured to Connie. "Have you seen your niece today? Do you have any information that will help us find her?"

"Yes, I saw her for a few minutes but I don't know where she went after that. And no, I don't remember what she was wearing. Didn't think I had to memorize her outfit." She planted her hands on her hips. "You all think I'm a crackpot anyway."

The detective handed her a business card. "Sometimes crackpots can have good information. If you do remember what she was wearing, or any other details, give me a call. I'd advise you not to leave the area as well."

"Me?" Connie said, close to hysterics. "What did I do?"

"Besides this boy, Matt, you were one of the last ones to see her. I would have thought you'd want to help find your niece?"

"Of course she does," Michael interrupted in a loud voice. "Both my sister and I will do whatever we can."

"Right." The detective handed him a card and told him again not to leave the area and to call if he remembered anything more. "Don't forget to email me her photo."

With that, he left.

Dennis tapped Michael on the shoulder. "I have an emergency call to attend to. An elderly woman lost her husband. I'm leaving now. Do you need anything?"

"A miracle."

"I'll try to find one for you."

He watched Dennis drive away. The crime unit vehicle lumbered down the hill behind him. A tow truck rolled slowly toward him, coming to a grinding, squeaky halt near his car. A hefty-looking man with an unlit small cigar protruding from his mouth got out. "Is this the one?" he said, pointing to Michael's vehicle.

"Yes," said one of the cops.

"What are you doing?" asked Michael.

"I have a warrant to impound this vehicle." He handed Michael a document.

"Why?"

The cigar-smoking man shrugged. "Just following orders."

Michael slapped the paper against his thigh. "Great. How am I supposed to get around town and find my daughter?"

No one answered.

"Do you want me to stay?" Connie asked.

He shook his head. Connie gave him a kiss on the cheek but he flinched and backed away. He walked back into his house and shut the door, not sure if he locked it, and not caring if he didn't.

He stood in the hallway for several minutes, listening to the quiet of the house and hating it. There was no Japanese music blasting its way downstairs from Elizabeth's bedroom. Her high-pitched giggles and hearty teenage laughter while chatting on the phone were absent. The sounds of her feet banging upstairs, sending pounding vibrations through the living room ceiling were missing.

It was just him in the big Northport house, all alone.

CHAPTER TWENTY-THREE

Jesus walked down the hill and headed straight toward the mountains. His figure faded into a stream of light that descended from the heavens. Elizabeth's body remained still.

"Where are you going?" Leah cried out to Him. She looked at her friends, confused over the preacher's disappearance. "Now what do we do?"

"We need to bury your friend here if you are unsure where her family lives," Jeremiah said.

"But this isn't our custom. We need to find out where her village is."

"But you do not know where it is," Sarah said.

Leah fought back tears. "We should take her back and bury her near my home."

"You cannot go back there," Jeremiah said. "The Roman will be looking for you."

"There is no easy answer," Sarah said, her voice hitched with a sob.

Leah touched Elizabeth's hair, removing it from her eyes. "Forgive me, child. We must take care of you here. I know no other way. I will look for your father and tell him."

"Let me ask the old man for some guidance," Jeremiah said, pointing straight ahead to a town nearby. "He might know someone who can help us bury Elizabeth."

Leah coaxed the donkey to rise as Jeremiah lifted Elizabeth onto the animal. They walked solemnly back toward town. The rain lightened and a soft, chilly wind skirted in from the west.

An elderly man greeted Jeremiah by gripping his shoulder in a conciliatory gesture. After chatting for several moments,

Jeremiah returned to the women. "Zachary is his name. He will help us. He has offered to summon a rabbi. Let us bring her body over there."

They were greeted by Zachary's wife, Margaret. She encouraged the group to come inside. "My condolences. Are you the mother and father?"

"No," replied Jeremiah.

"She was without a mother," said Leah.

"Where is the father? Husband?"

"She has no husband. Her father, I do not know where he is."

"How sad." Margaret gave her a hug. "Our home is your home. You have faced much today. Can I get you some drink or food?"

"I cannot eat or drink."

Leah waved off a chance to rest and watched Jeremiah carry Elizabeth's body into the house. He placed her on a bedroll which Margaret had laid out. Leah knelt beside her and prayed. Showing solidarity, Sarah did the same, wrapping an arm around her friend's shoulder. Leah spoke words of solemn passion. "Have mercy on Elizabeth. Guide her father to her passing. Have mercy on Michael."

Margaret placed four cups filled with water on a table while a small jug of wine stood near. She broke up several pieces of bread and offered it to them on plates. In the corner of the kitchen several long rods with sharp spears on the ends leaned against the wall. Several polished swords lay beside them. "Where do you live, Leah?"

"Not very far away, over the big hill to the West. Close to Jerusalem."

"Is this where you plan on burying this woman?"

"I do not know."

Sarah and Jeremiah glanced at Margaret, unsure how to explain the situation.

"I know our tradition and customs say we must bury Elizabeth outside the village where she lived," said Leah. "While she has not come from my womb, I feel she is like my daughter. Her father is likely at home, distraught, worrying about her." After a long pause, Leah concluded, "I do not know what to do."

Zachary walked into the kitchen carrying several small bottles. "We must prepare the body," he said. "We can help you take the woman back to her village."

"They do not know where she lives," said his wife.

"How is that possible?"

"It just is," responded Jeremiah. "She is lost but is a close friend to Leah. We do not know how far or near her family might be. But we must obey our laws."

"We shall," said Zachary. "Follow me."

He signaled to Jeremiah to help him take Elizabeth's body to the back of the house. The women carried clothes and a jug of water. Leah cleansed Elizabeth's face, neck and arms. Margaret and Sarah helped, making sure they removed all the dirt and debris.

Zachary took five small bottles and handed two to Jeremiah, as well as one each to the women. "Do you need any weapons?"

"Yes," said Jeremiah.

"No," Leah replied.

"Yes," said Jeremiah in a firm tone.

Leah anointed Elizabeth with different types of oils and spices. When they were done, Leah wrapped a clean garment around her and kissed her cheek. She looked at Zachary and Margaret, both holding each other. "Thank you. I must take her back where I live and bury Elizabeth. At least if her father returns, he can visit her."

"But what about the Roman soldier?" asked Jeremiah, his expression and tone laced with fear.

"It does not matter anymore."

"I will not let you get killed," reasoned Jeremiah.

"Please, Leah," Sarah said, "do not go back. While our customs are wonderful, your safety and freedom is important."

"How free am I? I have no one now."

"You have us," Sarah said, touching Leah's arm.

"Thank you, sweet friend. But I must go back and bury Elizabeth."

Sarah sighed. "We will do whatever we can to help you."

Leah bowed her head and put her hand over her heart as a way of showing her gratitude. "We should move soon now that the rain has stopped."

A local rabbi visited Zachary and Margaret's home, offering condolances. He prayed with them too. The words tempered Leah's fear and grief.

"Do you need me to help with the burial?" the rabbi asked.

"No. My gratitude to you."

"It must be completed before the next sunrise."

Leah nodded.

Although Sarah and Jeremiah worried about returning to their town and even considered Zachary's generous offer to remain in their home, their friendship was so strong they wouldn't allow Leah to travel alone.

"There is not much sunlight left so we should start our journey soon," Jeremiah said.

Leah agreed and while their anguish was deep, they managed to share a few fond stories with Zachary and Margaret as they ate lunch, welcoming a break from the duress. They repeated the story of Lazarus, who was well known in the town. Zachary's storytelling was spellbinding, tantalizing as he recalled the incredible, vivid details of what he saw that wonderful day.

"Women fell, others cried, some prayed," Zachary said. He tore a piece of bread and dipped it into his water cup. "We celebrated all day, drinking wine and dancing. The town was filled with joy."

"And the preacher you described was the one you spoke about being up on the hill?" Jeremiah asked.

"Yes. Did you see him?"

Jeremiah, Sarah and Leah looked at each other, not sure how to respond.

Leah nodded. "I believe we saw him." She swallowed hard. "But then he was gone."

"Where did he go?" asked Margaret.

Leah took a moment to compose herself before answering. "I saw him go off toward the mountains, following a long stream of light that peeked over it. Then he disappeared."

"What stream of light?" Zachary asked. "It has been dark and rainy all day."

Leah furrowed her brow. "You did not see the bright light?"

Zachary and Margaret shrugged their shoulders.

Leah glanced at Sarah and Jeremiah, hoping they would share their thoughts. "Did you see it?"

They nodded.

"Strange," said Zachary.

"We need to go," Jeremiah said. "Sarah, get the animal."

Zachary offered first a spear and then a sword. Jeremiah refused politely after seeing Leah's dissatisfaction. They followed Zachary outside where he handed them a makeshift cart to carry Elizabeth's wrapped body.

After waving goodbye, they left. The donkey pulled the cart as they walked solemnly beside it.

"Sarah, you look straight and to each side," Jeremiah said. "Let me know if there is any danger approaching."

It wasn't long before they saw the outer edges of their town. Jeremiah stopped briefly and took a deep breath. "We can rest her over there," he said, pointing to a place east of their village where the neighbors buried their loved ones. "Many are laid to rest into the side of the tall hills."

"I will need to leave a marker for her father," Leah said.

"Of course," replied Jeremiah.

They continued their trek toward the village, veering right toward a possible tomb area. They saw people watching their procession. Several stood in reverent silence. Elderly men and women dropped to their knees and prayed while children were shushed by their parents.

As Jeremiah guided the cart toward the hill, parents grabbed their children's hands and followed. Soon a long procession line formed. The workers in the field put down their equipment and joined them. Halfway to the burial area, Leah looked back and saw the procession line had extended back to town.

Leah was invigorated and comforted all at once from the demonstration of support, something that had eluded her when she had suffered the loss of her husband. Yes, Yochanan's death drew people, but the fear of retaliation for showing their affection haunted her mourning period. She grieved alone for the most part, keeping to herself, depressed in seclusion. She never understood why it happened until Marcus intruded into her life.

They halted the march near a cave by the hill as a hearty wind blew tree branches back and forth, unfurling Leah's hair.

The crowd formed a circle around them as they prepared to say their final goodbyes. A rabbi stepped forward from the line to offer a prayer. Each person held the other's hand as the rabbi said a few words to Leah. He directed Jeremiah to place the body inside the makeshift tomb.

The children stayed quiet as parents hugged them firmly. The elderly prayed as Jeremiah and two men pushed a stone in front of the tomb. Many in the crowd offered words of solace to them. Others mostly stared and nodded, acknowledging their loss.

Leah looked at the empty cart as the crowd dispersed. She stared at the tomb, wondering if she could have done anything to prevent Elizabeth's death. Leah fingered two chains, one bearing a cross and the other Elizabeth's locket. She smiled as she remembered teaching her how to weave a basket.

Slipping the cross into her pocket, she placed the locket's chain under a rock at the tomb's entrance to mark the spot.

"We should go," said Jeremiah.

Leah agreed. As they took their first steps back to town, a commotion startled them. A man on a horse was surrounded by several people shouting. The man gestured in their vicinity.

"What is going on? Who is that?" asked Leah.

"I do not know," replied Jeremiah, taking several more paces forward to see what the disturbance was about.

Three men on horses trotted up the hill in their direction.

"They are Romans," Jeremiah said, his tone filled with fear.

Leah's heart jumped. *This is it. This is where I will die. Oh, God, please let me join you without much pain.*

Sarah and Jeremiah scurried several yards up an embankment. "Run, Leah, run," Jeremiah implored. "Do not stand there. They will see you."

Leah shook her head. "I will not run any longer. What is my life worth if I have to keep running? I will let God handle my worries. Go and hide. Do not let the soldiers see you."

The Romans arrived with weapons. One of them – Marcus – dismounted and limped to her. Dried blood caked the side of his face from Elizabeth's blows. "You thought you could get away," he yelled, hobbling closer.

Leah stood straight, grinding her teeth. "I will not walk away in fear of you anymore."

He staggered one step and smacked Leah hard across the face, knocking her to the ground. "Woman, get on your knees and beg for mercy."

"I will not."

"You will die."

She rubbed her cheek. "So be it."

"Keep your hands off her," yelled Jeremiah from above.

Marcus pointed his spear at him. "Stay away or you and your woman will die too."

Sarah crouched behind her husband, her eyes wide with fear. "Please, sir." Her voice quivered. "Leave us alone. We promise we will not bother you."

Marcus shouted. "Silence. Where is the other woman?"

"She is gone," Leah said.

"Gone where?"

"A place that not even you can get to her."

Marcus jabbed at Leah's neck with his spear. "I should kill you here."

"Then do so," Leah said, pushing away the spear as she stood up. "Do you want to feel its pain?"

"Your spear cannot hurt me."

The other two Roman soldiers dismounted and stood beside Marcus. "There is no threat here. Can we go now?" one soldier asked.

"No." He faced Leah and again lowered his weapon, resting it on her chest. "Where is your friend?"

"She is home."

"I was just there. She is not." Marcus grabbed her arm. "You will come with me. I am going to search your house and town."

"You will never be able to hurt her again," Leah said in a calm voice as she allowed Marcus to drag her along the wet dirt and grass.

He growled and cursed like a madman, picking Leah up for a moment, slapping her across the face and dumping her to the ground. "I will show you fear, woman."

Jeremiah jumped down from the embankment to confront Marcus.

The other two Roman soldiers struck him, knocking him to the ground.

"My husband," screamed Sarah.

Leah struggled to sit up. "Leave him alone. He knows nothing. Let them go."

Marcus stomped his booted foot on Leah's leg. "You pig."

She winced but did not utter a word.

"Stop," yelled Sarah. "Leave her alone. Her friend has died. We buried her."

"Where?"

"Over there," Sarah said, pointing to the cave.

Marcus pulled Leah up on her feet and towed her to the cave. "Help me," he said to the soldiers.

Together they pushed the rock away and went inside. Moments later they exited the tomb.

Marcus glared at Leah. "You will stay with me and never leave your home."

She fell to the ground, refusing to go.

He tugged at her arm. "Get up." He kicked at her back several times.

"Stop," yelled Jeremiah.

"Back away or I will kill your woman."

Marcus pulled Leah's hair and twisted her neck back. "Do as I say."

She bit down hard on her lip, causing it to bleed, and with each kick she winced inwardly.

He struck her rib cage hard. "How do you like it? I learned it from your friend. How does it feel?"

As he got ready to strike her head, one of his soldiers pointed behind him. "Marcus. Look."

Leah looked behind as well and saw a long line of people trekking up the hill. Many were carrying rocks and sticks.

Marcus shoved Leah aside and waved his spear. "Stay back. This is not your business."

The group did not halt its march.

Leah stumbled to her feet as Jeremiah pulled her to safety with Sarah.

"Do not leave, Leah, or I will hunt you down," said Marcus, calling back to them.

The men held up their weapons and circled around the three soldiers.

An elderly man walked up to Marcus. "Leave in peace."

Marcus' face turned red. The blue veins in his neck tightened. "You do not give orders to a Roman."

"You do not belong here." The man stepped closer to Marcus. "You have terrorized us enough."

Marcus swung his weapon close to the man's face. "Old man, you do not tell me what I can or cannot do. Do you want to die?"

"If I must die so others may live, I shall do so. Look around you, Roman. How many of you are here? Now look at us. How many do you see? How many weapons do you have?"

Marcus glanced at the crowd closing in on him and the two soldiers. "We are not here to fight all of you. I am taking what belongs to me." He pointed to Leah. "She is my woman."

The elderly man crossed his arms in front of his chest. "Then you shall not leave at all."

Marcus lifted his spear and pierced the man's arm, drawing some blood as he fell to the ground.

Several men tossed rocks, one striking Marcus in the face. As the Roman fell, more jumped on him, swinging sticks. The other two soldiers defended their safety by drawing their weapons.

One man aimed a long, makeshift wooden spike at the two soldiers. "Leave and never return."

The two Romans mounted their horses and rode away.

The crowd cheered.

Leah, Sarah and Jeremiah joined the group surrounding Marcus who lay on the ground, dazed.

"Kill him," shouted a man.

"Let the woman kill him for what he did to her," another yelled.

One of the men handed Leah a spear. "It should be you who does this."

Filled with anger, Leah gripped the weapon and stared at the ground. She noticed how frail Marcus seemed. His breathing, rapid and shallow, reminded her of Yochanan's last minutes. His forehead bled and his right eye was smashed in.

With all the strength she could muster, Leah raised the spear high above her head and glared. "I hate you."

He whimpered and squirmed in pain.

"How does it feel, Roman, to crawl toward your death like a filthy donkey? Do you remember watching my husband die and mocking him? How does it feel to have God's wrath waiting to crush you?" Her eyes bulged with rage. The memories of being raped and beaten by him escalated her fury.

"No." Marcus begged for compassion. "I ask you for forgiveness. I ask you for your mercy."

She kicked at his injured side. "Do you remember my husband asking for mercy? Do you? Answer me!"

He squirmed and staggered to one knee, putting up an arm to shield his face.

Leah reached back with all her might, took a deep breath and rammed the sharp part of the spear into the ground near his head.

CHAPTER TWENTY-FOUR

It didn't take long for Michael to uncork a bottle of red wine and sink into his chair. As he rocked back and forth, his eyes stayed transfixed on his television set. He rested his head against the back of the chair, the coldness of the cushion matching the frigid fear running through his veins. He closed his eyes and a reel of his daughter played.

The memory was so vivid he reached out to touch her. The reel's sound soothed his anxiety. Elizabeth sat on the floor, flipping through travel magazines, enjoying a milkshake.

"I want to go to Japan and France and teach English," she said, her voice pummeling his injured heart. "I want to travel all over the world, Dad." She held up a magazine with a picture of the Coliseum in Rome. "There's so much out there to see."

"And what about me?" he had asked. "You're going to leave me here all alone?"

She rolled her eyes and let out one of her dramatic long sighs. "Oh, poor Dad, all alone with nobody to yell at. Maybe you'll finally get a girlfriend." She giggled. "Are you going to play the parent guilt thing on me until I'm like forty and too old to see the world?"

He pretended to throw a pillow at her. "Forty's not old."

She picked up another magazine, one with the Egyptian pyramids on the cover. "I'll come back and visit you for the holidays. You can come visit me wherever I am. I'll be your tour guide."

"I don't like to fly."

"You'll fly for me," she said with a smile that halted the argument.

It was a debate he never won. Michael was proud of his daughter's ambition and thirst to travel, something he had never done – until he discovered Jerusalem. Each time she talked about seeing the world, a small piece of his heart tore away. But now, thinking about her ambitions to see the world, he hoped she would be able to realize all her dreams, even if it meant she'd have new adventures without him.

He opened his eyes and finished off the remains of the wine, yet alcohol could not numb his pain. He withdrew upstairs to Elizabeth's room and sat on her bed, staring at the wall posters, cradling the Pikachu doll in both hands.

He absorbed the iconic picture of the Eiffel Tower, a poster showcasing the bright lights of Tokyo, another displaying an old church in the Holy Land, and an artist's rendition of Jesus holding a child. He sat in silence until jolted out of his trance by the loud ringing of his telephone.

He answered it. "Yeah."

"How are you doing?" Allison asked.

"Why are you calling?"

"I'm concerned about my goddaughter."

"I have nothing to tell you," he said, slightly slurring his words.

"Are you drinking?"

"None of your business."

"It is my business about Elizabeth."

"They took my car. There was some blood in it and ..." He gripped the phone in anger. *Why am I trying to explain this to her?*

"Whose blood?"

"I don't know. They think it might be Elizabeth's. So the cops took it."

"That's terrible," she said in a high-pitched voice. "I'll stop by tomorrow."

"Don't."

There was an awkward moment of silence between them. "Elizabeth will always be my goddaughter. Despite our differences and what went on between you and Vicki, I'm always there for her."

He didn't respond.

"I'd like to interview you for the local paper. This sounds so fascinating and would make a great story. Maybe getting this story out there would help find her."

"Fascinating? Great story?" he said, remembering what Dennis' concerns about a circus like atmosphere with the media. "There's nothing *fascinating* about my daughter missing. Goodnight. Don't drop by and don't call." He hung up the phone and continued to drink. Before he could finish his glass, the phone rang again.

He contemplated not answering it; he wasn't in the mood for another call from Allison, especially if she was going to make stupid comments about an interview. He reached for the phone, hoping it was good news about his daughter.

"Connie called me and said you were in trouble," his friend Susan said. "Sometimes I can't tell with your sister. She's such an emotional roller coaster and is always nosing in on everyone's business. Sorry to be so blunt but I've had it with her phone calls."

"Well, this time she's right."

"What do you mean? What's going on?"

"Something horrible has happened. Elizabeth's missing."

"Why didn't you call? Why didn't Connie tell me? Your sister is something. What happened?"

"I have no idea where she is. Well, maybe I do. She followed me down this tunnel and didn't come back. Or I think she hasn't. I'm starting to drink again. I'm going crazy. I need a hundred-foot couch to lie on right now."

"Michael, you're not making any sense," she said. "What do you mean?"

"Couch therapy. Going crazy. Need help."

"Elizabeth's got to be around somewhere. Have you checked with all her friends?"

"Yes, yes." He went to the cabinet and retrieved another bottle of wine. "I can't explain it over the phone. I know it's a lot to ask but can you drive down here? I won't be able to sleep and I really need to talk."

"Let me get a few things together and I'll be there as soon as I can."

He drank as he waited for Susan, knowing it would be at least five hours before she arrived from Massachusetts.

He glanced at the clock – nine-thirty. She would probably arrive by two a.m. He sat in the dark, his body and mind numb, sad, and shocked. He had so many emotions running the gamut through his soul, he couldn't even shed tears.

At some point he fell asleep as a ringing phone jolted him awake. "Yeah?"

"Michael, it's getting late and I want to go to bed. How are you?"

"Who's this?"

"It's Allison."

He rubbed his eyes and bit back a *leave me alone* retort. "I'm not doing any interviews."

She clicked her tongue loud enough for him to hear. "That's not why I'm calling. Have you heard from Elizabeth?"

"Nothing."

"I'll come by now. You shouldn't be alone on a night like this."

"I told you it isn't necessary." He yawned and stretched his legs to ease the cramping in his calves. "Anyway, I won't be alone. Susan's on her way now."

"Susan? The redhead?"

He took a deep breath. "Yes, that Susan."

Allison hung up the phone.

"Good. I don't have time for your drama," he said to the dial tone.

He exhaled, rolling his aching shoulder forward. He stretched his arms and picked up the half empty wine glass. He dumped the remainder of the alcohol into the sink and washed the dirty dishes. The noise of the running water was soothing, disrupting the unbearable silence of the house. He studied each plate, the grime in each part, before scrubbing it away. He took periodic glances at the clock, studying the third hand ticking away, much like he did when he was back in high school waiting for lunch break.

The doorbell rang.

Susan. Thank goodness.

He ran to the door, yanked it open wide and embraced her in a tight hug.

"I was just in the neighborhood." She patted him on the back and studied him. "You look terrible. You've been watching too many Mets games. Are you getting any heat from your Yankees friends for wearing the jacket I gave you?"

"Of course."

She smiled. "I know. Have you been wearing it?"

He nodded. "They call me Judas. Little do they know I knew the man."

"What? You must be in a state of shock. That makes no sense."

"It'll make sense later." He closed the door behind her. "Let's get you settled first."

"How about you get us both something to eat and drink?"

"Yes, of course. What would you like?"

She set her pocketbook down on the table. "A glass of cold water to start."

"Thanks for coming. How was the trip?"

Removing her shoes, she said, "Clear sailing on ninety-five." She waved her hand. "You'd do the same for me. Or I think you would? Right?"

"Sure." He led her into the living room. "How long can you stay?"

"How long do you need me to stay?"

"I'm not sure," he said. "I'm not sure of anything right now."

"Well, when you are sure, let me know. I have some vacation time I can use." She pointed to the hallway. "I'm going to freshen up."

Ten minutes later, Susan joined him in the kitchen. He filled a pitcher with ice cubes and water, cut a piece of chocolate pound cake, and set her a place at the kitchen table.

She sat across from him. "Mmmm. Chocolate cake. You do know a way to a woman's heart," she said with a wink.

He smiled weakly. "I have black licorice too."

She placed a paper napkin on her knee. "I'm impressed. You remembered."

"I did."

She smiled and drank some water. "Tell me what happened."

He took in her large, baby blue eyes, sparkling as they always did. Her hair looked more brown than the red he remembered and she seemed to have lost weight. "Please have something. I feel bad enough I asked you to drive all this way."

"Okay, I'll eat, you talk." She broke off a piece of cake with her fingers and popped it in her mouth. "And don't leave anything out."

He turned, opened a cupboard drawer and took out a fork. "Sorry, I forgot this."

She took it and cut into her piece of cake.

"Okay, where to begin?" He lowered his head and ran a hand through his hair. "I found this gateway in the old church on Main Street."

"Our church?"

"Yes. The gateway opened today. I went into it again. I'd been there before. Anyway, it led me to this tunnel and –"

Susan stopped chewing and waved her fork. "Whoa. I'm confused. I've been in that basement. There is no gateway or tunnel. You're not making any sense."

"I know. I'm trying to digest it all myself." He explained how the tunnel had opened four months ago, leading him and Elizabeth to first century Jerusalem during the last week of Christ's life. "I witnessed the crucifixion."

He mentioned Leah only for a moment, neglecting to share his romantic feelings for the Jewish widow. Susan remained silent. He described his experience at the Sermon on the Mount. "I met Jesus. I spoke to Him."

Her expression was vacant.

"He took me into this cave and it was like watching a movie of my life. I…I even saw Vicki briefly." He didn't go into the intimate details of his visit with his wife but he did tell her about the visions he'd witnessed. When he finished, he sat and poured himself a glass of water, gulping it down in one long haul.

Susan's eyes widened, her irises turning a darker shade of blue. She looked stunned. "I…I have no words." She poured herself a glass of water and took several sips. "I think I believe you, even though I can't get my mind around it all. Should I believe you?" Her expression glistened with wonder. "It's just so surreal. You met Jesus? Are you sure?"

"As sure as I see you sitting across from me now."

"Really? Jesus?"

He got up and paced around the kitchen. "You don't believe me."

"Come back in here. Can you blame me if this all sounds a bit far-fetched?"

Michael got on his knees in front of her and held her hands. "Susan, you're my best friend. I need you. My daughter is gone and I'm afraid I might do something crazy. I know this sounds like I'm ready for a strait jacket. But I know what I saw. And I know that my daughter is somewhere back there, perhaps alone in a dangerous world."

She squeezed his hands. "Connie told me she saw the tunnel or some opening."

"She's not sure whether Elizabeth went down there after me. She thinks she did but isn't a hundred percent sure."

"Why isn't she sure?"

He shrugged. "She didn't stick around the basement the whole time."

Susan sighed. "Figures."

"You sound like Allison."

"Don't even compare me to that woman." Her cheeks reddened. "You know how I feel about her. What she said about you after Vicki died."

"It doesn't matter. We know the truth."

"I know the drill." She rolled her eyes. "We're getting off track here. Who else knows about this trip you took?"

He got up and paced. "Dennis."

"Dennis?"

"Yeah, the pastor."

"Oh. What does he think?"

"He believes me." He stopped pacing and leaned against the fridge. "Or I think he does. I don't know at this point. He has this old book we found in the basement. He said there've been other incredible stories transcribed by the previous pastors."

She stared at him, not offering any advice. He found that odd since Susan had been his sounding board for years, lifting him up during his roughest days. "I'm at a loss for words. I don't know what to say or do. I'll admit I'm still in shock at what you told me." Her expression turned from wonder to melancholy. "I'm not any help at all with this."

"Of course you are. You're helping by just being here with me and not calling nine-one-one to cart me away."

She smiled. "Okay, let's look at this a different way. Nobody knows for sure if Elizabeth went through the tunnel." She held her hand up. "I know. Connie claims she did. But I'm not convinced your sister is one hundred percent on the ball half the time anyway. But for argument's sake, let's say Elizabeth did go into the tunnel. So she's back in Jerusalem and when she can't find you there, she turns around and comes back."

"Then why isn't she here yet?" Michael asked.

Susan chewed her bottom lip, seeming to be deep in thought. "Maybe, when she came back to this century, the tunnel led her to another city and she's trying to figure out how to get home. She's mature for her age, resourceful. I'm sure she's doing what she can to get back home. Did she have her cell phone with her?"

"No. She left it behind. Look, this all sounds plausible, but she knows how much I worry. Don't you think she'd get to a phone booth, a police station, even a church to get a message to me?"

"That's true." Susan nodded her head, then rubbed the back of her neck, sighing. "Let's try to get some sleep. We'll get up early, go to the church and take a look in the basement. Let's see if we can find out who else was in the church when this tunnel opened. Maybe someone saw her. We'll ask Pastor Dennis if we can read the book. Maybe there's something in there he hasn't seen that could help us. Have you looked in other places in the church for another opening?"

"Yes, many times."

"Well, let's get a look at that book. We may see something he hasn't."

"Good idea. But there's more. The cops found blood in my car."

"Whose blood?"

"I don't know."

He explained Detective Brady's suspicions.

"You've had a horrendous day," she said, her eyes sad. "I feel helpless right now." She went to him. "We don't know if anything bad has happened to Elizabeth. Stay positive. Okay?"

He nodded. "I need to find a way back somehow. Even if I have to dig my way back."

She put her hand on his shoulder. "Not tonight. Get some rest. Tomorrow morning we'll do everything we can to figure this out."

Susan's tone was reassuring, enough to relax him for a few moments.

"I could use something stronger than water," he said. "Want to join me?"

"You're on."

They moved to the living room where he opened a bottle of wine, sat and rocked in his chair, chatting idly with her. She talked about her new job and friends. When she told him there was no one special in her life, he was relieved though not sure what to do about it.

He glanced at the clock. Four a.m. "You must be wiped."

"Don't worry about it." She stood and went to the hallway. "I'm going to go and bring in my overnight bag from the car."

"I'll get some fresh sheets for the bed."

She waved her hand. "No need. I'll sleep on the couch. You go upstairs."

"I can't sleep."

"Then I'll stay up with you."

Michael smiled and wondered what had held him back from taking their friendship to a different level – a romantic one. He admired the way Susan greeted life with energy and enthusiasm. She walked in this world in a vibrant and positive light.

Perhaps she reminded him too much of Vicki?

She joined him in the living room and put her suitcase on the floor.

"Elizabeth missed you when you moved," he said.

"I know."

"How?"

"I got her emails."

"Oh."

He put his glass down. His heart ached at the mention of his daughter's feelings. Elizabeth was fond of Susan and encouraged her father to be more than friends. "When you left there was a big hole in my life." He was surprised to hear himself speak those heartfelt words. Maybe it was the wine or the emotional turmoil he was enduring. It didn't matter. It was how he truly felt.

He gathered the empty wine glasses before he said anything more, fearful again of getting too close to another woman.

As he retreated to the kitchen with the glasses, Susan put her hand on his arm to stop him. "I really do care about you," she said. "I worry about you every day."

"Then why did you leave?"

"I needed a change."

"A change from what?"

"From being disappointed."

His chest tightened. "Did I disappoint you?"

"My therapist told me when a situation gets stuck in neutral for a long time, you have to make some changes."

"Oh great. I drove you to the couch."

He put the glasses on the coffee table and pulled her in for a tight hug. She rubbed his back and he enjoyed the warmth of her body. "Did I push you away and make you run?"

She squeezed his upper arm. "I don't know how to answer that."

Michael let out a deep, sorrowful sigh.

She stepped back to look up at him. "What's wrong?"

"I'm scared."

"That's understandable. You're terrified for your daughter."

He pulled away slightly. Her gaze melted his vulnerabilities. *She's so beautiful I want to kiss her but I can't.*

The decision was taken out of his hands.

She pulled his head down and kissed him, a soft, tender meeting of the lips that mended part of his broken heart, giving it a moment's reprieve from sadness.

He pulled her closer, thankful for her decisiveness, and deepened the kiss.

CHAPTER TWENTY-FIVE

"You cannot go home." Sarah ran, catching up to Leah. "That soldier is still alive. He will not show you any mercy. You should have killed him when you had a chance."

"Has there not been enough killing?" Leah quickened her pace. "When shall it stop?"

"I do not know. But I do know you are not safe with him alive. You have to find a place far away."

"Where shall I go?" Leah stopped and waved her hand toward the rolling hills surrounding her town. "How far should I run? Do I run over there?" she asked, pointing to the farthest mountain. "Or there?" she asked, gesturing to the sea in the distance. "If I kill him, will the other soldiers not seek revenge on my brother and his family? Then what happens? Do others avenge their children and then later their children's children?"

Sarah touched Leah's shoulder. "Go be with your brother."

"Then he will not be safe."

"That is why you should have killed the soldier."

"What about our faith? What we pray for every day we are in the Temple? The Ten Commandments. Thou shall not kill. Are we a people of our word and faith or not?"

Sarah walked ahead of Leah and stood in front of her. "What good will our prayers do if we are dead?"

"Then go." Leah stepped around her and continued walking. "You have helped me and I will always be grateful, but I cannot bear to lose you and your husband too."

Jeremiah chased down the women and put his arm around his wife's shoulder. "Leah, come with us. We will keep each other safe."

"No, it is not safe if I am with you. It is best you find refuge far away from here." Leah swung her arms as she walked without fear.

"We are going to get some of our belongings and then we will go visit relatives," Jeremiah said. "Maybe someday we can return. If you change your mind, come by quickly."

Leah smiled and placed her hand on Jeremiah's face. "You are a good man. Sarah is blessed." She hugged them both. "Take care of each other. I will miss you. I will never forget what you did for me and Elizabeth."

They embraced each other one last time.

"We will walk you to your house to make sure you are safe," Sarah said.

"It is fine. Go and pack so you can leave. I am not going home right away."

"Where are you going?" asked Jeremiah.

Leah pointed to a neighborhood to the right of her town. "I will go to Yochanan's brother's house. He might know someone who can help me."

Leah continued, veering into a cluster of dirty, gray and white stoned houses. The neighborhood was alive with children, splashing in the puddles left by the rain, playing chasing games as the women caught the water dripping off the roofs with their buckets.

Leah stopped at the front door of her brother-in-law's humble home. "Calev, are you home?" She waited before calling out again. "Calev?"

"Who is here?" a woman answered.

"I need to see your husband."

A woman stepped outside, her hands on her hips. "What brings you here? Now?"

"Mira, I need his help."

"Why?"

"I am in danger."

"From who?"

Leah grimaced. "The Roman."

Mira narrowed her eyes. "Your husband?"

Leah bit back an angry retort. "He is *not* my husband."

Mira folded her arms. "Can he not give you everything you desire?"

"He beats me."

Mira sneered. "So be nicer to him."

"Let me in." Leah pushed past her, entering the house. She showed her a bruise on the side of her face. Mira touched the mark and Leah flinched.

"Cook him a nice meal," Mira said. "Take care of him and he will not hit you."

"No more." Leah's shoulders straightened as she held her head high. "Where is Calev?"

"He is not here. He cannot help you." Mira raised voice. "What can Calev do against a Roman? They will hurt or kill him too like they did to his brother. Can you not understand this?"

"I need him to speak to his friend at the prison where Marcus works."

She shook her head. "Leah, he was killed shortly after your friend and his daughter were here.

"What happened?"

"Calev loves you. He knew of the danger you were in." She wiped the sweat off her brow. "Against my wishes, he asked his friend to talk to that Roman. When Calev went back the next sunrise to see what happened, he was told the soldier killed him for interfering."

Leah stepped outside in a daze as a soft rain wept from the heavens, dampening her hair, the moisture intermingling with her tears. She leaned against the side of the house, defeated. She summoned her last bit of spirit and forced herself to head back home. Once there, she removed her wet clothes, oblivious to the bruises stinging from the beating on the hill. After clothing herself with dry garments, she climbed the ladder and sat in front of a dinner mat.

I should have insisted Elizabeth leave. I should have found a way to get her back to her home. Where is her father? Did he die here too? Why did she have to die? My God, I am trying to hold on to my faith. There are many unanswered questions and I cannot understand why this happened. I feel like I have lost two daughters. May they both find each other in any Kingdom.

Too exhausted to eat, she lay down and closed her eyes, hoping for a dream to take her away from all the misery. She slipped into a shallow sleep for a couple of hours, her body fidgeting as she twitched in and out of consciousness. She lifted her head several times wondering if the silence would ever give her peace.

The silence did not last long.

"Where are you, woman?" yelled Marcus from downstairs. He slammed several cups against the wall. Leah scurried up the stairs to the roof.

The rain continued to saturate the area as she stood at the edge, the same place from where Elizabeth fell.

She stared down at the ground. *Will this be my final resting place?*

"How did it feel to bury the woman?" Marcus shouted. "Did she cry before she died?" He laughed.

Rage ripped through Leah as she spun around to see him step up onto the roof. She noticed the dried blood on his face and leg.

Marcus pointed his sword straight ahead. "This is familiar. Jump off the roof and save yourself a bloody, slow death."

She moved a few steps to the left, maintaining a slight balance by putting her right hand down.

He bared yellow teeth, twisting his face in cruel ugliness. "You can try to get away. I will chase you until your last drop of blood falls from my sword."

She staggered, trying to get to the lowest part of the roof, the place where she and Michael sat that night watching the stars. She felt Elizabeth's cross in her pocket.

Marcus rushed her and picked her up by the back of her hair. "Meet your God."

She pulled the cross from her pocket and swung, gouging his eye. He stumbled backwards. "How dare you!" he shouted, covering his face.

Leah regained her footing as she ran several steps back to the higher part of the roof.

Marcus wielded his sword and hoisted it high.

Crack.

His eyes glazed and his body stiffened as a stone struck him. He fell face first into the roof's concrete.

"Run, Leah, run!" shouted a man.

Calev?

She looked down and saw another man standing next to him, waving at her. "Come quickly," he yelled.

Both men ran into her house and up the ladder. The soldier's sword lay by his side. "Leah, come with us, quickly," Calev urged.

"I will not run anymore," she said, clutching her chest to catch her breath. "Sometimes one must remove evil the only way possible."

Marcus rolled over and glanced up at her. "You will not kill me. You are weak like the other woman. I am a Roman. Others will hunt you down if you kill me. I know where your brother has gone. He is in Galilee. I have told other soldiers where he is." His grin formed the figure of a snake. "Leave us. This is none of your business," he said to Calev and his friend. "Leah, go downstairs. I will join you. We will be together again like before. It is too bad the other woman could not be with us too."

Calev pulled on her arm. "Come now, before it is too late."

She pushed him away.

"You will never be with me again." She picked up the Roman's sword with both hands and held it high over her head. "You have no God."

She rammed it straight into Marcus' chest.

CHAPTER TWENTY-SIX

The next morning Michael heard the shower being turned off and drawers opening and closing. He went to the bottom of the stairs and yelled up, "Susan, can you step it up a little?"

"What was that?" she shouted.

He cupped his hands around his mouth. "Can I help you with anything? We need to get going."

"I'm moving as fast as I can."

Not fast enough.

He grabbed his sneakers from the corner in the hallway, slipped them on, not even tying the laces. Now in a hyped up mood, he was ready to see what was written in the book.

What if Dennis doesn't let me see it? He's never allowed me to read the book. Maybe there's something terrible in there that he doesn't want me to read.

He sat on the bottom step and took deep breaths to calm himself. "Come on Susan," he yelled. "Let's go."

"I'm coming. Did you forget I arrived in the middle of the night after a long drive?"

He paced back and forth. "I know." He took a few more steps, opened the door and stared out at the street. "Seems like I'm always waiting for women in my life," he mumbled.

"What women are you referring to?" asked Susan from the top of the stairs.

"Right now, *you.*"

She hurried down the stairs and faced him. "You can be such an ingrate."

"Excuse me?"

She shouldered past him into the kitchen. "You heard me. I rush down here to be by your side, you bounce me around like an emotional ping pong ball and now you bust my chops over a stinking few minutes."

"I don't have a few minutes. Don't you get it? You know what, take a hike. I'll walk. I don't have time for your pity party."

She stopped rummaging through her bag. Before Michael could take a step out the front door, Susan yanked his arm. "Pity party? How many hours have I spent on the phone with you at night listening to your problems? Listening to you go on and on about your guilt? Then trying to dump a stinking guilt trip on me for leaving Northport."

Poking him in the shoulder with her index finger, she continued, "The endless crying sessions I've had to endure about why no one buys your book." Her face turned a bright shade of pink. "You've got some nerve. If this was my house, I'd kick you to the curb."

She slapped him in the face.

Michael backed away, holding his left cheek.

Without another word she walked outside.

CHAPTER TWENTY-SEVEN

After a silent ride to the church, Michael and Susan found Dennis sitting behind his desk, turning the pages in the old book. His eyes were bloodshot, his hair ruffled and his hand gripped a styrofoam cup filled with black coffee. Several empty cups topped his waste paper basket. He pulled at his sleeve, revealing a tattoo. *Never forget Dec 25th.*

He always keeps things in perspective, Michael thought. "Hey, Dennis," he said. "You look beat."

"I never made it to bed." Dennis gestured to the two chairs across from his desk. "Have a seat." He nodded at Susan. "I haven't seen you in a while. Have you joined another church?"

"I moved to Massachusetts," she answered in a cold tone.

"Good to see you." Dennis took a long draw from his coffee cup. "You look as tired as I feel."

He looked at Michael. "Any word from Elizabeth?"

"No."

Dennis closed the book and leaned back in his chair. "Anyway, I've re-read this book twice."

"Find anything useful?" Michael asked.

Dennis rubbed his eyes, pushing his reading glasses to the tip of his nose. "There were a few miracles and strange happenings that have supposedly occurred in this church." He yawned. "That is, if we believe the previous pastors who documented these cases."

Michael leaned forward. "Were there any time travel stories similar to what I experienced?"

"Yes."

"Why hasn't anyone talked about them?" Michael asked.

"I had heard stories about these events when I first joined this church." Dennis removed his glasses and set them down. "But I dismissed them, thinking they were tales told by overzealous people. That happens sometimes when people want attention from a new pastor. That's the way I looked at it anyway."

Dennis put his glasses back on. "But I think they aren't general knowledge for the same reason you haven't talked about it. You're afraid people will think you're crazy. Stories like this can cost someone their job. Their reputation. They'll be labeled religious kooks." He shook his head. "We spend most of our lives shutting out the everyday miracles that occur, why wouldn't we ignore the extraordinary ones? We spend more time trying to dispel them instead of believing in them."

"I could understand that," Susan said. "Rumors of time travel would make people think the person is living in some sort of fantasy land."

"It's not a fantasy. I was there." Michael tapped the side of his chair with his fingertips. "At least I believed I was there."

"I believe you believed you were there," she said, her lips drawn in a tight line.

Michael's cell phone rang. He looked at the call display; it was his sister. "Have you heard from Elizabeth?" he asked.

"No." Connie sounded out of breath. "It's about –"

"I'm busy now. I'll call you later. Bye." He was about to hang up when he heard his sister scream for him not to end the call.

"What's so important?" he asked, his patience thin.

"Turn the television on," she said.

"I'm not near a TV."

Connie screamed, "Well, go find one. Now."

"What? You're breaking up."

"Get … a TV…"

He put the phone down by his side. "Dennis, do you have a TV in here somewhere?"

Dennis got up, opened a cupboard and slid out a fourteen inch television set.

"Okay," Michael said to Connie. "I'm near a TV. Now what?"

"Turn on Channel 12."

He did as she suggested, leaned back against the desk and watched the breaking news story unfold.

Amber Alert: Elizabeth Stewart, brown hair, with bright pink streaks, fourteen years old, last seen in Northport. Her picture filled the screen. He dropped the phone to the floor as the reporter talked about the blood found in his car.

At the bottom of the screen, bold black letters shouted: *Blood found in father's car. Press conference at noon.*

"This is ridiculous," Susan said.

Dennis checked his watch. "Let's wait and see what this news conference is all about."

"Can I use the land line?" Michael picked up his cell phone and hung up. "I'm having a problem with my phone."

"Sure," Dennis said, pointing to the church phone.

Michael glanced at Dennis and Susan. "I'd like some privacy."

They left. Michael pulled out Detective Brady's business card and dialed.

"It's Michael Stewart. I saw the report on TV."

"Amber alerts are routine in these circumstances," Detective Brady said. "We're hoping that an appeal to the public will lead us to more information on your daughter's disappearance."

"Do you have any new information?"

"We're still investigating," he answered and Michael heard an accusatory tone in the detective's voice. "Make sure you don't leave the area. You're a person of interest. Call your lawyer if you need legal advice."

"I don't need a lawyer," he shouted. "Just find out what happened to my daughter. If you want to bring me in and put me under a bright light, give me a lie detector test, I'll do it. If it means you can get some answers."

"We've taken that under consideration. In the meantime, make yourself available for further questioning. Where are you now?"

"I'm at the church."

"We'll be in touch," he said.

Michael slammed the phone in its cradle, surprised it didn't break into a million pieces.

Susan and Dennis returned.

"I heard you yelling," she said.

"It's that detective," Michael said, raking his hands through his hair, not caring that it would make him look like a mad man. "I keep telling him I don't know where Elizabeth is."

"Michael," she said quietly, "that's not exactly true. You may know where she is."

He huffed out loud. "I can't very well tell the cops that I think she may have gone back to another century. I didn't see her go down into the tunnel and Connie isn't sure she saw her." He tightened his fists into balls. "And now there is no tunnel."

Dennis nodded in agreement. "The police would think he's trying to cover up something."

"Maybe you can dig your way back to the tunnel." Susan said.

"That may not be possible," Dennis answered.

"Why?" she asked.

"If what I read in the book is really true, it says that a way back will find you." He rubbed the area between his eyebrows. "It says it can be anywhere in this church."

"It didn't mention going back through a tunnel?" Michael asked.

"No."

Susan turned to the pastor. "Can we read the book?"

He hesitated for a fraction. "Don't remove the book from this office."

"We won't," Susan said.

"I have to go," Dennis said. "Help yourselves to water, soda or coffee."

He left and Susan sat in a chair with the book. "You try to relax for a bit and I'll see what I can find in here." She flipped through a few pages. "Looks like a lot of these miracles took place during charitable events."

Michael pulled up a chair and sat beside her. "Like what?"

"Food drives, bake sales to raise money for the needy, clothing drives." She fingered a page in the middle of the book. "One night they were cooking dinner for widows that lost their husbands back in the Civil War and a mist appeared by the front of the church. The pastor was making a plea for people to bring food for the hungry during a terrible disease outbreak here in town. Then the image of Jesus floated through the crowd."

"What happened next?"

He watched her scan the next few pages. "When the mist disappeared, the pastor looked at the first pew and saw several loaves of bread."

"Does it have any reference to the basement?

She turned another page. "Not yet."

He put his hand out. "Let me look."

She handed him the book. "How did Elizabeth's blood get in your car?"

"No idea," he said, speed reading through one of the pages.

"Are you sure?"

He shot her a dirty look. "You're seriously going to go there?"

She shrugged. "I had to ask. You'd do the same if it were me in this predicament."

He shoved his frustration aside and continued reading.

She leaned over his shoulder. "Wow. Some of these stories are hard to believe."

"I know." He was captivated by the historical scribing. Some passages were more detailed than others and a few annotations were difficult to read due the age of the book.

He flipped a page over and Susan put her finger on it, pointing to an entry. "Look at this."

Michael read it. "Not sure I see anything interesting."

She took the book from Michael's hand and pulled it closer to her face. "The name in this book. Tanner. That's my mother's maiden name." She handed the book back to Michael. "Read that page."

Michael read the story about a man named John Tanner. He appeared out of nowhere inside the church, his shirt stained with blood, screaming he saw horrific acts of violence. He read that sentence three times. "I wonder if he's related to you."

Her eyes widened. "It's not possible."

"What's not possible?"

"John Tanner." She rose from the chair. "He's my great-grandfather."

"Are you sure?"

"Yes," she said. "My grandmother told me a story many years ago about her father being sick, having to go to a special hospital. She never gave me the reason why. My mother rarely spoke about him."

"You should ask your mother more questions about him."

"I will." She opened the door.

"Where are you going?"

"To see my mom."

"She still lives around here? I thought she went with you to Massachusetts?"

"She did. But she couldn't sell the house down here so she came back." She put her hands on her hips and raised her hand. "Why don't you come with me?"

He opened the small fridge in the office and took out a bottle of water. "You go ahead."

"You're not going to be able to get into any tunnel right now. We didn't find much in that book to give us any answers, besides the reference to my great-grandfather. Maybe my mother will remember something and it may trigger some answers." She tugged at his arm. "Let's go."

He hesitated, maneuvering his arm away. "Okay."

Susan's mother Rita lived on the other side of Northport, away from Crab Meadow Beach, up a hill where several tall trees blocked any sunlight from reaching the street. It reminded Michael of the hundred acre woods. Susan's mother gave him the chills too, like she was ready to jump out in a corn maze to scare children.

When they arrived, Susan parked the car. A white-haired lady waved from the front door. "Susan. Why didn't you call to tell me you were coming?"

"I didn't have time," she said, heading up the front steps.

"You didn't drive all the way here for that man again, did you?"

Michael tried for a smile. "How are you?"

"Oh, it's you," she said. "I didn't see you behind Susan."

"I'm only a foot taller than she is. How could you miss me?"

"I'm not wearing my glasses."

As Michael offered his hand, she turned and walked away. He reluctantly followed Susan up the steps. She gave her mother a hug and kiss. "I'm sorry I didn't call you sooner. But I only got in last night. I'm here to lend Michael a hand."

"What does he need from you now?" Rita asked as she closed the door on Michael.

He waited a few seconds before tapping on the door.

"Sorry about that," said Susan, opening it. "Mom, you accidentally shut the door on Michael."

"It wasn't an accident," she said, scowling. "I'll never understand your relationship with that man." She shook her head. "Never mind him. Are you hungry? I know the man can't cook."

"I'm right here," Michael said, trying not to lose his temper. "I can hear you."

She glared at him. "I know."

Susan gave him a look that said to ignore her mother. "I'm not hungry, Mom. I just need to ask you a few questions."

"Let's go into the living room then," Rita pointed at Michael. "You might as well come in too. Just don't get too comfortable around here with my daughter again."

Susan rolled her eyes. "Mom, please."

Michael and Susan sat on faded gold chairs covered in plastic. The walls were papered with dull flowered prints and an old light bulb flickered in a dusty red lamp. Rita sat in a wooden rocking chair that looked like it belonged to Grandma Moses.

"Mom." Susan leaned forward. "Remember the story about your grandfather John?"

"He lived in a loony bin. What's more to say," her mother said.

"Do you know why he was in there?" Susan asked.

"Grandma never told me the reason. But we all knew the elevator wasn't going up to the right floor." She circled her finger around her temple. "Loco, that one."

Michael chuckled and Susan glared at him.

Rita rocked in the creaking chair, cracking her knuckles, sounding like milk poured into a bowl of Rice Krispies. "Why are you asking me these questions?"

"Mom, I don't think your grandfather was crazy."

She stopped rocking. "How would you know?"

Susan looked at Michael. "We have a theory."

Her mother slid a bowl of candies on the coffee table to Susan. "Have one."

Susan took a candy. "Would you mind if I see the box your grandmother left of his belongings? I know you spoke about it before."

Michael reached for the bowl and Rita pulled it away. He wondered if Rita's elevator never made it past the first floor as well.

"The box is up in the attic." She pointed to the ceiling. "I'm too old to climb up there."

"That's okay," Michael said. "I'll help her."

Rita huffed. "That's a switch. Since she's always helping you."

"Mom, please," Susan said, exasperated.

"Please what?" her mother said. "You travel all this way and I bet he didn't make you a decent meal."

"You're right," Michael said, standing. "I'll make it up to her."

Rita wagged a bony finger at him. "And keep your hands off my daughter too, unless you want to make her an honest woman."

Susan made a noise sounding like a frustrated growl. "Let's go take a look upstairs."

When they reached the second floor, Susan pointed to an opening in the ceiling. "There it is. Can you reach it?"

Michael stood on his toes and leaped up to push the small doorway open, prompting a small ladder to hurtle down, striking him in the head. "I bet your mother booby-trapped this."

"She'd think about it but not do it," she said. "Are you hurt?"

"I'll survive. I've already been slapped a few times."

"You deserved it," she said, with a hint of amusement in her voice.

They climbed up into the middle of a floor flooded with old cardboard boxes.

"My grandparents were good at keeping themselves organized," she said. "Look for a marking and let me know what it says."

For several minutes they opened boxes, examined the contents and discarded almost all of the items packed inside. Michael located a taped brown box with the inscription – *John Tanner What's left of my life.*

"I wonder what this is all about?" he said, handing her the box.

Susan pulled the tape off the top. "Looks like life insurance policies," she said, rifling through the contents. "He sure had a lot of coverage. Looks like my great-grandfather was obsessed with this."

Buried underneath the pile of papers was a dusty silver box. She gazed at the oval shape, holding it up. "Never saw one like this."

"Open it."

They found several coins. She flipped them a few times in her hands. "Very odd looking money. I wonder where these came from?"

Michael stared at them. "I've seen similar ones."

"On that antique show?"

He held out his hand. "Let me see it." She handed him one and he played with it in his hands, turning it over several times, trying to decipher the faint images on both sides. He stood and dug into his pocket, pulling out the one he had retrieved from Judas. He went to the window, pulled up the shade and held the coins side by side – Judas' blood money in his left hand and John Tanner's coin in his right.

"Look," he said, allowing the sunlight to hit the coins.

Susan gasped. "They're identical."

Michael's phone rang and he answered it. "Connie, I'm busy."

"What about Dad? Are you going to call him back?" she asked.

He sighed. "Look, I can't worry about Jim right now." He hung up.

"Everything all right?" Susan asked.

"Just dandy. Let's see if your mother knows anything about these coins."

Rita couldn't recall how the coins were obtained by her grandfather. She told them that she never talked to her grandfather much, as he was a source of embarrassment to the family. "We were little kids when we heard all these stories," she said. "We were scared out of our wits to even go near him."

She went on and told them that other family members didn't talk to him either and that her mother would visit him in that *place* only on holidays. She emphasized *place* several times during their conversation.

After they had said their goodbyes, Michael put the box of Tanner's belongings in the back of Susan's car.

"We should tell Pastor Dennis," Susan said, putting the key into the ignition.

"Maybe we should figure out what all this stuff about your great-grandfather means first."

She started the car. "Then where are we going?"

"Back to my place."

Michael didn't say much on the way home. He spun several theories through his mind as to why the coins he recovered during the last week of Christ's life matched the ones Susan's great-grandfather had.

The coins do look exactly the same. What does this mean though? Is this some sort of clue? Was John Tanner a fellow time traveler?

CHAPTER TWENTY-EIGHT

Michael dismissed the thought of taking Susan out to lunch for fear that people would stare. He was also irritated that she had slapped him. At the same time he could understand her anger. He decided to make lunch for her instead, serving her a tuna sandwich, a diet root beer and black licorice. She ate the sandwich quietly while he sat across from her.

"Did you see the licorice?" he asked.

She put the soda down and raised her eyebrows. "I'm not blind."

"I remembered it's your favorite."

"Do you want me to throw a parade?" She took a small bite of her sandwich. "It would be nice for you to remember other things too."

He flinched. "Your mom's right," he said. *The woman may be the biggest whack job in Northport but she loves Susan more than I ever will.*

"Right about what?" she asked.

"About me. I never appreciated you."

"Forget it," she said, sliding out a piece from the package and taking a bite. "It's delicious."

He focused on her striking blue eyes, trying to break inside her thoughts. "I should have taken you out for lunch."

She finished the candy. "This isn't a date. I know where I stand."

He cringed as she smiled, sliding two more pieces of licorice out of the package. "Thanks for the treat."

After lunch, they watched Detective Brady's press conference. A group of local reporters had amassed as he took the podium.

"Don't worry about them," Susan said. "Probably just a bunch of internet reporters."

The detective adjusted the microphone and propped up Elizabeth's picture next to him. "Blood was found in Michael Stewart's car. Mr. Stewart is Elizabeth's father and a resident of Northport. We found blood samples on the glove compartment, passenger side seat and door, and on a piece of tissue and paper. We also discovered a bloody sock in the Stewart's house."

"Bloody sock? I didn't see that in the house," Michael said.

Detective Brady then opened up the media event to questions.

One reporter asked, "Do you know where Elizabeth Stewart is?"

"Not at this time."

"Are the police searching for her?" another asked.

Detective Brady nodded. "Yes. Several officers have been assigned to the case."

Allison shouted out, "Are you treating this as a missing person case or is this a possible homicide?"

"What is *she* doing there?" Susan asked.

"Homicide? She isn't dead," Michael screamed at the TV.

Detective Brady held his hand up, halting the barrage of questions. "The main reason for this press conference is to appeal to the public for help." The camera zoomed in on Elizabeth's picture and Michael clutched his stomach. "If anyone knows the whereabouts of Elizabeth Stewart, please call the number on your screen. If you've seen this girl in the past forty-eight hours, we want to speak to you."

"Is Mr. Stewart a person of interest?" Allison asked, shouting over the other reporters.

"Anyone who is close to Miss Stewart is a person of interest at this point."

"The police found blood in the father's car? Correct?"

"Yes."

"And a bloody sock in the house?"

"Yes."

"Why the delay in arresting the father?" Allison asked.

"Why is she asking those questions?" Michael yelled.

The detective picked up Elizabeth's picture from the podium and held it up. "We have no reason to arrest anybody at this point in the investigation."

"Is Mr. Stewart your prime suspect?" Allison asked.

The detective didn't answer.

Michael grabbed his head, feeling like it was about to explode. "What is she trying to do?"

Allison continued to badger Detective Brady about Michael's possible involvement. To his credit, the detective gave ambiguous responses followed by the standard "no comment."

Susan pointed to the television set. "She's some friend."

"She was Vicki's best friend. She's no friend of mine. I know it now."

"Now you know this?" Susan said, shaking her head. "You're so dense sometimes."

"I don't care about her or what she says or thinks. I'm not going to waste my time or energy trying to figure out what she's up to."

"Oh. But I can."

"No. Don't. It'll only incite her. I can't worry about what's going on inside her head."

"This sounds like a witch hunt." Susan pointed to the TV again. "And the head witch is leading the hunt."

Michael shut the TV off. "I only care about getting Elizabeth home. Allison can have her fifteen minutes of fame. People are going to think what they want anyway. I know the truth. I would never hurt my daughter." He flung himself on the sofa. "I'm not going to stop until I can hold her in my arms. I won't ever stop looking for her."

"I don't know what we can do right now," Susan said quietly.

"I'm going back to the church." He shoved his grief aside. "I want to look through that book again. There has to be some clue. Maybe your great-grandfather was there too. Maybe he found a different way."

"I'll look through the box again."

"See if your great-grandfather left any information about what happened to him, where he was, maybe people he met."

"It sounds so bizarre though," she replied. "My mom said he was never the same person after he was found in the church raving like a madman. Where could he have been? She said people gossiped, saying he tried to kill himself with a knife."

"What do you believe?"

She rubbed her forehead. "I don't know what to think."

"Susan," he said, standing up. "I did not hurt my daughter."

"I know." She hugged him. "I'm coming with you."

"What about your mother?"

"I'm seeing her later for dinner. Do you want to join us?"

"I'm not exactly her favorite person."

Susan smiled. "She just likes to act tough to show people how protective she is of me."

"She'll poison my food."

Susan frowned. "She's grumpy, not evil."

"I'll pass."

She gave him a light punch on the arm. "She really gets to you, doesn't she?"

"She's a real kick. Even if she was friendly to me, I don't have any energy left in me to waste on anything other than my daughter."

CHAPTER TWENTY-NINE

Heavy rain pounded Susan's windshield as she drove with caution along Ocean Avenue. The conversation was sparse as both were immersed deep in thought. Susan focused straight ahead as condensation fogged the windows. "I can't see very well," she said.

Michael grabbed a tissue out of his pocket and wiped her side of the windshield.

Bam.

The car jolted and swerved. He fell head first into the steering wheel and sprawling onto her lap as the car skidded into some brush.

"Susan? Talk to me."

"My head. Geez, my head. Oh no, my neck."

The left side of the car was dented while the window was cracked. Pieces of glass scattered all over her back. She rubbed her head. Blood poured from the wound and onto the seat.

"My God, Susan. Your neck is really bad." She closed her eyes, her face was pale and her breathing shallow. "No, don't sleep. I'll call for help." He reached into his pocket for his cell phone to dial nine-one-one and pulled out the cloth Jesus had given him.

He stared at it for a second and wiped the wound with the cloth. "Stay with me." He pressed harder while holding her head with his other hand.

She opened her eyes. "What happened?"

"We got hit."

"By what?"

"A tricycle," he said, shaking his head. "What do you think? A car."

"You don't have to be sarcastic."

"The son of a –" He caught himself. "Whoever hit us took off."

"What?"

"How do you feel?" he asked, taking the cloth away to see how bad the wound was.

"I feel fine."

He stared at her neck. "Unbelievable."

"What? Is it that bad?"

"No." He paused. "It's gone."

He grimaced.

"What's wrong?" she asked.

"Oh Lord, I don't know if I was supposed to save this for Elizabeth. Oh, no, what have I done?"

Susan gave him an incredulous look. "Gee, thanks."

"No, no, I'm sorry, I didn't mean it that way."

"Then what did you mean?"

"Forget it," he said, staring at the cloth and looking at the red stain.

"Where did you get it?"

"You won't believe me."

"Try me."

"Jesus gave it to me."

She placed her fingers on her neck, moving them up and down and then in a circular motion. She touched the cloth and leaned her head into his shoulder. "I believe you now."

"Move over. Let me drive."

"No, I'm fine. What about you?" she asked. "Shouldn't you put that cloth on your head? That gash looks terrible."

"I'm fine. It's not that bad." He pushed her hand aside. "Just drive. No time to waste."

"What do we do about the car?"

"We can get a plastic bag or some sort of covering at the church for the window."

He put the cloth back in his pocket, never letting go of it as they arrived at the church. Once inside, Michael ignored Dennis and Susan's fussing over his bump. He went straight to the book while she filled Dennis in on what happened on their way over.

Michael read the first few pages, carefully handling the old, tattered paper. The handwriting was not as legible in the first section of the book so he took out a magnifying glass and examined the transcriptions.

Susan returned from talking to the police about the accident. "Where did you get that?" she asked.

"I bought it when I came back from Jerusalem. I wanted to see the detail of the coins."

He continued to study the early portion of the book. "This is going to take a while."

Dennis placed two bottles of water on the desk. "Is there anything else I can get you before I head out?" he asked. "I need to attend a wake."

"Anyone from the town that we know?" asked Susan.

"I don't think you'd know him," the pastor said. "Mr. Farmer died. He and his wife always attended our morning service. They don't have any family or friends. They always kept to themselves." He shook his head, sadness etched in his face. "Mrs. Farmer will probably be the only person at the wake."

"Where's the wake?" asked Susan.

"McMahon's, on Laurel Avenue."

"I'll see you over there," Susan said.

"That's kind of you," the pastor replied. "There are times when I don't understand my congregation. They're so giving during fundraisers but nobody seemed interested in supporting Mrs. Farmer after I made the announcement of her husband's tragic death."

Michael remained quiet, focusing on the book.

"How did he die?" Susan asked.

"She found him dead, all bloodied. A terrible way to find your spouse."

"Did someone kill him?" Michael asked.

"The police don't think so," Dennis said. "Susan, meet me there and we can discuss the book afterward." He went to the door, then stopped and turned. "Michael, will you be joining Susan?"

Michael placed a thin piece of paper in the old book to mark his spot. "I'll see you there."

"Compassion is a wonderful gift. Perhaps the greatest gift you can give to a stranger."

Michael downed a bottle of water and hurried to the basement. He climbed back upstairs, dejected. As they drove away, Michael talked about Elizabeth. "She grew up so fast. Seems like it was only a few months ago that I was lugging around a diaper bag at the basketball games I was covering. She told me all about her dreams, how she wanted to marry and have kids. She wanted to be a writer too."

"I know. She sent me some beautifully written poetry," Susan said.

"I didn't know that. When she came back from Jerusalem, she was a different person, so much stronger, more mature, assertive, and self-assured of what direction she wanted to go in her life. But I still had my own fears and reservations. I guess my fears were right."

"No they weren't," Susan said. "Kids grow up no matter how much you worry. You couldn't stop her from pursuing her dreams. Think back when you were her age and how you felt about the world and your life, your aspirations. It wouldn't have been fair to suffocate her dreams. I know you didn't like it when you felt your father was doing that."

"You sure do have a good memory."

She smiled. "Hey, we're confidants, remember."

"My own aspirations got Elizabeth trapped."

"What do you mean?"

He knew he had to come clean about how he felt about Leah. "I have to tell you about someone I met when I went to Jerusalem."

"Who?" She parked the car in the funeral home's lot.

"I met Leah the first time we were in Jerusalem. I fell in love in with her. Or I thought I did. Heck, I don't know what love is after I lost Vicki." He winced. "When I went back this second time, it was the wrong time period and she didn't recognize me. The first time I traveled there with Elizabeth, she was a widow. My real intention was to convince her to come back with me to Northport." He paused. "I thought I wanted to marry her."

She opened the door without looking at him. "Let's go inside."

* * *

The funeral home was empty; only one room was occupied. Michael's mind surged with sad memories of Vicki's wake. He had held his newborn baby close to his heart during those awful days, greeting friends and relatives and even strangers who heard of his plight.

It might have even been in this room.

Tonight he sat in the last row, reflecting. He was uncomfortable in funeral homes. Yes, he would occasionally attend a service to support a friend or relative who lost a loved one. For the most part, he had done what he was most skilled at – he'd shove his grief and emotions into the far recesses of his mind and mentally run from reality.

He remained pensive, his stare pinned on the coffin where the old man lay. He watched a lone woman sit in the front row.

I don't want that. I don't want people gawking at me. I have to tell Elizabeth this.

He hung his head.

"Michael, are you okay?" Susan asked.

He shook his head. "Time is so short, even if it's long."

"I know." She leaned her head on his shoulder. "Let's go up."

Mrs. Farmer wore a dark black dress and flat brown shoes. She was nearly eighty but strong and stable on her feet. Her white hair was neatly groomed, her hands folded, holding a small Bible with the prayer card stuck in it.

Susan knelt in front of the casket and Michael joined her, leaning against her for support.

He recalled his favorite memories of his deceased loved ones – the baseball games with his mother, playing with Sammie, the talks he had with Nana when he felt discouraged, the walks and dinners with his buddy Leo.

Lord, I'm scared. I'm worried about Elizabeth. Please give me a sign, anything that will help me find her. I'm begging you for your help. I'll do whatever you need me to do.

He looked at Mr. Farmer, so peaceful. *Is he there with you, Lord? Is Mr. Farmer with his relatives and family members who have died too? Tell me, Lord, what happens when we die?* Goosebumps chilled his spine and arms and he shivered. *Elizabeth? Lord, is my Elizabeth dead?*

He closed his eyes tight. *No, Lord I take that question back. Elizabeth isn't dead! She's so young. She has so much life left to live. Let me trade places with her. Take me. Take me tonight, Lord. Let my daughter live. Show me the way to bring Elizabeth home safely. I'll be ready to do your work. I promise.*

Susan gave her condolences and Michael followed. Mrs. Farmer asked if they knew her husband. He shook his head.

I wonder if once someone dies do they feel love? Anger? Remorse? Can they cry or laugh? Can they move around in heaven? Can they come to earth sometimes and visit their friends and relatives? Can they touch them? Feel them? Hear their hearts beat? Hug them?

Michael closed his eyes again. *My Lord, please protect Elizabeth until I can find her. Please guide Mr. Farmer into your Kingdom. Have mercy on me and forgive my sins. I would give everything up for Elizabeth's safety. Everything.*

He rubbed his shoulder, hoping to work out the knot that sent pain shooting up to the back of his neck.

Dennis gave a short eulogy, talking about Mr. Farmer's infectious smile and his unconditional devotion to his wife.

Michael patted Mrs. Farmer's hand and paid close attention to his friend's speech as he read a passage from the Bible. His voice was compassionate and energetic.

Dennis is amazing. He's been through a lot of tragedy and yet he's so positive about life and the community he serves.

Dennis spoke about Lazarus and how he was given a second chance to live. He compared that story to everlasting life. He said another prayer and closed his Bible. "I will see you tomorrow, Cecilia."

Susan and Michael took Mrs. Farmer home. She dabbed her eyes with a hanky from her purse. Sitting in the backseat with her, Michael rested his arm across her shoulder, remembering what Vicki had told him in the cave. "How are doing?"

"My best friend, the love of my life....He's gone." She covered her face with the hanky. "He'll never hold my hand again, or kiss me goodnight or ask me where I put the coffee beans every morning, even though I've never moved the can in fifty-five years of marriage."

He placed his hand into hers, not removing it until they arrived at her house.

She held onto Michael's arm. He noticed the cobwebs surrounding the door and the leaves scattered across the front porch. A motion detector flickered on, illuminating the final few feet of travel.

"George never did finish sweeping up. I don't know what I'll do if anyone stops by."

"I'll take care of that for you," Michael said. "Where's a broom?"

"In the garage."

"One minute." He grabbed the nearest broom and swept away the spider's web and leaves.

"That's kind of you," Mrs. Farmer said, opening the door.

"We'll walk you inside," Michael said.

The door squeaked as she opened it. "You're probably wondering why it isn't locked." She continued before Michael could voice his concern. "No one would try to break in to our house. People are afraid of us."

Michael and Susan followed her inside.

"I can't imagine why anyone would be afraid of you," Susan said.

"They are." Mrs. Farmer removed her coat and placed it on a wire hanger in a closet. "I'll make you both a cup of tea."

"I can't stay," Susan said. "Michael, do you want to stay with her for a bit?"

Michael hesitated and nodded. "Sure."

"Okay, call me if you need a ride home."

"Thank you for keeping an old woman company," Mrs. Farmer said. "I have to admit, I didn't want to be alone after the wake."

"No need to thank me, you're doing me a favor." Michael hung his jacket next to Mrs. Farmer's. "I won't be able to sleep much anyway. So you're helping me out as well, by keeping me company."

She led him into a living room where two chairs were placed together in front of an antique phonograph. A small, grungy looking couch was to the right and a tall pink vase sat on a battered, warped brown coffee table. The dark hardwood floors were dull and a lone picture hung on the wall. She lit a small lamp placed strategically between the two chairs.

"Sit down. Please take George's chair. He would be thrilled someone would be using it."

"Are you sure?"

"Yes. I'll be right back." She headed to the small kitchen off the living room.

He continued to take in the surroundings of the dim room. "Do you have a TV?" he asked.

"We've never owned a TV."

"Oh."

"Yes, people have called us strange. But we never saw a need for it. We've always had everything we wanted."

The floor boards creaked as he took a few steps toward the picture on the wall.

"Oh, that's something George started to paint many years ago," she said, peeking in from the kitchen. "He said going to church inspired him to draw it."

"It's hard to see. What is it?"

"George had an incredible imagination. The funny thing about this particular painting was he kept on pulling it off the wall to paint more, like he was re-writing a novel. I always thought he was doing this so he wouldn't have to rake the leaves or shovel the snow or go to the grocery store for milk." She smiled, looking pleased to have an audience to share her memories.

As he drew closer to the picture, he could see figures in a big field, running with what appeared to be an object in their hands.

"Sit down, Michael. I'll get you some tea."

"Could I help you?" he asked, turning away from the picture.

"I'm fine. Rest. We'll talk. George always said talking was better than any medicine a doctor could give you."

He relaxed in George's chair, feeling the texture, staring at the beautifully kept phonograph. "Do you still use this machine?"

"Yes, it still works," she replied over the clanging noise of a pot being filled with water.

His mind drifted back to Elizabeth, the church, and the tunnel. He noticed his cell phone was nearly out of battery power. Then he dug deep into his pocket to make sure he had his recharger with him. He tried to call out but couldn't get reception. *Stinking town. When are they going to put up a tower?*

"Would you mind if I use your phone?" he asked.

"Oh, I'm sorry. We don't have one anymore."

"Really?"

"Yes."

"Why?"

"Too many crank phone calls."

"How do you reach people?"

She smiled. "We walk. We write letters."

He plugged in his phone and the recharger as she placed a tray on the coffee table. Her hands shook as she poured the steaming water over a tea bag in a ceramic cup.

Michael listened to her delightful stories of George. The times they shared a dance while listening to their favorite songs, the endless walks around the town. Michael couldn't help but wonder why no one else showed up at tonight's wake. But it would be rude to ask so he remained quiet.

"I'm not sure what I'm going to do now without George," she said, her eyes filling with tears.

Michael put his empty cup on the coffee table. "When my daughter comes home, we'll both stop by and visit."

"Oh, yes," she said, taking a sip from her cup. "Pastor Dennis told me about your situation. Have you heard from her?"

"No." He glanced at his cell phone. "Not yet."

"Can the police people help you?"

"I hope so." He shrugged. "But I honestly don't know."

His stared at the small particles of dust on the floor.

She touched his hand. "George was right. He said many times we are only given what we can handle in life. We used to argue about that all the time."

"I'm not sure I can handle this one."

"You can and you will. You must stay strong for your daughter."

"I don't know how I'll ever find her."

"You must have faith. George always was vocal about this."

"I don't have much faith right now. I'll lose my mind if my daughter doesn't come back home soon."

She was silent for several seconds, deep in thought. A few tears trickled down the side of her face. "I have faith God will take care of me while George is away." Her voice trailed off as her final words broke up in sorrow.

Michael crouched down and held her hands. "It'll be okay. I'm here."

"I'm going to miss that big old lug. He was my best friend." She waved her hand. "No, I can't cry. George would want me to be strong and not be so sad."

Michael squeezed her hands tight. "I know exactly how you feel."

"You are such an affectionate man," she said. "Very different from my George."

"I don't know about that."

She gave him a surprised look. "What's wrong?" she asked. "You seem uncomfortable with the compliment."

He nodded in agreement. "Perhaps it's time I finally realized it's okay to show your emotions."

She gripped his hands back with some strength. "It is."

"Mrs. Farmer, could I ask you a personal question?"

"Why, of course. What is it?"

"How did George die?"

She hesitated, wiping her tears with a lace hanky. "So terrible. I found him outside the door, bleeding. There was a hole in his side."

"Do the cops know?"

"Yes."

"What did they tell you?"

"They're still investigating." She sniffed and shook her head. "They said all evidence pointed to suicide." She touched his hand again. "George would never do such a thing. He loved life. He loved me. No, he would never take his life."

"You seem certain," Michael said.

"Because I am," she responded, sitting straighter. "He talked to me before he died."

"What did he say?"

"It was hard to understand him." She paused.

"I'm sorry. I don't mean to upset you."

"No, I'm fine. George said a road man did this to him."

"A man on the road?"

"I guess."

"You told the police what George said?"

She nodded. "But they said there was no evidence of an intruder or anyone in the area who could have attacked him. They insisted this was self inflicted. But they did say they'd keep the case open."

"Did George describe this road man to you?"

"After he told me it was a man, I didn't wait around," she said. "I went to my next door neighbor and asked them to call for help. By the time I got back he had died."

CHAPTER THIRTY

The next day Michael went to the church to check out the basement. After spending a few hours waiting for a miracle to happen, he went home and checked his answering machine.

Allison left him a message. This time, it sickened his heart. He immediately erased it. *She's delusional. Vicki and I had separated at that time.*

He sat in his recliner and stared at the TV screen, waiting for Elizabeth to come dancing through the door like she had done so often after landing a great mark on a test.

The banging on the door shook him out of his wishful thinking. He opened it, hoping it was someone coming to tell him that they found Elizabeth.

It was Connie. She pushed the door wide open. "Come on, I'm driving." She grabbed his coat from the hall closet. "We're going to Dad's for dinner."

He walked passed her and slunk back into his chair. "Have fun."

"Let's go." She put her hands on her hips. "You need a hot meal and Dad really wants you there."

"Are you kidding me?" he said, exasperated. "He wants me there? The last time he invited me to dinner, Vicki was alive. Give me a break."

"Well, come for the food. You won't have to pretend to like my cooking today. He's ordering out and he's paying for it too."

"Like I said. Have fun."

"It will be good for you to get out of the house." She put her arm under his and tugged. "Like it or not, he's your father."

"I don't like it and I don't owe him anything, especially my time right now." He shrugged her hand away. "Does he even know what's been happening to his granddaughter?"

"I've told him a bit but not everything," Connie said. "He has enough to deal with right now and he's worried about you." She pointed to the stairway. "Go get washed up and changed, and fake a smile if you have to, but you shouldn't be alone today."

"I'm not going anywhere." He pounded his fist on the arm of his chair. "I'm not anywhere without my daughter."

She blew a strand of hair away from her face. "You're impossible. Call if you change your mind." She opened the door and left.

An hour later Detective Brady called. "I'm checking in to see if your daughter has contacted you. Or have you heard from one of her friends?"

"Nothing." Michael closed his eyes. "I would have called you immediately if I'd heard something."

"Just to remind you, don't leave Northport, Mr. Stewart."

Michael gritted his teeth and slammed the phone down. *And where I intend to go and find my daughter is off limits, even to the cops. Catch me if you can but if I find a way back into the tunnel, I'll be leaving Northport.*

* * *

The next day, Michael forced himself to shower and shave but had no energy to look for something different to wear so he wore the same clothes. He met Susan for George Farmer's funeral service.

Michael kept his head bowed, clutching his stomach at times, mostly staring at his fidgeting fingers. *Should I talk to Allison? She's been talking to them. Maybe the police know something I don't. Maybe I'm missing something she might have learned from the detective. She could help me.* He contemplated running downstairs to dig into the ground once more. *If I got back, why would I even return?*

"Everyone, please stand," Dennis said.

Michael rose like a robot as Susan sang along with the choir, her voice a pleasant interlude from his hidden turmoil. After the service ended, they walked out into the frigid air.

Black Friday clearance specials enticed shoppers to the streets while the firemen decorated Main Street in anticipation of Santa's arrival after the town's Christmas tree lighting.

As they followed the hearse in a black limousine, Mrs. Farmer dabbed a few tears away with a pink tissue. She held onto Michael's arm as they arrived at the cemetery. The rows of headstones chilled his spine as he helped her out of the car.

Dennis led them up a hill to a spot near a copse of trees. A cold wind smattered him in the face as the trees' vacant branches crackled back and forth. Dennis concluded the service with a prayer and the casket was lowered into the ground. Mrs. Farmer wept as Michael wrapped his arms around her for comfort. "I'm so sorry for your loss," he said.

They remained quiet on the trip back to Northport as Mrs. Farmer stared out the window. Michael was lost in his own thoughts.

Why are we here? What is the purpose? Am I here now for Mrs. Farmer? Is this the reason why I was able to get back and Elizabeth hasn't? Maybe God has a plan for Elizabeth there? What is the plan? Can you tell me, Lord?

He was distracted by the sights and sounds of the town's holiday celebrations. Men hoisted lights up onto the roof of the firehouse while vendors handed out hot chocolate and cookies.

After bringing Mrs. Farmer back to her home, Michael asked Susan to take him to the church.

"You're not going to go postal in the basement again, are you?" she asked.

He didn't respond, distracted by a motorcycle speeding away from the church parking lot. "Where's he going?"

"Who?"

"Dennis. Follow him. I need to ask him if I can have the book."

"Can't we wait?"

"No. He does this every Friday afternoon. He disappears sometimes for the rest of the day. I have to see the book now. I don't have time to search around for it and I don't know where he keeps it."

"I'm not going to be able to catch up with him on that Harley."

"I'll drive."

"All right. Do you know where he might be going?" Susan asked.

"If I knew that, then I would just give you the address."

She gave him an irritated look. "Call his cell."

"He won't hear his phone driving that noise machine."

Dennis drove onto the Northern State Parkway. It was only a couple of exits before he got off and pulled into a crowded parking lot. The black and white lettering – Mental Health Institution – stood out against the tall, five-sided stale yellow brick building that overshadowed two other small structures. Dennis utilized the narrow parking space up front while Michael whirled around the lot twice before finding a spot.

"Wonder who he's visiting here?" she said.

"No idea. Stay here," Michael said. "I'll be right back."

"You sure you ..." Before she could finish the question, Michael barreled through the main door.

The reception area was serene with soft music playing in the background. A woman wearing a bright red headband was answering the phone behind a black, wooden desk. She flashed a big smile as she hung up. "May I help you?"

"Yes, I was supposed to meet my friend here, Dennis. I saw him come through this way. Can you tell me where he's gone?"

"Oh, you mean Pastor Dennis?"

"Yes."

"Please sign the sheet and I'll give you a visitor's pass."

Michael became visitor number 328. He stuck the sticker on his jacket.

"Through those glass doors you'll see a bank of elevators on the left," the receptionist said. "Take it to the second floor. Pastor is visiting his friend in room 217."

As the door opened, he heard weeping sounds coming from down the hallway. He took a few feeble steps, bothered by the profound squeakiness of his sneakers. The number 217 was painted in black above the door frame. The crying was more audible as he slanted his head at an angle to look inside. Two men were holding each other, standing, and appeared to be grieving. He recognized Dennis' long hair.

"My son, I hope you can forgive me," Dennis said.

"Pastor, it wasn't your fault. Please let it go. I was looking for someone to blame. It's why I said that. But I've taken responsibility now. It's been a long time since I've accepted it."

"I know. It's just that at this time of the year it bothers me more. You are a wonderful friend. I thank you for your forgiveness."

The embrace ended and the men stepped back from each other.

Michael's knees felt like jelly and he almost dropped to the floor. He opened his mouth to say something but no words came out. He thought his heart would race right out of his chest. He clenched his hands into fists and stormed to the elevator. He rushed past the front desk in the lobby. "Is everything all right?" inquired the receptionist.

He didn't answer and instead sprinted to Susan's car. "Go home. Now."

"What do you mean? What happened?"

"I can't talk about it right now."

"Is something wrong with the pastor?"

"I have to talk to him alone."

Susan saw the determination and seriousness in his stance. She didn't question him any further and left.

Michael stood near the door with his arms folded and watched the sun start to give up its strongest light of the day. It was an hour before Dennis strolled past him. "Hello, Pastor."

"Michael?" he said as he spun around. "You scared me. What are you doing here?"

"I might ask you the same thing, *Pastor.*"

He tapped Michael on the shoulder. "What's with calling me Pastor?"

"*Pastor,* you haven't answered my question."

Dennis avoided Michael's glare. "I'm here to help a friend."

"Is this where you go every Friday?"

Dennis stepped back. "Is that important to you?"

"You might say so." Michael took a few steps toward Dennis, his arms still folded over his pounding chest. "When someone passes themselves off as my friend and I see them hugging the punk that killed my wife, I'd say it's important to me."

"Were you spying on me?"

"No. I was here to ask you for the book. But I'm glad I followed you." He clenched his fists. "Or should I call you Judas?"

"You had no right to follow me and listen in on our conversation."

"No right? The pastor or so-called friend of mine spends his Fridays consoling the monster who ruined my life, took away Elizabeth's mother and you say I have no right?" Michael raised his voice. "I don't know what planet or even century you come from, *Pastor,* but I would say you are the lowest of the low."

Michael stood directly in front of him, his face hot with anger, inches away from Dennis. "I should punch you right now. I'd go to hell I guess for striking a man of God. But it might be worth it to do so."

He pulled out a coin and showed it to Dennis. "Maybe I should give you this." Michael slapped the blood money into Dennis' palm.

Dennis closed his hand around the coin. "You need to forgive, Michael. You need to know that this person you have spent so much time hating made a mistake."

"Oh, is that what we're calling it now? We've changed the meaning of killing to *a mistake.* Well, let's all hold hands, sing

Kumbaya and watch the doves fly above us. That punk deserves to die."

Dennis shook his head. "No, he doesn't. He has much love to give. He's shown it to me. He deserves your forgiveness. He has given me his."

"Excuse me?" Michael threw his arms up in the air. "He's given you his? And why do you need his forgiveness?"

Dennis took a deep breath. "I should have told you sooner. You deserve the truth."

"The truth seems to be absent here."

"Not anymore." Dennis leaned against the building. "I know how terrible it was the night your wife died. Do you remember the article about the accident in the newspaper?"

"I remember every horrid detail."

"Do you remember what Robert said?"

"Yeah, he blamed everything and everybody that night. The weather, the road, how dark it was. The truck with the high beams on the other side that blinded him. So what? The cops never verified any of this."

"No, they didn't. And couldn't." Dennis lowered his head. "The guy driving the truck was me. And I did have my high beams on. Maybe I did blind him. I wasn't paying attention to the other side of the road."

Michael staggered a few steps back and didn't respond. He glared for a few seconds and walked back to him, grabbing the collar of Dennis' coat. "What? Are you saying you had something to do with my wife's death?"

"I don't know."

Michael tightened his grip, taking deep breaths, trying to control his rage. "Why didn't you tell me?"

"I wanted to. But I wanted to help you heal first." He could see Dennis' throat working. "I wanted to support you and Elizabeth. Help you both move forward and –"

"Stop with that healing crap," he shouted. "Don't say my daughter's name, you lying hypocrite." He pushed Dennis against the building and walked away.

"Michael, I made a mistake," Dennis called out. "I've asked Him for forgiveness. I ask you."

"Keep the coin, Judas."

* * *

A few hours later Michael was back at the church. Exhausted but filled with adrenaline surging through his body, he hurried to the basement. Small pieces of cement still lay on the floor where he had swung his ax. He fell, sweeping away the debris with his hands. "Lord, help me. Show me the way back to Jerusalem. Help me bring Elizabeth home. I'm begging."

He stared at the old, gray floor, hoping for a miracle, holding his aching head, rocking back and forth like he did in bed as a child, trying to fall asleep at night.

No miracle arrived. No sign was given.

How can I change this? What do I have to do?

He cupped his hands over his eyes for a brief second, then swung at the ground, yelling. "Open! Open now!" His anger echoed up the steps and into the church.

"Michael," Dennis said, catching his breath after running down the stairs. "I know I'm the last person you want to see but let me help you." He held out his hand.

Michael swatted it away. "Stay away from me."

"I'm not leaving."

Michael didn't say a word, numb from all the honesty.

"I'll stay with you all night if it's necessary." Dennis sat beside him. "I don't know why this has happened. But after reading about some of the situations the previous pastors have described, perhaps there are reasons for it. Maybe there's a reason why both of us are together now. Maybe we were brought together for a higher purpose."

"I don't care about some stupid higher purpose right now. How can you even sit here with me?"

"It's the only thing I know how to do. It's why I became a pastor. I'm trying to seek forgiveness like many."

Michael didn't respond.

"I'm trying to forgive myself like you are."

Michael stood. "Your problems are the least of my concern right now."

"I understand. But I believe we are being connected to each other for another miracle. There has to be a reason for all this."

"Are you saying you believe something more might happen?"

"What I'm saying is I don't believe your journey is finished."

There was a period of silence between the two for what seemed like several minutes. In reality, it lasted a few seconds. "How can I believe anything you tell me?" Michael asked.

"Let's put our animosity aside. You don't have to forgive me. You can hate me and end our friendship. But for now, let me help you try to find Elizabeth."

Michael took a few steps toward the stairs.

"I've spent a lot of time trying to understand the diary," Dennis continued. "I'm starting to see a pattern of sorts. I think I've discovered at least one."

Michael stopped as he put his foot on the stairs and turned around. "Are you trying to suck up to me now that I know the truth about you?"

"This has nothing to do with what I told you about myself. We need to put that aside." He held out his hand. "Truce for now?"

Michael stared at his hand for a few seconds. He put his own hand in his pocket. "How will I know when it'll happen?"

Dennis put his arm down. "I haven't been able to figure that part out. But there hasn't been a night where I haven't fallen asleep reading and re-reading it."

"Why should I trust you?" Michael asked, anger lingering in his gut. "I wonder what your motives are. Do you want my forgiveness?"

Dennis' eyes filled with regret. "You don't have to trust me as a friend. But I can help you as a pastor. I believe your story and I know I can help you," he said, his tone solemn. "I'll go through the book again. While I do this, would you please do me a favor?"

Michael looked up at the ceiling, shaking his head. "You have some nerve asking me for a favor. What do you want?"

"Can you stop by Mrs. Farmer's house and pick up something she's giving to the church?"

Michael clenched his jaw tight. "Do I have a choice?"

"We all have choices."

CHAPTER THIRTY-ONE

Michael stood in the doorway of the living room, ignoring the cup of tea and biscuits Mrs. Farmer put in his hands.

"Sit down, Michael."

"I can't. I'm a mess, Mrs. Farmer."

"Please. Call me Cecilia." She poured herself a cup of tea and dropped a cube of sugar in it. She looked up and he felt her intense stare as she stirred her tea. "I've lived long enough to see enough pain to know when someone is bottling up their agony."

"How are you able to stay so strong?"

"I'm not." She took a sip from her cup. "I've cried a great deal. But anger wears you down, takes away your energy."

"Then I have no energy."

"You should be angry, Michael. Your daughter is so young. I have no reason to be upset. We've had a wonderful, long life here. Now it's time for me to honor George's life by smiling every day."

"How do you do that?"

"You just do." She placed her hand over her heart. "He'll always be here."

She smiled, her eyes filled with understanding. "I know George would be upset with me if I wasted precious moments, crying and being sad. I remember him telling me after he was gone to dress him in his dungarees, sweatshirt, sneakers, hat and winter coat and put him in the garbage can out front." She laughed. "He told me to make sure to tip the garbage men because he was such a load to pick up." She shook her head, smiling. "But he would also say 'I'm worth the tip.'"

She laughed harder. He wasn't sure how to respond to the story. Taking a small bite out of a biscuit, she asked, "Has there been any news about your daughter?"

"No. The police are still looking for her." He blew out an aggravated breath. "I feel helpless."

She stood. "Stay here." She made her way up the stairs slowly, holding onto the railing, each step defined with its own unique creak.

He walked to the stairway and waited at the bottom to ensure she didn't fall. He heard her rummaging through a closet, pushing boxes on the floor.

"Do you need any help?" he called up to her.

"No. I'm fine. Have some tea and a biscuit. I'll be down in a few minutes."

He shrugged, wishing he could get back to the church and dig. He crept back into the living room, intent on examining George and Cecilia's pictures. Many of them looked to be about twenty or thirty years old, including one of them holding hands on Crab Meadow Beach, much like he and Vicki used to do when they first got married. *Why did we stop doing that?*

He turned to his right to glance again at the picture that hung on the far end of the wall in the dimmest part of the room. *I have to look at this again. What is it?* He put his fingers on the picture, feeling the texture and outline of the images. He turned his fingers sideways as he scanned the top, then the bottom. *This is so bizarre.*

Men and women ran in a field filled with tall grass, surrounded by mountains. Many of them carried a small clothed figure. Their faces expressed horror as red lines dripped down. One man in the painting was dressed in armor, his head encased in a helmet and his arms holding a spear. There was another red line protruding from his weapon.

Michael focused on the man in armor.

He looks like a Roman soldier. Is it possible? No, it couldn't be.

"You are fascinated by that picture, aren't you?" Cecilia said from behind him.

"It's interesting. I can't seem to take my eyes off of it."

"I didn't want to hang that picture. But George insisted. So I told him to put the darn thing all the way over there. He said it reminded him about the value of life."

Michael's eyes stayed with the painting. "Did he ever talk about why he drew this particular scene?"

"When I asked him the same question, he said he painted what he experienced."

His heart beat a little faster. "How could he live through something like that?"

"I think he lived through it in his imagination." She sat in her chair and poured some more tea for herself. "He was gifted that way."

"He certainly had an artistic gift. I think artists place themselves into situations whether fiction or non-fiction and paint or write their point of view so that people can feel as if they were there."

"George said he would never paint anything fictitious."

"Really?" Michael touched the frame around the picture. "Did he tell you how he experienced this and where?"

She reached down and pulled out a bottle of brandy, pouring a few ounces into her tea. "Would you like some?"

"No thanks," said Michael, surprised. "I have to drive, I mean walk. What about the painting?"

"I believed he lived through it," she said, sipping her loaded tea. "For the past three years, right after Thanksgiving he would paint a portrait of some kind. He scared off the few friends we had when they'd come to visit and ask him the same questions you're asking and he'd tell him that it was his life he painted." She shrugged, her cheeks warming from the tea. "He insisted it was real to him. Who was I to say it wasn't."

Michael swallowed hard and wondered if Mr. Farmer was eccentric or if by some miracle he had traveled back in time too. "Did you ever hear back from the cops about George's death?"

"Oh yes. They said it was..." She paused. "What was the word? Incon..."

"Inconclusive?"

"Yes. That's it. I told them no one knew George like I did. He was a happy man. He loved life. He would never take his life. He would defend life if it meant giving up his own."

"I wonder if he did," Michael said in a hushed tone.

"What was that?"

He turned around and noticed Cecilia was dabbing her eyes again.

"Oh nothing. I was just thinking to myself."

She smiled. "George did that often, especially when he was painting. I guess it was a release for him." She sighed. "Sit down. Let me show you something. I know this always cheered George up."

Cecilia opened a box filled with Christmas memorabilia. She took out a couple of wooden ornaments and an old angel, its white wings dirty from dust and put them onto the side table. "Usually George handled the decorations so I have no idea what else is in here."

As she dug deeper into the box, her face lit up. "Here," she said, pulling out a stunning replica of the baby Jesus. "George always smiled when we took this out. He said it brought him back to what was most important during this time. He would take it to the church to be displayed and come back to paint."

"He's beautiful," Michael said. "What do you want me to do with Him?"

"Bring it to Pastor Dennis. George would be happy to know that we have kept up the tradition of having the baby in the manger."

"I will. How old are the decorations?"

"Oh, they were handed down to us by George's great-grandfather. It meant so much to him to have the baby in the church every Christmas."

"I'll bring it over to the church tomorrow. Is that okay?"

She nodded. "Thank you for doing that. I don't feel much for walking alone." She looked at the vacant chair. "I haven't slept alone in over fifty years. He would snore a bit. At first it would keep me awake and I would turn the hair dryer on to drown him out. But then I got used to it. It was a comforting sound. Now the past couple of nights have been so silent and quiet. I thought I would never say this. I miss his snoring."

Michael half-smiled, filled a bit with gloom.

"I talk to him at night. I wonder if he hears me?" she asked.

"I think he does." He spotted a pen and paper on the coffee table and picked them up. "Here's my phone number." He wrote it down and handed it to her. "Call me if you need anything or if you just want to talk."

"How kind. But I don't have a phone."

"Right. Sorry."

She gave him a gentle kiss on the cheek. "I'll say a prayer for you and your daughter." She escorted him to the door, holding the box. The contents jingled, sounding like chimes in a gusty wind. He stopped.

"Is there anything wrong?" she asked.

"No."

He stepped outside and a cold, brisk spurt of air greeted him as he cradled the baby Jesus in his arms, cuddling him inside his overcoat. It was a good night for a walk.

* * *

The porch light was lit when Michael arrived home. Connie's vehicle was parked by the curb so he stood outside, watching a stray cat and a raccoon looking for a meal in his next door neighbor's garbage can. A light dusting of snow skirted from the heavens, drawing a breathtaking view, reminiscent of a Thomas Kincade painting that hung in the living room when Vicki was alive.

It was a beautiful, crisp night, the surrounding chimneys sending their smoke signals into the air while stars sprinkled blue streaks across the black sky.

Tap. Tap. Tap.

Connie knocked on the living room window. "What are you doing?" she mouthed.

Michael put his finger to the top of his head. "Thinking."

She shivered as she came outside, hopping up and down. "What is that?"

"A baby," he said, holding it to his chest and watching her eyes widen. "Not a real one."

"Why are you holding a doll?"

"I have to take it to the church."

"It's cold out here, come in. I've got some hot chocolate ready."

"I need some time alone."

She smiled. "I have little marshmallows."

"I'll come in soon."

She skipped back inside, her breath vaporizing into a frigid tranquil breeze.

He stayed outside until he felt the cold seep into his bones. He ran inside. The alluring aroma of chocolate intoxicated him as he took his coat off and placed the baby down on the couch.

"It's hot, be careful," Connie said as she handed him his favorite snowman mug that Elizabeth had given him a few years ago for Christmas. Five miniature marshmallows floated on top.

He inhaled the warm chocolate before taking a sip.

"Allison called again."

Oh, joy. "Did she leave a message?" he asked.

"Yes."

"What did she say?"

"She was rambling. I stopped listening after a while."

"Did any of Elizabeth's friends call?"

She shook her head. "Sorry. So how are you doing anyway?"

"How I feel isn't important."

"Do you want something to eat?"

"I don't feel like eating."

"I can cook a burger, order a pizza, Chinese, popcorn –"

"The hot chocolate will do. Thanks." He went into the living room and sat on the sofa, sipping his hot drink.

Connie sat next to him. "So what are you going to do?"

"For starters, I'm going to ask you to think real hard and try to remember every single detail of the last time you saw Elizabeth."

Connie twisted sideways and put her mug on the coffee table. "Okay, shoot."

"What was the last thing she said to you?"

She chewed her bottom lip. "She said she would come back upstairs after she cleaned up."

He spoke slower. "This is real important. Are you one hundred percent sure that you didn't see her come back?"

She rubbed her temple with her left hand. "Well, I did go upstairs briefly. But I'm sure I would have seen her come up the stairs if she came back. I was near the stairs." She squeezed her eyes shut as if replaying the day in her head. "But then again, there were a lot of people coming and going and I could have missed her if she did come back up." She opened her eyes. "I can't say for sure that she didn't come back before or after you."

He put his cup down on the coffee table, covering his eyes with his hands and rubbing the weariness out of them.

"This is still too hard to believe," she said.

Michael could feel the day's events frustrating him. "Look, you can either believe me or not. Frankly, I don't care what you believe right now."

She put her hand on his shoulder. "Let's not fight about this. I'm sure she hopped on a bus or train and took off to that concert. She's not perfect so she could have disobeyed you. She wouldn't be the first teenage girl to do this. I was a teenager and I know."

He put his hand out and slapped himself on the head. "I know what happened. I can't be in denial anymore. She didn't go to the concert. I would have heard from her by now. She's a good kid, not an angel. I know. I can't keep telling myself this didn't happen. It did."

Connie picked up his half drunk mug of hot chocolate and headed to the kitchen. "I'll get you a refill, and then…um…well, we have to talk about my conversation with the police."

He followed her. "What conversation?"

Her hands shook as she topped off his cup. "The police called me today, asking all sorts of questions about you."

"What kind of questions?"

"About you as a father."

"Yeah. And?"

She spilled hot chocolate on the counter. "They asked if you ever hit her."

"What did you say?"

She tore a piece of paper towel and mopped up the spill, her hands still shaking. "They know about the time you hit her at the zoo."

"How?"

"I don't know. But they knew."

She averted her eyes. Her face flushed.

"I had to or she would have lost her hand. I was scared."

"I know. I would have done the same thing. But it didn't help that someone told an authority over there about it."

"I explained it back then." He paced. "What else did they ask?"

"They asked whether you two spent a lot of time together, how your relationship was and whether you enjoyed being around her, how you acted."

"What did you say?"

She slipped her hands into her pant pockets and shrugged, keeping her head down. "I said I didn't really know since we don't see each other much. But they seem to think there were some problems at home."

He bit back a harsh retort. "That's just great."

"I couldn't very well lie to the police."

"Lie?" Michael slammed his fist on the counter. The mug filled with hot chocolate toppled over and crashed on the floor. "You're mind-boggling sometimes."

"Why are you mad at me?"

He threw his hands up in the air. "You remember one time that I tapped her hand and bottom and by the way, that does *not* constitute hitting, but you don't remember that she's my whole life?" His voice broke. "It's not a lie that I haven't been to every school event, raised her alone, provided a roof over her head, put food on the table, put aside my own goals and took care of every single need she had. Yeah, I made my mistakes. Many. I'm not proud of them. I'll probably have to live with a few until the day I die. I've been trying to avoid making them again. But I'm human. You know all this, you didn't have to be here all the time to figure that out."

"Well, when you put it that way –"

He huffed. "What else did they ask?"

"Detective Brady wanted to know why you hadn't been in a relationship after Vicki died."

"That could have been your cue to tell him that I was a dedicated father and spent my time raising my daughter." He took another gulp of air. "And how did he know about my social life anyway?"

"They know a lot about you. More than I know."

"How long were you on the phone with the detective?"

"Give or take thirty minutes."

"Anything else I should know?"

"He asked me several times if you took trips anywhere."

"What did you tell him?"

Her face turned a bright red. "I may have mentioned that you went to Jerusalem. Look, people think I'm crazy, like I'm some religious crackpot because I mentioned that snake. I don't know what to say and who to say it to."

He slammed his hand on the refrigerator door. "Are you kidding me?"

She raised her hands in annoyance. "Don't worry, he thinks it's some place in Pennsylvania."

"What else is there?"

She winced, looking down at the ground, embarrassed.

"Connie," he lowered his voice and forced a calm tone. "What else did he say?"

She backed up and leaned against the sink counter. "Now, don't be mad."

"Spill it."

"Well, he asked if I ever saw you touch Elizabeth…you know, like…in an inappropriate way."

"That's a disgusting question. How dare he even think that?"

"Calm down," she said. "I told him that even though we squabble at times and didn't see much of each other, you aren't that way."

Chills ran up his spine at the thought of anyone touching Elizabeth.

"The police have to ask these things," Connie said, interrupting the gruesome image he painted in his mind. "Especially when a young child is missing. That's what Kevin said when I told him all about it."

His wife's brother? That's all he needed. "You called him?"

"No. He called me. He saw it on the news and he said he's flying in to help us."

Michael balled up a dish cloth lying on the counter and threw it against the wall. "He doesn't want to help me! He hates me."

"No, he cares about you and Elizabeth and wants to help find her." She put her cup in the kitchen sink and turned the tap on. "Even if he can't do anything himself, maybe someone at the FBI can help." She finished rinsing the cup and opened the cupboard door to get a mop.

Michael took it from her. "I'll clean up this mess myself." He meant more than just the spilled hot chocolate and broken cup. As he patted the floor with the mop to soak up the liquid, he said, "Just go. I need to be alone."

"Um, another thing. The detective came by about a couple of hours ago. He gave me this piece of paper." She handed it to him.

""What is this search warrant for?"

"I don't know. But they took Elizabeth's computer and your laptop."

"Oh, great. Just great."

"Anything I can do before I go?"

"Yeah. Call Kevin and tell him to stay home." He put his hand up to stop the argument. "Tell him I'll call if I need him and that you'll keep him updated."

Connie left and he cleaned up the kitchen. He settled down on the couch, mentally preparing for tomorrow.

I have to bring the baby to the church. I'll do that first thing in the morning. Talk to Pastor Dennis again about the book. Maybe he's found out something else. Maybe another pattern? Check the basement.

He hugged the big, yellow Smile pillow Elizabeth had given him for his birthday. She told him to look at it when he felt sad and to think of her so he would smile.

He clutched the pillow closely to his heart.

CHAPTER THIRTY-TWO

Unable to sleep, Michael sat on Elizabeth's bed in the dark.

"What are you doing tonight, Elizabeth?" he whispered. "Are you safe? Is Leah with you? Are you warm and have a bed to sleep in? I'm going to find you. Somehow, I will."

Numb from all the emotional distress, Michael fell to the floor on his knees in the midst of the books, papers, clothes and stuffed animals. He let his body lie on the rubble, surrendering to sleep until the phone rang.

"Hello?" he said half asleep.

"This is Detective Brady."

"Yes, what can I do for you?"

"We spoke to Matt Jennison."

"Who?"

"Matt. Matt Jennison."

"Oh, Elizabeth's friend. Yes, what did he say?"

"Matt told us Elizabeth appeared to be fine, happy when she went into the church. He waited several minutes before going into the church and then coming back outside. He left to take his mom..."

Before the detective could finish, Michael interjected. "Yes, for an appointment. I know. I thought I told you this."

"He also said you put your hands on him. You've got quite a temper there, Mr. Stewart."

Michael didn't take the bait. "Is there anything else, Detective?"

"No. We'll be in touch soon." He hung up. Michael let the dial tone buzz the remainder of the night. He knew it would be impossible to sleep and he was in no mood to field any more phone calls.

The next morning, Michael shunned a quick shower and dressed in his worn gray sweats, a torn T-shirt and a sweatshirt. He put on his favorite black coat, picked the baby Jesus off the couch and wrapped it in a blanket given to him years ago by a young boy named Parker after Vicki died.

"Wrap your daughter in it," Parker had told him. "You'll feel better. I know I do when I put my blanket over me."

He and Parker became friends, sometimes meeting for an ice cream sundae on Saturday afternoons.

As Michael walked to the church, several cop cars zoomed past him, lights flashing but no sirens blaring. *Wonder what happened?*

He took a seat at the back of the church as Pastor Dennis began the morning service. The pastor spoke about how the community was planning to aid the hungry and homeless.

When the service ended, Michael met him in his office. "I have something for you." He handed the baby Jesus to him.

"Thanks for bringing this," said Dennis. "Cecilia and George have donated the baby for our manger since I've been here. How is she doing?"

"Fine. What's in the book that we didn't know before?"

"I do know this. I believe we're all here at this time for some-thing to happen. I don't know when it will be though."

"Did you get the parts that needed to be translated taken care of?"

"Most of them."

"Why is it happening in this church?"

Before Dennis could answer, his phone rang. "Hello? Yes, hello Detective. He's here but I've been appointed his spiritual advisor."

What? My spiritual advisor? Michael tamped down the urge to tell the pastor their friendship had not been renewed. The only reason he was managing to be civil to the man was to have access to the book.

"Are you sure the test is accurate?" asked the pastor. "Could it be a mistake?"

Michael could hear Detective Brady's garbled voice leaking from the phone. "What's he saying?" he mouthed to Dennis.

He held a finger up and gestured for him to stay quiet.

"He wouldn't do that." Dennis paused, his knuckles turning white as he gripped the phone. "You are way off base with this theory. Your assumptions about him are wrong." He shook his head as if someone waved a torch near his face. "I'm afraid I have to go now. I have an appointment. Have a blessed day." He hung up.

Irritated, Michael said, "Don't you think you should ask me first before you announce you're my advisor?"

"I'm sorry but I feel the less you talk to them the better."

"What did he want?" Michael asked.

Dennis scowled. "The DNA test concluded that the blood in the car belongs to Elizabeth." He waved to the chair. "Take a seat."

Michael leaned against the wall, folding his arms across his chest. "I'm fine."

He sighed. "The detective wants to bring you in for questioning."

"I didn't hurt her." He unfolded his arms and dangled them by his side. "I don't know how her blood ended up in my car."

"I believe you, Mike, but for some reason the police have the impression that you're some kind of a recluse who has a hard time relating to women and is prone to fits of rage."

Michael shoved himself off the wall, bunching his fists. "That's such nonsense and horse…" He stopped himself. "I did not hurt my daughter." He rubbed his face roughly.

Dennis put his hand up. "Right now you have to get yourself a lawyer."

"I'm not going to waste my time speaking to a lawyer." Michael leaned over, gripping the back of the chair. "It would look like I'm guilty of all the things the police are thinking and trying to weasel my way out of trouble." He straightened and let go of the chair. "And you know how lawyers can twist things."

Dennis sighed, frustrated with Michael's attitude. "Listen to me. I'm not a legal expert, but I do know enough that if you go down to the police station for questioning without a lawyer it could –"

Michael interrupted him. "I'm not leaving this church. I have to be here in case the tunnel opens up again."

"I can't lie for you, Michael, you know that. If they come here looking for you –"

"Then don't. You certainly had no problem lying to me before." He glared. "I'll take my chances. If they come in with guns blazing, I'll go voluntarily, but in the meantime, I need to do what I can to get back to Jerusalem."

Michael's cell phone lit up and he glanced at the call display. "It's Detective Brady."

Dennis surprised Michael when he yanked the phone out of his hand. "Don't answer it. Most cell phones have a GPS. He may be able to track you down."

Michael took his phone back and opened the door. "Then I better get myself downstairs again and see what I can do to get back."

"Wait." Dennis shut the door. "I have an idea." He picked up his office phone and hit several buttons. "Rabbi, good morning. Shalom. I need your help. Can I come over? Thank you." He waved to the door. "Let's go."

"Where?"

"To the Temple to see Rabbi Stedman. Maybe he can help us find shelter for you until we can figure everything out about the tunnel."

"I thought you couldn't lie for me? You know the cops will question you about my whereabouts."

"I'll think of something." He looked at Michael's surprised expression. "I'm sure there's a loop hole in the Bible for special circumstances."

Michael smiled for the first time that day but it was short lived as they stepped outside the church.

"Give me your cell phone," Dennis demanded.

"Why?"

"Trust me."

"Trust you?" He hesitated but gave it to him.

"Go to the Temple and tell the rabbi I'll join him shortly."

Michael jogged down Starlight Avenue and ran behind the old firehouse where the Temple stood. It was a place where many years ago rebel soldiers escaped the wrath of the British during the American Revolution. Last year Dennis told him that there were many tunnels that led to different parts of their town. He knocked hard on the wooden doors.

The rabbi greeted him. "Welcome."

"I'm Michael Stewart. Dennis, I mean, Pastor told me to tell you he'll join us in a few minutes."

"Come in, my friend." The rabbi ushered him inside. "You're the man on the news."

"If you're referring to my daughter's situation, yes, that would be me," he answered as he was led down a hallway into an office.

The rabbi invited Michael to sit and offered him a cup of coffee which he declined. The office was beautifully decorated with posh carpeting and a polished cherry wood desk. A painting of the Star of David hung on the lemon painted walls.

"Rabbi, I'd like to explain about the gossip regarding my daughter." He accepted the bottle of water handed to him. "I didn't have anything to do with her disappearance." Michael looked away for a moment. "I don't even know where she is."

"I've known Pastor Dennis for many years. He would never protect or want to help someone who would hurt someone else."

"Can I wait in this office until he gets here?"

"Certainly." The rabbi poured himself a cup of coffee from the pot brewing on the side credenza. "In the meantime, would you like to talk? Maybe we can help you find your daughter. We can ask our members to organize groups and check places she might be."

"I don't think that's the way to go."

The rabbi refrained from taking another sip. "Why not?"

Michael's face reddened. "I don't think she's in Northport."

"Where do you think she is?"

Conflicted, Michael busied himself with tearing the paper off the water bottle. He'd already lied to the rabbi. He took a sip of water, thinking of how to explain it to him without sounding like a complete lunatic. "Well, you see –"

The sound of blaring sirens interrupted him.

"I wonder what's going on out there?" Rabbi Stedman asked. He went to the window behind him and gasped.

"What's wrong?" Michael asked.

The rabbi didn't answer. Michael peered out the window and saw a commotion at the side of the church, near the Lady by the Bay parking lot. Four police officers surrounded the pastor's Harley.

Several police cars blocked off the street as traffic was redirected away from the church. He watched as Detective Brady directed the pastor into a police car as several cops raced into the church.

"I've got to help him. Let me find out what's happening," the rabbi said.

He opened the door and shouted, "Marla, take Michael downstairs to the safety room. Make him comfortable until I return."

A petite, dark-haired woman led him down a dark, narrow stairway. A cold gust of air pinched his face as he followed her into a room that looked like a 1950s bomb shelter.

"What is this used for?" he asked.

Marla smiled, opening a closet door and pulling out a couple of thick, black blankets. "It does get cold down here," she said. "We do our best to keep the place warm with electric heaters. But at night it can be downright chilly. There's a couch over there. Is there anything else you need?"

"I'm fine, thanks. I'll just wait until Rabbi Stedman comes back."

"If you do need anything, there's a phone located in the bottom desk drawer. Dial zero and I'll answer."

That's an odd place to keep the phone. The sound of her high heels clicking against the concrete steps faded seconds later as Michael walked around the room. No TV. No radio. No computer but they did have a phone. He wondered if he could dial an outside number to call his sister.

Michael opened drawers, searching for any modern day device that he could use to communicate. In the bottom drawer, he discovered the phone. It was an old style rotary one, dust covering up some of the numbers. He hadn't seen one since his college days. *Maybe if I dial nine I'll get an outside line?* He closed the drawer and continued to inspect the room. There was a wooden case, three rows high and filled with books, many of them personal memoirs of people who had survived the Holocaust. Another row displayed several self-help works in the area of survival. A gap between the bookcase and the wall caught his eye.

He tilted his head and placed his hand against the wall. As he slid it down, he felt a knob and pulled. When it wouldn't open, he kept running his hand up and down, then side to side, trying to decipher if there was anything else behind it.

It has to be a door. I wonder where this leads.

His concentration was broken by the rabbi's secretary.

"Excuse me," Marla said. "Can I help you with something?"

Michael jumped back, embarrassed. "No, no, I was just looking around. It's a very interesting room you have here."

He noticed Marla had changed into a pair of sneakers. No wonder he hadn't heard her approach.

Well, maybe she has to go up and down the stairs a lot. It's easier to do it in sneakers. Vicki did that all the time going into work.

Somehow he doubted that was the reason.

* * *

Holding onto his arm, Detective Brady dragged the pastor into a room with a table and chair. He shut the door hard. "Sit down, Dennis."

"You can call me Pastor."

"You call yourself a pastor? You wear an earring and ride a motorcycle. What kind of pastor does that?"

"Don't I get to make one phone call?"

"You're not a pastor here, Dennis. Do you want a lawyer?" He raised his voice. "Got something to hide?"

Dennis shook his head and smiled. "Not at all. What's your first name?"

"I'm not in the business of playing head games. Where's Michael Stewart?"

Dennis remained quiet and whispered to himself.

"What are you saying?"

"This pastor is saying a prayer for you."

"For me?" The detective let out a cynical laugh. "You're praying for the wrong dude, *Dennis*. Save your holy duties for your friend who's in deep trouble and getting deeper by hiding from us." He waved a cell phone in the air. "Why do you have Stewart's phone?"

Dennis didn't answer.

Brady scraped a chair forward, turned it around and straddled it backward. "It's going to be a long night if you keep this up. See, this is how it goes, *Dennis*. I ask the questions, you answer them. Not the other way around. Now, let's try this again. Where is Michael –"

A knock on the door interrupted the detective. Brady waved a woman inside. She handed the detective a long file folder. "Here's the background check for the suspect," she said.

The detective opened the folder and flipped through the paperwork, shaking his head. "No, not this." He scanned more pages and smirked. "Yes." He looked at the pastor with a triumphant smile.

The detective placed his clipboard down on the table. Dennis' throat seemed to close up and he started to cough. "I need some water," he said, trying to compose himself.

"First we talk."

Dennis continued coughing. The detective lit a cigarette and sent a few puffs his way, making Dennis gag.

"Tell me where Michael Stewart is and you can get all the water you want."

He swallowed hard and managed to stop coughing. "He's not in my church."

"Where is he then?"

"I don't know where he went after I left my office."

The detective got up and left for a few minutes, returning with a bottle of water. He twisted the cap and took a big swig. "Cold and thirst quenching." He shot Dennis another of his cynical smiles. "We can wrap this up real fast and you can have something to drink as well. Now, once more, where did he go after he left your office?"

Dennis licked his dry lips. "I have no idea."

Another man dressed in a gray suit stuck his head in the door and knocked at the same time. "Excuse me, Detective, but there's a rabbi here to see the pastor."

He laughed. "When does the pope arrive?" The detective left the room and shut the door.

Dennis took advantage of his absence. He grabbed the top sheet of paper on top of the file and started reading. A moment later he slumped and covered his face. He wiped his eyes when Rabbi Stedman walked into the room.

"My friend," the rabbi said. "Why did the police bring you here?"

"How is Michael?"

"He's fine. But you need to tell him the truth."

Dennis grimaced. "I have."

"How did he handle it?"

"He has a lot more things to worry about than me." He shook his head. "I will plead for God's mercy."

"I will plead with you too. But I'm here to help. I have a friend who is skilled in the area of law. He's in the process of getting an explanation as to why you are here."

Detective Brady returned, his lips set in a tight line. "You're free to go, Dennis. If I do find out you've helped Michael Stewart in any way that has obstructed the investigation, I'll bring you up on charges."

"Have a wonderful holiday, detective," said Dennis as he walked out into the hallway with Rabbi Stedman.

"Did they hurt you?" the rabbi asked.

"No."

"Do they know?"

"Yes."

"How did they find out?"

"I have an idea who told them."

"Move forward, my friend." The rabbi patted him on the shoulder. "Come. Let's go back to the Temple."

* * *

After a hot cup of tea, Michael lay on the couch, wrapping his body with the two black blankets. His curiosity regarding the door behind the bookcase had vanished for the moment, allowing him to sleep for an hour. Refreshed and alert, he paced around the room until heavy footsteps pounding the stairs alerted him to the doorway.

Dennis and the rabbi walked into the room.

Michael nodded toward Dennis. "Are you in trouble?"

Dennis waved him off and turned to the rabbi. "I can't let you get involved with this now."

"I can keep him safe if need be," the rabbi said.

"We may need to open up our passageway in case they come into the church."

The rabbi nodded. "I'll prepare this area and make it accessible."

"Wishing you a peaceful holiday," the pastor said. "Thank you for your help today. Do you mind if we take the passageway now?"

"Go ahead."

He led them several feet down another hall and pulled a lever, opening up a stairway leading further into the ground. The rabbi lit a candle and handed it to Pastor Dennis. "God speed."

The doorway closed behind him as a rush of cold air brushed Michael's face. The candle flickered several times as the pastor tried to steady it during the first few steps. "Stay close behind me."

"What's this used for?" Michael asked.

"It was first used to protect people from religious persecution as more and more immigrants made their way over from Europe. This even dates back to when the Pilgrims arrived. Then it was used in the 1960s to protect minorities against the Ku Klux Klan."

"I didn't know there were so many passageways in this town."

"There's more underneath the streets. Land owners don't speak publicly about them, they're afraid someone will try to use them for other reasons. So mum's the word."

They climbed several steps and entered inside the church near the front, not too far from where Dennis spoke at the podium. "Hold on," the pastor said, investigating the area. "All clear. Let's go."

He directed Michael back to his office and quickly locked the door. "Stay quiet. Allison told me the police were already here looking for you."

"Allison? What has she been talking to you about?"

Dennis furrowed his brow. "She's a volunteer. We mainly talk about what things she can do to help around here."

Michael rubbed the top of his head. "I don't trust her."

"I thought she was your friend."

"My wife's friend." He skewered Dennis with a dirty look. "I seem to misjudge a lot of people who I thought were friends. Look, I can't stay here all day."

"I'll lock up the church first. We have a candlelight service tomorrow for the children as we prepare for Christmas. The community is also putting on a play and they need to rehearse. Once I lock up, you're on your own."

"Should I stay in the basement? Is this where you believe the tunnel will open again?"

"I don't have the answers. It could happen anywhere from what I've read."

"How will we know where to be?"

"We won't."

Michael inhaled and glanced at his reflection in the glass mural located behind the pastor's desk. He saw more strands of gray creeping out and a small bald spot in the middle of his head. His hair had thinned noticeably and he looked gaunt.

"When was the last time you ate?" Dennis asked.

"It doesn't matter."

"It does matter. I'll have Allison bring you something."

"No. I don't want her around me."

The pastor shook his head, frustration clear in his expression. "She's concerned about you. Whatever your differences are, put them aside now. I'll leave you the key to my office in case you have to get back here for some reason."

Dennis left, leaving Michael stranded on the mini-couch in the office. He read through the first part of the black book and struggled to understand the writing. A knock interrupted his concentration. "Who is it?"

"Allison."

"I'm not hungry."

"Pastor said to bring you something."

"You eat it. I'm busy here."

She kicked open the door and brought in a plate piled with a hamburger, a baked potato and string beans. There was a biscuit, steaming hot and already buttered. She handed him a diet root beer.

"What happened to you?" he asked, watching her place the food down with one arm, her other in a sling.

"I don't want your pity, Michael. Take the food and eat it. Choke on it for all I care."

She slammed the door and left.

He locked it and pushed the food aside, plunging back into the book while her last phone message played in his mind, distracting his focus. He shook himself back to reading the book. An hour later he heard someone knocking on the door. "Michael, open up, it's Allison. I'm leaving now so I'll lock the church from the outside."

He slid open three locks, noticing a tape recorder sitting in her brown bag. "Just so you know," she said. "I am worried about my goddaughter. And yes, I do believe you did Vicki wrong when you left her."

"She asked me to leave."

"I don't believe it. She loved you."

"I don't care what you believe."

"I hope for God's sake you didn't hurt my goddaughter."

"Get out or I'll throw you out."

"Sure, pick on a woman. You're good at that."

Michael sat down and tried to ignore her.

"I hope you find her...and then I hope you drop dead for what you did to Vicki."

"You need help. You're bipolar."

She grinned, much like Judas smiled when Michael saw him after the betrayal. "If you need pillows and blankets they're located in the secretary's office in the cabinet to the left of the desk."

She widened her smile much like Judas did before he hung himself and walked away.

The church lights were shut off and the sound of the doors closing rattled his insides. Michael raced to the basement and sat against the wall, praying for a miracle. The wind shook the upstairs windows, creating a wheezing sound.

Elizabeth, I hope you're with Leah.

* * *

Michael occasionally slumped over at a sharp angle on the floor. His back tinged with pain, his neck was stiff, and his bones cracked as he stretched his arms toward the ceiling and moved his hips sideways. He pulled his shirt outside his sweats and zipped up his jacket, covering up a ketchup stain.

He stayed downstairs for most of the day as a group of people rehearsed their Christmas play. When they were done, Michael first listened at the stairway for a moment and fled to the top. The church, illuminated with lit candles, shone in holiness as the children's smiling faces glowed from their lanterns.

The organ played softly the strains of Silent Night. Dennis was guiding his flock like a maestro in front of an orchestra, singing the lyrics. Michael stood to the side, embarrassed over his wretched appearance. As the song ended, the blare of sirens shook the atmosphere.

The pastor ignored the warning sounds and spoke about the community coming together to bring the spiritual aspect into celebrating Christmas.

"Christmas isn't about how many expensive gifts we can get, or how many sparkly lights we can place on our trees. Christmas is about helping your neighbor, a friend or relative, and being there for someone when all seems lost and dark. Why not hold the door for the stranger coming out of a store all year long? Shouldn't Christmas always be in our hearts in July as it is in December?"

His talk was inspiring, poignant and heartfelt. Before he could finish, the sermon was jarred by the opening and slamming of the back doors. Detective Brady and several officers huddled in the back and broke up into three groups, walking down the two sides and the middle aisle. The churchgoers whispered, their voices elevating as they pointed at the officers.

"Children, blow out your candles quickly," Dennis implored.

The kids obliged, throwing the church into darkness. The crowd quieted as the Detective and the officers brandished bright flashlights, walking to the front.

Michael slipped into the first pew and sat.

"Detective, are you here for the service?" Dennis asked from the podium.

"Continue, Dennis."

As the flashlights moved from side to side, Michael got up from his pew but tripped, falling into the aisle. Brady gestured to the officers to take him.

"No," shouted Dennis.

Several people in the first few rows stood and surrounded Michael.

"Step away," yelled the detective.

More churchgoers abandoned their seats and formed a tight circle around him.

"We'll arrest all of you if we have to," Brady said.

"Then you'll need more cars to take us all away," shouted Mrs. Farmer, hobbling up the aisle.

By now many had formed a deep wall of humanity protecting him. "Detective, we don't have enough cars to bring everyone in," said an officer.

"I know."

"What would you like us to do?"

Frustrated, the detective made a call and a few minutes later signaled to his officers to go outside. The people clapped and cheered.

"My friends, Merry Christmas," said Dennis.

Many of the churchgoers remained behind for several minutes, chatting with their friends and family. Michael slid behind a curtain, opened a door and took several steps down into the dark passageway. He could hear muffled voices seeping from above. When the sounds died down, the doors closed.

"You're safe for now," said Dennis, returning. "But we've got company outside."

"What company?"

"Television stations." He looked at Michael with determination. "You'll need to stay here. I can give you sanctuary."

"You can do that?"

"I can try."

They took a quick glance out the window and saw the bright lights from the TV production trucks gleaming into the darkened skies over Northport, the humongous white satellite dishes on top giving it a surreal atmosphere.

"This is getting out of hand," Dennis said.

"I don't care. No one is stopping me from finding my daughter. No cop. No detective. No reporter. No one."

"Your sister Connie called before looking for you. I told her to phone me before she comes over."

Michael wanted to say thanks but he still wasn't comfortable renewing a semblance of friendship with the pastor.

CHAPTER THIRTY-THREE

The gawkers multiplied by the hour, seeking a chance to wave or pose for the media. Local New York stations fed reports to their national affiliates. Michael, who had been granted religious sanctuary in the church, had his picture splattered across television screens and internet blogs. Even the cheesy entertainment shows started to air on-the-scene updates. Everyone now had a story about what they knew of Michael Stewart and his daughter.

Detective Brady held press conferences in the morning and evening, further feeding the TV audience's appetite for an arrest.

Michael refused to meet with his brother-in-law, Kevin Holligan, despite Connie's pleas.

Dennis brought Michael back to his office. "How are you holding up?"

Michael took a seat. "I've been better."

Allison came into the office with her tape recorder. "Pastor, there's a man named Hewitt Paul upstairs banging on the back door."

"The former basketball player?" Michael asked.

"He said he's the lead agent in the New York FBI office for missing persons. He's demanding to speak to you now."

"Let me check on this, Michael." Dennis pulled open his desk drawer. He grabbed a set of keys and left the office.

Allison scowled at Michael. "Why don't you tell me what really happened to Elizabeth?"

"Leave me alone," he snapped.

'You've got some nerve. I could –"

He shot back. "Yeah, I know. You've made it clear with your phone messages. I don't care anymore. What happened between me and Vicki is none of your business."

"She was my best friend. It is my business."

"We've spoken about it, forgiven each other."

"When was this? I spoke to her an hour before she was in the car accident. She still sounded distraught."

Michael's hands clenched and he tightened his lips for a few seconds. "We were having a good day. Until she got into the car with Sammie. You don't know everything."

"I know that my best friend was in pain. That I know for sure. And it sure didn't sound like you guys had reconciled."

Michael opened the door. "Here's something for you and your stupid newspaper. I saw Vicki not too long ago. We spoke. We hugged. We told one another we love each other. We've forgiven each other. Go ahead and print it. Let's see what your readers think about your reporting skills."

"You've lost it. They'll cart you off in a strait jacket in a New York second." She laughed and turned her tape recorder on. "I have Michael Stewart with me. He's accused of a crime regarding the disappearance of his daughter, Elizabeth." She sneered. "Mr. Stewart has told me an interesting story about visiting his dead wife as his daughter has gone missing. Is he sane? Michael?"

She held the microphone in front of his face. "What happened to your daughter? Was she so oppressed at home that she had to run away? Does she know what kind of a dad she has? One that talks to dead people?"

Michael swung at the tape recorder, knocking it to the floor.

"You jerk," Allison yelled as she struggled to pick it up with one arm. "You're going to be sorry."

Michael helped her up and put the recorder inside her bag. Then he escorted her out of the office.

* * *

Dennis returned, looking worried. He sat down, sipped from a coffee cup and took the black book from Michael. He began flipping through it.

"What did the FBI guy want?" Michael asked.

He looked up from the book. "He told me the FBI now has jurisdiction in this case. This Hewitt Paul fella is now leading the investigation."

"So we don't have to deal with Detective Brady anymore?"

"Let's hope not."

"You don't think we've seen the last of him?"

"I don't know."

"But it's good news that at least there's someone else handling this, right?"

"I'm not sure."

"Why do you say that?"

"They want to take you in as soon as possible. While the detective seems to enjoy the spotlight, holding press conferences, this Paul character is a no-nonsense guy. He doesn't seem to care for the publicity."

"I know he was a good basketball player but quit years ago," Michael said. "I read some of the story when it happened."

"He quit in the prime of his career because of what happened to his daughter. She was kidnapped for ransom and they never found her."

Michael nodded, his memory refreshed by Dennis' recollections. "It was so sad. I didn't realize this was the work he was involved in now." Michael paused. "Then I'm just going to have to tell him the truth."

There was a long, awkward silence as the pastor nervously finished his coffee. "I've got to re-read this book again. Maybe I'm missing a hint of where you should be in this church."

Michael rubbed the back of his neck. "If it means I have to risk everything then I'll do it. She's my life. I not only owe it to her, I owe it to Vicki."

Dennis nodded. "They'll use the circumstantial evidence angle. Because the case has gotten so much publicity it means more pressure on these guys to finger someone."

"How do you know so much about this?"

Dennis looked down. "I've read up on some cases. I know all about the justice system."

Michael shook his head. "I may not be able to hold off justice here."

"You won't be able to help your daughter from prison. You need to be here. I'm sure of it."

Michael sighed. "I can't just sit here and do nothing."

"We're all taking this journey with you in some way. Never feel you're alone." The pastor poured another cup of coffee. "There's more. Your brother-in-law is outside with the FBI agent. He's working with him. Maybe he can help you?"

"He won't."

"Why?"

Michael hesitated about discussing his feelings about Kevin with the pastor. He had admired Kevin when he first met him and developed a close friendship during his marriage to Vicki. After her accident their relationship deteriorated. Kevin blamed Michael for letting his wife drive that night.

"Do you want to talk about this, Michael?"

He shook his head. "Not with you." He pointed to the book. "Let's keep reading this."

Dennis closed the book. "I think I should go speak to your brother-in-law."

Michael held his hand up. "You'll only make things worse. I don't need anyone else involved."

Dennis took off his glasses and rubbed his eyes. "Michael, I know you're still angry with me and now I can sense the anger you have toward your wife's family. Forgive us. It will help you heal."

"I can't deal with all this forgiveness and healing talk," he said. "You want to make it up to me? Then help me find my daughter."

A knock on the door stopped their conversation and Allison walked in. "Connie's outside asking to come in and see you, Michael."

Dennis nodded to Allison. "Show her into my office." He handed Allison the keys to open the door. "I'll give you and Connie some privacy." He clutched the old book to his chest. "I'll be in the dining room if you need something."

Allison left and Michael asked, "Do you think the FBI will recognize my sanctuary?"

"I don't know. But I do know that law enforcement officials don't want to barge into a church to arrest someone around the holidays with the eyes of the world on them. I'm sure their public relations department is advising them to tread carefully on this one."

Dennis walked out, leaving the door slightly ajar. A few minutes later, Connie came in, snowcap on her head, scarf around her neck, wearing blue gloves and a red coat. "It's freezing out there," she said. "Do you think we'll get a white Christmas?"

"You're not here to talk about the weather." He squinted at her. "I told you I didn't want to see Kevin. Why couldn't you at least do one thing I asked you to do and tell him to stay home."

Connie sat. "He can help."

"I've got to go," he said. He dialed the church phone.

"Where are you going?"

"I have an appointment."

"What about Dad?"

Michael didn't answer Connie. He finished his phone call and headed out of the office and down the passageway, hurrying to the Temple.

CHAPTER THIRTY-FOUR

Michael held his hip as he exited the hospital. He groaned in pain as Susan opened the passenger side door for him.

"Are you all right?" she asked.

"I'm fine."

"You were in there a while. What happened?"

"Took a test. I was there longer than I expected."

"You look like you're in a lot of pain," she said, sliding into the driver's seat.

"I've got Tylenol and some pain killers."

"I didn't know you had a problem with your hip."

"I didn't."

She gave him a perplexed glance.

"I'm okay." He smiled. "Can you take me back to the Temple?"

"Shouldn't you go home and rest?"

He shook his head. "Temple's the safest place to be right now."

Main Street was abuzz with holiday shoppers. He crouched down below the window.

"What are you doing?" she asked.

"Hiding."

"Do you have bail money?"

He looked up at her in disbelief.

"I need to ask you this just in case."

He inhaled a deep breath. "Thanks for being my best friend."

She stopped her car behind the old firehouse. "Should I wait here?"

"Yes. I just want to get something from the pastor. I'll be right back."

She gave him an odd look and turned off her lights and engine. "You mean Dennis?"

"No, I mean the pastor."

Michael limped to the door and tapped a few times. The rabbi's secretary greeted him. "What are you doing out here?" Marla asked.

"I need to use the passageway."

"Rabbi Stedman isn't here but come in."

She led him downstairs, handing him a candle and wished him well. When Michael reached the church side, he gently tapped on the door. He struck the wooden structure again yet there was still no answer. He sat down for a few minutes and listened, hoping to hear some movement. "Hello?" he said weakly, bending down near the bottom of the door. "Is anyone there?"

"Who is it?" asked a low voice.

"Michael. Is the pastor there?"

The door opened and Allison answered. "There are no dead people here. However, the pastor is waiting for you."

She led him to his office and banged on the door twice. "He's here."

Allison left and Dennis unlocked the door and pulled him in. "Where were you?"

He winced. "I had something to do."

"Are you hurt?"

"I'm fine." He hobbled to a chair. "I just needed to take a test. That's all. What about the book? We're running out of time."

"I know. One thing we do know for sure, you must stay inside the church. I've called Connie and your father for a special prayer service."

"Jim? Why him?"

"Connie asked if he could join us. I said yes."

Michael grimaced.

"He's your father."

"So I keep getting reminded. Is he even coming?"

"He is."

"What time are we doing this?" he asked.

"In an hour."

"Susan's outside by the Temple," Michael said. "Can you let her know she doesn't need to wait for me?" He stretched his leg out. "Connie told me this morning about the TV report regarding the headlights story."

The pastor paled. "I don't know how they found out. Only you, Robert, the rabbi and I know about it."

"Only them? Are you sure?"

The pastor shuffled the piece of paper around in the book.

"What is that?" Michael asked.

He handed a newspaper clipping to him and Michael read it in silence. "I don't care about this right now. I need your help to find a way back." Michael ripped up the article and tossed it in the garbage can. "It wasn't me. I didn't tell anybody."

Dennis kicked at the can. "Someone told the reporters. I should have come forth a long time ago."

"You can deny it."

"And continue to live a lie."

"I've lived one too."

"It's not the way to live, Michael."

He nodded. "Yeah, you're right. What's been the response from the people here?"

Dennis scratched the back of his head. "I've had hate emails and some heated phone calls. We've even had people threaten to remove their financial support from the church.

"I've made some big mistakes. I haven't had a full night's sleep since my wife and daughter left me. After the accident, I drowned myself in alcohol." He kicked at the garbage can again. "I drank so much I ruined my marriage and my relationship with my daughter."

"Dennis," Michael said. "It's time for both of us to forgive ourselves. I need you now. As a friend."

The pastor wiped his eyes with a stray tissue lying on his desk. "I'll go let Susan know she doesn't have to wait for you."

CHAPTER THIRTY-FIVE

The church lights dimmed and Dennis lit several candles.

Connie arrived early and sat in the first pew. "Allison left another message."

"What did she want this time?"

"She was so angry I couldn't understand most of it. She said you made her look like a fool or something."

"What?"

"About seeing Vicki."

"Forget about her." Michael fidgeted. "Where's Jim?" he asked.

"There he is," she said, standing up and waving to their father.

Dennis shook their hands and took a step toward the podium. A pounding on the back door disrupted them. "Open up, Pastor. It's Kevin Holligan."

He ignored the noise. "Let me say I'm happy to see your family here."

"Let me in, Pastor."

"Go ahead," Michael said. "Let him in."

"Are you sure?"

"It doesn't matter anymore."

Dennis took the keys out of his pocket and opened the door. The glare of the TV lights shone inside the church as a few men forced their way in. "Only Kevin comes in."

"Sorry, Pastor, but I've given you enough time with this charade."

Hewitt Paul was an imposing figure at six-foot-eight. He was wide shouldered, built like a brick house, and dressed like a

GQ model. His voice was clear, forceful and deep pitched, perfect for a high profile authority figure. Another man settled in the back pew, kneeling and praying while Special Agent Holligan stood beside Special Agent Paul, glaring at Michael.

Kevin walked in behind Hewitt Paul. "You should have listened to Connie," Kevin said. "Now I can't help you. Just like the night you didn't help my sister."

Michael got up and took a few steps toward the basement entrance.

"You can run but we've got all the doors blocked," Paul said. "I don't know how you got out of here to go to the hospital but it doesn't matter now."

Michael looked at the two agents in surprise.

"Oh, you didn't know we knew you were there?" Paul said. "I respected your situation. Now I have my job to do. I have no tolerance for adults who prey on kids."

"I didn't prey on my daughter."

"Why is her blood in your car? And in your house? And where is she?"

"I don't know how her blood got there. And I don't know where she is."

"He's lying," Kevin said.

"I agree," Paul replied. "I've seen enough cases like this. A man frustrated with his life, his inability to keep up with his bills, unable to forge a satisfying relationship, takes it out on his daughter, usually someone not strong enough to defend herself."

Dennis was finally able to lock the door, scolding the TV reporters who were trying to film the confrontation. "Can you people have some respect?" he yelled, waving at Allison who was standing to the extreme left. "No recording devices are allowed in here."

"Michael," Kevin said, "Come with us peacefully and I'll try to see if we can get you a reasonable bail."

"And what if you can't?"

"I'll try. I'll certainly try more than you have. Whoever heard of a father who didn't organize search parties for his missing daughter?"

Dennis appeared oblivious to the discussion, pulling out a box from a closet. He examined what looked liked pieces for the manger setup.

Paul turned to him and looked puzzled. "What are you doing, Pastor?"

"Setting up for our prayer service. Just go about your business," Dennis replied, walking up the steps near the curtain before placing the Mary and Joseph figures near the empty crib. He pulled out several animals and moved them around the nativity scene. "Michael, do you have your cloth for the baby? Can you help me with this?"

Inside the box was the baby Jesus, the one Mrs. Farmer donated. "Dennis, they're going to take me now. You know I can't go. Help me."

"Michael, I can't help you anymore. You now have to help yourself." He gestured for him to place the baby Jesus in the crib.

Michael picked the baby Jesus up and walked toward the crèche, knowing the FBI agents were right behind him.

Paul pulled his handcuffs out as Holligan reached for his gun.

Jim's cell phone buzzed. Michael stopped and looked at his dad.

"Hello? Yes, this is Mr. Stewart." He paused. "Oh hello, doctor." He listened for a moment. "He did? Thank you. Thank you very much." He shut off the phone and stared at Michael.

"Everything is set. You're a match." He paused. "Thank you, son."

Connie hugged her father as Michael knelt down, holding the baby tight, clinging to the cloth. Paul hurried a few more steps with the handcuffs in his hands.

"Leave my son alone!" his father shouted. He struck Paul in the face as he passed the pew, knocking the handcuffs to the ground. Jim fell on top of the special agent.

"Mr. Stewart," shouted Holligan. "You just struck an FBI agent."

"I'll hit you too," he said with anger.

Michael heard Dennis yell.

"Allison, what are you doing?"

She pointed a .22 caliber gun. Dennis stepped in front of Michael, putting his hands out. "Give me that before you hurt someone."

The special agents rushed to stop her. Paul pushed Jim off of him and yelled, "Put your weapon down."

Allison fired.

Dennis collapsed, holding his side.

"Why?" Michael yelled, running to aid his friend.

Blood poured out of Dennis' wound as he tried to stand up. "Michael, leave. Now."

Michael's legs wobbled as he held the baby wrapped in the cloth. A hot fire raged inside his head and seethed through his chest, arms, and legs. Dizzy, his mind flooded with images of his birth, baptism, communion, and his wedding.

Michael saw his father struggling with the special agents. Two men wrestled the gun out of Allison's hand and handcuffed her. Dennis didn't move. His eyes were open and glassy.

Connie screamed, running first to Dennis and then toward Michael. "Mike, are you all right?"

Michael's brain instructed him to speak yet he couldn't. *What's happening? Was I shot?* He felt lightheaded as his mind contorted random thoughts.

The baby flayed his arms and kicked his feet, crying.

What? This is a ceramic doll. How could it be moving and crying?

Michael shook his head, trying to clear his grogginess.

He closed his eyes tight as his stomach roiled with nausea. The air around him smelled like blood and death. Michael opened his eyes and looked around, confused at the unfamiliar landscape. He was outdoors, surrounded by heavy brush and trees. He shivered as he listened to piercing screams of terror.

Still lightheaded, he hid behind a large bush with the baby wrapped in a small, thin cloth, squirming with vigor. He opened the wrap a bit and realized it was a live baby boy. But whose?

"Leave my child alone," shrieked a woman, chasing a soldier armed with a sword and spear.

Michael sought safety to his right but witnessed a man pleading for mercy as another soldier ended the life of a newborn with a spear to the heart.

"Oh, God. No."

The soldier left the motionless baby on the ground as the man buckled, wailing as he picked up his son. *I'm back but when and where am I?* Michael understood his Biblical history well enough to know about King Herod and his ruthless pursuit to kill the baby Jesus by instituting an order to eliminate all young males. Could this possibly be the time? And how would he find Elizabeth now? Was this a sign that she had entered this time?

The screaming and mournful pleas quieted. Many men and women hugged, comforting and consoling each other. Michael kept himself hidden from grieving parents and leaned back to take the strain off his knees. The baby cried softly, moving his arms and kicking his legs.

"Shhh, little one. We need to be quiet."

He pulled the baby's face closer to his chest, trying to muffle the boy's tormented cries. "Here, feel my heart beat. It worked for Elizabeth. It can work for you." Then he did something he hadn't done in nearly fourteen years. He provided a baby with a natural pacifier – his thumb.

It seemed to soothe the boy as the couple to his right continued their mourning.

This has to be Herod and his order to kill the newborns.

"Who are you?" he said in a hushed tone, watching the boy close his eyes as his suckling slowed. Michael never let go of the baby. He sat up at an angle behind the bush so he could see both sides. In the far distance, there was a small town. Candles and torches glowed from the stone homes.

I'll travel that way when everyone has left. Maybe I can find the parents there. There has to be someone who left the boy here. Maybe this is why I'm here? To save a life so Elizabeth can come back? Maybe this is the miracle?

Michael waited until the last lingering pair of weeping parents staggered away. He rubbed the baby's gums, not only to keep the boy quiet but to calm his nerves. As he took a few steps in the direction of the town, a cool breeze sent a shiver up his spine. *This baby can freeze to death out here. I need to get him near a fire.*

What if this baby doesn't belong in this time? Maybe I have to get him back to our time? Is this your son, God? Tell me. Send me a sign, anything. If I return the baby, will this lead me to Elizabeth?

He struggled in indecision, wondering if he should wait for the parents to return. He put the sleeping baby down, stroking his legs and arms to warm him up.

I'll grab some branches and try to start a fire by this bush.

He crawled on his knees, keeping his head up, and gathered broken branches from a tree. He carefully pulled part of the bush down and sat on it, pressing it so it would give him a partial campfire. Then he rubbed the sticks together. *I can do this. I've done it as a kid. Yeah, it's been a long time. But I'm a modern day man, capable of doing anything.* He stroked the branches together in a feverish pace to light a spark.

Okay, no more doing it the caveman's way. He first whacked the sticks together and then massaged them with more force. A small flame ignited. He covered the stick with one hand and set it below some small leaves on the bush. It caught and the fire rose slowly. He moved the baby closer to the fire as the glow shone on his face.

"I'll get you home. Then I'll find Elizabeth and we can go home. And everyone can live happily ever after. Right? Just like our parents told us," he whispered to the baby.

The fire roared as it caught some more brush. Already the baby felt warmer.

A stinging pain poked at the lower part of his body.

Was I just bit by a bug or an animal?

He turned around and saw a soldier, holding a spear. "Please, don't hurt us," Michael said, picking up the baby and putting the cross around his neck.

"Where are you from?"

"Far away. Not of this town. We are no danger to your King."

"How do I know that?" the soldier asked, adjusting the position of his spear to Michael's neck.

"We got lost. I need to get my daughter back to my wife. We were visiting with friends," he said, hoping he had managed to deceive the soldier.

"I will not take the chance and face the wrath of the king."

"Please sir, please."

"What kind of clothes are these?" he said, moving his spear from his sweatshirt to his sweat pants. "And what kind of shoes are these?"

"I am from a far away town. We have different customs."

"Let me see if the baby is a girl."

Michael hesitated, trying to think of another lie. He began to remove the cloth and stopped. "I'm sorry. He's my son. I have to protect him. My wife would be devastated. She would kill herself if I didn't bring him back alive."

"I do not care. I would rather she die than have the king kill me." He poked Michael in the shoulder with this spear. "Lay the baby down on the ground and leave. I am not here to kill you."

"Please don't," Michael begged, noticing the baby's eyes had opened. The boy started to kick and coo a little, sucking on his thumb again. He gave the baby a kiss on the cheek and wiped away the drool from his thumb on the side of his pants, jingling some of the coins.

"Leave now. I will spare you the agony of watching your son's death."

Michael scrambled inside his pocket to unearth the coins. "Wait!" he shouted. "I have silver. Plenty of it."

The soldier lowered his weapon. "Show me."

Michael opened his other hand, displaying the coins he had found the first time during Holy Week. He also had the coins he took from Rita's attic in the other pocket.

The soldier grabbed the coins. "Do not go toward the lights," he said. "If my commander sees you are with the baby, he will know I did not carry out my orders from the king."

"Yes, sir."

"Go. Move quickly. Do not stop to rest."

"I will."

Michael snuggled the boy against his chest. *It's so dark out here. I don't even know where I'm going.* He could feel the baby shiver. Without a coat, the one he took off back at the church for the prayer service, he realized his options were limited to keep the child warm. So he removed his sweatshirt, with only his thin white t-shirt to fend off the cold breeze of the night.

Lord, what do I do now? Where am I going? Send me a sign.

CHAPTER THIRTY-SIX

Special Agents Paul and Holligan lifted Jim Stewart off the ground, dragging him down the few steps to the front row. "Keep him here," Paul said. The agent raced back up the stairway to the manger and looked behind the bright red curtain where several poinsettias stood. "Pastor, where did he go?"

In shock, Dennis clung to the animals in his hands, unable to move as an agent attended to him.

"Where did Mr. Stewart go?" Paul asked.

The pastor didn't answer.

"Holligan, get an ambulance here as soon as possible and call for some more agents. Let's tear this place apart. Keep all doors locked."

Paul retreated behind the curtain where Michael was last seen.

Connie sat down next to her father, hugging him.

"Where did he go?" Jim asked her.

"To find Elizabeth."

"Where?"

"If he told me the truth…to another century. A dangerous one. Oh, my God." She wailed, realizing her brother's story must be true.

"The FBI is going to eventually find him," Jim said.

Connie shook her head so hard. "Nobody will ever find him."

"Then why are you crying?"

"Because we won't be able to find him," she said. "Or Elizabeth."

"That's a bunch of nonsense," said Jim, handing her a tissue. "They'll both be back. Stop being so dramatic."

She threw her hands in the air. "You don't understand. He's in a lot of danger." She dabbed her eyes with the tissue and whispered, "I don't want to lose my brother too."

Jim crossed his arms. "He'll come back."

"We have a door that leads to some underground passageway behind the curtain," said Paul. "Get Special Agent Brown to ask the local police about any information regarding tunnels and where they lead."

Holligan approached Connie and Jim. "We need to talk."

"I don't have anything to say to you," Connie said.

"I think you do."

Jim held Connie's hand and helped her stand. "Let's go home."

"No," she said. "You need to get to the hospital."

"We'll make an appointment," Jim said.

They left through a side entrance, avoiding the mesh of TV camera lights and onlookers. Another special agent waited in an unmarked car.

* * *

Paul kicked in the passageway door and waited for some equipment to help guide him through the tunnel. He returned to Dennis, now sitting up. "How are you?"

"I've had better days."

"We'll get you to a hospital as soon as possible. You've lost a little blood."

"It really stings."

"You'll be fine. It's just a scrape. Pastor, we can make this easy or I can bring you in later for helping a suspect escape. Which will it be? Tell me where he could have gone."

Dennis shrugged. "I can venture a guess as to where he might have gone. But you wouldn't take me to an FBI office or any office for that matter. You would take me to the nearest psychological evaluation center."

"So you do know where he might have gone?"

"Yes. It's a guess."

"Where?"

"To find his daughter."

"Where, Pastor? Where? I don't have time to jerk around with you anymore."

"He went back in time. Christ's time."

Paul frowned. "Play it your way."

"I beg you don't proceed in this fashion any further," Dennis said. "Michael Stewart is innocent. He was taken against his own will and I think it was a way for him to find his daughter."

"If he was so concerned about finding his daughter, wouldn't he have organized search parties?" the special agent asked. "From what I saw, he didn't act like a father who was burdened with the loss of his daughter."

"Agent Paul, we all react in different ways to a tragedy. You have your way. A very admirable action you took, giving up all those millions to help others. Michael is different. He's a loving man but doesn't how to express it."

"I did mourn," Paul said. "I still do."

"I know. The result was just not the same for you and him. Michael loves his daughter so much he would give up his life for her. Like you. And he might have to do that if he's gone where I believe he may have gone."

"Where is that? Tell me the truth and stop with the religious tales."

"You can threaten me all you want," Dennis said. "That won't change the fact that nobody here can find him."

The special agent glared, looking frustrated. "Well, that won't be good enough for the law. You're heading for trouble."

"I know. But I am telling you the truth."

* * *

With a pair of night goggles and a sturdy flashlight, Paul led three of his colleagues into the tunnel. "Special Agent Brown, did you find out from the locals where the tunnel goes?"

"They said there are many underground passageways. They couldn't specifically say how many."

"Let's keep moving and find out where this tunnel leads us."

He navigated his men through the hallway with relative ease, stopping when they found the first door. Paul knocked hard with his flashlight.

It opened and a bearded man's grinning face greeted them. "Welcome, gentlemen. I'm Rabbi Stedman. Are you Jewish or do you wish to be?"

"Rabbi, my apologies," Paul said. "I'm Special Agent Hewitt Paul. We're looking for Michael Stewart. Do you know him?"

"Yes, I know the Christian chap. Why?"

"Did he come through here?" Paul asked.

"When?"

"In the past few minutes."

"No."

"Has he ever been here before?"

"A few days ago but not today."

"Rabbi, do you know if there are more tunnels down here leading to other parts of the town?"

"Yes. If you go further, you'll see another stairway."

"Do you specifically know where they lead?"

"I don't."

"Good day, Rabbi."

"Are you sure you don't want to convert?"

"Not today, Rabbi."

"A shame. Good day."

"One second, Rabbi. Special Agent Bender, take a look inside the Temple to be sure. You don't mind, do you?"

"Not at all. Come in, Mr. Bender. Are you Jewish?"

"No sir."

"Would you like to be?" the rabbi asked as he closed the door.

Paul and the special agents found another set of stairs about fifty yards further down the passageway. He climbed the steps, put his ear against the door and listened. Paul held his hand out, requesting silence. Then he tapped slowly with force. "Hello? Is anyone there?"

"Who is it?" a voice replied.

"This is Special Agent Hewitt Paul from the FBI."

"What do you need?"

"Please open."

The man unlocked the door. He wore a white garment and white cap and had a long beard which told Paul he had come upon a Mosque. "How may I help you, sir?"

He handed the man a photo of Michael. "Have you seen this man anytime today?"

"That's the man on TV whose daughter is missing."

"Yes. Have you seen him?"

"No."

"Are you sure?"

"Yes."

"Do you mind if we take a look inside?"

"Not at all. Come this way."

"Special Agent Smith. Go take a look."

"Thank you, sir," said Paul.

The man nodded and showed Special Agent Smith into the mosque. Paul leaned on the door. "What's next? The Buddists?"

"Maybe he never came down here," suggested another special agent.

Paul took out his cell phone and punched in Special Agent Brown's number. "You find anything in the church?"

"Nothing except some pieces of concrete in the basement."

"What about the shooter? What did she say?"

"She's a local reporter, sir, believe it or not. She said Stewart told her he visited his dead wife so she wrote the story. The publisher fired her after it went to print because it embarrassed the paper. I guess the readers tore her apart online."

"Visited his dead wife?"

"Yes sir."

"We've stumbled upon wacko land."

Special Agent Brown laughed. "There's always a few in towns like this."

CHAPTER THIRTY-SEVEN

Michael walked around in no particular direction. The baby was quiet as he held the boy's face close to his chest, limiting any movement. The child continued to suck his thumb. The temperatures of the evening dipped more, chilling his body. He covered the baby's feet with his sweatshirt. The desert wind picked up with force, sprinkling sand into his nose, eyes, and ears. He used his back as a shield, doing his best to deflect it from the boy. The terrain was rough in sporadic areas. Scattered rocks served as temporary markers, keeping him alert every step of the way.

Michael decided to wait until morning to proceed, unsure where he was in relation to the town of Bethlehem. He constantly checked the baby's breathing. He claimed a big rock for some rest while some shrub provided camouflage. He relaxed his body, closing his eyes for a brief moment. Or at least he thought it was for a few minutes.

He awoke shivering and dehydrated, the baby resting in his arms. His fingers and toes tingled, his knees numb. "I've got to find somewhere I can get warm, little fella. I'm too cold." He looked around. "Now what do we do? I can't see anything for miles."

Michael rubbed his hands together and stamped his feet, anxious to remove the pins and needles that pricked him. He removed his thumb from the baby's mouth. "I'm sorry, little one. I need to get warm so I can take care of you."

The wind picked up and sand pelted Michael's face again, entering his mouth. He spit it out and gagged. After recovering, he used his frame as a protective tent for the baby.

His stomach turned as an odor goaded his nose. *Where is that awful smell coming from?* Panicked, he picked up the boy and stumbled a few steps, his legs stretching like rubber bands.

"Where are you traveling?" asked a deep voice.

Michael didn't answer. He tripped over a small bank of rocks and fell, cradling the baby with both hands. The impact was minimal. *I'm sorry, little one. I didn't mean to fall. I hope you're okay.*

He hugged and held him close to the top of his chest, trying to soothe his angst.

"Are you hurt?" asked the voice, the odor now more powerful.

Michael staggered to his feet, grabbed his back, and jogged away.

"Do you need help?" the voice shouted.

The sand continued its assault, prompting him to hold up a portion of the sweatshirt so it wouldn't penetrate the baby's face. Michael slowed down, exhausted and famished. He waited to see who or what was behind the voice.

A large animal appeared, unlike any he had ever seen. Its head was huge, two lumps pitched high from its body and the legs were long and narrow. He cleared his eyes and took a closer look – a camel. On the camel's side were a small donkey and a man holding onto a thick string, leading them. "Where are you going?" the man asked.

"I'm lost."

"Where are you trying to go?"

"Somewhere warm."

He laughed. "No wonder you are cold. What is that you are wearing? I have never seen such garments."

Michael looked at his T-shirt, sweats, and sneakers. "These are hand-me-downs."

"What are hand-me-downs?"

"My sister gave them to me a long time ago," he lied.

"Your sister?"

"I have a baby. I need to keep him warm."

The man faced him a few feet away. He extended his hand and Michael shook it. "My name is Amun. You look tired," he said, pulling his donkey to him. "Sit, rest with your baby."

"Thank you."

Amun removed a blanket from a satchel he hung over his camel and wrapped it around Michael. "There are many more steps to go before we see the next town and it is colder there because it is by the water."

"What is the name of the town?"

"Yapu."

"Do they have a motel...I mean an inn?"

Amun looked baffled. "I believe so. I plan to sleep there."

I gave most of my money to the Roman soldier but I still have Susan's money. He moved the coins around in his pocket a few times to reassure himself. *I just have to get to a warm place and figure out what I should do next.*

Amun was a talkative man, chattering about his recent business deals in Nazareth and Bethlehem. He possessed several trinkets and silver cups in another bag that clanged together as they strolled in the pitch dark. "We will be able to eat for many sunsets," he said. "I have three boys now. They keep me busy with this. They are growing and their mouths seem to need more and more food." He laughed, finding his own thoughts amusing. "How old is your child?"

"Can't be more than a few months old."

"Months?"

"Sunsets, not many at all."

"What is the child's name?"

"I haven't named him yet."

"Boy or girl?"

"Boy."

"He's quiet. Is he sick?"

"He's been crying a lot. He's cold and probably hungry." Michael pulled back the top of the sweatshirt to see. "He's fine now. I have a daughter. She was a little tougher to handle when she was a baby."

"Where is your daughter?"

"I don't know. I'm trying to find her."

"She is lost?"

"Yes."

"My. This is terrible news. Do you believe she can be found along this way?"

"I'm going to try."

"Where is your wife?"

"I don't know."

Amun came over to the donkey where Michael was seated. "Was she killed up in the fields by the soldiers?"

Michael hesitated. *How long do I have to keep making things up? But I want to be safe and fit in right now.* "I'm not sure. I'll try to get back home later to see if she is there. I wanted to make sure the boy was safe."

"Well, you need to get warm and rest, get out of this misery." Amun kept up the chatter. "I hope you don't mind but it helps me on the long trips to speak what is in my heart out loud. Sometimes I allow my mind to wander. I even talk to myself. And that can be enjoyable."

His laugh was comforting, much like an uncle at a big holiday party. It was better than listening to the brisk wind circulating its colder temperatures. "Michael," he yelled.

Startled, Michael opened his eyes and realized he had slumped forward and dozed off for a few seconds. "What's wrong?"

"You were falling asleep with your son. Be careful. You don't want the boy to fall."

"No, of course not."

Amun regained his previous pace, head lowered at times to fend off the occasional spurts of sand gusting in his face, yet he still talked. He was obviously a skilled traveler. There wasn't much to see in the darkness of the desert, except for a bush blowing in the wind.

Michael listened to tales of Amun's travels to various cities. When he finished discussing the ports and big trades he made, Amun spoke eloquently about the cast of characters he'd met.

The one encounter that seemed to excite him the most was one in which he ran into a group of three men on camels and donkeys, possessing bags of riches such as gold, frankincense and myrrh. "Their camels were big, carrying many bags of gifts," he said so clearly now that the wind was still. "I tried to persuade them to an exchange. But they weren't interested. They were determined to find their friend's house. They said they were looking for a big star over the house."

"What were their names?"

"I don't know. They left so quickly."

"Maybe they were looking for a baby boy in a manger," Michael said with excitement.

"I do not think so. They never mentioned a manger. Then they told me their gifts were not for sale, rather for the family they were visiting."

"Oh."

Michael thought to himself, puzzled, yet still curious. *No manger. No star above it.* "Did they tell you what town they were traveling to?"

"No. They said their trip was their own and no one needed to know about it. Even a King wouldn't know."

"How long ago did you see them?"

"Not many sunsets ago."

I wonder if this is the path the holy family took to Egypt? "Amun, how far away are we from Egypt?"

"A couple of sunsets. Is this where you are going?"

"Yes, I am going home."

Amun gave a stoic look. "What about your wife?"

He dodged the question. "Amun, let me do that for a while. You sit and hold the baby."

He stopped. "I thought you would never ask," he said, handing him the string that pulled the camel and donkey along. He coddled the baby at first and opened the sweatshirt slightly to see the boy's face. "Michael?"

"Is everything all right. How is the baby?"

Amun stared at Michael, not holding the baby to his chest.

"Watch it, Amun, make sure the boy is protected from the wind and sand."

"If you say so."

"He is a beautiful baby," Michael said, gaining some momentum with his steps.

Amun didn't answer.

"He might be the most important baby in the world."

Amun still didn't respond.

Michael didn't expand any further that the boy could be the Christ child for fear it might scare off Amun and a chance to find a warm place to stay. Energized with purpose and now a direction, he welcomed the challenge of the gusting wind and pelting sand. It hit him hard with several bursts. When it died down, he heard Amun snoring.

"Amun," Michael shouted. "The boy! He's falling."

He assured Michael he was safe. "He's fine."

"What do you want your boys to be when they grow up?" he asked Amun.

"I do not know. They are young."

"I have a feeling this boy will become a carpenter."

"If you say so. Are you a prophet?" Amun asked.

"I'm a writer."

"You have a strange accent, one I have never heard before."

"It's how the people in my village speak. Have you ever taken your boys on a trip?"

"My boys will join me on my journeys someday. I will have someone to talk to, argue with, and discuss the world." There were a few minutes of silence as both men absorbed their opinions. "I think the boys will be salesmen. Yes, just like their father."

"Maybe someday the boy you're holding will sell you a chair or a table."

Amun changed the subject. "What is your wife like?"

"She had such beautiful eyes, a big heart. She strengthened me when I was weak, made me happy when I was sad, held me when I was cold, and hugged me when I felt alone."

An eerie wave crested over Michael. He wasn't sure who he was talking about. Was it Vicki? Leah? Susan? Maybe it was all three. Perhaps each of them reached his heart in some special, unique way. And it was fine to appreciate each of them.

"You talk as if she is no longer with you."

"In a way, she is not."

Amun shook his head, removing the cloth on the baby and taking a glance. "Did she die in the fields?"

"I don't know. I hope not."

"What is her name?"

Michael lowered his head, stalling for time to come up with something as he didn't want to give out Vicki's name. He was about to say something when he saw the first sign of the town silhouetted in the distance. "There, Amun. What town is it?"

"Yapu. It must be Yapu."

"Will there be a place to sleep?"

"There is. Let's hope there is a room."

"Let me take the animals for the rest of the trip. Thank you. Now it is your turn to get some rest, my friend. You have been through a lot."

Amun gave him the baby and took the string. He quickened the tempo, like it was urgent to get to the town as soon as possible. The pace irritated the camel, who sat down. "Get up!"

"Can I help?"

"No, Michael. He is a stubborn animal. Sometimes he is bothered when I go too quickly. Get up, you stupid animal."

The camel turned its head, ignoring the plea. Amun laughed. "He never listens to me."

"Hold on," Michael said, getting off the donkey. "I can walk the rest of the way."

"Are you sure?"

"I'll be fine."

"I will come back for the camel later."

He tied the animal to a small tree. Then Michael walked beside him, enjoying another reprieve from the wind as he talked about his life on Long Island. He didn't care whether Amun gave him weird looks. He just needed to unload some stress of the day and night. And his friend was a willing listener. They moved off the straight path and slanted to the left with their walk. "Why are we heading this way?"

"We need to head to the sea to get to Yapu. Keep the blankets on you. It will get colder."

"What about the baby? Do you have another blanket?"

"Yes. Will it make you feel better?"

"Of course."

Amun gave him a sorrowful look as he handed him a blanket.

CHAPTER THIRTY-EIGHT

Jim fidgeted in his pocket as they drove in the agents' car. He took out a cigarette. "Anyone have a light?"

"No smoking. Trumble Court," Holligan said to the driver.

"Why are we going back to Michael's house?" asked Connie.

"It's the closest place to talk."

"My father needs to get to the hospital."

"In due time."

"No. Now."

"I need five minutes."

"But I don't have the keys," Connie lied.

"I do."

Connie gave Kevin a dirty look. "I guess you can get anyone's keys."

"No. I got it from the pastor."

"Why would he give them to you?"

"Who cares how he got the keys," said Jim. "And just what do you expect to find there?"

"Maybe he left a note or something. Was he suicidal? Was he on drugs? Drinking a lot?"

"No and no," replied Connie.

"Maybe Elizabeth left another note?" Kevin asked. "For my sister's sake I have to try anything I can to help Elizabeth. Two people just don't vanish into thin air. Do they?"

Connie glared at him. "Well, you're the FBI agent. Why don't you tell us?"

"I'm getting a headache," Jim said. "I need a drink."

"Is that your answer to every crisis? A drink?" Kevin asked.

"You want a good smack in the mouth," Jim said, his face turning red.

"Give it your best shot, old man," Kevin leaned sideways to face him.

Jim reached over Connie and swung wildly, smacking him in the nose with the back of his closed fist.

Connie screamed as the enraged agent climbed over her to grab Jim's neck with both hands, squeezing hard.

"Sir! Sir! Do you need help?" asked the special agent driving the car.

"Keep driving. I need to teach the old man a lesson."

"Stop! Stop it, Kevin, you're choking him," she begged.

Jim coughed and tried to pull Kevin's grip apart.

Connie struck Kevin in the back of the head and bit his arm.

"You little whore," Kevin said, releasing his grip while catching some blood from his battered nose with his hands.

"I've been called worse." She turned to her father. "Are you hurt?"

"I'm fine," he said in a scratchy voice. "How's the nose, big shot?"

"I'll show you who's a big shot when I get out of the car."

"What are you going to do? I'm seventy-five years old. You're going to beat up an old man? You can't hurt me more than I already am."

"What would you know about being hurt?" Kevin asked.

"My wife died before she could see her grandchildren born. My youngest daughter passed away earlier this year. Now my son and Elizabeth are both missing and I don't know if I'll live to see them again. What are you going to do to me that will cause more pain?"

There was silence in the car as they rolled up the hill to Michael's house. No one moved. Kevin took a few tissues from the backseat compartment and attended to his bloody nose.

Jim asked, "What do you want from us?"

"Answers so I can do my job and find my niece." Kevin took a deep breath and sighed. "Bobby, stop the car and let them out."

"Sir? What about what Special Agent Paul said?"

"Let them go. I'll deal with him."

The special agent got out and opened the back passenger side door near the curb.

"I'll let you know if we hear anything," Kevin said.

Jim walked away and waved. "Don't drop by any time soon."

Kevin gave the keys to Connie. "Call me immediately if you hear from Elizabeth or Michael."

She nodded, caught up to her father and helped him inside.

"Now what?" Connie asked.

"I don't know. We wait, I guess."

Connie turned on the lights and adjusted the thermostat to give the room more heat. "I'm going to call your doctor for an appointment."

"I'll deal with it later."

"Why are you waiting?"

He didn't answer. She waved her hands in the air, shouting, "Men. I don't understand any of you." She sat at the kitchen table for a second and then poured some water into a kettle and lit the stove. "Do you want a cup of tea?"

"Tea?" he asked, walking into the kitchen, shaking his head. He opened all the cupboards. "Here we go," he said, grabbing a bottle. "Look at the year on this one. He doesn't drink whiskey, does he?"

"No, he doesn't drink that stuff. He kept it here for you in case you ever decided to visit him."

He took a glass out of the cupboard and poured himself a hefty fill and went back to the living room. He settled into Michael's recliner, rocking back and forth.

"In case you would rather drink this." Connie followed him with a cup of tea. She placed it on the end table next to him and sat on the sofa.

Her father took a long swig of his whiskey. "Life can be so cruel for some people. Why did your mother, Vicki and Sammie have to die before I did?"

You're so pickled with all that booze, you'll live forever. Connie watched the steam drift from her cup. "No clue."

"There's little left in my life."

Like I have time for this pity party. The man never changes. "Stop talking that way."

"There isn't. My life ended when your mother died. She was so young."

"Vicki and Sammie were young too." She took a sip of tea. "Michael was even younger than you were when he was widowed."

"You think I don't know that?"

She shrugged.

He took a big gulp and held the glass up to examine the liquid. "Did you know when Michael found a job and I found out he was going to move in with Aunt Adele, I got on the phone and told her not to help him?"

Connie shook her head. "No, I didn't know that. Why did you do that?"

"I wanted to give him the same tough love my father gave to me. Did I ever tell you when I came home from the war the first thing my father said was for me to get a job and my own place?"

She put her cup on the coffee table. "You told us he was wonderful."

"He was. But he wasn't sometimes. The only time we were able to talk to each other was when we shared a drink." He sipped the whiskey some more. "This world is cruel. Did I ever tell you I wanted to write a book but never had the time to do it?"

"Yes, many times," Connie said, finally sensing this was a moment her father wanted to bear his soul. "You have the time now to write. Why don't you?"

He took another big gulp. "I feel terrible for kicking your brother out into the cold."

"Yeah, well, I don't feel great about telling you to kick him out, too" she said. "Did you ever tell Michael how bad you feel?"

"No. He never wanted to share a drink with me. I don't why. Now I don't know if I'll ever be able to tell him."

He finished off the whiskey and poured himself another glass. Still rocking, he drained it all in one swallow and looked at Connie. His eyes were deadened and bloodshot as he held up his empty glass.

She looked at him in disgust. "Are we just going to sit here or try to do something to find them?"

"We are doing something."

He poured himself another drink.

CHAPTER THIRTY-NINE

Leah returned to her normal routine, finding strength in praying by the fig tree. She prepared a light breakfast. As the lamb brayed for attention, she closed her eyes and reflected on the past few days. A strange, yet familiar face appeared, startling her. He knelt. Closing his eyes too, he whispered the same words.

She smiled and grabbed a nearby bucket to retrieve some water from the well. The man carried a jug and followed her. He poured water into the container. Picking the jug up, he stepped ahead of her and brought it into the kitchen. "If you need any more help, please call upon me," he said.

His voice was clear, confident and strong, yet gentle in tone. His light blue eyes melted her and his dark black hair reminded her of Yochanan. Before he could leave, Leah called out. "Would you like to stay for some breakfast? It is not much this morning as I have not been to the market in a while."

"I would. I am sure it will be fulfilling."

She worked the meal with excitement and some relief. "May I ask you a personal question?"

The man nodded.

"Who are you?"

"I am Aharon, friend of Calev."

"I am Leah."

"I know. Calev has told me about you."

"He has? What did he say?" she asked, turning around.

"He said his brother was fortunate to have you as his wife."

She smiled, trying not to shed any tears. Leah handed him a cup of water as she returned to preparing the meal.

He sat, taking slow sips. "I am sorry for your loss."

She bowed.

"I am here whenever you need me."

"You are so nice to someone who is a stranger."

"I do not feel you are a stranger."

"Why do you say that?"

"Because of Calev, I feel I already know you."

She continued to cook the porridge, trying to calculate how she would ask the next question. "After you left and took the body, what did you do with him?"

"We paid a man enough silver so no one will ever know."

She nodded, moving the pan over the seething fire. "He will never be found?"

"He will not be."

Leah removed the pan from the fire. Her body shook back and forth as she burst into tears.

Aharon took the pan out of her hand, placed it down on the table and held her. His strong grip reassured her better days were ahead.

"I can live again, are you saying I can live again?" she asked through her weeping.

"You can, woman. And when you feel you can not, you tell me. I will be here for you."

"Why are you so nice to me? What have I done to deserve it?"

"Calev told me that you are a woman who deserves to be loved because you loved his brother so much."

She lay her head into his chest. "I know this is not proper for a woman to touch a stranger."

"We are not strangers," he said.

There were no initial romantic feelings surging through her body like she had with Michael. And this was fine with her. She had found a new friend.

CHAPTER FORTY

The candlelight's glow from the houses of Yapu shone brightly in the distance, a welcome site for Amun and Michael. The breeze off the water nearby invigorated their final steps in search of shelter. The chatter between the two slowed as exhaustion overran their curiosity about each other. They took their final few steps with smiles on their faces.

"Here we are," Amun said. "Home for the night."

"A wonderful sight too," Michael said.

Amun gathered up some silver. "I hope this is enough. If not, I can trade trinkets for a room."

"How much silver do they usually want?"

"There is no price. If there are many staying, the price goes higher. Let us hope many have not found their way here."

Michael frowned as his fingers danced inside his pockets with his one free hand, hoping to dig up the coins.

"Do you not have silver?" asked Amun.

"I have some silver. I did give most of it to the soldier to save the baby up in the field."

"This baby?"

"Yes. He's so good. Isn't he?"

Amun stared at the ground. "Michael, I do not know what to say. Stay here. I will be back."

"Sure."

He watched Amun negotiate with the innkeeper, handing him first the silver coins and a trinket. The innkeeper pointed to the right and Amun smiled, shaking his hand in gratitude. "Good news," he said. "There's enough room for both of us. We will stay next to each other, like good friends do."

"What about the payment?"

"No payment."

"Why?"

"We are friends. You helped me with my animals. I help you."

"You've been so kind to me. I don't think I would have made it this far if I hadn't met you."

His friend patted him on the back. "You need plenty of rest. Clear your head. I have carried some bread and water with me. Let me share with you."

"I'm grateful."

"Someday you tell your friends about me."

"I certainly will."

The two sat, drinking water and eating bread. The conversation was light, mainly focusing on what both had planned to do the next day. Amun told Michael he had a few more stops to make before arriving back in Egypt. "If you wish to join me, you may do so, but be up when the sun rises. I have to get my animal."

"The camel?"

"Yes."

"Won't he try to run away?"

"No, he was tired from the traveling. He is a loyal animal."

"I would like to travel. Would you mind if I take some water for the baby?"

Amun looked puzzled. "If it makes you feel better."

"It does. He needs to have something or he'll dehydrate. I'll ask around the inn to see if anyone is carrying food for a baby."

Amun's eyes widened. He tapped him on the back. "Sleep. Go to your room. Do not worry about the baby being hungry. He is fine. I am next to you if you need help, if you want to talk. There is a bedroll in the room. Keep the blankets. Stay warm."

"Thank you."

Amun smiled.

Michael planned out his trip to Egypt, the details baking in his mind. *Maybe I'm here to return the baby to them? Is this the Christ child?*

After nibbling on a piece of leftover bread, he lay the baby down on the bedroll. "You rest, little one. We'll find your parents and get you home safely."

Michael first placed a blanket over him and rubbed his tummy. "Elizabeth always liked this when she was young," he said with a smile. "Sometimes I think she was a puppy." He yawned and rubbed his eyes. "We've got a long trip ahead of us. I'm going to see if the innkeeper can tell us if there are any families with babies your age. Maybe they can spare some food." He stroked the top of the baby's head with the back of his hand.

Michael gave a last glance at the boy before scoping out the hallway. Each room was much like a cubical you would see in a Fortune 500 company, except they were filled with people wrapped in blankets and laying on bedrolls.

An old man missing his front teeth stood behind a beaten down table, illuminated by two thick lanterns. The innkeeper was attending to a couple and a small boy. They appeared distraught. The man, clothed in traditional garments, pulled at his brown beard, deep in thought as he held the boy's hand. The little one wasn't more than four or five years old, yet was bright eyed and bouncing with energy for this time of the night.

Just like Elizabeth was when she was his age. I wonder what kids do for fun here? How do parents keep their children busy?

The innkeeper looked at Michael. "What can I do for you?"

"Please take care of this family first."

"They are taken care of."

He couldn't remove his eyes from the woman wearing the blue veil. She moved it lower to speak to her husband, her concerns more visible. Her face was flushed, perhaps from the wind.

The man signaled the family to leave.

"Sir," Michael said. "May I ask what's wrong? Do they need silver to stay?"

"There is no room. You and your friend took the last two."

Michael called out to both the innkeeper and family. "Wait. Can they stay with me?"

"For a price."

"What do you want?"

"What do you have?"

Michael dug deep into his pocket and gave him the last two coins. "Sir, sir," he yelled, running after the family. "I have a room. Do you mind sharing it with me and my boy?"

The man gave Michael a gesture of gratitude.

"It's this way. Follow me."

The man and woman lay down three blankets. She persuaded the youngster to settle down on the makeshift bedroll and sang a short song, lulling her son to sleep. She fussed over him a few more minutes, kissing his cheek several times.

"Lay here," her husband whispered.

"Where will you sleep?" she asked in a higher tone.

"I will sit against the wall. Rest, woman. We have many more steps to take."

"Would you have any food you can share with me for my boy?" Michael asked the man.

"Yes." He reached inside a bag and pulled out a small pouch, filled with what looked like oatmeal.

"Thank you."

Michael decided not to wake the baby since he was sleeping, so he pocketed the pouch. *I'll use this for the trip to Egypt.* The woman and her son fell asleep while the man watched Michael, apparently not intending to close his eyes.

"You can trust me, sir," Michael said. "I'm resting before I travel again."

"I am not tired. Sleep. Do not worry about me."

"Where are you traveling to?"

"Very far."

"Egypt? That's where I'm going."

The man's eyebrows shot up. "No," he said in a stern, tense voice.

"Did I say something wrong?"

"Rest. There are many steps to get to where you wish to go."

The man's stare was unyielding.

"My name is Michael. What is your name?"

"My name is unimportant."

"Sorry if I upset you."

"You did not. We are thankful for your kindness and sharing your shelter with us. My wife is worried about our trip."

"I understand."

The man nodded toward the baby. "I see you have a little boy. Does he not cry? Or move? He is so still."

"He's sleeping."

The room was lit with one candle in the middle, shedding a low light.

"Close your eyes, Michael. Sleep."

"I will. If my boy wakes up, can you tell me?"

"Yes. I am not sleeping tonight."

CHAPTER FORTY-ONE

Michael was startled out of a shallow sleep as the couple's little boy hovered over him, sporting a huge grin. "Michael, why are you angry?" the little boy asked.

"Why do you say that?"

"You were moving your arms like this." The boy demonstrated Michael flailing his arms in a fighting stance.

"I had a bad dream."

The boy remained standing, his face only a few feet away from his.

"Go back to sleep." Michael looked around the room. "Where is my baby?"

The boy shrugged his shoulders. "Is he lost?"

"Yes. Yes, he is. Have you seen my boy?"

"I am a boy."

"I know. But there was another one. A baby. Wrapped in a blanket. He was laying here on the floor next to me." He looked around, adjusting his eyes to the darkness. "Oh, there he is," he said with relief seeing the baby still wrapped in the cloth in the far corner of the room. "How did he get over there?"

"I put him there," the little boy said.

"Why?"

"I was playing with him." The boy put his hand on Michael's face. "My father says you do not need to worry."

"Where is your father? I don't see him anywhere."

The child smiled. "My father is everywhere."

Michael's feet felt numb and when he tried to stand, his knees rolled over like jelly. He was unable to feel the texture of the ground. "I can't move. What's happening?" The boy placed two fingers on Michael's heart.

"What are you doing?" Michael asked, confused.

"Why is your heart sad?"

"I don't feel well."

"Tell me why your heart cries."

"It's a long story."

"I like stories."

"Can you get the man at the desk or ask my friend next door to come and help me? I can't feel my legs."

"You do not need them. You have my father."

"Your father isn't here," Michael said in a firm tone.

"He is. He told me."

"Where?"

"Close your eyes."

"How will I see him if I close my eyes?"

The boy grinned again. "My father says he need not be here to help you see."

"Is this some kind of game you play with your father?"

The boy didn't answer. "You are sad about your daughter. She is with my father now."

Michael gasped, his heart crushing against his ribs. "Your father knows where my daughter is?"

"Elizabeth is happy."

"Where is she?" He crawled on his knees to the boy, now sitting on his bedroll. "Tell me. Where is Elizabeth? I've come here to find her, to take her home."

"She is already home."

"Our home? In Northport? Tell me."

The boy gave a distressed look. "My father will take care of you. Do not be sad."

"How?" Michael asked, anxiety pounding through his temples, giving him a headache. "If you know where she is, tell me."

"My father is telling you."

"You need to get back to your parents." Michael gasped for air. "It's not nice to trick adults."

"It is not a trick. My father is here. You just do not see him."
Michael looked around, his headache easing, his lungs
slowing down. "I don't see anybody. What's your father's name
anyway? What's your name?"

"My name is Jesus."

Michael felt the blood draining from his head. "Where are
you from?"

"From far away. My parents told me to say that."

"Are your parents Mary and Joseph?"

"There." He pointed behind him to the man and woman,
bags in hand, signaling to the boy to come.

Mary gestured to Jesus. "We must go now."

Michael held his hand up for them to stop. "I came to bring
you the baby. The crying baby I found in the field," he said. "This
is the reason why I'm here. Am I right?"

Mary tilted her head, her brown eyes as warm as a mother's
caress. "It was not the baby crying for help. It was you."

"What?"

Mary knelt down beside him and opened the wrapping.
"See?"

The baby was still. Michael put his hand on the child's face,
feeling the texture. "It's the baby from the church. He's not
alive," he said incredulously. "I must look like a fool. I'm losing
my mind."

Mary helped him to his feet as Joseph continued packing
their belongings. "You are not a fool. You are a good man, a
wonderful father and loving husband who has made mistakes.
We have all made mistakes."

"We have many more steps to go, Mary," said Joseph. "Let us
keep ahead of the soldiers."

"Let me help," Michael said. "This must be the reason why
I'm here."

"You will be in danger," Joseph replied.

"You must go home," Mary implored.

"I don't know how to get back. I need to find my daughter.
Help me. I'm desperate. My daughter is lost."

"Then follow us," Joseph said, picking up the last bag. "We will do whatever we can to help you."

Michael composed himself and said goodbye to Amun. He rejoined Mary, Joseph, and Jesus outside the inn. They hurried in the direction of Egypt. Mary guarded her son, placing a couple of garments over his head. "Can you breathe?" she asked.

He giggled. "Mama, this is fun."

Michael stayed in front of the two donkeys with Joseph, holding onto the baby wrapped in the cloth. "How far?"

"Another sunset away," Joseph said. "Herod's butchers will be everywhere. Keep your eyes awake."

It wasn't long before they encountered a gathering of travelers waiting in a singular line. "Mary," Joseph yelled. "Cover Jesus well. Keep him quiet."

Her face grew white.

They reached the back of the line, some thirty or so weary men, women, some with children riding on donkeys and camels. Herod's soldiers, armed and brutal, pushed, shoved and battered many of those who resisted the theft of their possessions. The soldiers worked their way through the contour, pulling aside only a few children but mostly grabbing anything of value. And when an elderly man objected to the treatment of his wife, the soldiers delivered a fatal blow, leaving the woman weeping, kneeling by his side. Michael turned away in fear. Jesus started to fidget. He whispered, "My father will punish the wicked."

Mary shushed him but he resisted. "Mama, they are not nice men."

As a soldier stared at them, Mary tightened her grip, cupping part of the garment over Jesus' mouth. Joseph stayed silent, smiling and bowing, anxious to move forward upon the soldier's approval. Another Roman crept a few more steps back.

Oh no. They're going to get him.

Michael ran, clutching the baby and the cloth. "I've got a boy," he yelled.

"Stop him!" the soldier demanded. "He has a child."

"Move on," the soldier screamed at Joseph.

A group of five pursued Michael as he ran back in the direction of the inn. "Leave me alone," he shouted. "I need to find my daughter."

Out of breath a few minutes later, he stumbled to the ground, clinging to the baby as the cloth fell off a few feet away.

"Get up!" commanded one of the soldiers as the others drew their spears, surrounding him. They grabbed the baby, studied him for a few seconds, and threw him to the ground. The soldier growled, "You are a fool."

The soldier jolted Michael in the head with one sharp thrust of his spear, opening a gash as he fell backwards. He struck the side of his head against a large rock.

"Leave him," the leader said. "We need to get back. More silver to take there."

The baby lay silent and motionless; his arms glued upright. Dazed, Michael reached for the cloth with his right hand. Pain plunged through his neck and lower back. The stars above him spun around in a fast, circular direction.

Jesus towered over him, his parents a few feet behind.

Joseph extended his hand. "My friend, you are hurt. We need to get you help."

"No. Go. Your family is in danger."

"My Father is near," Jesus said.

"My daughter. Where is she?"

Jesus picked up the cloth and placed it over Michael's wound. "She is here."

Michael's body floated and a foggy mist engulfed his head. His body, once aching with pain and exhaustion, filled with an internal heat, soothing his soul as he elevated above the three.

Am I dead? Is this heaven? Vicki? Mom? Sammie? Are you coming to get me?

CHAPTER FORTY-TWO

Michael's world had gone black for what seemed like a few minutes. Just as quickly, the sun shone and he took in the mountains surrounding him on all sides as if the tips of their terrain scraped the clear blue sky. He heard sheep in the distance and people's chatter.

Where am I?

He rubbed his eyes and shook his head. Taking a deep breath, he stepped sideways down the hill, unsteady.

While shielding his eyes, a sparkling glare near a mountain opening alerted him.

What is that?

He increased his speed, the momentum of the slope propelling him into a slow trot. He sprinted the last few yards.

Out of breath, he leaned down, staring at the gold chain as if in a trance. He lifted the rock and picked it up, holding it in his hand. A chill slivered up his spine, making the hairs on his neck tingle.

My daughter can't be here.

He fell to his knees, clutching the chain and wiping off the dirt. "It's not Elizabeth's," he said in a whisper. "I'm sure of it. She doesn't own something like this. Someone else must have dropped it."

It was a chain and locket like no other he had seen in Jerusalem.

It could have been from someone else who came through the tunnel.

He held on to the locket for several moments, allowing the sun to create a glare from it, hitting the top part of the cave.

Michael trembled and picked at the locket.

It opened and he shut it just as quickly, squeezing his hand around it.

He walked up and down a small hill several times until anxiety tired him. He clipped at it again with his fingernails.

He closed his eyes before it opened again, praying as he peeked at the picture in the locket.

Matt.

"No. Please. No." Falling to his knees, he hugged the chain. "It can't be."

Michael crawled into the cave and pushed away a stone.

A figure swathed from head to toe in white cloths lay before him. The ointments intoxicated his nose.

He leaned over and unraveled the top of the body.

Bile rose up in this throat and he let out a growl, so animalistic, he thought a wild animal was nearby but realized it was him.

He picked up a rock and hurled it against the wall and looked up. "You did this," he shouted. "You, God, you did this. Why did you take my daughter? Wasn't my wife enough for you?"

He retrieved the rock and sharpened its edges and swung it at his chest. "Why did this have to happen? I've done everything you've asked of me. I've given my life to you, God. This is my reward? Talk to me. You're God! You're supposed to help the good people. I'm good."

He cried and threw another rock against the cave's wall.

"You win. Kill me. Take me." He stood up and fell down just as quickly, heaving and sobbing. "I'll kill myself. Take me, Lord."

He picked up Elizabeth and pressed her against his chest, rocking back and forth, kissing her face. His wails echoed off the hollow stone walls of the tomb.

"I want to die," he yelled. "I want to be with my daughter."

CHAPTER FORTY-THREE

Michael leaned on his refined walking stick, his arms more muscular yet his eyes weary. He pulled his hair tightly together, feeling it touch his shoulders. His legs were straight as he walked down the hillside. He took a deep breath and stopped, finding cover a few yards away from the mountain.

He watched a man and woman holding hands as they approached the cave. They embraced as she leaned her head against his chest. The woman whispered words he couldn't comprehend.

Michael hid behind a bush, removed the wooden cross from his pocket and placed the chain around his neck. He peered out and smiled.

It's Leah coming here again. She looks happy. She looks so beautiful.

Leah and the man went into the cave. It was several minutes before they reappeared.

The man and Leah walked away, holding each other's waists. She looked up and Michael hurried behind the burly bush. *Did she see me? I hope not.* He retreated a few more yards back up the hill. When it was clear, he descended again, his steps measured.

He kneeled down inside the opening and touched the clothed body, enjoying the sweet smell of the oils. He whispered the words he had said so many times as a little boy. "Our Father, who art in heaven…."

After Michael finished, he closed his eyes and let his mind drift back to Northport.

Elizabeth was sitting next to him. She was ecstatic that her Daddy had taken her to the movies for the first time.

"Remember, no eating the popcorn or candy until the movie starts."

She nodded, grinning.

"Do you promise?" he had repeated.

"I will cross my heart." So she did. As her hand swung down it tipped the bag on her lap over. A few pieces tumbled to the floor. She jumped down, retrieved the fallen popcorn, and wiped them off with her shirt. "Five second rule, it's okay to eat," Elizabeth had said.

She sported a sly smile, melting his heart. He patted her on the back and leaned over, whispering in her ear, "I was teasing. Enjoy your popcorn."

With enormous glee, she took a handful and began munching. He had laughed. "Like father, like daughter."

Michael crashed out of the memory, wiping a tear with his sleeve. "How much is that doggy in the window?" he sang softly. His voice broke and he couldn't get through the song. He closed his eyes for several minutes, trying hard to convince his mind to travel back to another time. He was startled as a hand touched his shoulder. "Who is that?" he asked in the dark.

"It is me," a soft feminine voice said. "Why did you not tell me you were here?"

"Leah?"

"Yes."

"Why, Michael, did you not come back to my home?"

He stood and noticed her tired green eyes, a few wrinkles below them, demonstrating she had endured more stress in her life. "I saw you many times with a man here. You looked happy, holding hands, hugging each other. I couldn't intrude on your happiness. You have moved on and I'm grateful you have found someone again. You deserve it."

Leah shook her head. "Michael, I loved you. I would have wanted to know if you were here."

"I don't think you understand how much I loved you, Leah."

She bowed her head. "I do understand." Leah hugged him. "You should be proud of Elizabeth."

"I am," he said, absorbing the embrace with his heart. "How did she die? Tell me."

She hesitated for a brief moment. "She was brave. Courageous and strong. A woman without fear. She defended me against Marcus. She fought him."

Michael sobbed, holding her tight. "Was she in a lot of pain?"

Leah didn't answer. "She told me to tell you she loved you." She wept and leaned her head into his chest, wiping her tears on his garment.

"She also told me to tell you she didn't mean to leave the lights on. I do not know what she meant."

Michael shook and sobbed. "I do."

He squeezed her. "I miss her so much," he said.

"I do as well."

"Are you in trouble," a man's voice called from outside.

She turned from Michael's embrace. "I am fine."

"You should go," Michael said.

"I cannot let go of you. I cannot bear to lose you again."

He tried to remove her grip. "You must. You have a wonderful life ahead of you, many more sunsets to thank God for, live and love for."

She released her hold as Michael wiped tears away with his hand.

"I will always keep the rooftop here." Leah pointed to her heart. "I am so glad we found each other."

She kissed him on the lips and left. Michael watched the two fade into the hillside before returning to the tomb. The sky had darkened and there was some thunder in the distance. He stood at the lip of the cave's opening, admiring the stormy weather. A heavy rain drenched the ground, forming little pools. He looked down and saw his reflection. *Boy, would I love a warm shower.*

He waited several more minutes before pulling his hood over his head to begin his walk back home. The mud soiled his sandals so he took them off. He stopped and let his feet feel the sloppy sludge. It was an oozy feeling yet he relished the soft comfort.

Michael took a few more steps and stopped again. He looked around. *It looks big enough. No, I can't do this. But there is nobody around.* He dropped his sandals to the ground and laughed. *I hear you. Do it with me?*

He bent down and lay flat on his back, relishing the moisture soaking his face. "Okay, now!"

He swung his arms up and down. "Can you see me Vicki? This is for you. Thanks for saying yes."

Michael continued, smiling and crying at the same time. As he finished his mud angel, a man stood above him. He jumped up. "My Lord."

He smiled.

"Why are you here?"

Jesus' grin widened.

"Why are you smiling?"

"I witnessed a beautiful act of unselfish love – the greatest gift you can give to another person."

He smiled again. A raging wind whipped through the small cave opening. Voices swirled around him. Snippets of conversation could be heard nearby in the cave.

"Who is there?" Michael asked, walking back to opening of the tomb.

He saw the stone displaced. "What the…"

"It's time for both of you to go," Jesus said.

"I don't want to go back to Northport," Michael said, turning around. "There's nothing left there for me."

"There is much work to be done for both of you here."

"Both?"

A woman walked out from the cave.

"Elizabeth?"

She stood in silence, touching and feeling her face.

"My God, Elizabeth!"

Michael hugged her.

"Where am I? What happened?" she asked.

"My God, my God, thank you."

He embraced her tighter and kissed the back of her head several times.

"There is not much time," Jesus said. He gave them His instructions.

Before Michael could say a word, He disappeared into the cave.

ABOUT THE AUTHOR

Michael John Sullivan graduated from St. John's University with a communications degree and a promising future in the field of journalism after working for the official school paper the previous two years. Six months later, he found himself washing his hair in a toilet at the same university as he prepared for a job interview.

Riding a New York City subway train at night, his only companion was a green plastic bag of belongings. During these bleak days, he began writing his most reflective and emotional childhood and adult memories now featured in two of his novels, *Necessary Heartbreak* and *Everybody's Daughter*.

Sullivan spent almost a month on the E train at night until he was rescued by relatives. After spending much of the past two decades raising their daughters while working at home, Sullivan returned to his notes in 2007 and began writing *Necessary Heartbreak: A Novel of Faith and Forgiveness*. It was published by Simon & Schuster's Gallery Books imprint in April 2010. He finished *Everybody's Daughter* in 2012 and recently finished the last book in the series, *The Greatest Gift*. He is also the author of *An Angel Comes Home*, a prequel novelette to *Everybody's Daughter*.